Incarnation

LAURA DAVIS HAYS

Incarnation

Pam,

It is such a pleasure knowing you both professionally + as a friend!

Happy reading!

Love + blessings,

Laura

Terra Nova Books
SANTA FE, NEW MEXICO

Library of Congress Control Number: 2015951936

Distributed by SCB Distributors, (800) 729-6423

Published by Terra Nova Books, Santa Fe, New Mexico.
www.TerraNovaBooks.com

ISBN 978-1-938288-44-9

For My Beloveds

Acknowledgments

I am grateful to my husband, Jim Hays, for many years of faithful support of my writing, for his love and protection and our beautiful life together, and for building me a perfect room with a view.

Thank you to Susana Guillaume for her always-insightful and gentle reading and highly perceptive editorial suggestions, and for her generosity in friendship and impeccable taste. I am appreciative beyond words.

Thanks to Lisa Sandlin for much early and professional reading and for our long, enduring, and deep friendship. You are my true sister.

I appreciate my early writing group and their patient reading and rereading of *Incarnation*: Susana, Lisa, Carolyn K., Carolyn S., Francis, and, of course, Brian.

Thanks to Anya Achtenberg, my writing mentor and teacher of Story I through IV, and all the beautiful participants of that workshop.

Thanks to Marty and Scott Gerber of Terra Nova Books for their patience and professionalism and believing in *Incarnation*.

A special thank you to Linda Durham for our lovely salon afternoons at The Wonder Institute discussing writing, spirituality, art, and music.

I could not be the person I am without the support of my church community at Everyday Center for Spiritual Living. Thank you Gayle and Paul.

Thank you to my friends who have spent years tracking the progress of this book, and to my current writing group at ECSL, all of whom have showed faithful interest in *Incarnation*.

I am most appreciative for my family, Gabe and Holly, and the beautiful girls, Sadie and Gemma. I love you with all my heart. To my extended families, Davis and Hays and Taylor, you are the backbone of my existence. Thank you to Hal Davis for your profound influence on my life and your generosity.

To my mother, Elaine Davis, for your constant love and sweet example.

And, especially, I am grateful to Donald Holm Davis, my father, who taught me I could do anything I wanted, and be anyone I wanted to be. I will miss you always.

A White Place

I live in a white place, a place as long as the sky and full of starry light. Sometimes a little color floats past—a sunrise tint, an azure sparkle. Then I stare at the horizons and wonder what's out there. Instantly, I am floating at the edge of infinity; shifting colors rush past like thoughts. A stream of pure joy flows through me. I know everything at once. I am the whole. I am love.

More often I sit with One-God, chanting, praying, learning with the others. Many souls have gathered here to review the lives they once lived. We atone, we forgive, we plan our rebirth: You will be my mother, brother, sister, friend. Together we will not do, not do, not do again. As we once did, twice did, thrice, couldn't help but be the same.

Then I place my hands against the skin of the world and remember. Warm waters, a midnight swim, the surf moving in the dark, a beach fire, my beloved Jarad close at my side. We watch Muamdi's hands dance over the herbs, casting spells. Sparks fly, stars wink. The night glows and the sea makes its constant sounds, sighing in and out.

Hush, hush. Hush, hush.

Oh, how I've tried to forget that life! A life filled with sweetness, but with terrible sad things too. Did I cause them? Perhaps. For that, I've done my penance, once, twice, tenfold. Yet there is something I cannot finish, something that grinds like a bone in the throat. One who once desired me, one who blamed me, will not let go.

With him, I bargain still.

Can you help me, soul descendant? For strangely we are becoming linked, my thoughts, your thoughts. I don't understand how or why except to believe that you can free me. If you are brave, you will. And then?

And then I will free you.

PART I

DREAMTIME

Chapter 1

Kelsey Dupuis, a young dark-haired woman, went running in the early morning light through the dirt streets near her house, then turned into the foothills. She didn't stop to take in the view that opened to the city of Santa Fe below, the sparkling valley, the snowy mountain ridge beyond—just kept going through the warren of tight lanes lined with mud houses, some with growling dogs chained in the yards, others with Mercedes SUVs guarding their remodeled exteriors. She was not running away this morning, rather she ran toward something, seeking, in the rhythmic movement, the breathing-induced meditation, an understanding of the mystery that lay coiled inside her.

Yesterday, catapulted out of bed by the nightmare, she'd driven halfway to Clines Corners, found a pullout, ducked under the barbed wire, and bolted into the desert. The ground felt soft and pliable under her feet, and there was sound in her ears, a gentle water sound, like hushing or sighing. Behind it, she could hear the eerie mix of distant highway noises, calls of waking birds, a coyote howling. And then the voice came through, speaking so clearly she stopped and turned, though she knew she was alone out there. *You will be my brother, sister, lover, friend. Together we will not do, not do, not do again. As we once did, twice did, thrice, couldn't help but be the same.*

Suddenly a hallucination, straight out of the nightmare world, bloomed before her eyes. Standing in a narrow wash where water had funneled for millennia, scooping away the sandstone walls until they were cupped like two ears, she'd first imagined, then heard, then seen. She would not think of it now. Not today. Today she was just a person who dreamed, a person alone in a new city with a new job. A person with a plan to find normal again.

When Kelsey entered the lab at BioVenture Enterprises, the lights were blazing, geometric screensavers dancing, alternative rock blaring as usual, but Molly, her supervisor, was nowhere in sight. Kelsey logged in and set to work, got frustrated because she couldn't find her notebook, her printouts, her data stick. What could have happened to them? Was she losing her mind? Then Molly came waddling through the lab's doorway. Big to begin with—a former college basketball star—Molly had become enormous with the pregnancy, and twice as loud too.

"You're late," Molly boomed. "Again. Still having those nightmares?"

Kelsey regretted, once more, the confidence she'd shared with Molly. Of course she was still having the nightmares. Of course that was why she was late, why she felt so scattered despite her best efforts. And yes, she'd dreamed again. It was relentless.

"I can't find my data sheets anywhere," Kelsey said.

Molly grinned. "I'm having these irresistible nesting urges. Cleaning up wherever I go. They ought to be studying me, instead of these glorified maggots." She pulled open a drawer crammed with Kelsey's papers. "Happy now?"

"That's my junk drawer," Kelsey complained as she sorted through it. "And yesterday's logs aren't here. Or my backups."

"Well, that's not my fault." Molly scanned Kelsey head to toe. "What are you wearing, anyway? I've heard of casual Friday, but you've taken it to a new low."

"It's just jeans," said Kelsey, looking down at her legs.

"Well, they're muddy. And your shirt is too."

At 10:00 A.M. just like every other day, a messenger arrived from engineering with the day's samples. Not the usual sloppy man, Franklin, but a new guy, young, clean-cut.

"You Kelsey?" he asked after he'd deposited the microscopic animals next to the sink. "I'm George. Got a message for you from the boss." He dropped a company-embossed envelope in front of her and stood staring, memorizing her face, it seemed, then executed a kind of masculine pirouette, and was gone.

"Cute, huh?" said Molly, eyeing her from across the room. "Don't get your hopes up, though. I hear he's married."

Kelsey studied the envelope with her full name typed, perfectly-centered, on the front.

The note inside was hand-written, almost illegible. *Come in for a chat. 11:15. M. Crouch.*

Molly rolled over, still in her lab chair, feet scooping the floor, and grabbed the paper out of Kelsey's hands. "He writes like a monkey. What's it say?"

"Crouch wants to see me."

"Myron F. Crouch, the thirty-fifth? Sounds like you're fired." Molly squinted, then frowned. "What the hell am I going to do without you to cover for me?"

~~~

An hour later, wearing a lab coat over her clothes, Kelsey made her way through the first-floor construction, past the roped off elevators, up the outside stairs to the far end of the third floor where the executive suite was located. Before stepping inside, she tried to conjure a picture of her boss from her childhood—he'd been her father's student, a favorite, she was sure—but the memory was hazy and she'd had no chance to refresh it since her arrival at BioVenture. Not counting the cursory handshake at orientation, or her back-of-the-class seat at staff meetings, this would be her first face-to-face with Myron Crouch.

Left in the waiting room, Kelsey picked up a Sports Illustrated and stared at the bikini-clad cover model. Behind the girl was the beach: bright sand, the line of turquoise water, a white ruffle of wave, the deeper, darker blue lurking behind it. Kelsey turned the magazine over, and suddenly a picture from the past formed behind her eyelids. A youthful animated face with a rim of auburn hair, and flashing hazel eyes. Her father sat at the desk, gray and digni-
~~~

fied as she'd always known him, watching the pacing man. She could almost hear the arguments, the younger man challenging the elder as they discussed science. Again she felt that heady sensation as her mind stretched to catch a familiar word, to understand one sentence in five. Crazy, she'd been only eight or nine at the time. How could she have hoped to understand graduate level work?

But she could now, couldn't she? She was one of them now, wasn't she?

Just then, the door opened.

"Kelsey! Great to see you!"

Myron Crouch, hair shorter, still thick but no longer red, more a uniform chestnut brown with a little gray painted at the temples, had emerged from the inner sanctum. He pumped her hand, clapped her on the back, then guided her inside.

The room was done in an Old West style with paintings of Indians in huge gilt frames on several walls. A bronze figurine of a rearing horse dominated one corner of the desk. Besides a pen set, a green pad, and a lone file folder, the desk's surface was bare. Kelsey glanced at the folder to see if it had her name on it.

"Sit," said Crouch, taking a seat himself. "Take off your coat. Make yourself comfortable."

She shifted into the leather chair across from him.

"So how's the job going? Like it here? Sherman treating you all right?"

"She's a good scientist," said Kelsey.

"She still pregnant? She'll be out how long?"

"Three months," said Kelsey. "She's planning three months."

"They always take longer once they get a taste of the good life."

Kelsey traced the brass grommets on the arm of her chair. What was there to say to that?

"How long you been here now, Kelsey?"

"Seven weeks."

"Like it?" he asked again. "Like your job? Your work?"

"Yes, Sir. Thank you, Sir." She could almost see the other face, the younger, thinner one, not superimposed, but embedded. The past there within the present.

"But," he prompted, "you're a little bored maybe? Not up to your full potential?" He gave her a wink. "So with Sherman out, there'll be room for advancement. What do you say?"

"You mean Molly's job?"

He turned toward the painting, an Indian brave on horseback, all flying hair and hooves and dust. "You're a smart one, aren't you? A real little Einstein. Your father's pride and joy." There was a ferocity in his demeanor, his glowing, almost orange gaze. "What were those sonnets you used to recite? In Latin, no less."

Latin sonnets? Pride and joy? What was he talking about? She had the sudden revelation that maybe she *had* been precocious, maybe her father *had* been proud, though it was his disappointment he'd mostly showed her. Again she pictured the darkened study, her father's sanctuary, curtains drawn, fan spinning, the smell of pipe smoke, sweet, on a sultry afternoon. She'd heard raised voices and stopped in the doorway. She was invited inside, so she'd perched on a straight backed chair, sat swinging her feet, waiting and listening. When her father focused his attention on her at last, commanded her in perfect German to recite for his guest, she knew what he wanted—the periodic table, or the quadratic equation, in German, of course. The slim red-haired young man who moved restlessly in his corner by the window turned those same angry eyes upon her. Terrified, she sang then, *Twinkle, Twinkle, Little Star* in French, and her father sent his displeasure her way, saying . . .

Crouch's voice interrupted her reverie. "Saw a yellow Karmann Ghia in the parking lot," he said, "Couldn't be the same one, I'm thinking."

"What? My car?" She kind of blurted it.

"Hot little ride in its day. Your brother was quite the man." Crouch picked up the folder, opened it, closed it, put it down. "Your father wouldn't sell it, of course. So now you have it."

"He gave it to me when he was . . ." Kelsey stopped. "I couldn't just leave it . . . ." She lifted her hands to cover her cheeks.

"Of course you couldn't." Crouch smiled nicely. "So," he said after a moment more of staring until she felt the blush spreading to her ears, "you're not like your father? I mean you're over it. The death of your brother—devastating, of course, I'm not belittling. Just too bad Cecil lost . . . But no, I'm thinking you're intact. Not carrying around a bunch of emotional baggage."

She felt the old sense of being unmoored wash over her. "I hate that, calling it 'emotional baggage,'" she said at last.

"Feisty, I like that. All I'm asking is are you ready to go to work for me?"

Her bafflement grew. "I am working for you."

"I mean give your all to this project. I like to make bold moves. Are you with me? Can I count on your support?"

He was telling her something. That more was at stake than she'd realized. That she was like, or unlike her father—she didn't know which. "I always try to contribute," she managed.

"Keep your eyes open then. You know what's at stake?"

She had the right answer now. She'd heard him say it often enough at staff meetings. "It's groundbreaking, Sir."

"Right," he said, smiling and standing to shake her hand. "World class."

Kelsey stood on the third-floor landing, her hand on the cold metal railing, the bright winter air lapping her skin, the view spread before her. Suddenly the landscape shifted—a white expanse with infinite horizons, bright and compelling—she blinked, and it shifted back. New Mexico brown, the dots of evergreen. She took in a slow deep breath and as she exhaled, closed her eyes. That's when she heard it again, a voice, not quite inside, not quite outside.

You will be my mother-brother-lover-son . . . Together we will not do . . .

Kelsey's eyes flew open. "Who's there?" she called. "Is somebody there?" She firmed her grip on the railing, and the world came rushing back.

What did Crouch want from her anyway? Some scientific brilliance she'd yet to demonstrate? Some information about her father? And why bring up Galen as though he was the family weakness? She should barely remember her older brother, killed when she was only six—but she did—he'd doted on her, and she'd adored him. Kelsey was taking full breaths, feeling the sun on her face, almost warm at midday, when she heard the door open behind her.

"Going down?"

She spun. The man was tall, blondish, not bad looking, wore a beard and glasses like so many of the scientists. Behind the lenses, his soft gray eyes were friendly, intelligent, and kindly.

"Harrison?" she asked, remembering.

"Kelsey?" he echoed. "Heading back to the cesspool?" He started down the stairs at a gallop.

She followed, caught him as they entered the lobby. There, four men struggled with a massive bubble-wrapped object. They set it down in the midst of the construction where the barricades and plastic had finally been removed to reveal plumbing pipes poking into the air.

"That's what they call the lab?" Kelsey asked. "I was actually thinking of lunch. I'm starving."

"The cafeteria?" he asked. Then, "Sure. Why not."

He slowed for her now, waved at the construction as they passed it. "They're setting the glass today. All one piece, curved too."

"I thought it was supposed to be a reception desk," Kelsey said.

"It's a fish tank and a desk. An aquarium desk."

"But why? I mean, it's so impractical, so extravagant."

"Imagine a Roman colonnade. Complete with spouting nudes." Harrison gestured toward the rim of the atrium.

On the way to the cafeteria, he told her everything she'd somehow missed. How the three-story atrium with its tropical plants and centerpiece aquarium was modeled after the one at the main branch in California, that the renovations were costing close to fifteen million, that the company was opening a European office, and that Crouch was being considered for CEO of the whole operation.

"Really? Myron Crouch?"

"You knew him before," Harrison said. "That's the word on the street."

They entered the cafeteria, a large pleasant room with light streaming in from a bank of windows. Kelsey was accustomed to getting the salad bar or an occasional made-to-order omelet, and having lunch by herself, reading a book or a magazine. She wasn't the only one who did that. She avoided the groups of men who sat together and made a lot of noise—sometimes they seemed quite juvenile. Today they called out to Harrison, but he took a sunny table away from them.

"Crouch was a student of my father's," Kelsey said when they were settled. "I was just a kid."

After a few quick bites of his sandwich, Harrison said. "It was Berkeley, right?"

"What? Did we know each other?"

He shook his head. "I didn't mean you. But yeah, I was there."

They started comparing notes and found they *had* overlapped as students, same years, same department, both getting a master's, his an interim degree in biological modeling, hers in microbiology, but they'd never met—how strange was that? Harrison's expression softened. "I must have seen you, though. You looked so familiar. Kind of a déjà vu, you know?"

There was an awkward pause. She couldn't reciprocate.

"But your father," he continued. "Berkeley's where Crouch studied."

"Yeah. Daddy taught there. Crouch was a graduate student. But I was a kid," she said again. "I didn't pay much attention."

"But he's why you came here. Why you got the job."

"No," she said, toying with her salad, "I mean . . . Daddy's dead."

"I'm sorry," said Harrison.

She nodded. "He was old."

A look of curiosity came into his eyes. "So Crouch didn't solicit you?"

Kelsey shook her head. "I responded to a form letter—it was sent to all the graduates—then I was hired on the phone by HR. Crouch signed the letter, and maybe he knew it was me, but I didn't put it together until we met." She pressed her palms to the table. "At orientation he gave a big speech, welcomed each of us by name." She hesitated, but something in his open face made her continue. "He made a remark about a stuffed bear I used to have." *Mu Bear.*

"Establishing rank?"

She nodded. "I don't think anyone else caught it. It just . . . I don't know, warned me." She was thinking of the meeting they'd just had.

"Did your father do research," Harrison asked after a moment, "as well as teach?"

"A little, I think. He was really known as a writer. History of Physics primarily."

"Not Cecil Dupuis? I thought he did his writing in the '40s. He was your father, not your grandfather?"

As they left the cafeteria, she gave the quick explanation to the familiar question. Her father had been sixty when she was born. He'd had a whole other family before them. Before Galen and finally Kelsey, the afterthought to the afterthought.

"So you're following in his footsteps?"

"You mean as a scientist? I didn't have much choice really." She remembered her father's white mustache quivering with contempt when she told him she'd been considering switching to psychology, philosophy, something softer than straight science. "It's funny," said Kelsey, "now that we're talking about it, it's coming back to me. I think they were working on something together. Some kind of experiment."

"Crouch and your father? What was it?"

She shook her head. "I was just a little kid," she said for the third time.

Now they were back at the door to the lab, and Harrison seemed to be waiting for something. "Do you ski?" he asked "Snow's pretty good right now."

"I don't know why I haven't gone. I used to ski a lot in California."

"Well, look, some of us are going up tomorrow."

"Not tomorrow. I can't tomorrow." She was thinking of her plan.

"Sunday?" he suggested when she again raised her eyes to his.

"Sure. That would be fun."

"Great. OK. I'll e-mail you."

Molly, always tired in the afternoons, grew grumpy as the day wore on, complaining about the heat, turning the thermostat down to sub-arctic levels, doing deep knee bends at her desk, until Kelsey worried she'd go into early labor. Plus, her missing backups had never showed up. But there, before her, distracting her, engaging her, was her protozoan, cilia wiggling, as she prepared the next murderous chemical. Kelsey paused, eyedropper in hand. As the drop hit the slide, the face of the animal—it looked like a face anyway—changed. It seemed to grin and blush purple, its hairy bristles quivering. Then it was suddenly dying, pulsing, pushing the strange color from its tiny nucleus heart as it struggled. Kelsey watched it weaken, throbbing bloody purple.

Afterward, as she cleaned up, the inert organism dead on the slide, some of the new color slipped onto the table. The lavender stain spread quickly, damming against the fingers of her right hand. The sensation was surprising, a tingle, like bubbles bursting, a pleasant sting, then numbness. That was stupid, she thought as she scrubbed her hands in the sink. There was a sudden ruckus in the hallway and Kelsey looked up.

"Rodman," Molly yelled as the noisy group of scientists passed. "What's up?"

"We got the retrovirus vector to carry," Rodman answered. "Want to get a beer? Oh, I forgot. You're pregnant."

"That means they've met the criteria?" Kelsey asked Molly. "They have the specimen?"

"It means more work finding out."

"But we'll be getting a look at the real animals now, right?"

"We're always the last to know anything."

A gangly graying man slouched along behind the group. His odd appearance—delicate spectacles perched low on his nose, scraggly ponytail—was accentuated by horn-like protruding eyebrows which he wiggled at her. "What are you gaping at, Pie Face?"

Kelsey retreated into the doorway. "Who was that?"

"The reclusive Dr. Wickstrom. Watch out for him. He bites."

Though Molly padded after the others, Kelsey stayed behind, feeling like a misfit in her father's world. This was the kind of breakthrough he would have reveled in after months of tedium: first isolating the traits, then microscopically attaching them to the carrying virus, finally bringing it into the cell. Kelsey shuddered, imagining the little protozoans, the sharp intrusion of virus thrust into their nuclei. They'd writhe, helpless, fighting the forced change.

Chapter 2

She's awakened by rain hitting the windows, pelting, tapping like fingernails. Lightning flashes, and she sees where she is. The house is all glass—floor-to-ceiling windows—and is perched on the edge of a bluff overlooking the ocean. She wanders from room to room, each exposed, each with its view of the storm-tossed water. The scant furniture is modern, flat, and low to the ground. At first she thinks she's safe up here, then another flash illuminates the pools that are creeping toward the foundation. Waves crash against the rocks; spray begins to streak the glass. She presses her nose to the window and looks. Out to sea, the tsunami gathers.

She wakes again.

When Kelsey got up, her yellow tabby, Pedro, ran to his dish, his back broad, his tail high as he waited for his food. Kelsey poured kibble out of the bag, made coffee, and went to sit on the sofa in front of her unlit fireplace. The room was cold, the mud walls radiated the morning chill, and she gripped her cup for warmth. Pedro jumped up, and as she stroked the cat's fur, her hand, the one that had soaked up the solution in the lab, began tingling again. In that instant, her dream came back. She could see the water moving. She could feel the fear building in her chest.

Shivering, fighting off panic, she felt as though her world was breaking apart. Much as she clung to the knowledge that it was only a dream, she was afraid of being swallowed by that dream world. What was real after all? Something's going to happen, she thought. Something's got to change.

That's when the house phone rang.

"Kelsey?" A pause. "This is Stan Dresser." A resonant, masculine voice, not unfamiliar.

Pedro ran to the back door and arched against the glass, meowing loudly. Kelsey followed, phone to her ear, and fumbled with the knob.

"Go on, Pedro." But the cat sniffed the cold air and ducked back between her legs.

"Is someone there with you?" the voice on the phone asked.

"Sorry," Kelsey said, closing the door. "Do I know you?"

"We met at that party."

She scanned her memory of the Sunday afternoon potluck at Molly's. Mostly people from work, like Rodman and his wife. "You're Molly's friend?" she asked.

"I don't know any Molly."

"I haven't been to any other parties."

"That's too bad," he said. Then, "Maybe you don't remember. New Year's Eve. Karen Simpson's." He cleared his throat. "You know, the art collector?"

"You're an art collector? Oh right, the hostess."

The party was in a big, sprawling house set at the edge of the thirteenth fairway, and was crammed with people. The owner, a sixtyish woman from Dallas, had some connection to Molly's mother. Kelsey had understood the charity behind the invitation when she got the phone call—she was a stray, brand new in town—but she'd gone anyway, had had a predictably awkward time talking to women twice her age and their drunken husbands, going along on the hostess tour of the house, looking at the art, the overt sexuality of which made her uncomfortable in the company of a lecherous balding bachelor who'd attached himself to her.

"Is it Richard, did you say?" For that was the name of the man she'd escaped from.

"No. It's Stan." He paused. "I'm the one who kissed you."

"Oh." A little thrill ran up her spine, and she felt herself blush.

"Well," he said. "It was a mistake."

Just after midnight, as she was making her way back through the crowd, someone had flipped the breaker, causing a blackout. She'd kept threading between the guests in the dark, mainly by feel, listening to the excited chatter, when she'd been suddenly pulled aside and kissed. No tongue, not at first anyway, just the hands on her shoulders, pulling her to him, the lips against hers. After the first shock, the quick flare of her arousal, she'd closed her eyes and surrendered. It was what she'd been missing, longing for in some suppressed region of herself. Then the lights came back on, and the sound rushed into her ears, and he'd apologized profusely. He was movie star handsome, dark hair, perfect cheek bones, sultry brown eyes. He was wearing a tux, and his date had on a slinky silver gown that plunged to her waist in back. His forehead was perspiring lightly as he tried to explain himself, looking back and forth between the two women—Kelsey, embarrassed at her own flagrant participation, his date growing angrier with each word. Afterward, Kelsey had drunk another glass of champagne and watched as they drifted through the party. They were the most glamorous couple in the room, a drama about them, heightened by the woman's anger and Stan's solicitous attention to her.

"It took me this long to track you down," he was saying. "Can you believe it? I didn't even know your name."

"We weren't properly introduced," she said, sitting down on her bed.

"I was hoping to make it up to you." He paused. "Thing is," he said, disappointment permeating his voice, "they didn't tell me you were living with someone."

"I'm not," she said, running her fingers through her hair.

"Who's Pedro then?"

"My cat."

He was laughing now. "Why don't you ask him if I can take you to dinner?"

She felt charmed by the inclusion of the cat. "He says OK, as long as it's fish."

"Well, good. Great. Say, eight o'clock?"

"You mean tonight?"

"You're busy?" The disappointment again.

Kelsey's gaze rested on her unmade bed, then herself in the dresser mirror, dark hair messy, looping over her face, eyes shadowy, serious. "Well," she said. "I guess I could."

"Great. That's just great. Shall I pick you up?"

"I'd better meet you there. That's standard on a blind date, isn't it?"

"If I was blind," he said, "I wouldn't have called."

After he hung up, she brushed her hair until it was silky, wondering if she'd done the right thing. By then, Pedro was again at the back door, looking out through the glass, meowing. This time, when she opened it, he ran out and disappeared over the back fence.

The afternoon was clear and cold, and the sky, swept by tiny horsetail clouds, foretold in-coming weather. Kelsey drove the mile or so to the quiet neighborhood of neat bungalows and found the house. There were no other cars, so she stalled a moment, watching the trees in the yard, their bare branches windblown and fragile against the harsh sky.

The woman who answered her knock was in her early forties, slender, small-boned and flat-chested, with an abundance of light brown curly hair. Her face was slightly flat, too, almost concave around her eyes and her little up-turned nose. She had red-rimmed glasses perched on that nose, and she peered at Kelsey over the tops of them.

"I came for the dream class," Kelsey said. "In the paper?"

"I'm sorry," said the woman, "we're not having it today."

"Oh," said Kelsey, starting to turn away.

"Wait." The woman touched her shoulder. "I'm being rude. Would you come in for a moment?" She smiled for the first time as she held out her hand. "I'm Marigold, by the way."

"Kelsey Dupuis. You're the dream therapist?"

Still holding Kelsey's hand, Marigold briefly closed her eyes, as though getting a transmission. "You're really hot," she said when she opened them. "Are you ill?"

Startled, Kelsey looked down. Her hand had turned an alarming shade of red, and her fingers were visibly swollen. "I guess I touched something in the lab. It doesn't hurt," she added.

"I have some salve that might help," said Marigold, and pulled her inside.

There were shoes by the front door, so Kelsey took hers off while she waited. The room was open, the furnishings spare: pillows, cushions, a futon, some low Japanese-style tables, and an array of crystals in the picture window that sent rainbows spinning across the bare oak floor. Kelsey was immediately reminded of the house in her dream. Just then Marigold returned with a jar of salve that smelled like vanilla ice cream and began applying it. As the cool sensation penetrated, Kelsey relaxed.

"All herbal," said Marigold, "and it's been prayed over." She had a high tinkling laugh. "Want to sit a moment? I'd like to talk a little. Maybe hear one of your dreams."

Tentatively Kelsey took the futon. She was thinking this was not going as she'd planned. It was too fast, too direct, she was not prepared for a one on one. But she didn't see how to refuse this strange and now-friendly woman. Marigold pulled over a round cushion, sat cross-legged in front of her, and perched the red glasses low on her flat nose. "You have nightmares?"

Kelsey felt a shock run through her body. "How did you know?"

Marigold tapped the center of her forehead, then laughed again. "It's a common reason."

"For the last two months," Kelsey said. "Since I moved to New Mexico."

"And what is the primary symbol in the dreams?"

"Symbol?" asked Kelsey. For a moment, the word held no meaning.

"Yes," said Marigold. "Is there repeated imagery?"

Kelsey took a breath. "Water."

Their eyes met, and Kelsey noticed Marigold's were quite blue behind the lenses. She started to shiver, and Marigold leaned forward and touched her shoulder. Her fingers were long and narrow like her body, and the touch conveyed both sympathy and encouragement.

"Just breathe," Marigold said and closed her eyes.

Waiting again, Kelsey stared out the window. The clouds were thicker now, drifting rapidly. The sun came and went, causing the crystals to blink on and off hypnotically. She was trying not to think about the big dream, the one that had sent her running in the desert, the one she'd been trying to push away. Just as Kelsey felt the pressure building again, Marigold opened her eyes.

"I can see you're troubled, and I'd like to know what's troubling you."

"It's more than the nightmares," Kelsey blurted out. "I thought maybe they'd go away." She took a breath. "But now, I think . . . I think I'm hearing voices."

"What do they say?" Marigold asked.

Kelsey shook her head. "Something about my dead brother." *You will be my brother, lover, sister* . . . "I just get snatches of it, like a bad phone connection. And then I can't really remember." Should I be doing this? Kelsey wondered. Doesn't she normally charge people? "Do you think I'm crazy?" she asked.

"I hardly know you," said Marigold.

"But voices are standard for crazy people, aren't they?" She'd been worrying about this.

"And saints." Marigold smiled and glanced at a clock on the wall. Red-rimmed and modern, like the glasses, it read 2:17. The number flipped. 2:18.

"Want to tell me a dream? Any one will do. Since you came all this way."

Kelsey took another breath and studied the face in front of her. The flat bridge of the nose, the china blue eyes. And there was the slight swaying of the upright torso, the body movements, almost cat-like. She suddenly felt she was in the presence of some kind of animal, powerful, neutral, intuitive, only half-human. Her mind flashed to the tunnel she'd waded through in the dream, the sounds—water rushing, dripping—the briny smell, the moonlight and the beach below. When the bird dove, it made a sound, clear and startling, and then the water was rising, towering, beginning to crash as it moved up the beach. She remembered sinking to her knees and feeling the earth give way. She remembered the hallucination that followed.

"I can't," Kelsey said. "I'm afraid if I go back there, it will swallow me."

Marigold's face changed. She was not the cat any longer, but a therapist, a helper.

"Listen," she said. "We've just gotten started, but I get the feeling there's something important going on for you. Something that I could help you uncover."

"Like what?"

"An unresolved issue in your life? Something you're not looking at? Childhood abuse? Maybe even an outside influence at work."

"You make it sound like I'm possessed."

Marigold touched the middle of her forehead again. "It could be a past life coming through, your dead brother, even an entity that's chosen you for a channel."

"I don't believe in any of that," said Kelsey. "I'm a scientist," she explained.

Marigold got up and Kelsey followed suit. She sat by the door and put on her shoes while Marigold again disappeared into the back room. When the therapist returned, she handed Kelsey a flyer about the dream circle, and a business card. Marigold Starflower, MA, LPC, Dream Therapy, Hypnosis, Life Path and Soul-Based Counseling. Individuals and Groups.

"Starflower?" Kelsey asked. It was not her main question, rather the one that popped out.

"My parents were hippies back in the day."

"Well," said Kelsey. "Maybe I'll come back for the class. It's next week?"

"Would you rather do individual work? I have a sliding scale, if that's the issue."

Kelsey shook her head. What would her father say if she used her small inheritance for this kind of therapy? Entities? Past lives? Dreams? He'd hate it. Certainly.

"Nightmares equal repression," Marigold said now, stepping between Kelsey and the door. "I personally believe they're a beautiful gift, a chance to see inside in a dramatic way. An opportunity to break free."

Kelsey had read an article that espoused this viewpoint. She shook her head. "I'd just like them to stop."

"Listen," said Marigold. "It's very important, essential, that you not run away. I've seen ignored dreams break into the daylight, as yours are starting to do. The danger is daymares, things like accidents, car wrecks, marriage break-ups. Some dreams are prophetic." Marigold had her hand on the door handle. "Literally your water dreams could mean drowning. Or lung issues. Are you ill?" She lifted Kelsey's hand again, but it was almost normal now. Cool, pinkish.

The knock that Marigold must have been expecting came at that moment, just as the therapist pressed a baggie into Kelsey's hand. It contained several greenish ill-formed pills.

"All herbal, but you should sleep dreamless. Just don't overuse them. Call me, Kelsey." And she opened the door.

The woman who entered smiled at Kelsey, and hugged Marigold. She seemed to be looking forward to her session.

"I'll think about it," Kelsey said as she walked to her car.

Chapter 3

I am asking this of you: a brave stance, wisdom greater than mine, deliverance of a verdict. I pray for your safety.

I am watching every move you make.

It had grown cold outside, and shifting clouds haloed the moon. Kelsey had spent the afternoon resting and thinking, but not sleeping; she was too excited and uncertain. On the way to the restaurant, her muscles tightened to the verge of a shiver. Now, she stood in the red velvet foyer, staring at the swinging doors that led to the bar. Through the doors came laughter, sounds of clinking glass. Someone laid a hand across the piano keys, and the laughter grew louder.

The dining room sparkled with candlelight, white china, and crystal. Diners were nestled in red leather booths, but she didn't see Stan. Then he came striding around the corner, a drink in his hand, and she recognized him with a jolt. Tall, wearing an elegant black jacket, he approached with that same physical confidence that had mesmerized her at the party. She saw his angular bone structure, the slight furrow in his brow, his flashy smile, the dark shadow of beard lurking beneath the translucent skin. When he took her hand, a pale thrill coursed through her body.

"What lovely flowers they have," she said as they settled into his booth. A large arrangement of pink rose buds, baby's breath, and wild blue iris dominated the table's center.

The smile flashed. "My apology to you."

"Oh, they're yours?" she asked. "Thank you."

When the waiter came, Kelsey, recognizing his accent, ordered a glass of wine in French, starting a conversation in that language that went on a little too long.

"Where did you learn to speak French?" Stan asked when the waiter finally left. His drink was amber colored around the remains of ice. He'd not ordered another.

"I was born in Paris."

When she countered with a question about his origins, he said without a twinge of accent that he was from the South, then changed the subject back to her. "You must have had a sophisticated childhood. Wine, pastry shops, all that."

"I was little. I stayed in the nursery."

"Oh right, the nursery." He made a sound, half laugh, half grunt and she understood he was making fun of her privilege, or maybe his lack of it.

"You're a lawyer, didn't you say?" she asked to cover her embarrassment.

"I hadn't said. But yes, good guess." He gave her a slow look. "Or maybe you were checking up on me."

She *had* called Molly who'd called the hostess, Karen, and reported back. (Molly would never let her hear the last of it.) She found out he worked for a law firm that specialized in high-profile cases, was engaged to a former Miss New Orleans, an heiress to a pipeline fortune, but, as the hostess told Molly, a real bitch. "You were checking up on *me,* weren't you?"

She saw the perfect gleam of his teeth. "OK," he said. "We're even."

"Sometimes it doesn't seem like enough, though," Stan said. Show jazz had started in the bar and the crowd was growing louder. "The education, I mean."

Kelsey sipped her wine, feeling the warmth spread through her thighs. "No, it doesn't. Not quite."

"But for you, it's just the finishing touch, right? I mean, your family's well-off."

"Just comfortable. My father was a . . . an academic."

"All I meant," Stan said, "is that my childhood wasn't nice like yours."

The revelation startled her. Was it poverty? Abuse? She watched him watching the crowd, his profile turned her way, and noticed a tiny scar across his eyebrow. But she could not imagine a parent striking that face. No, she decided, he'd probably suffered some family dysfunction, drinking perhaps, divorce, maybe an uncommunicative father who'd had affairs. Then Stan turned back toward her, and she felt a pulse of warmth. When his knee brushed hers under the table and he covered her hand with his, she, too, had to look away.

They ordered new drinks and Stan raised his glass. "To us," he said.

"To us getting to know each other," she countered.

He took a long swallow. "Tell me something about yourself. What brought you to town?"

"A job," she said. "A coincidence, actually." She told him about the old connection, Crouch in his late thirties, her father well past retirement age. "It must have been a kind of last chance for both of them. That was the attraction." She smiled as her memory loosened. "Cecil had lots of students, but Myron Crouch was his favorite."

"You call your father by his first name?"

"It's just that he didn't always seem like my father. He was . . ." she searched for the right words, ". . . grand in the world, I guess. He died six years ago."

"I'm sorry." He looked away, lost in thought for a moment. "I read something about your company, I think. Bio-engineering? You're going after oil spills, right?"

"And chemicals. The organism would thrive on any variety of pollutants."

"Land or ocean?"

"Both," she said, and a prickle ran up her spine. *Water.*

"You like your job?" Stan asked after a pause.

"Sometimes."

"Seems like a big commitment if you're not into it."

She heard an echo of Harrison's remark. *Following in your fa-*

ther's footsteps. But thoughts of Harrison vanished as Stan touched her hand.

"I always wanted to be a lawyer, ever since I knew what justice meant. When I'm in the courtroom, defending someone . . ." He stopped. "You don't think ill of me, do you? A lawyer? Admitting he likes it?"

"No," she said, laughing, "of course not."

"It just suits me, that's all. Well, you'll see."

Waiters were running back and forth carrying loaded trays, a cork popped, diners were shouting to be heard. In the bar, the crowd was enthusiastically clapping after every number. Kelsey was hungry, but she hardly cared now. Stan's thigh was so near she could feel the heat flowing across her lap. It was practically all she was aware of. That and her growing giddiness as she drank her wine and listened to him talk. Stan flagged down a busboy who returned a moment later with their appetizers. Microgreens, a scattering of scallops.

"Mostly men in your profession," Stan said, when they'd polished off the scant food.

"I guess so," she said. "Well, there's Molly."

"Good odds for a woman."

It took her a beat to understand.

"Some of the guys are pretty nerdy." She laughed. "I mean really nerdy."

"What about back in California? Someone waiting for you?"

She thought of Joe, her last serious boyfriend, two years ago. She'd dropped out of school to be with him, but he'd left her, and the humiliation had been deep. Now she saw they'd really been unsuited for each other. Joe with his appetites for intoxicants, sex, and thrills, his casual lack of ambition, his inability to commit. She shook her head. "Long over with."

"So you're free to see me? Forgive me, if I'm being too direct."

Again she shook her head. "But what about you? That woman you were with?"

"Broke up," he said. "Going that way for a long time." Then the smile flashed and he said, "That kiss was the best thing that ever happened to me."

So she understood she'd been part of it.

After that they sat, empty plates in front of them, water glasses dry, drinks drained. They complained to each other, enjoyed the complaining, then tired of it. Stan went in search of the waiter, returned with two more drinks. She got a whiff of something sweet as they clinked, and she realized he must have switched to ginger ale.

"But I'm intrigued," said Stan, "by something you alluded to earlier. You agreed with me about education not being enough. For me it was necessary, maybe insufficient. But for you . . ."

She was very hungry now, and definitively getting a little drunk, but the overriding thing was the attraction. He was looking into her eyes with undeniable intensity. Plus he'd gone straight to the core of something she'd been thinking all day. Who was she, if she got away from her father's influence, from the scientist she'd become?

"I had no real choice," she told him. "Education was expected. A particular kind of education. I've become what my father wanted me to be, but maybe it masks the real me. Maybe I'm a totally different person inside."

"How so?"

"Not so conventional, so good girl," she took a chance, "so smart." She laughed. "What if I have a secret self? A wild self? Someone I've never let out before."

"I'd like to—"

Just then their plates arrived. The trout was served whole, butter-toasted almonds covered it like oily scales, and the white cooked eye stared up at her. Suddenly, Kelsey was back in her nightmare. She saw the wave crashing; it was full of jewel-eyed fish, their high-pitched voices whining in her head. A warning. *Too late. Too late.* Then the room came rushing back with its clatter of dishes and roaring voices.

Stan had slid away across the red leather cushion, as though giving her the space to regain her equilibrium. She'd left the fish untouched, was eating bread and butter and drinking water instead of wine now, though perhaps it was already too late.

"So tell me more," Stan said when she finally sat back, "about the wild Kelsey who's hidden inside the demure and sophisticated scientist." His brown eyes were soft, and held, not so much curiosity, as longing, which made her feel sad.

"I met a therapist today," Kelsey said. "She told me I'm probably not crazy." She could hear her own voice sounding tinny, growing over-excited.

Stan slid closer. "What made you go?"

"I dream." He draped his arm across the booth behind her and she felt some dark core of herself rush up toward the light. "Nightmares. Tidal waves, floods, anything to do with water."

"You're afraid of water?"

She started trembling in earnest now. "I don't like being afraid. I've never been afraid like this. I'm usually a pretty brave person."

His knee was pressing hers, his arm, behind her, didn't quite touch her shoulders. She could stop, or she could go on. "Marigold thinks there's an outside influence at work. I think . . ." her teeth started to chatter ". . . I have some kind of change . . . some kind of . . . quest . . . I need to pull the pieces of myself back together." She looked up and when Stan dropped his arm around her shoulders, she burst into tears against his chest.

"It's OK," he said, stroking her arm and kissing her hair. "I'm here. I'll take care of you."

In the ladies room mirror, her eyes looked washed out and mismatched, her mouth enlarged, as though she'd been kissed. She repaired the best she could, adding lipstick and splashing her cheeks to bring down the blush. When she got back, Stan's credit card receipt was on the bill tray, and he was gone.

She thought he'd left her, but then he was there again, the flowers in one hand. As he walked her to her car, she recast the evening. The flirtation, the sexual excitement were gone; in their place, chagrin. She'd gotten drunk, lost control. Maybe he'd taken advantage, sought out her vulnerability, but she could only blame herself.

"I'm sorry." She faced him under the streetlight. "I don't know what happened. I think I drank too much. I don't usually cry like that."

"Is that still bothering you?" He set the flowers on her car and moved closer.

She'd been anticipating the kiss all evening, but it felt ruined now. He seemed to sense it. He grasped her shoulders like the night of the party, kissed her lightly on both cheeks, barely grazing her lips in between. "When can I see you again?"

"I'm sorry," she said again. "I'm so embarrassed."

"Don't be crazy, Kelsey." He bent close and whispered. "I think I've been looking for you my whole life."

She couldn't believe she'd heard right, yet she wanted it to be so. As she sat in her car, watching him walk away, she knew she'd been ambushed by his deliberate spell. But she could still feel his hands on her shoulders, and her mouth thrilled from the light brush of his lips.

Chapter 4

Why can't you hear me? Must I crack you open like an egg?

Kelsey lay back and watched the day come up, yellow, behind thick clouds. Snow drifted down in soft flakes, and the patio was already covered. She was groggy from Marigold's pill, a little hung over, and she was thinking about Stan.

He'd called to make sure she'd gotten home all right, had assured her she'd been fine, lovely, in fact. Then he told her his secret: he'd kissed her on purpose that night at the party.

"Why?" she asked.

"I don't know," he said. "I just had to."

Kelsey lingered in bed, savoring the memory of his voice, his breath on the phone. Too late, she got up and fixed breakfast. She was sorting through a box of ski gear when Harrison knocked. He stood in her doorway, wet flakes gathering on his beard and in his hair.

"Hope you like powder," he said. "It's going to be deep."

"I'm almost ready. Come in a minute." She pulled a red ski hat out of the box. "I lost my helmet in the move," she said. "What's the report up there?"

"Thirteen inches overnight. Could snow all day."

Pedro came running out of the bedroom, tail erect, meowing a greeting. Harrison bent to pet him, and the cat brushed against his legs, then shied from the wetness with a loud protest.

Kelsey laughed. "Serves him right. He doesn't usually like

strangers." She picked up her boots and her bag of gear. "Well," she said, "I guess that's it."

"I'll grab your skis," Harrison said.

She turned to see them, leaning against the wall. They weren't right—one tip was dangling, the fiber glass ragged at the break. She blinked hard and they were whole again. As Harrison picked them up, she squatted to pat Pedro, and to compose herself. *It must be those herbs*, she thought. *I'll have to tell Marigold.*

"They're calling it the Siberian Snowman." Harrison said as he drove up the plowed and sanded road toward the ski basin. "A wet storm off the Pacific, colliding with a cold air mass from the Rockies. Denver got three feet last night. It's supposed to get bitter cold."

"I didn't know it was coming," Kelsey said, staring out at the steady flurry.

He glanced over at her. "It's been all over the news."

The parking lot was only half full, but traffic was steady behind them. Quickly they unloaded their equipment, layered on their warm gear, and started toward the base, boots squeaking on the snow.

The lift took them up over trees flocked with frozen clumps of white. A ski patrol zigzagged through powder at the edge of the slope, then disappeared into the trees. Fat flakes settled on their thighs.

"Groomer to warm up?" Harrison asked, shifting his poles to unload.

Kelsey smiled as her skis made contact and exhilaration took over. She made a little hop in front of him, then two tiny wiggle turns. She danced her way through a puff of untracked powder on the edge of the trail, before looking over her shoulder to make sure he was following.

Harrison proved a match for Kelsey. Where she had grace and style, he had lightness and speed. Where she had fluidity, he had strength. And his sheer boldness took her breath away. He flashed in and out of trees, and plunged down steep gullies without the briefest hesitation. She paused a heartbeat before following.

They found the lightest powder, floated as though through clouds, skied camouflaged fields of bumps with the snow flying in their faces, working their knees up and down until their thighs burned. Late morning, the sun winked out and he showed her a tight little glade that opened into a hidden bowl, glistening with crystalline pinpricks of color. They made the pitch, then crossed back and forth through the flats, leaving a print behind them like a double helix.

When they stopped in the bar for a beer and a burger, Harrison told her about a run down the undeveloped back side of the mountain. Outside, the sky had turned black, and snow fell thickly. On their next ride, they could hardly see the chair in front of them. As they got off the lift and moved toward the ridge, the wind whipped the flakes into hard stinging crystals. Tracks diverged in several directions, but they saw no other skiers.

"This way," Harrison yelled, and they dropped into a sheltered bowl. It was a heavenly pitch, filled with virgin snow, up over their thighs in places. Then they were in a tight runout following a frozen streambed through the woods. At last the trail opened onto an old logging road covered with cross country tracks. From there, they hitchhiked, taking a ride in the back of a truck with a bunch of hyped-up snowboarders.

When they got back to the parking lot, Kelsey was seriously cold and ready to call it quits.

"It's been such a great day," Harrison said. "Just one more ride?"

Kelsey stood, deciding. He hadn't moved toward the lift or toward his truck either, but he was grinning, she could tell, even under all the gear, the goggles, the neck warmer, his frosty beard. He stood, square, alert, ready to go. She laughed and followed him, infected by his mood.

They took the first lift, then raced after each other to catch the second to the top. Icy wind blasted them as the chair swung away from the first tower. She shook her hands, sending a tingle of blood into her frozen fingers. At the top, the snow blew sideways. Kelsey crooked her arm over her face and followed the tails of Harrison's skis.

Snow had accumulated over the old tracks, so everywhere was fresh, though rugged from irregularities underneath. Kelsey's body rose and fell as she skied blindly ahead. After a time the trail steepened, and Kelsey realized Harrison had led her down the wild back side again.

Pine gave way to aspen, spindly and silver in the falling light. They stayed high and traversed, then abruptly Harrison pulled up in a hockey stop. Beneath them, the mountain fell sharply away. Boulders lined the bottom of the cliff a hundred feet below.

"I didn't see that one coming," Harrison said through heavy breath.

Kelsey's heart pounded. "Look," she said, "I really don't like this. I'm cold, and it's getting late. And we're lost."

"No," he said. "If we traverse a little farther, we should come to a big open area, and then we can drop down easily. I've seen it from below. We'll hitch a ride to town, and I can get my neighbor to bring me back up for my truck."

Too cold to stand there and argue, she sidestepped up the hill to firmer ground. She led now, past frequent rock-filled gullies that became the norm of the terrain. But each ravine grew gentler, and the rocks less numerous. She began thinking that a steep descent would get them quickly to the access road, and they could get back to the pavement in minutes. She didn't count on finding the open slope Harrison had described. Finally she came to the chute she'd been looking for. It was steep but rock-free. It looked skiable. Barely, but skiable, yes.

Harrison pulled in behind her. "You're not thinking of . . ."

She made the plunge while she still had the nerve. That first instant she was weightless, flying into the white void. When she landed, pitched slightly forward, it felt like a gentle tripping, like a shoelace or a hem undone. Her left ski caught, her tips crossed, poked under, then it all speeded up. Flung into the air, landing hard on her back, bouncing, rolling, tangled, everything coming apart—skis, poles, chunks of powder, her scream, Harrison's yell—she was sliding backwards, out of control, grasping at the snow with her hands. She hit something, her feet went over her head, a branch whapped her face, then all was still.

Her hat was gone, her goggles hung by a thread, and she tasted blood. Shakily, she tested her limbs, pushed upward, and waved. Harrison shouted, and then she heard the rumble.

The slide of snow swept down in a quiet thunder. She had the presence of mind to grasp a small pine and cling to it. All she felt was the cold and the wet, and that she couldn't move. Oh, God, she thought, when she could think at all. Oh, God.

Kelsey's entire body, even her face, was encased in snow. She'd struggled at first, but that ate up her little air, and now she lay still, feeling the icy coffin solidify. She was no longer cold; sleepy warmth numbed her. In growing resignation, she relaxed her grip on the little tree, and her hand fell. Then she knew: she'd found an air pocket.

She began to dig, expanding the hole toward her face, pulled off her gloves and clawed at the snow with bare hands, freeing her nose and mouth. She took a big gulping breath.

The air was only slightly richer than before. She let her heartbeat slow, then dug again, hands aching with cold. Inch by inch, Kelsey slid into the space under the tree. She could smell the running sap. She thought she saw light. Inside the light, she saw a sparkling wave cresting in the desert. Then the world shook like it had once before, and the land was covered in water. A second rumble, another warning, and in that instant, an icy hand seized the back of her head and slammed her face forward. She saw black, then white, then rich, old vision.

Childhood, her brother Galen, her mother's face—so young!—bent over her crib. White metal, a hospital, nurses gathered around her incubator, a black tunnel, and she shooting backward, down it. Flying.

At the end of the tunnel, brightness exploded. An old woman in colonial dress, bonnet pulled tight over her ears, waded through a snowy woods. Then the flying pictures again, the tunnel, an Indian cave, a Cossack horde thundering on their horses, a white temple, blue sky through an arched glass-less window. Kelsey reeled away, spinning wildly through time. She saw the ghostly shape of her own girl-child and slipped inside it. Now another girl appeared, dark braids streaming down her back, sandy feet lifted in disdain above the snow. The barefoot one fingered a crystal, her green eyes blazing an invitation. She reached out and they clasped hands like old friends. Together they skipped backward through the layered ages toward their ancient destination . . . .

Commotion woke her and the spiral of time unwound. Kelsey opened her eyes to a sinking red sun. She wanted to go into the red.

Kelsey.

Blinking, she saw multiple faces. Chattering, incomprehensible, insistent. Slowly she came back, cold, so cold, and everything throbbing.

She felt them wrap her. She struggled inside her mute body as they lifted her and took her away, jostling, close to the ground. Someone was moaning and wouldn't stop. *Hush, hush.* At last it grew quiet and very dark. Only a swishing noise and she could sleep. Then many voices again waking her, and jarring light against the darkness. She was burning up now, the steady pain a backdrop that slowly filled everything until it burst open like fireworks, scattering the last pieces of her awareness against the night sky.

The dream took hold. It was strong and deep. Kelsey dreamed another world. Someplace distant and warm. Someplace she'd known a very long time ago.

The Moment We Knew

For you, I must remember everything. My ignoble death was of little consequence against the context of a lifetime. There are far worse things than such a death. Sudden shock, the dawn of terrible loss. Guilt? Unfathomable sorrow? Loneliness that feels like wood in the heart. Still, my strange new life went on from there, those many years afterward. What suffering was that, to long for a death that all the others had been granted?

Instead I will think of something else now: my one true love and the moment we knew.

A spring night, soft and moonless. Jarad and I take my grandmother down to the beach where she's promised to show us a marvel or two. Muamdi, despite her blindness, is surefooted as we wind our way between the houses. She knows the path by heart, while Jarad and I, used to relying on our sight, stub our toes before we reach the open dunes.

This almost-summer evening, the sand retains the sun's heat, and the first marvel becomes evident: the delicious way we sink to our calves, like into the comfort of our beds and then into sleep. Muamdi hums as she walks, then waits while we climb a dune and slide down. We do it again, though we're not children. We do it because it is a relief to let go our seriousness for once.

When we finally tire of our game, we sit on the sand with Muamdi. Our eyes adjust to the dark, and we see the ocean is almost silvery tonight. It sings a lullaby—hush, hush—as the waves pulse to the shore. My grandmother conjures a fire from beach sticks. There is vision in the crackling fire, the shifting flames, and potency in the shimmering air, so we sit and wait for what will come. Muamdi has trained me to this posture of waiting, though it goes against my nature, but Jarad seems to hold it easily. He is alert, something is out there, and after awhile, I see it too. Spouts at the edge of the sea, just outside the surf. "Look," says Jarad as another one blows high into the air.

"This is what I wanted you to see," Muamdi says, smiling. "There are babies, too."

I have been alive long enough to know that the whales move past our island this time of year, but for some reason I have forgotten this truth in my excitement at Muamdi's invitation. "Your artistic friend," she said, "the one we saw at market the other day." Tonight I am doubly disappointed in myself for momentarily losing my second sense. I can usually hear the fish and the sea creatures, if I listen, and can feel them moving through the water.

Tonight it seems as though Jarad is the one with the second sight, for he calls out in advance when each whale breaches. One of them, no two, a baby and its parent, come closer to shore, as though to have a look at us. We wade into the tide pools, the water still body-warm, and follow them as they move across the shallows of the bay. Muamdi laughs and raises her tunic above her knees. I dance in the shiny surf, spinning with happiness.

Jarad twirls behind me, mimicking my turns at half-speed. He is graceful and boyish at the same time. And so I know the last of the marvels. A swelling in my heart for him. A special liking I've not felt before.

Abruptly, I stop the dance, and walk beside Muamdi who's been watching us through her blind eyes, knowing it would be so. She's planned this. But why? When I glance at Jarad, he looks quickly away. And in that quickness, that sharp movement of his head, that swishing of his hair as it settles against his face, I find all the reassurance I need.

PART II

REGRESSION

Chapter 5

What has come of the world, turned upside down by water? The ocean rages, and I am but a bit of cork stuck to its skin. My father's boat, so battered and broken, clings to life, tenacious as a mussel. Yet I would not live, for Jarad is drowned with the others. Do you hear me say it? I would not live without his love.

Kelsey woke in an unfamiliar bed, in an unfamiliar room. The white ceiling squares formed a wavering path that led to a heavy door; she opened it with her mind and stepped through.

Must I live again the events that wrought this terrible pain? Must I scrutinize the things I did, ere once more they're laid to rest? No. You ask too much of me. I've already paid my price, double, and tenfold.

Kelsey tried to sink back into that place where pleasant beginnings blurred unhappy endings. Something had come before this torment, something softer, something more certain than this pain.

If I could go back to the day I was welcomed by the world as a woman—an azure day, so beautiful and harsh, the smells of roasting lamb and spilled wine, the sudden hush as the guests lean forward to listen—would I say yes to Gewil instead of no?

Gewil takes my hand and kneels. The people smile and coo; they know what comes next, for I've long been promised. They wait to hear the happy words, and any pretty sentiment I might add. I could tell them how this alliance brings great good fortune to my family, and that I've always longed for this day. Instead, I say my soul weeps at the thought of this marriage, its bounds and duties. I say I'm not ready for love, that I may never be.

What did I know of love on that day so long ago? Red now, livid and wounded, it was only a bud then, sweet and pink. I had a child's sense of love, Muamdi first, then Mama and Papa, the little ones when they were good.

But Gewil? If I had loved him instead of Jarad, would all this be different? Would thousands have lived instead of died?

Even so, I could never say anything but no.

Listen, friend of my soul. I travel far and at great peril to bring you this news.

Kelsey jolted awake at the sound of footsteps coming toward her. She struggled to get away, but something unyielding had her by the neck. Pain rode down her vertebrae, and she saw a blurry face. She blinked and the face came closer. It was old, the skin folded by tiny lines. Red lips puckered but didn't kiss.

"Mama."

"Don't talk, Lamb. Just forget about it now."

"Mama?"

"You gave us a scare. But it's all over." The voice cracked and Kelsey felt her mother's hand come into hers, like a child's.

"Wednesday," the nurses told her when she asked what day it was. "You've been unconscious since Sunday."

"I was dreaming," Kelsey answered, before drifting back to sleep.

On Thursday, Kelsey made better sense of things. She was in a private hospital room; her face was swollen on one side, her neck was in a brace, and her back in traction. She ached in any position, and her spine ricocheted pain at the slightest movement. She was told she had a concussion, severe whiplash, and two broken ribs. The coma, they couldn't explain.

Despite her discomfort, Kelsey had an inexplicable feeling of completeness. For the first time in a long while, she welcomed sleep, slipped into it willingly, unafraid of her dreams. The high emotions—sorrow, anger, and joy—seemed only the painful outer shell to the dream. She'd penetrated further; some important truth lay within her grasp.

She'd heard of near-death experiences, where you approached a brilliant white light and were surrounded by extraordinary love. She couldn't remember anything like that. In fact, she remembered nothing between going to work on Friday and waking up in the hospital.

Her physician told her it was normal to forget events surrounding a trauma. It might be days or months, even years before she remembered, if at all. The nurses told her how cold her body had been when the ski patrol brought her in, how the doctors thought she wouldn't make it. And how attentive her boyfriend had been.

"Boyfriend?" asked Kelsey. "What boyfriend?"

Jackie, the night nurse, winked. "The one who brought you in. He sure was worried about you. He's been here every night."

On Friday it was light in the room when Kelsey woke. She felt cranky and all slept out, the transcendent feeling gone. Her mother dozed in the chair, mouth open, white head thrown back. Though they'd kept their distance in the six years since her father's funeral, Kelsey was glad to see her. She seemed old and harmless, vulnerable even, as she slept.

"How are we feeling this morning?" The day nurse asked. "Ready to eat something?"

"Oh, nothing for me," Kelsey's mother said, sitting up, and Kelsey immediately adjusted her assessment of her parent.

"Coffee then?" The nurse smiled brightly. "For both of you?"

They drank the coffee and ate, Mrs. Dupuis's jaw working on a piece of Kelsey's toast she'd buttered for herself. "I went to your apartment this morning," she said as she wiped crumbs from her mouth. "That cat nearly drove me mad, rubbing my leg and making noises like a strangled bird."

"Pedro! Is he OK?"

"I arranged with that Mexican woman to clean up around there. To her credit she refused payment when I told her about our tragedy."

"Mrs. Rodriguez? My landlady?" Kelsey asked.

Mrs. Dupuis warmed to her topic. "I don't see how people live with all this dirt. Dirt roads, dirt houses. It's so . . . primitive." Her mother's mouth puckered, and it all came rushing back. The poisonous tongue, the judgment, the superiority, why she'd stayed away so long.

"Oh," Mrs. Dupuis said, pulling something out of her purse and slapping it down on Kelsey's tray. "They gave me this, but it's broken. I thought it was a transistor radio. It kept playing the same song over and over again."

"It's a cell phone, Mama," Kelsey said. "You must know that." There was a text from Molly teasing her about her date, and seven more from the same number, a contact she'd not yet programmed in.

Her mother sniffed. "I certainly never knew how to use one of those silly things."

"No," said Kelsey, remembering this meddling, spying side too. "But I bet you do now."

The next time Kelsey opened her eyes, an extravagant bouquet sat on her tray table, roses, still tucked into tight buds, red as nail polish.

The card read, "Hope you get well soon. Love, Stan." The handwriting was loopy, feminine, obviously done by an employee at the flower shop. The message meant nothing, but slowly, his voice came back to her. She had the sensation of a word on the tip of her tongue. As she reached, it receded into her throat. She stared at the flowers, hoping they'd trigger something, but the roses were mute and their perfume suggested nothing but dreams.

"You have a visitor," a nurse said later that afternoon. "Shall I let him in?"

A sprig of yellow daffodils poked its way around the heavy metal door, and the visitor, dressed in denim, his light hair damp and curling at the temples, followed. His eyes, behind his glasses, looked intelligent. This was Harrison she knew, though he was only vaguely familiar. She sniffed his flowers and waited for the jolt of memory. None came.

Harrison stood at the foot of the bed, shifting his weight, and asked how she was feeling. "I guess I owe you an apology," he said.

"For what?"

"For taking you up there. For being so stupid."

"Shouldn't I be thanking you?" she asked. "Didn't you rescue me?"

"It was the ski patrol. I only—"

"Please stop." Kelsey said. "I don't care about any of that."

Harrison slipped his hands into his pockets.

"Sit down," she said. "It's hard to see you way over there."

He came around and took the chair.

"Look," she said. "I don't remember the accident, I don't even remember going skiing. But I know you couldn't have stopped it. Nothing could have." She sat up higher in the bed. "Something changed when I was under the snow. It's like I . . . retrieved something. It's slipping away now, but it was real. Yesterday it was . . ." Emotion closed her throat.

"This is too much for you."

"No, please. Help me, if you can."

He placed his hand briefly on the bed beside hers. "Kelsey, I felt so bad. The first night they wouldn't let me see you. After they moved you out of intensive, I sat here and read you poetry, psalms, Buddhist prayers, stuff I grabbed off my shelf. But I didn't feel like I was reaching you, so I just watched you sleep."

"I think I dreamed that."

"I remember thinking you were somewhere else, because your face was so altered. Then for an instant the coma broke, and you opened your eyes; they were very clear, and you mumbled something, and just for a moment I understood."

"Understood what?"

"I couldn't make out the words. But I was sure you were telling me it was all right. That you were home maybe."

She took a breath. "I must have seen things. I don't remember.

I woke up feeling near to something . . . ." Her gaze wandered to the ceiling, to the white squares. "I released some fear."

"You didn't talk about it that day, but—"

They were interrupted by the click of the door. Kelsey's mother, dressed up in a navy suit, stockings, and heels, trotted into the room. Harrison rose and extended his hand. "I'm glad to meet you at last, Mrs. Dupuis. I'm sorry our first conversation was unpleasant."

She gave him three limp fingers and averted her eyes.

"God knows I shocked you. We still didn't know . . ." Harrison glanced at Kelsey.

"I don't see how she got into such trouble. She's a wonderful skier."

"That's true," said Harrison. "She's a terrific skier."

"Mama," Kelsey said, "Harrison saved me. You should be grateful to him."

"I can't believe he's such a hero. If he were, he would have prevented—"

"You're right. I should have done more," Harrison said. "I apologize to you both."

Mrs. Dupuis blazed a smile at him. "Then we do agree." She waved toward her daughter. "Kelsey's too independent. She takes too many risks."

Harrison seemed to be deciphering this last.

"Well you might as well take a chair, young man, and have your visit," Mrs. Dupuis said. "I don't bite, you know."

They made an uneasy group, the visitors stiffly adjacent, and Kelsey half-turned to face them, her blankets pulled up for warmth.

"So you're a scientist?" Mrs. Dupuis asked. "A Ph.D.? You seem young."

"I'm thirty-seven. I've had my doctorate six years now."

"Cecil had his when he was twenty-two. Of course I, didn't know him then."

"He must have been a remarkable man."

"They were like gods, you know, those scientists. They made such leaps toward progress. Nothing since comes close. Don't you agree?"

"Nothing I've seen." Harrison gave Kelsey a hidden smile, then reached into his jacket pocket. "I almost forgot. From work."

It was a picture of a bunny sitting in the snow, a cast on one leg and a ski on the other. Inside it said: Hope you're not on your tail too long. The card was signed by almost everyone, including Myron Crouch. "We want you back in the saddle soon, Kelsey," he'd written.

"Let's see." Her mother put on her glasses, and her face suddenly gathered color. "Myron Crouch," she said before dropping the card onto the bed. "That can't be the same one."

"He runs the company where I work, Mama. Didn't I tell you?"

"Well, I never. He's nothing but a two-bit liar and a thief."

Her mother's remark produced a memory as visceral as it was visual. Kelsey had not understood the particulars of her father's sudden retirement, but she remembered the endless arguments between her parents before her mother's outrage turned to icy silence. All of a sudden, Kelsey pieced together the fragments of the scandal: the press coming around, the hearing, her mother's urging, and Cecil's final acquiescence. There'd been a student at the center of it. With a chill, Kelsey realized that student must have been Myron Crouch.

When the conversation returned to skiing, Mrs. Dupuis dropped her contentious attitude. "My husband and I used to ski the Alps. Everyone wore black, not those gaudy things you see nowadays." She lowered her voice. "And we always saw Royalty."

"Was Kelsey with you?"

"On no, she came along much later. We had Cecil's boys—I was his second wife, you know." As Mrs. Dupuis talked about the children and Europe, her face grew softer, and her voice became low and melodic. "Kelsey was such a wunderkind," she concluded. "A marvelous little girl. Quite a natural athlete. Better than any of them. Except Galen, of course."

Kelsey started. She'd not heard her mother speak her brother's name in twenty years.

"Galen's your brother?" Harrison asked.

"He died," Kelsey said quickly. "In the Peace Corps. The train was ambushed."

Mrs. Dupuis sat straight-backed in the chair. When she realized the attention was on her, she spoke. "So, Dr. Stanton, tell us how you rescued my daughter."

"Stillman, Mama."

Harrison turned to Kelsey. "Perhaps you're tired. I should go."

"Not yet," she said. "It might help me remember."

Harrison nodded and folded his hands in his lap. He talked about how it had snowed, was still snowing, how the powder was soft and light. He named the runs, the order they'd skied them. Mrs. Dupuis showed a keen interest.

"It was an undeclared competition," Harrison said to her, "who was the better skier."

"Kelsey, of course," Mrs. Dupuis answered.

Kelsey closed her eyes as Harrison described skiing the back of the mountain, how beautiful it had been. Then he told of the last ride up the chairlift in the bitter cold, and his decision to go down the undeveloped run again.

"There was a particular open slope I'd found one summer when I was hiking, but I'd never skied it before. It would have been spectacular in untracked snow with a view of the sunset. The conditions were perfect. But we got a little off course and started getting into rocky terrain and aspens. They're trouble, you know."

Harrison's description had a hypnotic effect. Kelsey saw blowing snow that gave way to rain and wind. She smelled salt in the air.

Harrison's voice broke through. ". . . too far to climb up by then and Kelsey got in front of me. Suddenly we were at the top of this bare ravine, and I could see she was going to go for it. I yelled, but she didn't stop."

"She went down on purpose?" Mrs. Dupuis asked.

"I guess she thought she could ski it." He paused. "Then she was just gone."

Kelsey shifted deeper into her bed and closed her eyes. There was a great calm now, a white sun slowly collapsing. Then darkness. And that feeling. Distant pleasure, flooding warmth.

Her mother was asking something, and she felt Harrison gazing at her. It had only been an instant, but she had been back there, in a world of warmth and the sighing sound of the sea.

"The ski patrol saw our tracks in the sweep," Harrison said. "Came over the top to see if we'd gotten down. I guess they heard me after all."

"What would you have done if they hadn't?"

"I tried to dig," Harrison said. "It caved a second time." His face grew red, and Kelsey wanted to help him, but the spot of warmth released her and her teeth began to chatter. Harrison and her mother stood simultaneously. Mrs. Dupuis rang for the nurse.

"I'm sorry, Kelsey," Harrison said as he took his leave. Light glinted off his glasses, obscuring his eyes as the metal door swung shut behind him.

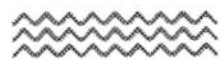

It was about five that afternoon, when Kelsey had a second visitor. The nurse had called in a psychologist because of Kelsey's memory loss. The psychologist's name was Marigold Starflower, and though the name did not ring a bell, Kelsey recognized her at once. Marigold gave a little startled laugh and said, "Well, I guess there are no coincidences." There followed a long and fruitful talk about Kelsey's childhood, her brother Galen's death, why he'd gone into the Peace Corps against her father's wishes, daytime hallucinations, giant waves, near-death experiences, fear and not-fear, and pleasant dreams of warmer climes. It had grown dark in the room before Marigold left her to sleep again.

Chapter 6

"I didn't expect you this early," Kelsey said as she ushered Stan inside. Still dressed in his business suit, exuding masculine confidence, he was larger than life against the backdrop of her tiny living room. She watched him take in her shabby surroundings, the smoky fireplace, the sagging vigas, the closed door to the bedroom where her mother was napping. She thought of the text messages he'd sent her, a casual invitation, a more formal one, then some reassurances, and finally a plea to call him no matter what. All before he'd learned of her accident.

"Sorry I didn't visit you." Stan kissed her good cheek. "Work's been nuts."

"That's all right." She'd gotten the impression he didn't want to come to the hospital—but now, almost two weeks later, with the swelling and bruising finally going down, she was glad. She'd looked a fright. His gaze settled on her, and she caught something, a quick assessment, disappointment maybe. She pulled her sweatshirt up over her neck brace.

"You'll be perfect again in a day or so," he said when they were seated at the kitchen table. He touched the exact spot where the swelling still lingered. Then he smiled and began telling her about a new case he was working on, defending a Mexican client against U.S. seizures and import charges. "Customs has slapped them with huge fines. It's financial, certainly, but more that that, it's the principle. Their guilt can't be presumed. We expect due process."

"Innocent until proven guilty, that's our motto," said Mrs. Dupuis, coming out of Kelsey's bedroom. She was back in her dress and stockings, her white hair combed fluffy, and a bright smear of lipstick on her mouth.

"It's not a motto, Mama," Kelsey said. "It's the law."

When Stan stood and held out the chair, Mrs. Dupuis turned her face up to him and beamed. "Now there's a proper gentleman."

"Always a pleasure to assist a beautiful lady." Stan's smile included Kelsey.

"You are too kind," Mrs. Dupuis said, batting her eyelashes.

After the introductions, Stan drew her out with small talk. As her mother launched into her favorite topic—the ugliness of the town, the dust, the dryness—Kelsey watched with muted astonishment. Her mother had been so unkind to Harrison who'd been attentive and helpful, bringing in the rollaway and groceries twice. Now under Stan's attentions, she was acting like a schoolgirl. "I'm told you have a nice little opera," Mrs. Dupuis conceded, "and some decent restaurants. Of course, we haven't been out of this house once."

"Why don't you let me take you and Kelsey to dinner?" Stan asked.

Kelsey objected that she was still too tired at night, so Stan suggested Sunday brunch. "We could have a lovely meal at one of several places, Mrs. Dupuis."

"Call me Betty, please." She tilted her chin as Kelsey had seen her do countless times.

Kelsey excused herself and went into the bedroom. Her body ached as she struggled into her jeans and a nicer shirt, but wasn't this flirting too much to bear? For a second longer, she stared out the window at the spring afternoon and the few crocuses poking through the snow. Beyond the winter landscape, she sensed a warm place with sun and sand, and deeply familiar people. She closed her eyes, but already the laughter from the other room had spoiled the mood.

"Oh, look what you've done all by yourself," Kelsey's mother said. "And where's your neck brace?"

Stan rose to pull out her chair. "Betty said you went skiing with a friend from work. She said you can't remember anything."

"I'm up to Saturday night," Kelsey said. "After that it's a blank."

"You remember we went out? And talked on the phone?"

"What about?" Betty Dupuis looked from one to the other.

"Love," said Stan, and Kelsey felt her cheeks go hot.

"See, you don't need that quack," Mrs. Dupuis said, clapping her hands. "She going to get hypnotized," she added in a stage whisper to Stan. "If I thought she'd listen, I'd forbid it."

"I'm old enough to make my own decisions, Mama."

Mrs. Dupuis sniffed and got up. Stan rose to help her, but she turned her back and disappeared into the bedroom. Stan put his elbows on the table and leaned closer. She could smell his masculine scent under his cologne. "She's worried about you, that's all."

"I can't help it. She gets on my nerves."

"I'm just saying, lighten up a little, Kelsey. She's your mother."

Kelsey felt angry with him, betrayed even, and at the same time, like a spoiled child. He took her hand, and then Mrs. Dupuis reappeared, freshly made-up, carrying her purse.

"Stan is taking me shopping," she announced.

He confirmed it with a nod.

Moments later, Kelsey watched from the doorway as Stan seated Betty Dupuis in his car. When he was done, he came back and stood with his hand above her head, braced against the wall in the afternoon sunlight. Something about his face, their positions, felt deeply familiar.

"Thanks for taking her out," Kelsey said. "It's helpful." Suddenly, the present melted away as Kelsey saw a girl, maybe fifteen, on a promontory, overlooking the ocean. She was thin-limbed, agile and energetic; her dark, braided hair hung down her back, and brown legs, below her tunic, flicked together once, twice, as though she was brushing away a fly. The girl intently watched the water as sails edged across the bay. Slowly the background came into focus: white buildings, colonnades and statues, gleaming in the sun. Dappled shade from an ancient, gnarled tree spread across a stone patio. Then the scene shifted another level and Kelsey was *there.*

Bare feet against rugged flagstones, salt air, approaching footsteps. The hairs on her arms prickled as his shadow fell across her. She turned, and the sameness clicked.

Kelsey blinked and Stan was still hanging over her, smiling.

Only a second had passed, a brief flash of time. She waited, but he did not kiss her. Instead, he inclined his head toward the car where Kelsey's mother's face was pressed to the window, watching them.

Harrison arrived shortly afterwards. Kelsey was back in her sweats, making tea.

"You alone?"

Kelsey nodded. "Mama already went shopping," she said. "She liked my friend's BMW."

"Better than my truck?" Harrison smiled a little quizzically but didn't ask about the friend. "How does the Caribbean sound?"

"You thinking of taking me there?"

"As a matter of fact, I got one of the assignments. And ... " he straightened up, "I get a lab person. I didn't think Molly would want to go."

"What are you talking about? The project?"

"We're taking it to the beach. Crouch announced it yesterday, and everyone's sucking up to get an assignment."

"You sound cynical."

"I think he's got it all planned out. He knows who he absolutely needs, I'm in that category. As for the others, he's testing loyalty." He met her eyes briefly. "It might be fun if you were there, though."

"I don't know," she said. "This is kind of new." She felt uncomfortable suddenly, anxiety pressing in, the water idea gathering up its malevolent force. "Why the Caribbean?"

"We can't duplicate ocean conditions in the lab. Warmer water is better because of biodiversity and rapid generation, plus the current application is Gulf of Mexico. Probably going to be a private island off Belize. Rodman's down there scouting now. He's team leader." Harrison sniffed the air as they sat down at the kitchen table. "Reeks of after-shave in here."

Kelsey pushed her hair back and coughed. "I'm coming back to work next week," she said. "Half time."

"Great. That's great news."

"At least I'll be out of the house."

"You and your Mom not getting along?"

"She'll be gone by then. Thank God."

"I don't think she likes me much."

Kelsey shook her head. "She puts a shield around things she doesn't want to see."

"Like your friends?"

"You don't understand. When Galen died, she went to bed for a year." Kelsey gazed out the kitchen window at the late afternoon light. "We were in France still, and my father brought in a woman to do the housework. Mama stayed behind the closed bedroom door. It was a perfect little world in there; she wore beautiful peignoir sets; her hair was always done; everything was brought in on a silver service. She ate, but only fancy foods in tiny portions. She let me help with the crossword puzzle, printing in the letters, until I made a mistake. Then she sent me away. I felt ... that her retreat was somehow my fault." Kelsey started scratching a spot on the table.

Harrison's glasses glinted. "Children always think that. How old were you?"

"Five," she said. "But it was true. I'm sure it was."

He poured more tea. "So she doesn't like this accident. It reminds her of the other one. What else? The thing you were dreaming?"

She looked up at him. "I can't get back to it while she's around. If I talk about anything deep, anything . . . mystical . . . unscientific . . . she'll fight me with every fiber of her being."

"Why?"

Kelsey shook her head.

"But she might know things from your childhood, things that could help. Maybe if you gave her a chance, asked her . . ."

Kelsey went back to scratching the table. "I can't," she said. "I really couldn't."

Friday morning, Marigold arrived to pick her up for the hypnosis session—Kelsey couldn't drive yet—wearing tight red jeans and a lacy top under her black leather jacket. Mrs. Dupuis eyed her, then announced she was coming along.

"I'll read a magazine in the waiting room. I won't bother you at all."

"I don't have a waiting room," Marigold said. "I work out of my home."

"What kind of doctor are you?"

"I'm a licensed—" Marigold started.

"You don't want me to come," Mrs. Dupuis interrupted.

"No," said Kelsey. "Not really."

"Well," said her mother, sitting down with a plop, "I can take a hint."

Marigold helped Kelsey with her coat. "Can we pick something up for you while we're out, Mrs. Dupuis? A pastry maybe? Cappuccino?"

"Don't trouble yourself."

Outside, the air smelled clean, and the sky was deep and clear. Kelsey breathed in the fineness of the day. "I don't know why she wanted to come. She hates the idea of this."

Marigold was silent a moment. "Do I sense a deeper issue here?"

"She's driving me crazy, that's all. She thinks she's got to oppose me in everything, then she tries to push herself into my business on top of it."

"Well, that's a clear feeling," said Marigold.

As they pulled into Marigold's driveway, Kelsey noticed the flowers, yellow forsythia, the pink crab apple in bloom. Inside, they slipped off their shoes and hung their coats. Kelsey looked out through the plate glass window and saw a black BMW slowing in front of the sidewalk. Now it eased away, and she was suddenly sure.

"I think that was my friend Stan," she said. "Someone I had a date with the night before the accident."

"What's he doing here?"

"I have no idea," said Kelsey.

They'd planned a hypnotic regression that would take Kelsey back to the place she'd gone when she was in a coma, the pleasant and familiar place, not the frightening waters of her dreams. Marigold started the recorder, and Kelsey felt herself slipping easily into the induced peaceful state. "Let go of your old fears," Marigold said. "Put them behind you now. I'm going to whistle once to take you there. When I whistle again, you'll return, or at any time that you wish." Marigold whistled.

Kelsey lifted her head at the sound. Pounding waves crashed nearby, a gale force wind blew salt spray. Inside the wind, she recognized a human voice, speaking softly, repeating the same two questions. Kelsey, where are you? Kelsey, can you hear me? Kelsey . . .

Then the storm was gone, replaced by a cloudless blue day. She stood on the edge of a bluff overlooking the calm turquoise sea. The sand was warm under her bare feet, and a path wound across a line of dunes that seemed to go on forever. She was still half-aware of the room, but as she walked along the cliff, it faded away.

A voice droned, but she didn't listen to it as she hurried along. Below, the deserted beach beckoned. Finally she came upon an opening between the bluffs that led toward a beautiful aquamarine cove. She sank to her ankles as she slid down the chute. At the bottom, white sand and water sparkled; a solitary gate stood ajar in a short section of fence.

She knew she had to go through the gate, not around it. She was getting instructions from somewhere. The sand grew blistering hot, burning her feet. She could see the cool water, smell the salt in the air. She felt her legs elongate, her braids fly behind her as she ran. The gate slowly shut.

Suddenly she was back in the storm, the sea rising. She cried out. A gull descended from the sky, hovered close by, and whistled a single high note.

~~~

"You were getting agitated, so I pulled you out," Marigold said. "How do you feel?"

Kelsey's feet were still burning. "I heard a voice."

"You were speaking in a strange language."

Kelsey yanked off her socks and rubbed away sand. The soles of her feet were red and blistered. As they both watched, the blisters retreated, leaving small red marks which slowly turned pale and healed. "What was that?" Kelsey asked.

"Transfiguration? I don't know. I've never seen it before."

"But the sand." Kelsey looked on the floor, searching for remaining grains, found them sparkling as though in sunlight, then watched the sparkles fade too. "Did you see that?" she asked.

Marigold shook her head.
~~~

"Sand," Kelsey insisted. "It came in on my feet."

"I just saw the red marks," said Marigold. "They were faint. Maybe you . . ."

"What?" asked Kelsey. "Maybe I hypnotized you?"

At that they both laughed.

Kelsey told Marigold the facts of her vision, the beach, the cove, the white gate, the sudden storm. "If I'd just gotten through that gate before it closed, I could have put my feet into the ocean and everything would have been OK. I was supposed to go through the gate. I just know it."

They played the recording. Marigold's questions were clearly distinguishable, but Kelsey's voice was low, speaking in incomprehensible syllables. Then an English phrase.

"Let's play that part back," Marigold said.

They listened to Kelsey's altered voice, the unknown language, then a single, lilting English phrase. *Iriel is talking now.* Hearing it made Kelsey feel suddenly heavy, as though coming over the top of a roller coaster.

"What was that name?" Marigold asked. "Ariel?"

"Iriel." Kelsey said, feeling a lift in her stomach again.

"You know who that is?" Marigold asked.

Kelsey shook her head. "Just the name. I know the name."

"Everything looks brighter today," Kelsey said as Marigold drove her home. "Tilted, different. I feel like I was . . . almost inside someone else." She thought suddenly of the kiss with Stan, the almost kiss, and how it had been like that too.

"You said before that you didn't believe in certain types of . . . shall we say . . . mysterious other worldly events. Do you remember? You said you were a scientist."

Kelsey shook her head, silent now, feeling the facts of a strange afternoon settle in. Speaking in tongues. The soles of her feet still warm in her shoes. Unscientific? Certainly.

"So you say you were in a body. A foreign body." Marigold pulled into Kelsey's driveway and turned off the engine. "This person is Iriel, perhaps?"

Kelsey looked at Marigold. "That doesn't make sense."

"Everything you've said," her therapist began, "the feeling when you woke up in the hospital, the water you couldn't reach, the amnesia, the foreign yet familiar entity, makes me think there's another realm opening up. It's still hidden, still coming to light. The closing gate represents that."

"I don't understand," said Kelsey, though she did understand what Marigold was saying. More strongly, she felt the surrounding blankness, as though she was encased in something clear and invisible, akin to air or water, but impenetrable.

"You're getting closer, but it might not be safe yet."

"But I *want* to go through that gate. I'm tired of being afraid. What do I have to do?"

"Hypnosis. Guided meditation. Do you keep a journal?"

"No," said Kelsey.

"I think it would be a good idea."

"What should I put in it?"

"Everything. Feelings, dreams, anything about our work, any visions. Writing it down will make it more concrete, less frightening."

Kelsey leaned against the seat, staring at her front window. The curtain moved.

"What about your mother, Kelsey?" Marigold asked gently. "Can you talk to her?"

"Impossible."

"Let me make a suggestion. Try to forget her difficult personality for a moment. Concentrate on what you need to learn from her. What is she afraid of? What is she avoiding? What does she know that you've forgotten? If you don't mind me saying so, your relationship seems extra charged right now. Doesn't she have some part in all of this?"

"How could she?" Kelsey asked. But as she opened the car door and felt the rush of air on her injured shoulder and ribs, the answer came in with the cold: How could she not?

Chapter 7

As they drove to the restaurant on the last Sunday of Betty Dupuis' visit, Kelsey stared at the back of Stan's head and listened to her mother come to life under his attentions. She spoke of her friends, a book group, senior singles. Later, when they were seated in the restaurant, she mentioned her gentleman friend who'd been taking her to church every Sunday morning for the last several months.

"I didn't know how much I'd missed it," she said, her mouth shaping itself into a red heart. "Cecil was an atheist, you know. He didn't believe in anything that couldn't be proven by scientific means. He said religion was the opium of the people."

"Opiate," Kelsey corrected automatically.

Betty blinked and looked from Kelsey to Stan.

"What else did he say, Betty?" Stan prompted.

Mrs. Dupuis opened her mouth, then closed it abruptly. Her hand trembled as she reached for her water glass.

"He read Karl Marx?" Stan asked.

"All the philosophers," Kelsey said. "It was his hobby. He could argue from any of their points of view. You never knew what he truly thought."

"Kelsey understood him better than I," Mrs. Dupuis said, watching her daughter. "They were always studying together. She inherited his brains, you know." She gave a nervous laugh.

Kelsey's intention, contrary to Marigold's and Harrison's suggestions, had been to let the time until her mother's departure pass without touching on any serious subject. With effort, she'd held her tongue, let the subtle, and not so subtle, digs go. Now, on her mother's last day, she was in danger of letting her temper loose.

"I'm reading Nietzsche now," Stan said conversationally.

"Why him?" Kelsey asked, feeling her impatience escape in his direction.

"I like some of his stuff." A furrow appeared between Stan's eyes. "His concept of will to power. The possibility of human perfection. It makes sense to me."

"What about his elitism?" Kelsey asked.

"Not everyone has the ability to sort out the difference between parroted dogma and . . ." Stan pressed his temple.

"Nietzsche's critically examined values?" The familiar words jumped out.

Stan looked away into the crowded dining room. "Uneducated people are like animals. They shouldn't be allowed to—"

"What? Vote? Breed?"

Stan lowered his eyes. Color had risen in his cheeks. "Your education was a given. Am I right? You were always part of the thinking upper class."

"And what? You've risen from the underprivileged? The nearly-animal state?"

Mrs. Dupuis' head had been turning back and forth, as if she was watching a tennis match. "Tais-toi. Tu exagères, Kelsey!" she warned now.

"Laisses-moi tranquille, Maman," Kelsey shot back.

When Stan lifted his lashes and looked at her, Kelsey saw he was deeply wounded.

"Can't we order now?" Mrs. Dupuis asked.

"I'm sorry, Stan," Kelsey said. She turned to her mother. "I didn't mean anything by it."

"You're just like your father," said Betty nervously.

The waitress poured champagne, and Stan raised his glass. "To two beautiful ladies." He nodded at Kelsey. "And to your wit and charm."

Throughout the meal, Kelsey watched her mother's cheeks blotch pink under Stan's flattery and attention. Toward her, Stan seemed watchful, though perhaps stimulated by her display of temper. His knee knocked hers under the table, and he touched her arm often as he talked. Once, when Kelsey returned from the bathroom, she knew they'd talked about her. When they got back to her house, Kelsey waited while Stan helped her mother inside, saying a lengthy goodbye. The wind had calmed, and there was real warmth to the afternoon sun. Kelsey leaned against the wall, feeling loose from the champagne. She closed her eyes and drifted. Suddenly, she saw the ocean sparkling in the distance, felt the sea breeze against her cheeks. Then she heard the door and Stan came toward her. He bent closer, kissed her, his body sheltering hers.

"I've wanted to do that all day."

She didn't change her position, nor open her eyes. The ocean seemed within a few steps. When a second kiss didn't come, she looked up.

"Your mother said I might have some competition."

Kelsey smiled and shook her head. Her mother's tactics amused her now.

"Good." Stan kissed her deeply, and this time, she felt the tide running over her feet.

"What did Stan want out there on the porch?" Mrs. Dupuis asked.

"A lady never tells." Kelsey smiled at her mother.

"I thought you'd lost him for sure in the restaurant."

"Lost him?" Kelsey's mind was still on the kiss.

"You should never let a gentleman think you're smarter than he is. Even if you are."

"You want me to pretend I'm stupid?"

"You'll be an old maid."

"That's obsolete. I have a career. I—"

Her land line rang. "I just heard Betty was in town," said the man on the other end.

"Yes," Kelsey said, still brusque, "she is."

There was a pause. "Myron Crouch here." Another pause. "Point is, we'd love to see her, have you both over next week."

"She's leaving tomorrow morning."

Unceremoniously he put down the receiver. She heard voices, then his footsteps.

"Tonight then? We'll have dinner at the house."

"I don't know. I'll have to ask her."

"Better yet. Let me talk to her."

Kelsey's mother had taken a seat on the sofa and was rapidly flipping the pages of a magazine. When Kelsey handed her the phone, she put on a stiff smile.

"Well, I certainly couldn't, you know." She listened again. "What do you mean by that?"

During Crouch's long response, Betty continually smoothed the fabric of her skirt. "For Cecil's sake?" she asked once.

After that the conversation still went on, so Kelsey retreated to the bedroom. Through the door, she could hear the rise and fall of her mother's voice, the familiar cooing. Then Mrs. Dupuis burst in without knocking. "He's sending a car at seven." Her face was rosy.

"I guess I'm not surprised." Kelsey mumbled.

"Don't get fresh with me, young lady."

Kelsey's face grew hot. "A few days ago you called Myron Crouch a liar and a thief. " Kelsey took a breath and plunged in deeper. "I know this has to do with Daddy."

"You leave him out of it."

"Damn it." Kelsey jumped up from the bed. "I'm sick of being treated like a child."

Mrs. Dupuis whirled to face her daughter. "Until you act your age, I have no reason to—"

"My age? *You're* the one—"

"Sulking and always staring out the window, skiing like a house afire—and your friends, that Maryflower, we used to call that cheap in my day."

"Marigold has a master's degree from Bryn Mawr for your information."

"Well, she dresses like a prostitute."

Kelsey took in air. "Marigold is smart and . . ."

Her mother put her hands over her ears.

"Mama! I have something else to say! Listen to me!"

When Betty didn't move, Kelsey grabbed her wrists and for a moment they were caught in a combative embrace, inches apart, her mother's expression full of terror. Realizing the absurdity, Kelsey let go first. Betty separated her fingers just enough so she could hear.

"Listen Mama. Je t'en prie. All my life you've made me suppress things. All the secrets, the pain we never talked about. And now ... no, listen! You can't deny me this. It's all mixed up. Galen dying. Daddy's grip on everybody. My lonely childhood. The way no one ever let me ..."

Mrs. Dupuis let her hands fall to her sides.

"I've been having nightmares. Terrible nightmares."

"Oh," said Mrs. Dupuis, brightening. "That old thing."

"What?" Kelsey inhaled through her teeth.

"We thought you'd outgrown it."

Kelsey let her breath out and turned away. "Why can't I remember anything? I *must* be going crazy," she muttered half to herself.

"Your father hated that kind of talk," said Mrs. Dupuis rubbing her wrists.

"Well, he's not here. Mama? He's gone, you know. Dead."

"Don't," Mrs. Dupuis said.

"Why won't you talk to me? What are you afraid of?"

Mrs. Dupuis' lips quivered. "I'm all alone now, Kelsey. As you so aptly pointed out."

Kelsey felt helpless as she watched her mother sit on the edge of the bed and cover her face with her hands. She knew she'd never reach her once the performance started. "What would he have said?" Kelsey pleaded. "What possibly could he have said about any of this?"

"He would tell you to stop being so silly. He would tell you to get control of yourself."

Suddenly her father's pure logic entered the room and killed the last of Kelsey's temper. She saw the dreams, the speaking in tongues, even her blistered feet as the result of her own weakness. No, she wouldn't be talking about it if he were around. She wouldn't let him see this irrationality. She imagined him in the corner, sitting in her chair, smoking his pipe. She shrank as his disapproval came out of the grave and settled on her shoulders like a cold, damp wrap.

Kelsey lay on the couch the rest of the afternoon trying to make sense of the new clues her mother had given her. The childhood nightmares she couldn't remember, but the struggle with her father came vividly back to life. Once, when she was perhaps six, she'd rushed to him, excited that she'd just read a book all by herself. He took it out of her hands. A fairy tale? Did she believe in magic? When she said, yes, oh yes, he let loose his terrible scorn.

The afternoon waned, and Kelsey heard Betty moving about in the other room. When Kelsey entered the bedroom, Mrs. Dupuis was in her slip and stockings, facing the mirror. Her upper arms swung loosely as she raised her hands to take the pin curls out of her hair. She seemed dazed from her nap, and wary too, as she glanced back at her daughter.

As her mother twisted back and forth on tiptoe, surveying her still-stately torso, her slim dancer's ankles, Kelsey looked for some piece of herself. A physical resemblance yes, but she saw nothing in the personality or the mind. "Am I really like him?" she asked. "Like Cecil?"

Mrs. Dupuis spun so her back was reflected in the mirror, the tug of the white slip across her derriere, the circles of uncombed hair, a single pin she'd missed. For a moment Kelsey wondered if she would attack again, but her face grew soft as she gazed at her daughter. "You're really more like . . ." Tears started tracking through her mother's powdery make-up.

Kelsey helped her mother sit on the bed. Betty Dupuis turned her streaked face toward her daughter and reached for her hands. "You don't understand. Everything about you, your face, your voice, the way you talk . . . you remind me of Galen every single day." She began to sob.

"Oh Mama." Kelsey was crying too, a child's tears for the brother she'd been crazy about. It went deeper than that: It was cathartic to sit, hip to hip, and feel the gentle, tentative bond of grief.

Mrs. Dupuis told story after story about Kelsey's brother—

Galen's classes at the university, how he'd saved a dog's life when he was ten, how he'd tutored ghetto youths in Oakland. Just when Kelsey thought her mother was done, she'd start up again. "Galen was a natural gentleman. He was too romantic for Cecil. He could never please him."

"What kind of a man do you think he would have become?" Kelsey asked.

"Oh," said Betty tearing up again, "He had a lovely mind. Maybe he would have been a poet. I kept them, you know. In a box."

Kelsey pictured it, a Chinese lacquered box covered with pink flowers and blue vines. "I think he would have made a great teacher. A professor, classics, perhaps."

"That's when he should have lived." Betty said suddenly. "Before all this science."

Emma Crouch extended her hand offering them each a warm squeeze. She was a petite, hennish woman in her late fifties, with bobbed, brown hair that settled around her face. "I feel remiss we haven't had you out before, Kelsey."

She ushered them into a gigantic living room, traditional northern New Mexico style with a cathedral ceiling made of carved beams. Huge windows revealed a panorama of western sky, still pale with the falling light, and the outline of the mountain range across the valley.

Myron Crouch entered from a side wing, wearing a bright patterned cardigan and casual slacks. He went straight to Mrs. Dupuis, took her hands, and kissed her on both cheeks.

"Why young Myron Crouch. How you've grown up."

Crouch threw back his head and laughed. "It *has* been a long time."

Emma excused herself, and Crouch led Kelsey and her mother to the sofa across from a roaring fire. He mixed martinis at the copper wet bar, opened wine for Kelsey, then sat, legs crossed at the knee, in an oversized chair upholstered in Navajo weavings.

"Betty and I agreed to dedicate the evening to Cecil." Crouch raised his glass. "To Cecil Dupuis. A man who exemplified greatness." They leaned forward and clinked.

"He was a very important influence in my life," Crouch said, leaning back and taking a sip of his drink. "I've already shared that with Betty."

Betty's smile was tentative. "He used to say you had such promise."

"I hope he's up in heaven tonight, looking down on us. I think he'd be proud." Crouch waved an arm toward Kelsey.

Betty began to reminisce about her husband, his honors, the many books he'd written. "Cecil didn't have a proper education growing up. You never would have known it. He was so worldly."

"They were poor?" Crouch asked, his eyes glittering with curiosity.

"His parents owned a dairy farm in Switzerland. I never met them. They didn't come to the wedding and we never went back while they were alive."

Crouch nodded.

"Cecil was the only one who got away from the farm. The others stayed and took care of things. It caused some feelings, you know."

"They didn't approve of his success," Crouch said.

Emma re-appeared with a large tray of shrimp and caviar. Crouch appraised the food as she bent to serve. "The staff has Sunday off," he said, "so we're taking our chances tonight."

Emma settled onto the arm of a chair and smiled reassuringly. "When did you two meet?" she asked Betty. "You and your husband."

"I was studying fashion design in Paris after the war, and Cecil was a widower with two young children. A girl from my school was his nanny, and she introduced us. Right away, we were the talk of the town. I was very young." Betty's face glowed with the memory. "We were married six weeks later."

"How romantic," said Emma. "You must have had a fascinating life, surrounded by all those important people."

"Oh well, there were the children, you know."

"Your husband must have been a wonderful teacher, Betty," Emma said.

"Cecil was much more than that, Emma," Crouch said. "He was a chemist first and foremost and certainly a writer before a teacher."

"Oh, I know," Emma said. "I was just . . . how many books did he write?"

"Dozens," said Betty. "I never read a one. I don't have that kind of mind, you know."

But I do, Kelsey thought, so what's my excuse?

Crouch uncrossed his legs and placed his hands, palms down, on his knees. "Cecil chronicled the progress of the early atomic physicists, Fermi, Teller, all the greats. He knew them before they were famous. They probably even came to your house."

Betty's back stiffened. "I never got involved in his work. You should know that."

Crouch was quick. "Everyone thought of you as Cecil's right arm. All of us knew Betty," he said to Emma and Kelsey. "We loved them both equally."

"Cecil was adored by his students," Betty said, blushing. "We always had them in for Sunday dinner. They'd discuss everything, philosophy, politics, history, and always in the end, science. I was mostly busy with the meal, though. I didn't have that girl then."

"Lilya," said Crouch. "I'd forgotten she worked at the house."

Kelsey remembered her, long dark hair twisted around her smooth face as she bent over the stove, her bare legs covered with more black hair, and under her arms the heavy patches she displayed so freely. She saw the face up-turned toward her father, shining with infatuation, then incongruously, animate with the discussion at the table. Was she another student?

"Well," said Emma, "that's wonderful. Anybody want another drink?"

The conversation turned to Betty's years alone in Paris. Emma had spent three weeks there in the summer and seemed anxious to have her impressions confirmed. Crouch's boredom became evident. "Oh," Emma exclaimed suddenly, "the roast." She and Betty headed for the kitchen leaving Kelsey alone with her boss.

Crouch dipped a shrimp into red sauce and popped it into his mouth. He gave Kelsey a slow look. "I understand you're suffering from amnesia. Convenient, I suppose."

Though she didn't know what he was implying, she'd seen him pressing Betty all night for some kind of juicy detail about Cecil, so she decided in the brief fiery instant when their eyes met, to turn the tables. "Something happened between you and my father at the end. My mother won't talk about it."

"She's right. It's water under the bridge."

"I believe I have a right to know."

"Who's stopping you? Look it up. The press had a field day."

She pretended to adjust her weight, and when she moved everything hurt. She'd left the brace at home, a mistake, she realized. "I'd hoped to understand him better, that's all."

"If that's what you want then." He leaned forward and she felt as though his gin-laced breath would scorch her. "Betty might idolize him, but Cecil was basically weak. That was his ultimate downfall. Get my drift?"

Kelsey's thoughts spun. Weakness? She'd never seen a scrap of it. "I can't believe it." She searched for words. "He was always . . . very correct. I never saw him waver."

"Ah." Crouch put his feet up on the footstool. "Cecil's famous self-righteousness. But he couldn't stick to his precious principles and still get what he wanted in the end."

"I don't know what you're talking about."

Crouch opened a silver box and offered her a cigarette. When she refused, he lit one for himself. "It was the moral fall he couldn't face. It didn't reconcile with his precious self-image."

Despite her shock, a new possibility formed in her mind: her father, not as the man who intimidated her with his perfection and his principles but a rigid authoritarian with cracks in his character. Was it true? She looked Crouch in the eye and plunged in further. "You were part of this moral fall, I take it?"

"I was witness to it."

"You and he were working on something. An experiment. As equals?" This last came out of the blue but seemed to hit its mark.

"Equals." Crouch waved his cigarette. "There were those above him, the scientific gods he wrote about, and the rest of us below."

"He didn't want to share the credit with his student?"

"You are a babe in the woods, aren't you?"

Kelsey flushed. "I don't know the first thing about it. I was a child. I assume you and Daddy had a falling out."

"Falling out." Crouch exhaled generously. "I took the fall all right.

He had the position. He exploited it. That was the extent of it."

They could hear the women in the dining room, setting the table. "Almost ready, you two," Emma called out.

Kelsey turned back to her boss. "But what went wrong? What was the moral choice?"

Crouch stubbed out his cigarette. "Get your ski buddy to help you out. He knows about that kind of thing."

"Harrison?" She lifted her glass to cover her confusion.

"Yes. The brilliant Dr. Stillman. He's not immune to scandal." Crouch twirled the last of his martini, keeping his gaze on her. "You know what I regret more than anything, Kelsey?"

Kelsey glanced toward the dining room. The women seemed to be simply talking now, heads bent together over the buffet.

"It would appear to the casual observer that I have everything." Crouch waved at the cavernous room. "But your father denied me the ability to do research. Research is the ultimate frontier, Kelsey." Crouch stood and chivalrously extended his arm to her. "I can have all the Ph.D.'s in the world working for me. That's my compensation. But Kelsey, love, I will never have that big prize. Of course then, neither will he."

The bed creaked as Mrs. Dupuis settled herself. She'd been excited all evening, flushed from wine and attention. Toward the end, she'd let her face go slack once or twice, and Kelsey had insisted they leave. "I'm not tired at all," Betty said now. "I think I'd better start packing."

"I'll help you in the morning."

"I manage very well on my own, you know," said Mrs. Dupuis, rolling to her side.

Kelsey's rollaway was wedged in next to the window, and she stared outside as she listened to her mother's breathing deepen. The moon hung over the mountains, illuminating the white face of the slope, and Kelsey felt a wave of melancholy.

"Are you asleep, Mama?"

Her mother's white hair flashed in the moonlight. "I was just thinking, do you like your name, dear?"

"What?" Kelsey asked. "Yes, I like it fine. Why?"

"Once, when you were small, we'd gone to a dinner party and you fell asleep on the downstairs bed. Someone threw a coat over you, and your father had to dig you out. You scratched and kicked, just wouldn't wake up. I tried to talk to you, but you got very mad, very adamant. You didn't want to be called by your name."

The moon rose out of view, and the room darkened. This was the part, Kelsey thought, the part that couldn't be mentioned. She whispered her question. "What did I want to be called?"

Betty Dupuis rolled to her back. "Cecil wouldn't . . ." She stopped. Then her voice came back, quiet and hurried as though she was sneaking it past her dead husband. "I think you had a doll, or maybe an imaginary playmate, named . . . Rill . . . something like that. Yes, I think you called her Rill. You were only five or six at the time. That was the name you wanted."

"Rill," said Kelsey, and a chill of recognition raced up her spine. *Iriel.*

"Of course your father discouraged it."

"Yes," said Kelsey, and she reached across the gap between the beds and took her mother's hand, letting the warmth pass between their palms.

Chapter 8

Kelsey was managing pretty well on the abbreviated schedule she was keeping at BioVenture. She hardly saw Molly, who had an ever-increasing number of doctor's appointments, birthing classes, and "sleep tank-up" absences. Meanwhile, her mother was gone, and Stan too, traveling south, gathering facts for the case. He kept her updated via cryptic and enthusiastic text, his preferred method of communication: All Gr8!! Miss u!! Nor was she dreaming, as though it had all come out at once, spurred by the accident. She and Harrison had discussed this. Plus there were Marigold's green pills. In short, life was peaceful.

Wednesday, after work, she had an appointment with Marigold. She felt eager and optimistic, with the new clues they planned to examine.

"Do you remember Rill?" Marigold asked right off.

"I've been trying," said Kelsey. "I think she came to my room to play. I must have been five or six."

"Would you like to lie down? Perhaps it would come more easily."

There was a gauzy Indian bedspread on Marigold's futon. On a whim, Kelsey draped it over her face. Marigold sat on the floor, legs crossed in half-lotus, and started the relaxation process. Listening to her therapist say the ages, twelve, ten, eight, Kelsey regressed, easily imagining her childhood bedroom. When she reached six, the other girl entered the room and stood with one bare foot crossed over the other, her stubby braids sticking out from her head. Kelsey raised her hand, signaling Marigold, as they'd agreed.

"Now focus your inner eye and let the picture form fully. Tell me what you see."

"A dark child, Asian face, or Indian. Mongolian maybe. Her features are wide, a prominent bone structure, her skin is olive brown, and her eyes . . . why, they're clear green, like seawater." The bedspread settled over Kelsey's face, resting on her eyelashes, her nose, her chin. When she exhaled, it floated up and away.

"How old is she?"

"My age or a little older. Seven maybe."

"Look around the dream space. Where are you?"

"I see sparkly sand, blue water. It's warm. I can almost . . . Oh! It's going now."

When Kelsey opened her eyes, Marigold was leaning close, her thin arm extended. "Relax. Close your eyes again and breathe deeply. Let the pictures come. That's right."

Little Kelsey was in her bedroom, looking around at the frilly decorations, everything brighter than normal. She felt a lightness in her stomach as though she'd just jumped down from a high place. Then the sunglow on her skin faded, the turquoise light went out from behind her eyes, and everything grew plain again.

"It felt so real," Kelsey said coming back. "After she left, I'd look for the shells, something. But there wouldn't be a single grain of sand or salt to prove where I'd been."

"Can you see the beach? What's it like?"

Water foaming around chubby feet, gently rushing, inviting dance. Oatmeal-colored sand, very fine and soft, sticking to wet legs. The sun seemed huge, golden red.

"It's no place here on earth, not now anyway. It's so deserted, so pristine, so . . ."

"What?"

Kelsey looked up. "Familiar?"

"OK," said Marigold, as though she'd just proven something. She leaned into her folded legs, her back straight as a reed. "Surely Iriel is a grown-up Rill. Don't you agree? And she's obviously connected to the water that's been such a constant. What interests me though, is the way you described the beach, both strange and familiar. What does that mean to you?"

Kelsey watched her therapist. "You mean the past life thing, don't you?"

"How does that make you feel?"

Kelsey inventoried the sensations that had overtaken her body. The excited trembling, internal heat building, a race of fear. "As though . . . if I even think about it . . . I'll be punished." She opened her eyes. "That's odd, isn't it?"

Marigold patted her arm. "Let me ask you something else. When did the visions stop?"

"Around the time of Galen's death. Everything changed then. My life was cut in half."

It was a relief to cry, her head back in the pillows, the cloth twisting in her hands.

"You may never have grieved properly," Marigold said. "Do you want to work on that?"

Near the end of the hour, after Kelsey had exhausted the storytelling and this new rush of grief, Marigold led her back into meditation. "Try to remember a pleasant playtime with Rill. You're children, innocent, happy. You feel the sun on your face, hear the sound the water makes. Just relax and enjoy it."

Kelsey was upstairs in the white room, sitting on the bed under its lace canopy. A place in the wall blurred, and Rill emerged, laughing. She shook her head, and her braids flew furiously, spraying drops everywhere. Gleefully, Kelsey jumped down to join her. They held hands and ran toward the ocean. The breakers rolled continuously, tight green curls.

Iriel was older now, about thirteen, her slim arms circling with the pulse of the waves as she swam. Way beyond, a storm whipped the sea, pushing toward shore. Kelsey waded after her. She saw the towering darkness and Iriel pressing into it. Then the bottom disappeared, and Kelsey twisted in the water, struggling to swim. Couldn't. Had never learned how.

That night, Kelsey dialed her mother's number in New York.

"Is everyone all right?" her mother asked, her voice sleepy.

"Mama. It's me, Kelsey."

"I know who my only daughter is."

Kelsey paused. "I didn't realize it was so late. Go back to sleep and I'll call you in the morning."

Betty's breathing sounded muffled. "Has Galen gotten there yet?

"What?" Kelsey asked. "What are you saying, Mama?"

"He told me he was coming to see you."

Kelsey waited, a terrible unease gripping her.

"Galen said, 'Tell Kelsey I'll help her as soon as I can find her again.'" Two breaths, then the whisper. "I can't talk about it now. Cecil will be angry."

Of course, he would, Kelsey thought, and she hung up without asking her question: Why hadn't she been taught to swim?

It was the weekend before she and Stan met. They talked about his work—the pre-trial hearing coming up in Las Cruces, his client's wealth—then he encouraged her to tell him about her therapy. "I went through plenty of it myself," he said.

"I realized this week that I never learned to swim," Kelsey said. "It's so strange that I'd forget something like that. Then these dreams came up and now all I want to do is get back to the sea. Does that mean I'm getting better?"

Stan looked at her. "I didn't tell you before, but I share your fear of water."

"Really?"

"A huge wave hits me, and I'm underwater. I swim hard, but it gets darker, colder. Suddenly, I realize I've been going down, not up. The surface is way above me. With my last strength, I kick, and finally burst out, gasping for breath. Then over my head, another wave—"

"Stop it! That could have been my nightmare. It's uncanny."

He took her to a French movie which she thoroughly enjoyed, and whose nuance he seemed to understand almost vicariously. Afterward, they strolled through the dark streets. The invigorating air, his hand on her back, her warmth under her coat, all excited her. He'd been complimenting her all evening.

"My beautiful queen of the night," he said, brushing aside a piece of her hair that had twisted into her eyes. "Your perfection has returned."

When he pressed her into an indentation in an adobe wall, she sank into his lips, and then she was seeing flashes of another world through parting leaves. *Faces, and the smell of the sea, its sound rushing in her ears.* Stan's hands, his mouth, his breath brought it, as though he were playing an instrument. And she, the cello, sang with full body, sending brightness into dark.

A third presence, someone else's consciousness . . . *I am . . . I can't . . .* She pulled back in confusion. Stan's face hung over hers, and she stared into his eyes, trying to recognize him. His hands went under her open coat, and then full vision was upon her.

A flagstone courtyard in the moonlight, the sea glistening below. A young man, desire in his dark eyes, stood across from her. She knew him, and she didn't. He moved in, she was near surrender . . .

"Did I go too fast?" Stan stood back from her.

"No. No."

"Why did you fight me then?"

"I was . . . something happened." She wanted to tell him how his kisses brought the smell of the sea and a dark, familiar world, even transformed her into another self. But something had been going wrong with it. Now he stood in front of her, a flesh-and-blood man, separate from the vision. Which one had she been kissing?

"I think I'm falling in love," Kelsey told Marigold the next week. "Well, maybe."

"You're not sure?" Marigold asked.

"He's loosening me up," Kelsey said.

She'd written about it in her journal, the last kiss, and the feeling of the sea nearby, the hint of confusion, the way she'd pulled away. Why had she done that? She thought about him all the time. But now, on the futon, her therapist's keen gaze upon her face, she wanted to keep her feelings about Stan to herself a little longer. Sweet and secret. So she tried to change the subject. "I talked to my mother the other night."

Marigold didn't take the bait. "What's confusing about this relationship?" she asked. "What's his name again?"

"Stan," said Kelsey. "Well, my mother liked him for one thing."

"And that's your recommendation of him?"

"That's my reservation." Kelsey laughed.

They sat a moment longer.

"No, really," Kelsey said "He's very sexy."

"OK," said Marigold. She tapped the frame of her glasses with an index finger. "So tell me about your mother."

Kelsey recounted the gist of the phone conversation. "I hated that she went off like that, as though she has permission to make stuff up, just because she thinks I do."

"You think she was making it up?"

"Of course she is," Kelsey said.

"Have you considered that maybe she's not?"

"You're saying she's got some clairvoyant ability?"

"Why not?" Marigold asked. "You do."

Later, stretched out on Marigold's futon, Kelsey felt jumpy. They'd decided to do their meditation on Galen, to see if it illuminated her mother's claim in any way.

"Go back to before Galen's death," Marigold said, "maybe the last time you saw him. Can you remember?"

Kelsey's body felt leaden. She got a whiff of something—pipe smoke—and then she knew. "I think my father's here."

"Good," said Marigold. "Let's talk to him."

Kelsey shook her head. "He's blocking the way. He doesn't want me to do this."

"Greet him, look behind him. Is Galen there too . . . Kelsey?"

She felt a lump form in the pit of her stomach, something utterly dead. She stared at Marigold's pale skin, the honey-striped curls. "It's not working."

Marigold shifted up into her chair. "What's your father's name?"

"Cecil."

"I'm going to talk to him. Is that OK with you?"

"You can try."

Marigold took an audible breath. "Cecil, your daughter Kelsey is here. We ask for your help and permission. She needs to contact her brother, Galen, to remember the time of his death. Please tell us any objections you have to our work, so we can go on with it."

"Oh my God," said Kelsey. "I think I know."

"What?"

"Galen came back to me after he was dead."

Kelsey sat on the bed waiting for Rill. She'd dressed herself in a fancy velvet dress with petticoats and white tights. Her room was neat; she kept it that way by herself, though she was only six. Her teddy bears were lined up on her bed in a row, the covers carefully smoothed by her little hands. Usually Mama helped her, but Mama had been too sick lately.

Kelsey said a prayer of a sort. It was a wishing prayer, not like the ones her friends said before eating supper with their families. It was something she'd never been taught but did naturally. She closed her eyes and pictured Rill in her mind, and wished as hard as she could.

Usually the wishing prayer brought her ghostly friend to visibility. But today Rill didn't come. Wouldn't, thought Kelsey, angrily. She crawled up onto her bed and pulled Mu Bear onto her lap, squeezing its head.

She was hunched over, eyes focused on the curtains blowing at her window, when she heard a shuffling noise. It was the sound she usually associated with Rill. But Rill did not appear. In fact, whoever it was, played at being invisible. This annoyed Kelsey further. Rill's friends sometimes came along in this way, not letting her see them.

Galen spoke immediately. "Don't be angry, little one. I'm not able to let you see me. But you can hear, can't you?"

"Oh, yes!" Kelsey jumped down and ran toward Galen's voice. She made crazy circles around and around while Galen laughed.

"Enough!" he said, and she stopped. "I can't stay long. I'm not solid enough."

"You're not solid at all," Kelsey said in her small voice.

Galen's laughter spun around the room, as though he was on an invisible carnival ride. "You're so funny, little one," he said at last. "You make me laugh so hard."

"Do you live with the angels now?" Kelsey asked.

"I don't live anywhere," Galen said. "I'm learning to be . . . it's so strange being dead."

"What does it feel like?" she asked, staring at the lamp where she'd last heard his voice.

"It's getting stranger all the time," he said from in front of her closet. "Do you know what it's like to fly?"

"I wish I was dead too. Then we could play together every day and fly all over and see everything from the sky."

"Don't wish that, Kelsey." His voice sounded distant and stretched out. "You're just a baby. Besides, there is no here or there, or now or then. I'm usually not even me. Just for you, little one, for you I can be, for a little while."

"I know." She folded her hands in her lap. And then he was gone.

"How many times did he come, Kelsey?" Marigold asked

"Five or six, I think. I've suppressed that for such a long time. It makes me so sad. Happy too." *To have heard Galen's voice. To have felt his presence.* "I feel as though he's come all the way back again just to tell me . . ."

"Tell you what?"

Kelsey closed her eyes and tried to reach Galen again. Betty's face at forty came instead. "One day I told my mother. I wanted her to be happy, but it devastated her. She was so upset," Kelsey covered her face with her hands, "and Cecil was furious." She could still hear his booming voice and see the physicality of his anger as he approached her. Had he hit her?

"That wasn't your fault," Marigold said.

Kelsey looked up at Marigold. "Don't you see? Cecil was protecting Betty from me, an innocent little girl. It was who I am at my deepest core that hurt her. That's why I couldn't ever be that person. That's why it's so hard for me now."

Kelsey felt the deeper anger rush in. "He was the one who killed it in me. Or made it grow into this . . . this repressed monster." Her voice shook with fury. "He tried to take away my dreams and give me logic instead. Logic!"

Marigold was silent during this outburst. Now she got up and walked around the room. "You've gotten a lot of information today. I think we may need a little time to digest this."

"No," said Kelsey. "I want to go back in. I want to find out what Galen wanted."

Marigold slipped back into her chair. "We have a little time left."

It was just evening; Kelsey had already been called to supper. A breeze from the garden blew through the room, and she sat quietly, watching the lace curtains flap. She knew Galen was nearby; she'd already heard his breathing.

"Tell Mama I'm happy," Galen said. "She's so sad. I wish she'd let me . . ." His voice trailed off and the white curtain fluttered like a butterfly wing.

Kelsey put her chin on the wooden sill and looked into the garden. For the first time, she could see him, in the middle of the vegetable patch, the sky behind him filled with feathery clouds. He was in profile—his young face was clean-shaven—and he was gazing into the orchard. The new leaves were the color of pale green apples.

"Kelsey," he said as he reached through the open window for her hand. "You must remember something for me."

She heard her mother calling, and the pressure of Galen's hand faded ever so slightly.

"Kelsey," he said, turning to the trees. "I don't have much time left. But listen to me, little one, listen carefully. You are very close to the spirit world. You can open that door and look through. That's your curse and your gift. You may not understand it now, but just remember, you must always be true and brave and always look through doorways and listen to voices, no matter what they say."

She heard her father's footsteps on the stairs and started to cry.

"Hush, now. Don't forget what I told you. And don't forget me. Je t'aime, ma petite."

She turned at the sound of the door, and when she looked back, Galen was gone. Only wisps of scarlet cloud and the tingling of her hands told her he'd been there at all.

Chapter 9

Kelsey's third Monday back at work, Molly was furiously typing up her most illegible notes in preparation for her impending maternity leave, and Kelsey was bent over the microscope. Though her neck hurt—she was supposed to pace herself—Kelsey had been glued to the instrument all morning, for today, the face was back. Beard hairs wiggled, eyes about to open, mouth puckered, ready to kiss, nose twitching as if to sneeze. Kelsey watched it, thinking, it's just a unicellular animal that looks like a face, not a real face. And then, suddenly, someone grabbed her shoulder, pulled her backwards, and they were both falling.

"Oww!" Molly cried. "Ooh! Ooaf!"

Kelsey, cushioned by the softness that was Molly's hip, rolled away, hugging her own aching ribs, circling the pain from her wrist, feeling the wetness spreading under her side. Molly, leaking amniotic fluid, raised her feet in the air dead-bug-like and panted. After a moment, she exhaled, curled toward Kelsey.

Later, after the ambulance had come and gone, after Molly's husband, pulled out of his third-grade classroom, had arrived too late and rushed off to the hospital, after Kelsey had mopped the floor and straightened up Molly's work station, Crouch came into the lab. He didn't ask about Molly. Instead, he wanted to know who had delivered her samples that morning.

"Franklin," she said.

Crouch moved closer, hovering over her microscope. "How's the rate of propagation?"

"Faster. Every . . ." she checked her sheets ". . . twenty minutes on the average."

"Great." Crouch's face flashed two emotions—excitement, then agitation. "Let me take it to the sequencing room. I want to check the DNA again."

"But I'm not done with my tests."

"Doesn't matter." He bustled around, collecting her tubes, then stopped.

"Great to see you and Betty the other night. She's a great gal. Brought back memories."

"Yes," said Kelsey, watching him.

"You know, she's right about Cecil. Terrific man. Can't seem to forget his influence. Lucky to have known them both . . . during the golden era, as it was." Then he rushed out the door, her work in his hands.

Kelsey met Harrison in the lunchroom. After they discussed Molly and the nine-pound baby named Bernadette Jasmine, she told him about Crouch. "He was in a dither this morning. He came and took my animals away."

Harrison took a bite of his sandwich and chewed thoughtfully.

"The only objective difference was slightly faster propagation, but I had a feeling the samples were different today. Aren't we supposed to get new ones next week?"

"Who delivered them?"

"Franklin. That's the same question Crouch asked."

Harrison looked around. "Let's not talk here."

Watching him recycling his lunch trash, cans, paper, compost, Kelsey decided something. "You know that night we had dinner with Crouch?" she asked. "I told you what he said about my father."

"I remember." Harrison's eyes were mild behind his glasses.

"Well, he took it back, just now in the lab. He said how much he admired my father." She shook her head. "I researched it, a little, but I couldn't find much on-line. Too old, I guess."

"Yeah," he said, looking away.

"What? You did too?" She didn't have time for more because

Harrison tapped her elbow. Franklin, the sloppy tech assistant was approaching. He dumped everything into the garbage and shoved his tray into the window.

"How's it going, Franklin?"

"Stillman," Franklin said, "with New Lab Person. Interesting. Kelly, right?"

"Kelsey." *Asshole, you know my name.* "By the way, Crouch already picked up my samples, so you don't need to get them this afternoon. He seemed kind of miffed."

"Tell me about it. Already got my ass chewed."

"See," said Harrison when Franklin was gone.

"I had the prototype this morning, didn't I? Don't I usually?"

He lowered his voice. "I think there's more than one strain being developed."

"What makes you say that?"

"Crouch has broken up the team. I think he's getting two different sets of data on two different versions of the organism. There must have been a mix-up because George mentioned his results were a little weak. I think he usually has the hot samples."

"Why separate the results?"

"To keep any one of us from having the whole picture. To cheat on the precautions." Harrison shrugged. "I can think of lots of reasons."

"You were an Indigo." Marigold was up and pacing in front of the window, bright with late afternoon light. They'd just finished a session on Kelsey's childhood.

"What's an Indigo?" Kelsey asked.

"You've not heard of it?" Marigold bent over her bookshelf and drew out a volume. The cover showed a child with a huge psychedelic aura, predominantly violet in color. Angels hovered, embedded in the purple.

"I don't know," said Kelsey.

"The phenomenon's well-documented. An increasing number of children are being born with extraordinary psychic abilities, very high intelligence, memories of past lives. They're still close to the other world, as all children are, but these are specially gifted. They often lose it, between over-medication and parental repression. Or they simply outgrow it."

"You're saying this was me."

"I'd say you started out that way; certainly, your brother's and Rill's visitations proved your ability. Then it was interrupted—due to your father's disapproval, your scientific training. But you're a gifted adult too—we've seen that—so I think it's important that we—"

"You want to train me," said Kelsey.

"I didn't say it," said Marigold. "But see? You just read my mind."

Kelsey smiled because Marigold had been trying so hard to hold back her opinions, and now they were flooding out. She started pulling books off the shelf and handing them to Kelsey. *Edgar Cayce, Soul Retrieval, ESP For Dummies, Many Mansions.* "Whether Iriel is a past life, a channeled entity, or an 'imaginary' playmate, you can't let your talent go to waste. Plus there's the danger."

"What danger?"

"Surely Iriel's been warning you."

Kelsey felt a chill as she slipped her shoes on at the door. "But what can I learn going over the same ground again and again? My father's denial, my mother's sudden awakening to every kind of emotion? I need to know who Iriel is, where she's from, and what she wants. I need to hear her voice."

Marigold had been in motion, and now she stopped. "You're dissatisfied with our progress?"

"The thing is, *she* was trying to reach *me*, and now I'm trying to reach her. What if I start having the nightmares again?"

"Maybe if you came another day a week."

"I don't know," said Kelsey. She had her hand on the doorknob.

"What?" asked Marigold. "Is something else going on?"

"Not really."

"That man?"

"I'm cooking dinner for him Friday night."

"What else?"

Kelsey just shrugged as she left. The day felt very fine as she walked to her car.

Kelsey bought a nice piece of fish, and when she got home from work, made a lemon soufflé for dessert. As she was setting the table, she popped a few berries into her mouth.

Stan arrived a little after eight, tired from his flight but effusive about the candles and the table cloth, the tulips she'd cut from the garden. He took her in his arms. They were sitting on the couch, necking, when her house phone rang. It was Kelsey's mother. After a moment, Kelsey put Stan on and they chatted while Kelsey dressed the salad.

All day, Kelsey had felt excited, thinking about the night. But suddenly, the flutters in her stomach became waves of nausea. She poured herself some fizzy water and sat down.

"You OK, doll?" Stan asked when he'd hung up.

No, she wasn't. She spent the next thirty minutes in the bathroom, vomiting up her lunch, the few blueberries, and then pure bile. Stan was not much help—he couldn't stand to watch her sickness, couldn't stand pain of any kind, he said—but when she came out and said she'd better go to bed, he brightened. "I'll help you get undressed."

Not as she'd planned it, but still. Gently helping her out of the jeans and into her nightgown, looking, barely touching. Not sexual but erotic as hell. She almost thought she could do it, but then she was back on her knees in front of the toilet. When she came out, he was gone. He left a nice note on her pillow saying he'd check on her in the morning. She was up most of the night, but finally, about four, it was over. She showered, got back into bed and slept deeply, through the ringing of her phone, the knocking at the front door, her name being called, the text-whistling, until suddenly she woke to the sound of the back door creaking open. Then Pedro was streaking away from his place behind her knees, and she was wide awake clutching the covers to her chest.

For a moment all she could see was the intruder seeking entry. A dark man, face pressed to the glass, silently slipping through the opening, suddenly inside. It took a few heartbeats to realize it was Stan.

"I'm sorry," he said. "I didn't mean to startle you. I just couldn't wake you, and I was worried. You should lock your back door," he added.

"I can't," she said. "It doesn't work."

She closed her journal and tucked it into the drawer of her bedside table, put on a bathrobe, and brushed her teeth again. When she came out, he was sitting on the couch, waiting for her. She said she didn't want to give him her bug.

"You won't," he said, but he wouldn't kiss her on the mouth, just her face, her neck. They started sinking down into the sofa. His beard was prickly on her skin; he gave off a faint odor of alcohol and she thought maybe he'd been drinking. He was on top of her, pushing her robe open. Just past his shoulder, a dark-haired girl of about sixteen materialized. She held a small green crystal between her fingers, and it flashed in Kelsey's eyes. Kelsey blinked, and slowly the apparition disintegrated, leaving only a trace of emerald color.

Someone was knocking on the door again.

"Don't answer it."

But she had to because she remembered the escape valve she'd set up for herself. In case Stan had wanted to stay the night. In case she needed an excuse to tell him he couldn't.

The air felt cool on her hot face. Harrison, hands thrust into his pockets, glanced at her, then averted his eyes. She could feel her nipples standing against her thin nightgown under the open robe.

"Sorry," she said stepping aside. "Come in."

She watched his face fall when he saw Stan, but there was nothing she could do about it. The two men approached each other and shook hands.

"Stan. This is Harrison. From work."

"Stan Dresser," said Stan smoothly. "Counselor at Law. At your service."

Harrison raised his eyebrows. "Harrison Stillman. Ph.D. At yours."

"I work with Harrison," Kelsey said to Stan. "I promised him . . . we're going for a hike."

Harrison was the taller and leaner man, but next to Stan, he seemed pale and ordinary.

"Stan just dropped by. Just now. Well, I was sick last night." She brushed her palms on her robe which she'd tied shut. "I'll go change," she said, not knowing what else to do.

When she came back, the two men were seated at the kitchen table, and Stan was talking intently to Harrison. "Routine drug charges. The trial starts Monday, so I'm leaving tonight. Going to hole up in the Holiday Inn and prepare for the onslaught. This client is high class. Somebody set them up, wanting bribes. That happens all the time in Mexico."

"I thought it was a Customs violation," Kelsey said.

"That too."

Outside, there was an awkward moment. Stan opened the truck door for her. "I'll call you," he whispered. She was startled when he bent to kiss her in front of Harrison. She pulled away, and he was left with only her hand, which he captured and pressed to his sullen mouth.

Kelsey thought she should explain Stan's presence to Harrison, how it wasn't what it looked like. But why was she feeling so guilty anyway? Harrison was just a friend, and Stan was . . . she wasn't sure what Stan was. She glanced over at Harrison. "Where are we going?" she asked.

"Your friend asked me that too."

"What did you tell him?"

"Albuquerque." They were headed in the opposite direction: north.

"You lied?" she asked.

"It is April Fools Day," he said, grinning. "I just thought it wasn't any of his business." Harrison seemed different. She couldn't place it. His chin, his lips.

"You shaved," she said at last.

"Got tired of it," he said, grinning again.

Just past the casinos, Harrison turned left. The land took on a rural feel—the trees still in winter undress, the looming mesas, a suggestion of peaks ahead. He pointed out Black Mesa, a spectacular flat-topped formation that was sacred to the Indians, and she began to get the idea. She was about to make another playful guess when his expression changed.

"You know, I found some more stuff about your dad."

Her stomach tightened. "Me too."

"You first."

She told him how she'd gone to the library, found some old newspaper reports on microfilm, which led her to the student newspaper. "They really liked the Cecil story."

"I bet," he said.

"Anyway, the Tribune wrote about a student and professor involved in a publishing dispute. The student, Crouch, accused the professor, my father, of plagiarizing student writings, including his own. Crouch sounded crazy, young and fiery, and, according to the article, had withdrawn from the university just shy of his degree, his Ph.D. The student newspaper took Crouch's side, of course. Then another student came forward and accused Cecil of the same thing. They built it into a story about professors taking credit for students' ideas, using them to bolster their own publications, how it was accepted practice in universities all over the country."

Harrison glanced over at her. "Kelsey, it was worse than that."

"They called for his resignation," she said. "There was an investigation, and a hearing."

He brushed the hair from his eyes. "There was an accident."

"Accident?" she asked. "That wasn't in the papers."

He explained as they crossed the Rio Grande, rushing with runoff, that he'd researched the scientific journals of the day. Ahead the road widened and rose steeply. "A grad student was exposed to a dose of iridium-based radiation."

"Did he get sick?"

"She. I don't know. The article was sketchy—a survey of radiation-related accidents—and this got only a paragraph. It had a hyper-link on Cecil's name; that's how I found it."

"God, I feel so stupid. What were they working on?"

"Radioactive-enhanced growth patterns in cells. Creating cancer, as it were."

"Prize worthy work?"

"Could have been. But your father never published a paper, as far as I could find out."

"Yes," she said. "That was a condition of the settlement. That he not publish anything student-related."

Harrison downshifted and pulled into the passing lane. "Only reason it came to light is her roommate complained. Found that out by reading the dean's memoir. He didn't name names, but the facts and dates matched. Must have been protecting Cecil."

"Wait a minute," she said. "Crouch was almost demonic that night at his house talking about Cecil's moral weakness. It almost makes more sense if it was plagiarism."

"Yes, but why did Crouch leave the university if he was the victim?"

"You're saying my father forced him out? Well," she said, thinking back, "that would explain some of what he said about my father taking away his ability to do research."

"They were working on something together, we've guessed that much, there's an accident, someone has to get blamed. But Crouch gets his revenge by making a stink—hence the plagiarism allegation. Might have been completely fabricated. But back to what you were saying. If Cecil really wanted that prize—"

"He did," said Kelsey. She was sure of it.

"So they were on the brink of something big, or thought they were. They were taking short cuts, someone gets hurt, they cover it up—"

"That's the moral fall? A cover-up?"

"Or the circumstances leading up to the accident in the first place."

"But why didn't Crouch publicize the accident instead of making something up about plagiarism?"

"Maybe it was his fault," Harrison said. "Or maybe the prize was still on the line."

She suddenly heard her parents, Cecil pacing the hall in the middle of the night, Betty wailing, the argument so loud Kelsey, inside her bedroom, had to stop her ears. Her mother had screamed the name again and again. "What was the victim's name?"

"Perhaps it was a pseudonym. Lilya."

"Lilya," said Kelsey. "She worked at the house. If my father was a younger man, I'd have thought it was sexual. But ambition was more to the core of his being. Like Crouch said."

"With Crouch's youth, his risk-taking, your father thought he could realize his dream."

"Yes," said Kelsey. "That would have been seductive."

"But they essentially destroyed each other," Harrison said.

They drove through White Rock, the bedroom community for

Los Alamos National Laboratory, then started climbing into forested highlands, passing a group of bicyclists.

"Scientists," said Harrison. "You can spot them a mile away."

Kelsey looked over at him and took a breath. "There's something else, Harrison. Crouch said you knew about this kind of thing. You weren't immune to scandal was how he put it. "

"Shit, Kelsey." Harrison pressed the steering wheel. "Why didn't you tell me?"

They began to pass chain link enclosures posted with warnings of radioactivity and high explosives. "Don't be angry, Harrison. I'm sorry."

"It just pisses me off, that's all. Crouch recruits me out of the blue, not because I'm good at what I do, but because he thinks he has something on me."

She had a flash of insight. Maybe he'd recruited her too. "What was it?" she asked him. "Can you tell me?"

As they crossed the mesa, deep in atomic country, Harrison told her about his job for a small company that developed robots for military intelligence. "There was this other rookie—Frank was his name. He hid behind this nerd act, but he was truly brilliant." Harrison shook his head. "God, what a waste."

"Waste?" Kelsey asked.

"They called it a drug overdose. Only thing was, Frank was clean. No drugs, no alcohol, not even beer. Coffee was his only vice."

"I don't understand."

So Harrison told her about the intelligence robot, supposedly designed to collect data, but actually equipped to kill. "Frank and I weren't supposed to know about that function, but he figured it out. He started playing around, putting in code so the robot would spout out random insults as it got closer to its target, 'Stalin was a fucking pig,' in Russian, for example."

"He spoke Russian?"

"Seven languages, including Farsi and Chinese. The guy was a fucking genius."

"They found out?" she asked. "You got fired?"

"At a demonstration for the brass. It was messy, but Frank took the entire rap, claimed it was a political prank. He started acting like a nutcase and wouldn't return my calls. He was protecting me, I understand now. About two months later, I saw his obituary."

"It could have been something else."

His mouth was open, jaw loose. "Don't you see, Kelsey? Every move he makes. This secret project. The way he lies."

She felt herself spin. "You're talking about Myron Crouch?"

"The system is corrupt. It's naïve to think otherwise." They were high on the mesa, passing trees left blackened by forest fire. "When I was cleaning up after Frank, copying his phrases to get translated at the library, I sometimes felt he was watching over me, pointing the way. He had it all embedded in there, where the code was going to branch, where someone was going to patch in the program that turned on the weapon, that activated the trigger. Someone was going to get assassinated. Someone high up."

"Who?" she asked

"I never got that far. I just knew I had to get out of there. The only safe thing was to go back to school."

"That was it?"

"Someone followed me for years. I know the FBI has a file on me."

"Crouch knows about it?"

"Listen Kelsey," his eyes were so intense she could barely return his gaze, "I don't know quite how to say this, but if you're going to be my friend, you have to be on my side. I'll never believe anything else but that they were terribly corrupt, and that they killed him. And deep, deep down, I know Crouch is cut from the same cloth."

Chapter 10

As they drove into Bandelier National Monument, a breathtaking canyon opened up below the road. Harrison told her the cliff face was full of caves where the Indians once made their homes high above the canyon floor. They avoided the museum, and the main ruins trail, crossed a footbridge, and entered a shady woods along the creek. The air was rich with the scent of pine.

"You see dozens of them here," Harrison said when they came upon a grazing doe and her fawn. "They're practically tame."

"What about the Indians? Were the deer tame then?"

He cocked his head. "I've never heard of domesticated deer."

Walking the soft trail, feeling dwarfed by the towering vertical walls of the canyon and the long history of the place, her large question surfaced.

"You know I've been reading those books Marigold gave me about reincarnation." She'd come to rely on Harrison's free and sometimes wild ideas in relation to the strange events of her therapy. Now Kelsey moved in front of him as the trail narrowed. "It would explain a lot of things. But I can't see it, or feel it? Right? No one has any certain experience of it."

"There are lots of things we can't see that are true. We've learned that through science."

"But in science we have proof."

"Proof is the tedium, the washing of dishes after the intuitive feast. Maybe some things are beyond proof."

They followed an animal trail through dense brush to the creek and sat on rocks beside a tiny pool. Kelsey watched a leaf bobbing in the eddy, stuck, going round and round.

"How's this, then?" Harrison said. "The past, the present, people, nature, chemicals, space, time—it's a big web of energy interconnected in ways we've yet to measure. A person is just energy moving through time and space; therefore, one soul is not separate from any other soul no matter when they lived. Supposing there is specific attraction, or a . . . a replication, like two mirrors set facing each other, creating an infinite array of reflections—"

"I don't even know if I have a soul," she interrupted.

"Don't you?"

"Well, I must. I just don't know what it is. I don't feel it."

"Who is it who observes then?"

"Observes?" Kelsey laughed. "That's one way to think about it." She looked at him, impatient. "All I want to know is who is Iriel, how is she connected to me and my life? I think the nightmares came from her. And there was the accident. Not that that has anything to do with water, or waves."

"An avalanche is basically a frozen wave."

"But how did she know? How could she possibly know that in advance?"

"Maybe she met her death in water. Drowned as a witch."

"Witch, yes." Kelsey felt the zing in her head as she watched the water bubbling around a rock. "The thing is, I feel her hovering, trying to communicate. Warning me . . . which is something else I've been meaning to tell you. I can't go to the island. I know this sounds stupid, but I can't even swim."

He gave her that look again, cocked head, half-smile. "They have classes for adults."

She stared at the water gliding by. "I don't know. Maybe. Let me think about it."

They got up to walk again. Harrison crossed the creek and veered into an open field of golden grasses. He squinted into the light. "There's a cave up there."

"I see lots of caves," Kelsey said.

"I'm looking for one in particular. There." He pointed, bending closer to show her.

They followed a faint path to the base of the cliff. Indentations in the soft rock formed a ladder to the opening, twenty feet above. She went first, wedging her toes into the carved places, staying light on her feet against the sun-warmed rock. The cave was dark and cool.

"Look," Kelsey said. "Pictographs. Is that the word?"

"Pictographs are the paintings. Petroglyphs are carvings. They're both here."

"A spiral, some kind of animal, a deer maybe, and look ... a handprint." Kelsey examined the print, the color of dried blood on the flaked mud plaster.

"I thought you'd like it," Harrison said. "Look at this sleeping space. Child-sized by today's standards, but I'd say it was probably a young couple. No children yet."

"Why do you say that?"

"They lived so far up the valley. They were independent. Independent means no babies. They would have moved back down sooner or later, if they'd lived."

"You think they died young?" Kelsey asked.

"I found some things." Harrison used his pocketknife to lift a flat rock embedded in the floor and pulled out several objects. Kelsey picked a delicate white circle from his hand.

"It's bone. Carved with a knife. Like this one." Harrison held up a perfect flint blade, then laid out a turquoise nugget, and a pale pink seashell, not much bigger than a thumbnail.

Kelsey examined the shell. "Where did they get this?"

"Traded probably."

Kelsey imagined someone first learning about a vast ocean from the tiny shell she had balanced on her palm. "I don't get the feeling these people are dead," she said.

Harrison laughed. "Well, they'd be about eight hundred years old."

"That's not what I meant." Kelsey looked across at the opposite canyon wall. She thought about climbing it in the dark of night. "I think they lived a normal life span somewhere else."

"Why would they leave this stuff behind?"

"They left in a hurry maybe."

The sun had reached the cave, the warmth expanded, and the light whitened the powdery floor. Kelsey took off her jacket, rolled up her jeans, and hung her legs over the ledge. They ate the food Harrison had brought—thick avocado and cheese sandwiches, apples, cookies, and two bottles of beer. Kelsey leaned back into the shadows. "I feel like a nap."

"You could try the sleeping alcove."

Out of curiosity, she crawled into the curved space. The contour of the floor was soft, though it was too short to extend her legs, and the ceiling was less than a foot above her face.

"Here, hold these." Harrison placed the bone bracelet, the turquoise, and the shell on her stomach. His face was next to hers.

"You've planned this," she said.

"Just now, when we were talking at the stream. I thought something might come up."

"OK," she said, closing her eyes. "I'll try."

Pictures did come. Kelsey saw a man's round face. He was outside in a snowstorm, wrapped in skins, walking among a small herd of deer, throwing out grain; one ate directly from his hand. Later she saw him in summer, bending over plants, dropping pollen from one flowering head into another. Then shifting scenes of people working in gardens, herding turkeys, and hauling logs out of a denuded forest. The man was arguing, pointing to the trees. Later the man and a woman in knee-high moccasins walked wearily through the snow. Then there was just landscape, a rushing river, snowy mountains. After a time, all she saw was redness, like the aftermath of a flashbulb.

When Kelsey opened her eyes, she was alone. The cave's entrance was a bright fissure against the dimness. She crawled over to look at the paintings; they had a magnetic draw, an energy she'd not noticed the first time. The deer seemed to dance on the wall, and the spiral started to spin. She lifted her palm and pressed it to the reddish brown handprint. It was an exact fit, and like a key turning a lock, everything suddenly changed.

Crooked Twig places Long Bow's hand into the dish of red paint, then presses it to the cave wall. He pulls back, but she laughs and holds his

wrist firmly, her smaller hand on top of his. Behind them the fire snaps and sends a spark, like a shooting star, over their heads.

Later they sit by the fire wrapped in the new feather blanket Long Bow's mother made. The snow swirls outside, but they are warm on their pile of mats and skins. They don't talk; they don't need to. She thinks of the deer she will paint tomorrow, if the storm doesn't clear. Long Bow might finish her bracelet, and glue the blue stone into place. She loves to look into the stone and imagine Big Water, the very same color. One-Who-Speaks-Many-Tongues talked forever of Big Water's warmth, and the bright-colored fishes, and the dangerous ones that could eat a man alive. He and Long Bow talked and talked of the world. Many Tongues gave Crooked Twig a tiny pink bone when he left. He said it was worn on the outside by a water animal, with another bone, just the same, only backward, on the other side. This, she can hardly imagine.

Still later, Crooked Twig buries her face in Long Bow's chest and imagines the red handprint glowing on the wall. She feels her own palms glow. They glow with love. She holds Long Bow's back. She hears the wind and the crack of the coals. Then she sleeps.

Harrison was waiting below in the tall winter grasses. They sat, backs to the cliff, watching the sun drop behind the bluff across the valley. A little bird with black and yellow markings flew past. Kelsey felt keenly alive.

"So this Indian man was ahead of his time, a botanist, an early environmentalist." He spoke with growing excitement. "You know they think sites like Chaco and Bandelier were abandoned due to climatic change and erosion. They cut down all the trees, lost most of the topsoil, had a few dry years, the game was gone, and they had to leave."

A slight breeze rustled the grasses at their feet. "A lesson for our time," she said.

The valley had gotten cool and shady, winter creeping back into the air. Kelsey sighed and pulled her coat closer. "It's so beautiful here. These trees."

"It takes half an hour to cut down a tree, and two hundred years to grow it back," Harrison said. "A terrible karmic debt, in my view."

"The earth is like God," Kelsey said. "It has a long memory, and infinite capacity to heal." She felt the chill enter her bones.

"Cold?" he asked. "Should we head back?"

"Not yet." She didn't want to go because of the purpling light in the valley. She watched a rabbit in the grasses. Nibbling, then hopping, nibbling again. "You know, Harrison, I was inside that woman. I felt her thoughts, her love for the man. It was so vivid."

His coloring was ruddy from the day in the sun. He pulled his legs in and didn't say anything more.

The swinging headlights spotlighted the dark forest as they wound their way back over the mesa. Kelsey stared out the window. "Harrison," she said, "what made you take me there?"

"My affinity for the place, I guess."

"So you thought, or felt, maybe I'd share that affinity?"

"The history . . . the landscape . . . I thought it might reveal a past. And it did."

Ahead, the lights of White Rock cast a disturbing brightness against the night. Soon they'd pass out of the beauty into the artificial light. Kelsey closed her eyes and suddenly felt Long Bow's silky skin under her hands. For a moment her fingertips and palms were warmed by Crooked Twig's love. It was like a hot breath came through her hands. "Here," she said. "Feel." She placed her palm against his smooth cheek.

"Warm."

She felt a flash of love for him, just between their two skins. She recognized Crooked Twig's heart, beating within her own. Reeling with surprise and embarrassment, Kelsey broke the touch. She placed her fingers, cool again, against her own cheek. "I can't sustain it," she said.

Harrison put his hand to his cheek. "Could you imagine that I might have been . . ."

"You mean in my vision?" For the first time all day her thoughts turned to Stan, that rush that came with their sexuality, the flashes of Iriel. "You're my friend, Harrison. I need you to be the sounding board, not part of the dream. I'm sorry," she added quickly.

"Forget it," he said. "I was indulging in a little romanticism."

They pulled up to Kelsey's house. Harrison turned off the truck and faced her. "I just wanted to ask . . . is Stan your boyfriend?"

Kelsey had been waiting for this. "I know how it looked. He just dropped over."

"He's hurting you?"

"What made you say that?"

"I got the impression."

Kelsey shook her head. "Not at all."

Kelsey flashed on Stan's bloodless face pressed to the window of her bedroom, like a still frame from a nightmare: the intruder seeking entry. For a moment she considered it—that he was part of the danger. Then she let the idea slide away into the dark of the night.

Chapter 11

There is much for us to talk about, much I need to tell you. For now, here is my little wisdom. Be better than I was. Be wiser and more courageous. Be kinder. As you wade into dangerous waters, be mindful and take good care. You are my future, and I offer you this: I will protect you with all the power of my past.

"Kelsey." It was Stan's voice on the phone. "We won."

It was Sunday afternoon, and she was covered with sweat, back from her first run since the accident. "What happened, Stan? You didn't call. It's been a week." Her heart was racing.

"Last time I saw you, you were going off with that Ph.D. character, remember?"

"But I called you," she said, "more than once."

"The towers are sketchy down here."

He seemed in a great mood. He told her about his week, how the ice machine was right by his room, how the other lawyers liked to party. He'd been staying in to prepare, but then he was too wound up to sleep. "I did some soul searching." She sat in her armchair, feet draped over the side, listening to his voice. "I thought a lot about us, Kelsey. Why don't you come over? There's something I need to tell you."

Kelsey showered and tossed back a glass of wine, dressed in velvet pants, a bare top, and a little silk jacket. The evening was cool and she was underdressed, but excitement warmed her. She followed Stan's directions into the foothills and found the house deep in a web of dirt roads. To the west, flamingo wisps floated over the dark spine of the Jemez Mountains.

Kelsey hesitated only briefly before climbing the steps. The doubt came from a memory: Harrison's hands on the wheel as he steered the truck across the mesa into White Rock. But when Stan opened the door, his eyes met hers, and it all came rushing to her, his magnetism, everything there behind it. He kissed her hello, and she was back, all the way back.

He gave a tour of the house starting with the curved living room with its expansive view, the deck where they could see the lights of the city, the huge kitchen, and finally the tasteless master suite with its round bed and massive Jacuzzi tub surrounded by pink marble.

"It belongs to my Mexican client. He's rarely here. Occasionally he comes and I move into the guesthouse. Other than that, the house is mine."

Back in the living room, Kelsey settled in a corner of the sofa, across from the fire. She took off her boots and buried her toes in the fur rug. Stan returned with champagne and frosted flutes and when he sat beside her, she could feel his heat.

"I believe we're soul-mates, Kelsey," he said. "We were together in another lifetime."

A slight dryness came into her throat. "Tell me."

His fingers were warm against her skin. "I had a dream about us. We were by the sea." The light in his eyes flickered.

Her head began to pound. Just today, she'd found something in one of her books, Edgar Cayce, the sleeping prophet, the ancient time he'd described in detail. She took a sip of champagne. "When?" she asked. "Do you know when and where?"

"Atlantis."

"Iriel," Kelsey said, breathing at last. "Iriel was from Atlantis."

"It explains everything," he said, "our common fear of drowning. Why I can't get you out of my mind."

She'd hardly dared think it, the mythical time and place. Now a white monolith rose up in her child-mind, a city with turrets and flags and a sparkling seaport. *Atlantis.*

"You're so beautiful, so mysterious," Stan whispered, his breath warm on her ear, his hands in her hair. He pulled back to look at her. "Your eyes are like a stormy sea, tonight."

She watched him take off his jacket, his muscles moving beneath the shirt. He kissed her bare shoulder, her neck, moving in so fast she could hardly breathe. Her top was gone, he circled her bare nipple with his tongue. She rose to meet him, to fall into his kiss, then separated to look. Then they were naked, rolling onto the fur rug, his hands cupping her ass, his beard at her neck sending goose-flesh. She rode him, her hair falling across his bare chest, ends alive as though they could feel.

She stayed there afterward, luxuriating in the soft fur, spent, not wanting to move. She had a sense of Iriel hovering nearby. Stan built up the fire, brought her pillows, covered her with a blanket, and she dozed. She woke with him standing over her, a glass of wine in his hand. He'd made pasta and a salad. They ate rapidly; they were both famished. When he offered more wine, she covered her glass. "Tomorrow's Monday. I'd better go home."

"Stay."

Kelsey felt a tug in her gut at that and let him lead her to the bed.

\~\~\~

In the morning they slept late, wound together in the covers. At ten, wearing a robe she'd taken from the closet, Kelsey called in sick. Stan came into the study with tall glasses of Bloody Mary. The fine hairs on her neck stood up as he bent his lips to her skin.

He made her wait in the darkened library while he went for two more drinks. She blinked at the bound volumes of fine books. The leather chair slipped beneath her thighs as she rocked back and forth, eyes closed. She could hear creaking boat timbers; she could smell the ocean.

They made love in the dark corner behind the massive desk, each stroke of his hand heightening her trance, her feeling that Iriel would step out of hiding. But once they were done, Iriel's ghostly presence receded, and Kelsey felt hungrier than ever.

That afternoon, Stan brought out drugs. He offered no explanation, just casually invited her to join him. She found herself laughing and reeling and thinking this was the most fun she'd ever had. She'd never liked cocaine before, but somehow now, with Stan, she found it natural and liberating. It was all leading somewhere.

Kelsey began to see Iriel's world in her mind's eye, vague, enticing images that flickered in and out. It seemed when she paraded naked in front of him, when she shivered at his touch, he was becoming someone else. Once, when she caught him studying her, he truly seemed that other person: someone darker, moodier, dangerous even. She didn't care. It was what she wanted.

But Stan was the perfect gentleman, and tender too; he brought her juice and tea, made a bubble bath. He sat fully clothed on the tile and washed her with a streaming cloth. All the blinds were down, and even though it was mid-afternoon, it seemed like dusk.

"I want us always to be together. I love you. I want . . ." and he continued speaking words of love as she sank into the water, surrendering to the warmth.

"I've never had anyone so fine as you. I want to give you everything. I want to live like this always."

After she dressed, he began to talk about what he'd held back. "We were dirt poor. Ma . . . my mother cleaned houses for a living. That's how I got a taste for this. Wouldn't have known it existed otherwise."

"I wouldn't have guessed. You seem so natural. You have a natural elegance."

"One can learn. One can overcome anything."

"Being poor isn't anything to be ashamed of."

"We were worse than poor. We were trash."

She took his hands in hers. "Your mother allowed it?"

"All she wanted when she got home was whiskey. They had that much in common." A slight hint of accent came through, widened syllables, a Southern swinginess. "She hated his guts."

"Did she have reason?" Kelsey asked after a pause.

"Him." Stan's brow furrowed, and Kelsey saw it was Stan who hated his father. Then he seemed to shake it off. He smiled, showing his even teeth. "He was an asshole. Started in the mines when he was young but ended up on disability."

"What happened?"

"Cut off his pinkie. Did it on purpose. Had a high pain threshold." He fingered the tiny scar across his eyebrow. "Unfortunately, I didn't."

They sat quietly, shoulders brushing. She could think of nothing to say.

"I ran away when I was fourteen, after Ma died." He took a breath. "Makes me feel like washing my hands."

He returned with another drink. They ended where they'd begun, on the rug in front of the fire. When they were through, he stroked her leg gently. The air in the room was warm. She drifted, half-conscious. A face appeared clearly.

The young girl was amber-skinned, her black hair braided loosely. She unclasped the braid and let her hair fall down her back. Glow from a campfire glinted off her high, wide cheekbones. As she turned, Kelsey saw the green depths of her eyes. It was a startling look, as though the girl saw Kelsey too.

Stan lifted his hand and the picture faded.

"I saw her, Stan," Kelsey said, breathing rapidly. "I saw Iriel. She was looking at me."

"Your young queen from Atlantis?" He pulled her to him and kissed her. His brown eyes were slightly unfocused. "You can't ever leave me, Kelsey."

"Why not?" she asked lightly.

"Because I'm your only link."

It made her gasp. "Yes," she whispered. "I know."

That night Kelsey fell asleep instantly. She dreamed she and Stan were making love. The passion exceeded anything they had experienced together. It built slowly to a forceful climax, orgasmic waves shaking her body. But the sensation did not subside. More revelation than satisfaction, it grew until it overwhelmed her. Her mind felt infinite, her spirit filled with clarity, and in that instant she woke.

Immediately she knew something had changed. The room was dark and quiet, save for Stan's shallow breath. For once he slept. She scanned the walls, the blank night outside the glass, the shadowed hallway. She saw nothing, only felt it, no, *him.* Someone watching.

A dark young man dressed in a white tunic stood in the corner of the room. He was bathed in an eerie green glow, and he stared at her in a way that invaded her whole being.

Kelsey got up from the bed, thinking she would banish the hallucination, but the man did not vanish; he rose to greet her.

"I have come for you," he said in a voice she recognized.

A hole opened in the wall, and she followed him into a strange landscape. Black lava rock, wild gigantic vegetation, and a steaming pink and purple fog trailing against the ground. The young man held out his hands.

"*Iriel,*" he said. *"At last you are mine."*

PART III

KARMA

Purple Mists

The glowing mists come down the mountainside and cover the blackened land. Though I marvel at the pulsing lights, the softly changing colors like a thousand false sunsets, I feel uneasy. The mist is crystle-formed, of that I grow certain. I sense the hard behind the softness and the brittle magic in the air-borne water.

A pale tendril creeps toward my feet, moving like a snake. It joins another, then a third. Soon the rock where I sit is afloat, a tiny island in an ocean of purple mists. Before me, the white desert stretches to the shimmering horizon—an impossible stretch of sand we somehow managed to cross.

Jarad and I, lost for so many days after we'd veered from the rugged mountain trail Quiri had laid out for us, desperate and desolate after the flood that took most of our supplies, didn't want to climb all the way back into the high mountains. We could almost hear Quiri's voice in our heads, instructing, "Keep to the path at all costs." Yet we questioned his wisdom, for he was no longer with us. In our minds, we had only to cross the bit of white sand before rejoining the mountain chain at the far side. Why not cut straight across the pristine and sparkling whiteness, the innocent sand, toward the beautiful colors that mirrored the sunset, toward the violet-shrouded mountain, so beautiful, so seemingly close, so enticing?

We soon understood our mistake. The daytime heat was like the heart of fire, the nights so frigid we could not sleep, and the distance so much farther than we'd imagined. Nothing grew save the spiny plants whose sweet flesh we sucked until even those failed to appear. Soon we had no water left, only the poisonous liquid in the hollow gourd that even the animals could not drink. But for our chance meeting with the trader Bracto riding his two-humped lecmel, we would have died of thirst. But for our luck and courage in overcoming him, we would have remained his prisoner, instead of he, ours.

Now I sit on a rock as black as the shimmering sand before me is white, surrounded by this low-slung, ground-hugging, swirling mist. A wandering vapor kisses my face. Color fills me, and a tingle of prescience. I'm blind inside a lavender fog, and yet I see: a future of molten rock, red as flames, and our group, tiny on the edge of a massive burning caldron. Jarad, the captive Bracto, Dtaner and Gewil, the three beasts.

"Iriel." Jarad's voice behind me. "I was worried."

"I saw a terrible volcano," I say. "We were all there. I was afraid."

"You were using the crystal again."

Indeed, despite my promise, I clutch my green stone. The tiny crystal, warm as a kitten, sings a small protest as I tuck it back into its pouch.

"I think I've found a trail," Jarad says. "A rock slide's blocked the beginning, but after that, it seems clear enough."

"Where does it lead?"

"Up."

Into the mists. Into the cloud. Though no one's actually said it, it's what we've agreed, our little mismatched troop of humans and animals. The agreement is communicated in our upward gazes, our driven pace. We seek the source of the mysterious mist—a shifting pink and purple cloud that sits on the mountaintop. It beckons, no, compels us. We want to be inside it, shrouded in soft color, feeling more of this budding joy: knowing things.

"Who's guarding Bracto?" I ask.

"I set him free," Jarad says.

I glance into the nearby shrubbery, half expecting ambush.

"He's left?" I ask.

"He would not," says Jarad. "He says he wants to make the journey with us as far as the mainland." I listen patiently while he explains. We were expending too much effort guarding him. The alliances in our group are unclear enough without a prisoner in our midst. The trader may have knowledge that helps us. "Anyway," he says at last. "I believe he is harmless."

"What are the others doing?"

"Cooking," says Jarad. "They have supplies left, and Dtaner caught two fish."

"He is always hungry," I say, laughing now.

"He is twice as big as you are. He cannot live on fruit alone."

I have been feasting on this lush plum-like fruit, sun warmed and sweet as honey. "She-Beast will eat the fruit but not if the others touch it first."

I have a keen affection for the shy half-woman, half-cat who has followed us all the way from home. I helped her once, and I suppose that is why she furtively trails us. I suppose she would help me in return, if she could.

"She can pluck it herself," says Jarad, patting my hand. "It's everywhere."

This verdant lushness is astounding and unlike anything I've seen before in my sixteen summers. The myriad fruits, the multi-colored grasses that Quiri's donkey, Gijhaad, munches side by side with the lecmel. And then there are the flowers in rainbow colors and a variety of shapes that remind me of the coral gardens under the sea. This thought brings a wave of homesickness. I think of Muamdi and what she's lost, and I am once again glad that Quiri has returned to her.

"Does Dtaner still guard his pack so closely?" I ask.

It is not the pack but its contents that I am fixed upon. Muamdi's green star casts a flood of azure light right through the rough cloth and onto the sand. I've come to think of the stone, stolen from my gentle grandmother and used to track us, as mine for the taking. It is certainly not Dtaner's. Dtaner carries it for his master, Gewil, for truly Gewil commands him. Gewil commands Dtaner because he needs him and the stone to follow me. Gewil follows me because he must; he is obsessed with me, with reversing my rejection of our arranged marriage. He brings me Muamdi's stone in the hope that it will lure me back to his side.

Now Jarad grows quiet. "Iriel," he says at last. "You must forget this notion of yours."

"It is more rightfully mine than his."

"It is rightfully Muamdi's."

"I would take it back to her," I say. "But first it will help us. Of that, I'm sure."

He knows me well, for we have had nearly two moons together since leaving home, and in that time, we have shared every thought and every deed. He understands that the green stone, the mother of my little egg, is dear to me in a way I can barely describe. I love it, not like I love humans or animals, but like my arm or my leg—a part of myself I could not imagine doing without.

"Iriel," Jarad continues. "The crystal is a greater danger to you than to the others. Let Dtaner carry it for now. We will see the mainland, we

will perform our duty. You will fulfill your purpose as the One. Then we will return it to her in good time."

"What if she dies of grief in the meantime?"

"You must not covet her stone. There is much tragedy in that crystal."

Muamdi, my grandmother, with her tragedies and her secrets, the green crystal the greatest of these, is dying of madness and grief since they stole her treasure. This I know from my dreams, and it worries me more than anything else.

"I want to show you something," Jarad says as he leads me to the black edge of the mountainside. We step over plants, a fragrant boxy flower, a traipsing fern. Jarad squeezes between two rock sentinels and into a dark passage that emerges in a lush canyon, narrow as a room. Because the walls curve together at the top, the mists have barely penetrated here. It should be dark, but it's bright as midday. Bright as the sheen of endless sun on endless sand. Bright as the light of my green crystal when it woke again. The piece Muamdi gave me at the outset of our journey, gave me despite all her warnings and counsel against crystals, gave me at great cost to herself. "It is my truest belief that you will need this," she said as she pressed the fragment into my hand.

Vines cascade down the walls of our little room; a silvery stream washes over jewel-colored pebbles, and mosses grow thick at our feet. I watch a tiny green and yellow bird hopping from branch to branch; it breaks into song. A huge butterfly lands on my outstretched palm, its delicate feet pressing lightly before it lifts away.

Jarad stops before a mass of red flowers that covers the canyon walls, the ground, everything. Just ahead is a bubbling pool and the source of the light, a huge crystal embedded in the cliff. It emanates white radiance, like a star brought down from the heavens.

In the white crystal's light, I see Jarad in all his perfection—his wondrous beauty, his kindness and love, his wisdom. Desire invades us. We fall onto the ground, and surrender to our animal nature.

After our pleasure rushes, I grow vaguely aware of another presence. It steals some part of us, so our delight is diminished, our happiness penetrated by tender doubt. Jarad and I stare at each other, bashful though not quite ashamed. We scan the heavy vegetation, the twisting depths of the canyon, the distant rim. There, a fleeting shape shifts and is gone.

As we dress in the false brilliance of the crystal's light, we do not talk. Our hearts feel the lingering chill of that passing shadow, and we know something has been irrevocably changed; jealousy is fed, anger boiled hard.

Outside the chasm, it is night. Bracto and Dtaner huddle near the fire, making some plan. Dtaner's big head moves up and down. Gewil is not there. We feel him hiding in the darkness, still watching us.

Chapter 12

When Kelsey returned to her little house, the porch light was still on and someone had neatly stacked the newspapers by the front door. Inside, Pedro had torn open the bag of cat food, and little star-shaped kidney bits were scattered across the floor. She felt a stab of guilt that she'd left him alone, but he seemed no worse for it; he rubbed against her leg and purred.

Kelsey moved through the rooms seeing everything—the crooked picture, the chipped night stand, the books by her bed, the dusty hiking boots, the residue-stained wine glass, all detritus of her recent existence—with new eyes. For everything had changed; she'd been truly inside Iriel, felt the alien self as though it was her own, known her brave center, her confusion, her bursts of power and confidence. She could close her eyes and feel the other's braids running down her back, the longer, thinner legs, her whole body lighter and stronger, as though the earth's gravity was once weaker.

She felt uplifted by a buoyant mood. The mood was Atlantis, strange and powerful with its oversized landscapes, mists, and exotic plants. It filled her with a need to find the place where things could happen, where they had happened. Deeper still was the sensation of something held between her hands. Alternately hard and cold, then suddenly hot, the thing transmitted ecstatic and terrifying emotions: pleasure, sadness, fear, intense longing. Kelsey tried to drop it, but it seemed to absorb through her skin, infusing her with feeling.

Then everything faded into smoke. Kelsey sat petting Pedro in the dim morning light. With Iriel gone, she was left with Stan. She understood now that Stan offered a possible shortcut to Iriel. There was an element of weakness in it, an emotional betrayal even. To what or to whom, she wasn't sure.

She thought about their sex, his love talk, replaying it until she tired of it and went to shower. But Stan lingered in the rise of her flesh under the hot water, and the soreness between her legs. And when she closed her eyes, she saw his smile and felt the thrill of his caresses. Yes, she would go back for more. Of that, she was certain.

There were messages on her land line: Marigold, and Harrison twice. The phone seemed to vibrate as she hit the numbers.

"Kelsey?" Marigold said. "I'm just surprised, that's all. It's not like you to miss a session and not call."

Kelsey repeated the story she'd told them at work. "I was sick. I had the flu."

"I thought you sounded vulnerable when we talked on Sunday."

"Did I?" She went deeper into the lie. "Maybe I was already coming down with it."

"I have Thursday noon open."

"This week is bad for me. I . . . have a lot of catching up to do."

"Call me then. I'll make time for you."

A big paving machine was running in the parking lot when Kelsey got to work. She'd come early, hoping to get to the lab before she had to talk to anyone. But as luck would have it, Crouch's bronze Mercedes pulled in behind her.

"Kelsey! Just the person I was looking for. Just got back from Atlantis."

"What?" Were her ears playing tricks on her?

"Atlanta. Capital of Georgia, you know?"

She trotted to keep up.

"Course we were down in Brunswick most of the time. Toured the facilities."

She stared at him, trying to see what her father had seen all those years ago. They passed the completed front reception, the new curved fish tank already full of bright tropical fish.

"Pretty snazzy setup," Crouch said, waiting for her to enter the new glass-sided elevator. It was attached to the outside of the building, so they could see both sets of mountain ranges through the cold glass as they rose.

"So," Crouch said casually as they stopped at her floor. "You teaming up with Stillman?"

"He asked me to be his lab support."

Crouch waved his hand. "I mean friends, lovers. You two tight?"

The safe answer was obvious. "No," she said, "Not at all."

His voice lowered and he moved closer. "You know, he got in trouble at his last job—sabotage of government equipment."

"Really?" She dared not meet his eye.

"A real rebel. Smart, though. Never pinned it on him."

"Why'd you hire him then?"

Crouch laughed. "Paying him half what he's worth."

She didn't answer, only gave a little snort. He could take it how he would.

Crouch was beaming now. "You hear I bought the island? Walk-The-Plank Caye." He laughed loudly. "Pirate named Rafael kept his mistress out there. So the story goes." He stepped aside. "Well, Miss Kelsey Dupuis, just say the word, and I'll send you down there. You can be *my* lab support."

"I've been thinking I'd say no. I have . . . things going on. With Molly out . . ."

"Sure. I need team players here too." But his disappointment was evident.

She nodded and briefly met his eye. Then she escaped him.

During the morning, slides passed under her microscope, samples of dead or dying organisms and the pollutants that killed them. Kelsey watched as a single-celled animal spasmed wildly, then split apart, the two halves dying before her eyes. She wondered about a stronger membrane, something to ward off the invasive substance and keep the tender core safe a little longer.

All the while, she was thinking about Harrison—why she'd not acknowledged their friendship to Crouch, why she wanted to avoid him, why she couldn't go to the island. It was Stan, of course, who would make Harrison impossible. It was two-thirty before she took a break to eat, safely late enough, she thought. But Harrison entered the cafeteria while she was in line.

"How are you feeling?" he asked.

"I'm starving," she said looking at the salad line-up, not at him.

He waited while she loaded her tray with a weird array of food: a single enchilada, mashed potatoes, and coconut cream pie.

"I was worried about you, Kelsey. You never answered either phone, so I came by, and it didn't look like you were even there."

"I was in bed mostly." Immediately she wanted to bite her tongue.

"You look good," Harrison said. "In fact, really good."

Kelsey knew she was broadcasting something—robust sexiness—she couldn't very well hide it. She took a greasy bite.

"Well," he said, after a moment. "I'm leaving Monday."

"So soon?"

"The schedule's been moved up—Rodman's down there already, and a couple of the engineers. Making the palapas habitable. It used to be a hippie dive resort, you know."

"I thought pirates lived there."

"That too." He gave her a little smile. "I just wanted to tell you . . . I put your name down. I made it tentative, but I thought it was just a matter of a little encouragement."

Her fork clattered against the plate. "I've got to get back to the lab."

"But you've hardly eaten anything."

"I'm not hungry."

"A minute ago you were starving." He followed her, watching curiously as she slid her tray through the window. He touched her arm, startling her. Involuntarily she thought of Stan, his mouth on her body.

"I'm really sorry, Harrison."

It was almost 5:30 when she looked up to see him standing in the doorway. By then, she was calmer, less guilty. She had a right to the sex with Stan. It had felt good and she wanted it. Harrison, on the other hand, was angry.

"Come in," she said.

He straightened but didn't come closer. "I heard you talked with Crouch. Told him you weren't going. You didn't feel like telling me at lunch?"

"It was new," she said.

"Even George yelled it out to me in the hall. He's on the list now. He was really excited." He stood staring at her, his elbows angling out from his side. Then he said almost under his breath, "You weren't really sick, were you?"

Staring back at him, trying to gather her thoughts, she wondered for an instant if she could have him and Stan too. Then she shook her head, not in answer to his question but to rid herself of the new depravity that made her have such a thought.

"Well," he said finally taking his hands out of his pockets. "At least we should go over some things before I leave."

"Sure. Fine." She motioned him in.

Harrison closed the door to the hallway. "I need you to do some extra work for me. You're the only person I can trust."

She winced.

"Crouch doesn't have what he wants yet. If he did, he'd be out of the labs by now."

"What kind of samples did Rodman take?"

"They'll be flown in later." Harrison paused a moment. "When you get the organism, the one Rodman gets, I'd like you to do some extra tests. Nothing different, just extra."

"Why?" she asked.

"For a broader statistical base. I'm interested in the one-in-a-million mutation."

He walked her to her car, Galen's old Karmann Ghia. Leaning against it, his slim legs crossed at the ankle, he seemed at home again. He asked if she wanted to get some dinner.

Startled, she shook her head. "I . . . I can't." She was thinking of Stan.

"Well," he said, unfolding awkwardly to stand. "Guess I'll see you around." His eyes were clear and bright with hurt.

Betrothal

I suppose it had been going on since I was a little girl, this idea that I would marry Gewil. A plan made between my father, Rotan, and his boss, Marlane, Gewil's father. I was not a pretty child, rather gangly and wild, sand in my hair, salt on my skin—I was always in and out of the sea—and my strange green eyes were unlike any others. Perhaps with the taint on Muamdi, Rotan did not think I would be marriageable, and so when Marlane spoke . . .

Marlane was a hungry man. Though he had ships and wealth, and many men to work for him, he wanted more. The crystal work that left Muamdi a societal outcast, the scandal which I did not learn of until much later, presented no deterrent to a man used to wielding power and wealth. Rather—and he passed this idea on to his son—the possibilities seemed rich. No, Marlane was not afraid of me or my raw talent, he was not afraid of the council or the bay guards, or any of the rules that had kept us, in our village of Yabeth, from traveling to the far shores of our isolated island, let alone to the mainland. No trade, no crystals, certainly not activated ones—those were the rules. Yet the stories enticed us: aircars and mutants—half-man, half-beast—who did the work in the mines, the Ari, that pale race said to come from the stars, clever machines, and crystal-driven weapons. Weapons? We had not thought of enemies or war, for in the years since our isolation, we'd been protected from such horrors.

Nor had we imagined armies. Gewil was the first of our kind to amass one.

Would you understand if I told you about Muamdi, my gentle grandmother, and the healing arts she taught me, the way she once experimented, and the grief it brought her? Perhaps I could tell you of the priestess who comforted me in my first exile, when I was but a girl of fourteen, who taught me the gentle love of One-God, and opened my heart to my destiny. Or of the evil queen Lyticia and her dwarf, Gopwy, who ruled in the time of the first disaster, and how she founded our settlement and claimed her redemption, though her face was disfigured by half.

No, while the conduit remains open between us, I must show you how it was for me those times when my love for Jarad was young, and my destiny was forming. I must tell you about Gewil's obsession, and how I fed it. About that journey to the mainland, when he trailed us, and the second journey I made alone to a place so far not one of us had imagined it.

I must make you understand all of this, and the lure of the crystals too. Muamdi's crystal madness, the power of the green one, and why I threw it away. Perhaps that was the real beginning of the end.

I remember it like this, a little package of sorrow whose meaning I've spun for all these millennia. Perhaps that is not enough. Perhaps the careful interpretation impedes my progress. It seems the pictures saved up in my mind's eye must now flood out. I must live it again, as I've already started to do.

This I pledge for our common good, my soul sister. I give you this gift as warning and as plea. For, despite my karma, you have your own free will, and your own life to live.

How it will solve mine, I do not know.

Chapter 13

Kelsey went back to Stan's that night, and again the next night. They had dinner, a little wine, talked about work, made love, but she didn't stay over. It was sweeter that way, the days spent apart, thinking about each other. And the prospect of the weekend, spending the whole time in bed as Stan promised, made Kelsey almost light-headed. Friday night, when she arrived carrying her overnight bag, he was in the kitchen. He picked her up and twirled her around, then showed her the little vial he had in his pocket, and when she refused, offered her champagne from a half-empty bottle. They made quick work of it. After that, she followed him into the wine cellar where he chose a ten-year-old bottle of Bordeaux. She knew something about the label: it had to be worth at least a hundred dollars.

"Should we be drinking his wine?" she asked.

"He'll never miss it," Stan said, waving at the rows of bottles.

She let it go because her excitement was building, down in the musty cellar. The dark timbers, the paneled walls, and the smell of polished wood reminded her of something. A boat; she remembered a boat. He touched her hand, and she began to feel the boat rocking gently in the waves. She heard the seabirds calling overhead; she could almost smell the salt air. When he stepped away, reaching for the wine, she followed. The wooden timbers creaked with every step. She caught him at the base of the stairs and pulled him back into the cellar, unbuttoning, going for what she needed. Once they came together, the boat began to pitch wildly. The storm whistled, waves slapped the hull. Now the others were crowded with her in the ship's hold. They all watched her, especially the dark one. *Gewil.* His name came to her in a flash. Cold seawater poured into the hold and swirled them against each other. She felt his hands on her in the melee; the water covered her, and she couldn't breathe. Too many unclean bodies, and someone had vomited. She gasped and pushed away.

Stan left her there on the floor. When she found him in the kitchen, he was scowling.

"Don't," she told him when he started to uncork the wine. "I don't want any."

"Well, I do." He poured himself a glass, drained it in one gulp.

"Don't you think you're drinking too much?"

"Don't *ever* tell me that. Understand?" His eyes flashed anger.

"I don't like your tone." She reached for her purse.

"You got what you wanted. Now you're going to leave?"

"That's right," she said, turning her back.

He grabbed her and spun her around. "I'm not done with you yet."

The defense sprang out of her mouth. "You learn this from your father?"

Color bloomed in his face, and he dropped her arm. "I'm nothing like him." Then he pulled her against his body and began to work her throat with his mouth. At first, she resisted, but his roughness, his need, excited her. This time the sex had no otherworldly accompaniment, was only harsh and urgent. Before long, she was meeting his need with her own.

The fight spoiled the weekend mood, though. They were careful with each other, and Saturday, when she refused the morning Bloody Mary, they parted. She went home, thought about calling Marigold but didn't, wrote in her journal, read, then fell asleep, and slept all afternoon, right through dinner. Her phone remained silent until early the next morning when his text came in. He needed to talk to her right away, he said. He arrived in minutes, clean-shaven, moving confidently through her house, filling the rooms with his scent.

"You were right," he said. "I *have* been drinking too much. I'm ready to admit I might have a problem."

"Really?" she asked. "You're sure?"

"I've already been to a meeting. Well, maybe you'll come with me sometime." He took her hands, and his smile faded. "There's something else. I don't want it to be like it was, the way you attacked me down in the cellar." His voice got softer. "It didn't feel like you were making love to me. Not to me. Something else was going on. Something really sick."

She could barely meet his eye. "You remember what you said the other night? The last night before I went back to work?"

He frowned. "You mean my old man? Maybe I shouldn't have told you."

"No," she said. "It was all right."

"I'm over it, you understand? I've done all the processing there is to do, and he's done screwing up my life. That's why what you said . . ."

She was trembling now, feeling the energy building between them. They were still face-to-face, hands connected. "Don't you remember? You said you were my only link. And it's true. You connect me to something. It's not always pleasant. But you see I need to find out." She was pleading with him, "I need to find out what happened to her."

"Your young queen." His eyes were intense. "I have the power to make you see her?"

"I thought you knew," she said into his chest.

"I just didn't realize how much it meant to you." He was rocking her gently.

"It means everything," Kelsey said.

The day was lazy, her little house full of their languorous lovemaking. Around three, she got out her tool box and they started working on her back door. Stan was handier than she; he pulled off the knob and lock and was testing the parts when he pinched his finger.

"Shit," he said and dropped the pliers. He got to his feet, shaking his hand, asked for ice, sat on the couch with it. She sat with him, making soothing sounds like to a small child until the ice had melted and his smile came back. Then he told her he was going away. That he had to leave right away.

She pulled back, reeling. She'd been in a semi-trance all day, getting shifting pictures of a blackened landscape, the smell of fire strong in her nostrils. "Now?" she asked.

"My suitcase is in the car. I've already stayed too long. I need to be in Las Cruces in the morning."

"But you didn't say anything."

"This was perfect, Kel. Just a perfect day. I'll treasure the memory—it will keep me going. Don't worry, I'll be home by the weekend." And then he was gone.

Kelsey was left to reassemble the lock and put it back on by herself. It worked no better than before. In fact it was probably worse.

Home alone that night, she couldn't get away from her thoughts of Stan. She wanted to feel his hands stroking her, exciting her, his mouth finding hers. She fantasized about living with him in the beautiful, big house. And Iriel, in full flesh, would be living there beside her.

As the fantasy played out, Kelsey imagined letting it be known that she was attached, introducing Stan at a company party: a handsome young lawyer, stylish, smart. And there it fell apart. How could she ever face Harrison with Stan at her side? Had she made her choice already?

When she closed her eyes, she saw Harrison's eyes, not hurt, as they'd last been, but lively with thought. It wasn't midnight yet, so she tried him. "I couldn't sleep. Were you up?"

"I was working on my taxes." There was a long pause. "But that's not why you called."

Kelsey wrapped the covers around herself. "I'm sorry about not having dinner. I wanted to wish you bon voyage."

She could almost hear him thinking on the other end of the line. "You sound scared."

"No," she answered quickly. She hadn't meant for the conversation to take this turn.

"Something new is happening. Tell me if I'm wrong."

"I can't talk about it."

"Why call then? Why get my hopes up in the middle of the night?"

She turned on her back, held the phone away from her mouth, and stared at the ceiling. She must have known it was coming, this declaration, yet it shocked her still.

"Tell me, is it me? Something I said?"

"Not you." She shook her head. "Nothing about you, Harrison."

"This sounds like . . . shit, Kelsey."

"It's just . . . the timing is bad."

"I thought that too."

She grew confused. Did he know about Stan, then?

"You know when I met you, I thought, wow, an interesting woman, a little delicate maybe, but smart, we could talk, and beautiful, besides. But that day on the mountain, I felt a connection that was . . . extraordinary. I was already caught up, feeling like . . . it was so exciting to be out in the wilds with you. You were angry; I even liked that. I thought we'd laugh about it later. Then that avalanche. I went through hell. But I already told you all that."

She felt like a wild animal, listening to his voice in the night.

"And then you came back as though from the dead. Changed. Since then, I've been waiting, watching you get stronger. I thought it was the right thing to do. But now it's too late," he added softly. "I waited too long, didn't I?"

She felt as though darkness was closing down upon her.

"It's that lawyer, isn't it?" A tone of bitterness had crept into his voice.

"No," Kelsey shook her head vigorously. "Not at all."

"Why don't I believe you?"

Kelsey felt her breath start to catch. "What if I told you?" There was a long pause and she could see she'd already done it.

"OK," he said. "Spill your guts."

"Somehow he . . . he's connected to . . . to her. That's all it is. I swear."

"What an idiot," he said after a pause. "What a fucking idiot I am."

"I'm the idiot," she whispered. But by then, she was talking to the empty air.

Muamdi

I run into her house—it's dark, not a candle lit—squeeze past the loom that takes up most of her main room, then move into her kitchen. I drag my hand across her wooden table, thinking of the training we are to start. Herbs, healing arts, Muamdi's minde-read ability. I close my eyes and smell supper—fish, and tea. But when I try to picture where she's gone, I get nothing but an ache in the middle of my forehead.

Going out, I bump the loom with my hipbone. I'm about to kick it when her voice, calling my name, stops me.

"Grandmother! I didn't think you were home."

She points to her meditation pillows. "I was right here all the time."

I join my tiny grandmother at our customary sitting place—cushions against the wall. She lights a candle, and arranges her shawl across her legs. All the while, my story lies coiled like a snake in the back of my throat, but I must wait until I'm properly calm and settled, so the words come out straight and right. Muamdi has trained me on this since I was little. She says that I, like the sea, am best when my breath is still or steady: too much wind and I'm as sensible as a storm.

Muamdi places her hands in prayer position to signify One-God is with us in the room and that Her wisdom will guide us, in this matter as in all. Then I feel three taps on my leg, the signal that I may begin.

"Today when I was walking on the road to Kdoty Sker, I met a stranger. At first, I thought he was a monk, but he laughed too much. Then he grabbed my arm and called me by my name and told me I was named for my eyes. Iriel, a living green rock that clings to the old stone that formed it. He said I was a stubborn girl, like the Iriel-stone. Is that true, Grandmother?"

Muamdi's hands fly up to her cheeks. She inclines her head, the slightest nod, and makes a little murmuring sound before her hands flutter back to her lap.

"He made me take him up to the school," I continue. "He said he didn't remember the way, but he must have been pretending because he and Shemmabdis cried like girls to see each other. And then he taught our class, but it wasn't like any teaching we ever had. He made us sit as still as we could, and then he jumped up all of a sudden and we had to do everything he did. He stood on one leg for the longest time, and he could fold himself in half and touch his ears with his toes. At the end, he jumped into the air and did a backward flip."

Muamdi's breath whistles out. "Quiri."

"Master Quiri, that's the name he gave. You know him?"

"It's been so many years."

Something I'd thought nothing of at the time comes into my mind. "He told me he once knew a girl who looked just like me. Was that you, then?"

She grows quiet, a familiar sad quiet. Muamdi has, as long as I've known her, retreated behind a still face. Sometimes for moments, sometimes for days. Though she is sitting right beside me, I cannot penetrate her thoughts, so I wait as I've learned to do, wishing I knew what troubles her so deeply.

"How was he?" she asks finally. "How did he look?"

"Old," I say. "His hair is all white and flies about his face."

"White," she repeats, touching her own hair.

"He brought wondrous things—sticky stones called magnets—and he speaks of the mainland and . . . Will he teach us about crystals do you think?"

"That would be the height of foolishness!"

"But why? I want to learn about crystals more than any other thing."

She looks into the darkness. "Do they have such power over you, even so? You've had little contact with them, I've been careful of that."

"Gewil had one. He held it to a candle and it glowed for a long time afterward."

"Did you touch it, child?" Her blind eye turns my way. "Of course you did."

"Grandmother," I say. "It was not activated."

She sighs. "If the ban is lifted, everyone will have crystals and everyone will be professing crystle-minde. And some may have it. Then we repeat the disasters of the past."

The candlelight seems to flicker, then grow brighter. Muamdi prays, waits, prays again. When she turns to me, her eyes look white and filmy. "Now that Quiri has returned," she lets out a long breath, "I fear I cannot shield you forever."

She takes my hand, and I feel her struggle. "Long ago, when I was young, despite the ban and the cautions of the elders, I was more interested in crystals than any other thing. It was before that last lava flow at Kdoty Sker. People used to come in that way. And things. One day I met a trader who sold me a small green stone. It had been activated by a healer from the mainland, he told me, but later I learned that it was Gopwy who'd done it."

"Who's Gopwy?" I ask.

"A sorcerer. Lyticia's dwarf."

"Who's Lyticia?"

"Ah, Lyticia," says Muamdi, shaking her white head. I feel her mind unwinding, coming closer to me. "Lyticia was a powerful queen born to the mainland. She had an evil thing, a white monolith crystal of such power and magic that she could not control it. It resulted in terrible destruction not only to the land but to herself."

"She died?"

"No, she survived, disfigured by half—and reformed. She took her exile here in Yabeth with a small crew, founded what she hoped would be a perfect society. It was she who made the rules against crystals, the bans on history and travel."

"I thought crystals could heal."

"Sometimes the most sensitive people, the most talented, have no defense. They are so open that the strong stones eat them piece by piece. The craving is torture." Muamdi looks wild now, her hair lifting, her eyes searching the corners of the room. "Iriel, I was a healer, but I went too far. We did. Quiri and I."

Perhaps it is the way she says it. Perhaps the way her cheeks flush, but I get an inkling of something I don't fully understand.

"You have the gift of empathy, child. It is why I would spare you such tales."

"But what happened?"

"Your grandfather and I met Quiri when we were newly married, and he'd come back to Yabeth the first time. I had Gopwy's crystal, and Quiri had several of his own, so we began working as healers. Before

long, they were lined up at the door. But we weren't satisfied with curing sniffles, or helping with a difficult birth, or straightening a lame leg. Quiri wanted to try things: flying, for instance, tricks, like invisibility, spirit talking. He was wild, and I was too. Between it all, we fell in love. And so your grandfather left. By the time he returned, I was pregnant."

My mind reels, for Muamdi has but one child, my mother. I'm thinking Quiri is . . .

"No," she says reading my thoughts. "This baby died. She was mad with the crystals that made her, and so . . ." Muamdi's eyes fill with tears. "It was my punishment too, you see."

We sit quietly together, digesting, and then she adds, "You see why I put my stone away? Why I buried it?"

I nod, all the while lingering on the fact of her power stone, buried where I might find it. I'm thinking of the shed outside and the old Gwatalpa tree, the garden. But a few days later, when I search for it, there is nothing there.

Chapter 14

Monday, Kelsey signed up for a class for adults who couldn't swim. She told no one. That first evening, as she stepped out of the locker room, the pool, sliced into ribbons by shimmering black lane lines, seemed to spit and seethe at her approach.

Several people were already bouncing in the shallow end, mostly middle aged to elderly, and one pimply teen. Kelsey eased down the ladder. Clutching the cement rim, she edged toward the group, feeling the water lapping her ribcage. Rosemary, the instructor, told them to pair up: the idea was for one partner to provide support while the other filled his lungs with air and floated. Kelsey's partner was old, white, and shriveled, but he floated with his chest rounded and firm as a barrel, and his legs stuck out military straight. When it was her turn, Kelsey lowered the back of her head, wincing as the water sucked at her hair. She stiffened at the touch of her partner's arthritic hands but panicked when he took them away. Finally, Rosemary came to help.

"Breathe," she said as she lifted Kelsey almost all the way out of the water. "Fill yourself with breath and let the water do the work. Relax."

"I can't." Kelsey buckled awkwardly, trying to stand.

"Can't," repeated Rosemary, still holding Kelsey in her arms. "I take that word as a personal challenge."

That night Kelsey called her mother to ask why she'd never been taught to swim. She could remember sitting on the dock in upstate

New York—she would have been about eight—while her mother and her grandparents paddled around in the lake. She was so frightened she'd gotten a stomach ache, and wouldn't get in the water, though they coaxed and promised treats. Then, in boarding school, she'd developed a rash; later, when it came up in college phys. Ed., she'd broken her arm. Coincidence? Maybe not.

"Well, I don't know what's wrong with your memory, Kelsey Anne. We took you to the Mediterranean every week when you were little. You had your inflatable wings and you swam like a fish. But when we moved to California, you wouldn't go near the water. You put up such a fuss we even took you to a child psychiatrist your father knew from the University."

It must have been about the time Galen died, Kelsey thought.

"That's when everything started going wrong," Betty said, echoing her thought. "You weren't a very happy little girl. None of us were. I know I wasn't a good mother," she said suddenly.

"No," Kelsey said. "You did the best you could."

"I really should have given Cecil more support. I almost left him, you know."

Kelsey hardly breathed. Was Betty talking about that later time, now? For her mother's thoughts seemed fluid tonight.

"You remember that trip we took to New York to see Granny Jo?"

Kelsey nodded even though Betty couldn't see her. She felt as though the conversation could be tipped either way with a word: more precious information, or hysteria.

"It was our trial separation. All because that Lilya got sick." Her mother sniffed. "She called me up after Cecil died, you know."

"I didn't," said Kelsey.

"And I got a Christmas card from her this year. Well, I always do. But I haven't written her back. I don't know what's wrong with me these days. I just don't seem to get around to things anymore."

There was a slight pause, and then her mother added something, "Oh, and that nice young man of yours called me again."

After a beat, as her mother waxed on about his charm and manners, Kelsey realized it was Stan, not Harrison. "What did he want?" she asked.

"Oh, nothing much. Just to chat."

"What about?"

"He just wants to make sure he has a chance with you. And he wanted my blessing. Of course I gave it to him."

And then her mother changed the subject abruptly, and Kelsey could get no more about Stan out of her. She did manage Lilya's address, however. After much fumbling, her mother found the envelope in her desk drawer and told her daughter to write an apology on her behalf.

Tuesday night Kelsey stayed late to begin the extra tests for Harrison. They had received the latest version of the protozoa that morning, named CR-787. CR for Crouch, Molly had pointed out when she came in to visit with her baby, a gargantuan girl.

Because Molly was on leave, Kelsey was doing two sets of tests at once: growing the organisms in friendly media for reproduction, and testing the protozoa's tolerance for irritants. The new organisms, engineered for thicker cell membranes, held up longer against the irritants. Surprisingly, the two lists had some items in common—mostly petroleum-based compounds, and salts. That seemed a little strange, but as Molly said, "food and poison might be the same thing to these guys."

"Going to get through before you leave?" Crouch asked, coming into the lab.

Kelsey moved back to her station and began cleaning up. She watched Crouch walk around the lab, making himself at home. Lately he'd taken to wearing a lab coat over his suit. "Stillman say anything to you before he left?" he asked. "Give you any special instructions?"

"No," she said, shaking her head. "Nothing special."

"I want a copy of anything you send to him. That's an order."

Kelsey decided to cover her tracks. "He did say something about running a few extra tests, if I have time. He wants a bigger statistical base."

"Fair enough." Crouch appraised her. "I want that data too."

"But there's too much to test," Kelsey said. "I can't even keep up with the regular lists."

"Double them up then." Crouch waved his hand. "We won't be in a lab much longer."

She stared at him. "Whether I can accurately control it or not?"

"Smart girl." He was walking around touching things. He went to the sink, turned it on, pulled test tubes off the shelves. He shuffled through her logbook, then Molly's. Finally, he turned to her. "I don't care what you do. Just keep it to yourself."

The probability for accidents, noxious combinations, results that couldn't be duplicated, was raised tenfold. But she knew hers wouldn't be the only shortcut Crouch was taking. If she was going to combine substances for testing, the lab was the safest place to do it. Tentatively she put equal portions of the first two proteins together, saw the organism's growth rate speed up but its life span shorten. She noted it, then looked at the list again. It would take too much time to test all the permutations in any kind of organized fashion, so she chose three substances, ones she knew wouldn't create a bad reaction, mixed them together, dropped another CR-787 into the solution, and stood back to await the results.

"Good," Rosemary said Wednesday night as she supported Kelsey in a float. "You're doing this just about by yourself."

Though the rest of the class was already ahead of her, Kelsey was encouraged. She put her face in the water and blew bubbles. With her right eye shut and her left eye squinting open, she watched the pretty foam grow. Kelsey held her breath against the hallucination, but the froth got bigger, engulfing her head. She swayed, lost the bottom of the pool as the wave roared past.

Standing in the waist-deep water, Kelsey heard Rosemary tell the rest of the class to float on their backs and kick. Kelsey bounced, then stood directly over a line in the bottom of the pool and holding her breath, put her face in. When the black line wavered, Kelsey lifted her head and focused on the bleachers. As soon as she could, she dipped in again.

By the end of the hour, Kelsey had a strong sense of the pool around her. She'd trained herself to listen to noises that told her where she was. If she concentrated strongly enough, she could force out the terrifying images.

Still, in the shower, she felt shaky. As she was dressing, Rosemary came in. "I've seen a lot of fear in here, and it's always something . . . but with you it's different, I don't know, almost like your life depends on it. Mind my asking why?"

"I thought . . . it might come in handy."

"Well, I appreciate your determination. Maybe if I gave you some private lessons . . . you know, I've gotten a lot of people over their fear of the water."

Kelsey agreed to come the two alternate weeknights. On her way home, she felt a touch of optimism. Was it Iriel? Were they becoming one? She imagined herself running down a beach, feet slapping in the surf, then diving into a wave, wrapped in the pleasure of warm water. How wonderful that felt! How familiar! Yes, swimming might forge that strong connection she'd had as a child, and lost. For a moment she imagined that was all it would take.

There was a message from Marigold, asking for a call back. Though they had talked, Kelsey had not made an appointment. She was busy catching up at work, back full time, covering for Molly, doing extra tests, learning how to swim. But underneath it all, she knew she was avoiding her therapist because of Stan.

Why? She'd have a hard time explaining Stan to Marigold. Their fight, his sudden leave-taking, Harrison—all the recent events of their relationship had left her feeling a little queasy. Who was he, after all? Her lover, of course, and his connection to Iriel was unmistakable. But she felt he was cheating somehow, or lying to her, or maybe it was she who was cheating, taking the shortcut to Iriel that Stan provided.

Sometimes, when he was gone, she believed she could get along without him. Iriel was coming to her now, wasn't she? But whenever she thought that way, she knew she didn't want to let go of him. There was something hungry in her need for Stan, something deep in her psyche that only he could satisfy.

The night was chilly and windy, and now she felt melancholy, so she got into bed to read more of Edgar Cayce. *On Atlantis* had a cover that was a deep sea blue. Cayce, the Sleeping Prophet, a clairvoyant who'd transmitted his information in hypnotic trance, spoke of three periods of destruction in Atlantis and the resultant chain of islands formed from the remnants of a continent. She read about the volcanoes and earthquakes set off by huge, destructive crystals, the hybrid half-human half-animals called "things." She read about progress in the fields of electricity and transportation. Aircars! That sounded familiar.

Kelsey switched off the bedside lamp and stared out through the glass into the back yard. It was a small private space, connected to the front only by a narrow path between her house and the fence, and secured by a gate. Now she became aware of a sound she'd been hearing: her gate banging in the wind.

Kelsey's slippers crunched through the remnants of snow along her north wall. She latched the gate, and while she was out there, thought to bring in the spare house key she'd hidden under a loose stone.

Back inside, things suddenly seemed disturbed, invaded. She couldn't pin anything down, but perhaps her bookmark had not been in the same place, perhaps the pages of her journal were smudged. But who would have meddled with her things—no, spied on her—if not Stan? But he was gone, wasn't he? Out of town and miles away? Except for the texts, all some variation of *Hi beautiful*, or *Missing you*, she hadn't heard from him all week.

She tried to call then, but his cell was out of service, and when she tried the desk at the Las Cruces Marriott, they had no record of a Stan Dresser registered as a guest.

Cove of Secrets

Seen from the high cave where I sit, the pool is almost perfectly oval. The water is clear and green, and filled with light. It is the most beautiful hidden place in the world, and it's mine, my secret place.

I haven't come back here since Quiri came to Yabeth, almost a moon now. I have been home weaving, and learning other feminine skills in preparation for my ceremony of womanhood when all will be made official. I had to beg Mama to allow me out for school even. She said, "That crazy magician will bring trouble to us all."

She's right, in a way. Although Quiri is teaching us new things, like how the stars whirl in the heavens, he will not speak of the mainland, and he no longer wears his crystals. Worse, we are forced to do torturous balancing exercises and make speeches whenever he calls upon us. Quiri says it is to show him what knowledge we have. I think it is to show our ignorance, for the boys ramble on like fools, and usually resort to teasing and insults. Though it is not yet official, they know the arrangement my father and Marlane have made, the arrangement that brings my family so much good fortune.

I watch the sunlit water slosh back and forth below me, brilliant as a blue-green crystal. Fish swarm in the shelter of the cliff, a huge red and yellow panfish circles the reef, and I glimpse a bit of crimson as a blood eel pokes its head out of a coral hole.

It's blazing hot on this ledge where the sun gathers, and I begin to think I'll go mad if I don't swim. Still, I wait, wondering how it would be to be locked up inside, being a dutiful wife—Gewil's wife. When I can stand it no more, I jump—and sink into cool relief. The water is as clear as air. I can see sky and a white puff of cloud above me, and my own rising bubbles. Then I'm up, floating in the sunlight, wishing I were as free as a fish.

To slide into the minds of fishes is a pleasant sensation, simple, watery, instinctive. They have a narrow, shifting vision; the world spins at the flick of a fin, the lazy stroke of a tail. I close my eyes and listen to my breath amplified by the cliffs. Then I'm sinking with a school of red millers. Above, I see my own back, and a cloud of minnows sheltering there.

Then a new breath mingles with mine. I sense dolphin-mind before she clicks her hello. I know things: She is young, a female, wandering farther than usual. And she's never seen a human this close before.

Water shudders against my skin, bringing a silent invitation to play. I slither beneath the surface as she circles, goes to the heart of the cove, and dives. I take a breath and follow, going as deep as I can, then deeper, holding my breath until I'm ready to burst. We try again; she leaps and I raise my arms and sing, she dives and I chase. Finally I rest, floating in the sunlight, waiting for her to come close. The dolphin noses me with her beak, and glides beneath my back. Her skin is slick, and passes a clear message—a liking, a promise to return. She whistles, nudges me, and drops away. When I look up, she is beyond the rocky barrier that protects my cove from the sea.

Then my mind stretches far out to sea. I see the little dolphin as she speeds through open waters. I hear the shape of the distant schools, and sense the pod rushing to join her. She tells her story of the human she met, and our time of play. Somehow, I remain connected, listening to the pod's answer—shifting tales of human encounters—so I'm filled with dolphin mind and breath. All past is present, all present now; the whole future comes after the next exhale.

Fish in my gullet, not quite swallowed. I choke, and our mind link breaks. I am only Iriel, a creature of the land. I begin to make my way home along the rocky shore.

Chapter 15

The next night, Kelsey had her first extra lesson. The water felt friendly and invigorating, and by the end of the hour, she managed to cross the shallow end with a kickboard. She left the pool, hair still wrapped in a towel. The spring evening was lingering, and she stayed a moment at the park, listening to the kids squealing, the birds. But there was something else she could almost hear—a muffled rhythmic whisper. It was the ocean, she decided, washing in and out, gentle waves on a soft shore. Jubilant, she headed home.

Stan's car was parked in front of her house, and instantly her mood changed. She was wary as she approached the vehicle. But he wasn't waiting outside. He was inside, sitting on the love seat, facing a blazing fire. His dark hair swirled at the back of his neck, longer, deep brown. For a second he didn't move. Then he put down the book with the blue cover, turned, and rose.

"How did you get in?" she asked. "Are you reading my book?"

He produced a blue key from his pocket. "Where were you?" he asked. "You've been gone all day."

"I go to work. I take swimming lessons."

He kissed her, stepped back, and stared at her face. She'd forgotten how he looked at her. She reached and kissed him again. This time his lips sent her spinning back toward Atlantis, *her* Atlantis. She had the crystal in her hand, felt its power merge with her own. She lifted it sparkling to the brilliant sky. She would change the world. She would save—

Stan pulled back. "Wow," he said.

Still tasting his kiss, she ran a hand though her hair, feeling a twinge of surprise that it stopped at her shoulders, didn't run down her back in two long braids. "You felt it too?" she asked.

"I feel everything you feel."

She believed him then, believed he'd been with her in that other world. When he took her by the elbows, she nearly swooned; she could not have stood without him.

"You should tell me where you're going" he said later. They were in Kelsey's bed, twisted in the sheets. "I like to know where you are."

"Why? I never know where *you're* going to be. You were supposedly in Las Cruces, then you just show up."

"It doesn't matter," he said. "I can take care of myself."

She felt as though he was drawing out her venom on purpose. "Where did you get that key?" she asked.

"Had it made."

"What if I said I wanted it back."

"I wouldn't give it to you." He kissed her cheek.

"No," she said, pushing away. "You're taking too much liberty with me. I don't know if I can trust you," she said petulantly.

"Can you trust this?"

She didn't know how he'd smuggled it into the bed, but he pulled out a velvet box.

"I can't take this, Stan."

"Not now maybe." He snapped the lid shut; the sparkle vanished. "Just know it's there whenever you're ready."

Despite her refusal of it, the ring kept coming into her mind over the next few days, sometimes making her smile, and sometimes stopping her in her tracks. She'd believed his love words hollow before, but now she thought them true. Then in the night, she might wake, thinking the diamond was glittering on the night table. She'd stare, trying to see the stone which winked at her, thinking all she would have to do is say yes, and the pact would be complete.

Stan stayed two more nights before again dashing off to Las Cruces. "Do you need to go now?" she asked him sleepily when he got up at four on Sunday morning.

"It's a big week," he said as he kissed her goodbye.

"But I thought you'd already won."

"Just a preliminary hearing."

He was starting to wear thin anyway. He never left her house, not for work or anything, protested whenever she went out. Didn't drink in front of her but sometimes seemed as if he had been drinking. Plus Pedro had developed an aversion to him, hissing then running into the depths of the closet or under the sink to hide. Stan disliked the cat too, kicking him away whenever he thought Kelsey wasn't looking. Even now with Stan gone, Pedro was skittish, following Kelsey from room to room, jumping into her lap when she sat down, leaping away when she petted him.

Kelsey settled into a quiet day. The weather had turned beautiful, warm and clear, the spring wind stilled for now. She sat in the yard and basked in the sunshine, closing her eyes, leaning back and letting her book drop, feeling the burn on her face, not caring. Iriel seemed right beside her, ready to go out for a lazy swim. And Stan, the agent of this wonderful state, was conveniently out of the way.

It was getting late, the sun gone behind the house, evening's chill not far away. Kelsey looked out across the garden, and suddenly beyond the budding green plants, an open stretch of desert appeared. She blinked, but the vision stayed.

Two figures approach from a distance. One is slight and dark, moving with a lithe determination. The other, huge, carries a sagging pack on his back, cupping his hands under the base to support its weight.

It was the smaller one who held Kelsey's attention. He had a moody concentration, a steely conservation of energy. Though ragged, he seemed patrician. As he came closer, she saw his face, the black eyes, the elegant, sharp nose. He looked at her with the familiarity of a lover, with the confidence of a possessor. She went into her house, huddled in her bed, and fell asleep with her cat clutched in her arms. Funny thing was, by morning she felt fine. Better than fine.

The week brought more perfect weather. Everywhere around town, lilacs were opening. And now suddenly in the pool, Kelsey was progressing rapidly, feeling herself waken to the pleasure of the water. Work too seemed in the groove.

Kelsey had a culture of CR-791 growing in a super-oxygenated saltwater solution. She'd been adding nutrients all day, making careful notes of the proportions. In a separate experiment, she had mixed an aggravating combination of pollutants to test on a robust mature specimen. She had an eye-dropper full of the nasty stuff when she suddenly looked up to see a young girl in the doorway.

The girl was dark-haired and barefoot, wearing layers of flowing white garments. She raised a hand, something flashed, a stone or jewel, and when Kelsey blinked, she was gone.

In her confusion—for Kelsey knew immediately the girl was Iriel, and an apparition—she dropped some of her liquid poison into the wrong dish. She watched in horror as the dark, viscous drops spread, for this would mean starting over, hours of extra work. But almost before her eyes, the organism began multiplying at a phenomenal rate. She could see it unaided by magnification. This is impossible, she thought, and took the petri dish to her microscope. There, as though seeing a repeating vision, she watched the rapid bloom of propagation.

She knew the mixing of dishes was no accident, that Iriel's visit had caused it, and she was more firmly embedded in the strange world of serendipity than ever before. She hadn't presumed to mix the pollutants and the nutrients. Now she saw she could get some fantastic results if she did. But why would Iriel be getting involved in her scientific experiments?

That night Rosemary took her to deep water for the first time. "Remember they're the same skills whether you're in two feet of water or two hundred." Rosemary treaded water just beyond the ladder, her feet circling hypnotically. As Kelsey watched, the water swirled faster and faster until it swept upward and threatened to pull her beneath the surface. Then a sleek animal body rose, nodded its gray head, and seemed to wink at her. Kelsey felt a foreign kind of electricity, a spark of creature love. It was a dolphin, then it was Rosemary sitting in front of her on the deck.

"What just happened?" asked Rosemary.

Kelsey shook her head. "I'd like to get into the water again, if you don't mind."

Kelsey was able to swim across the deep end with the kick-board, and then, spider-like, on her back. Rosemary, ecstatic with her progress, suggested they try a little underwater work. Kelsey planted her face and watched through her goggles as Rosemary slipped under the surface and sank to the bottom of the pool. She rose for a breath, then dove under, then up again, doing an occasional tumble or stretch, always floating up in rhythm, steady as breath.

"All you need is one breath," Rosemary said. "Here, drop under, and I'll push you up."

Kelsey lifted her arms, letting her weight pull her down, feeling the pressure in her ears, her lungs. She felt Rosemary's hands on her hips, she gave a pull, and there was air. One breath, she thought, as the water closed over her head again.

Up and down they went, Rosemary at the off-cycle, pushing, Kelsey doing a kind of underwater jumping jack. When she surfaced, Kelsey caught a golden glint, like a flash of sunlight, and she could hear laughter and seabirds before she sank back into the aqua depths. Rosemary again became the creature, brushing past her, playing in the water. When finally Rosemary pulled her to the side, Kelsey was dazed, otherworldly, but happy.

"This was amazing," Rosemary said in the shower. "Let me buy you a beer to celebrate."

They went to a bar and sat in a quiet section. They were savoring the last of the beer, Rosemary telling Kelsey about her favorite resort in Mexico, when Rosemary raised her eyes to a spot just behind Kelsey's head. There was Stan with a margarita in his hand. Another man, small, with a two-pointed beard, stood behind him. "What are you doing here?" Kelsey asked him.

"Just got in," Stan motioned her to move over. "Hey, man," he said to the other man, "pull up a chair. This is Eddie. A colleague. Kelsey. My fiancée."

Rosemary was already gathering her things.

"Waitress," Stan called out, "we need some drinks over here."

Kelsey followed Rosemary into the bathroom and began thanking her. She broke off when she saw Rosemary's flushed face, the hardening features. "What's wrong?"

"What did you say your boyfriend did?"

"A lawyer. Why?"

"Just that Eddie's no lawyer." There was finality in Rosemary's tone as she turned to leave.

"Wait. What do you mean? You know him?"

Rosemary stopped, her hand on the bathroom door. "I don't *even* like to think about that scumbag. But maybe, just maybe, you don't know who you're dealing with." She moved forward now, crowding Kelsey against the sink.

"A few years ago my little brother developed a very bad drug habit. Basically ruined his life. He's locked up in the State Pen right now." She brought her face close, and Kelsey felt the cold porcelain hit her back. "That Eddie was his main supplier. And *he's* already out."

The table was deserted except for some cash and the empties, beer bottles and two drained shot glasses. Kelsey settled the bill and waited for Stan's change, thinking he'd come back and she'd talk to him about the holes in his story, and whatever urge had drawn him to this very same bar, this very same night. That more than anything. But she grew tired of waiting and went out to the parking lot. There, in the shadows, she saw the two men next to Stan's car. They didn't seem to see or hear her, though she started toward them. Stan was lecturing Eddie, who moved like a cat in a cage. Then Eddie turned and stared. Just the single blazing look, and she ran for the safety of her car. Only when she started the engine did Stan look up, his smile momentarily frozen in her headlights. She drove home, put the chain on the door, and dialed Marigold's number.

"Kelsey," said Marigold.

"Sorry to call so late."

"What's going on?"

Now it came out in a rush. "I think I'm in trouble." Not what she'd meant to say.

Marigold waited, the silence an open invitation.

"I've been . . . I started a relationship . . . with that man I told you about. He . . . it's consuming me. And I can't trust him anymore."

"Why not?"

She paused, thinking how to put it. "It's like he always knows where I'll be. He just shows up and I never know where he goes, or how to reach him. He even calls my mother."

"Stalking," Marigold mumbled.

"What?" said Kelsey as she felt the zing run up her spine. "I guess we need to talk."

"Yes," said Marigold, and Kelsey could hear the pages of her appointment book flipping.

That night, even with Marigold's assurances fresh in her mind, even with the prospect of their upcoming session, Kelsey couldn't sleep. She kept remembering Stan in the bar, Eddie's staring, and Rosemary's angry face, inches away. She lay awake for a long time watching her own back door, even though she'd hung a curtain across the glass, even though she knew he wouldn't come to her tonight.

Spies!

Jarad and I hide in the bushes near Shemmabdis's rooms which Quiri now occupies—our old teacher mysteriously absent and replaced by our new—and wait until he goes off, whistling, into the hills. We often see him leave that way, threading through the boulders, disappearing into the trees. He usually does not return for hours. What he does up there, we are not sure. All we know is, this is our chance.

The rooms are darkened, heavy curtains drawn; the smells of a recent fire and a meal linger in the air. We pass through the work room, glance at the open scrolls on the table—in Phyrian script, probably, though, of course, we can't read—and go right into the inner room, the sleeping room. There in the middle of his tightly made bed, prominently displayed, as though he meant for us to find it, is his cloth sack. A tiny singing comes from the sack, inviting us closer.

I open the bag with Jarad at my shoulder. Inside are four tiny crystals, each a different color. One is crimson, red and clear, another yellow, one pale blue like Quiri's eyes, and the last, the tiniest, is dense and white.

We look at each other and at the four stones that sparkle and wink and seem to jump around in my palm. Jarad's eyes are wide and bright as the moon, his mouth round in surprise—a mirror of how I feel. Then we plunge back into the little world that I hold in my hand.

I am most drawn to the red and the blue that shine even in the dark room. Jarad fingers them too, and with the red I feel something, a kind of gnawing in my gut like when the monthly blood comes, only pleasant. Jarad must feel it too, for he turns away in embarrassment.

Just then we hear Quiri's whistle outside. Back? Already?

Hands trembling I stuff the small stones into the sack. The white one seems to jump away and I must search the floor for it. Precious moments pass until Jarad, on hands and knees, finds it in a dust pile. I spit on it to clean it; the dirt only smears and seems to stick more. Finally Jarad puts it in his mouth before returning it to its sack, streaked and muddy. We have just gone out the back way and are pressed against the house, catching our breath, when we hear Quiri enter by the front. His footsteps pause. He utters one word.

"Spies!"

Jarad and I have nowhere to go but across an open expanse of ground, and this we do as though on wings. In Shemmabdis's garden we are ill-hidden among the vegetables and flowers. We leave the shelter of an artichoke bush and creep through the orchard into the shrubbery lining the school building. After a short while, we hear laughter coming from the cottage. It is crazy and loud, and it frightens us deeply. Still, we have to pass by the house to get to the path. The laughter seems to invade us and make us want to laugh too. Because we must express this rumbling discontent, this mirthless mirth—we can't help it—we begin to laugh so loud the birds scold us. It hurts our bellies, our mouths open wide, our tongues hang out. Long after the laughter from the cottage dies out, we continue.

Finally, sides aching, breath catching, we steal away, past the little house, down the path. Quiri does not come out to confront us. All is still inside.

Jarad and I decide the laughter is our punishment. For the rest of the afternoon, we fight the urge to be loud when we should be quiet, to give in, as though to an itch, and let the sound roar out. We finally overcome it by talking of every sad thing we can think of, things that have happened, things that might happen still, everyone we love dead, ourselves maimed, suffering. We are finally sober, if not exactly sad. Mainly, we feel deeply embarrassed. We decide the only thing to do is to face up to our crime. We will admit our guilt and beg Quiri's forgiveness.

Jarad and I part reluctantly. He heads away from the dense part of Yabeth where I live, up into the fertile valley where his family's vineyard is located. I've been there only once, to a harvest festival where everyone tasted the old and the new wine, and his older sister and brother teased him a lot and his father was forever pressing his arms around him. I'm sure whatever he has done wrong will be forgiven. For me, the reckoning might be harsher.

I sniff the air as I enter Muamdi's unlit house. It is quiet, though maybe not empty. Is Quiri hiding in wait for me? Will I have to face him alone? I feel the laughter ready to rise, and I push it down. A sound escapes, a hiccup, a half-swallowed guffaw. I cover my mouth and sob.

Muamdi emerges from the darkness. She shakes her head at me, takes my hands, and pulls me toward her kitchen. "I have something to show you." When I resist, she says, "Don't worry, he's not here."

And just like that, the itch to laugh or cry is gone, and my anxiety dissipates. I light a candle, and we take it to the smooth kitchen table made of polished obsidian. The stone is covered with neat bundles of dried herbs.

"Here, close your eyes." She blows out the candle and takes my left hand between hers, rubbing it lightly and rapidly. "Now pick the herb for stomach trouble."

I open my eyes. "No," she says, "by feel and intuition."

I close my eyes again and put out my hand, thinking of my stomach, and begin to feel a slight ache in it. I pass my palm over the table, until my stomach feels really terrible and my hand warm. I pick up a scratchy bundle. Instantly I feel fine.

"Good!" says Muamdi. "I thought you'd have a talent for this."

We go through four more cures. When I choose a tiny yellow flower for menstrual cramps, Muamdi corrects me. "Those will smooth labor pains, and speed the dilation and birth. Find the other one." I close my eyes, the cramping changes to a small, fiery pain, and I pick a bundle of flat, fuzzy leaves. I am suddenly very tired.

"We will make a soothing tea and relax," Muamdi says. "One should always rest after psychic work." I lie on the soft sleeping mat among the pillows while she boils the tea and hums softly. I close my eyes and push my nose into a frayed pillow. The musty smell reminds me of childhood.

I dream of the earliest times when Mama and I lived with Muamdi and my grandfather. I was watched by one or the other, always at someone's feet, usually Muamdi's. I remember the sounds, the soft shush of yarn against yarn, the goat's milk squirting into the bowl, Mama's groans as she hoed the garden or carried water into the house. And the light. It seemed I was always looking up, and the light at the top of a room was full of floating shapes. I liked to watch those shapes as I'm doing now—twirling dust, lulling me to sleep.

Suddenly I'm awake and there is Quiri, so close his nose is almost touching mine. In his hand is the pouch with the crystals. Muamdi is not anywhere around.

"You must tell me which ones you touched. Precisely how."

". . . all, I think."

"And with which part of your body?"

"My hands?"

"Try to remember. It's important."

"Jarad put the white one in his mouth."

Quiri winces, the left side of his face contracting until his eye is squinted shut and his lip raised as if in a sneer. Slowly—I can see his will at work—it releases, and his lip drops. His cheek is reddened but soft again, the wrinkles hanging loosely above his mouth.

"I have already been to him," Quiri says. "We have done what we could."

"Is he sick?"

"Not much," says Quiri, "Are you?"

I don't feel sick, just more tired than I can ever remember being, and still denied sleep. But I see he won't let me be, so I think back and tell him, yes, I'd held the red, even rubbed it between my palms feeling the delicious warmth of it, and the blue, clear and cold between my fingertips, a sensation like plunging into water on a hot day. "The white rolled over my arm, I think. I didn't notice it."

"The white is precisely the one I am interested in." Quiri's eyes, like blue fire, seem to burn me.

I begin to cry. "I'm sorry. I don't remember."

And then I do. The little white crystal had not rolled away but had burned me, like Quiri's eyes are doing now, only right through my skin and mind at the same time. I'd seen something then, like the inside of clouds opened up by lightning. I'd flung it, for I'd been terrified.

"Yes," Quiri says. "Do you understand now?"

"I should never have touched it," I say. "We shouldn't have been spying. I'm sorry."

"No, you're not," he says.

I see he is right. A little question starts to creep in. Why had I not remembered about the white? What was the power it contained?

Quiri has my hands now. Between his feet is the pouch, close enough I could touch it, were my hands free. He is in trance, and I feel his energy begin to take my tiredness away. I look again, but the sack is gone, perhaps was never there at all. I close my eyes and see blue. It is his color, I know, cold and calm, his eyes, water, the morning sky on the rare cool day. Then Muamdi is there too. She has a bowl and a cloth and she is washing me, my hands, my arm where the white crystal rolled off. I'd tried to fling it, but it stuck to me. I now remember a struggle, my growing panic. Later, the dirt stuck to it. It is a sticky little power, the white crystal. That part was real.

Muamdi bathes the place with tea, letting the liquid run over and over my arm, which is red as a streak of sunset on a cloudy day. It does not hurt as the mark fades away. I simply feel drained again. They let me sleep.

When I wake for a moment, deep in the night, they are sleeping too, entwined on the sitting mat, leaving me the bed. Like kittens, innocent, content. Sleeping the sleep of babies.

Chapter 16

Kelsey sat on Marigold's front stoop, thinking about what she had to do. She'd made up her mind she would tell Marigold everything: Stan's drinking, Rosemary's accusation, and her own vague suspicions. That was the easy part. But how could she explain her complicity?

After the night in the bar, Kelsey had truly wanted to break it off. But when Stan called, all smooth and contrite, she'd agreed to see him. He took her to dinner at one of those elegant restaurants where the food is invented from disparate ingredients and tastes heavenly paired with delicate wines. Stan didn't drink, nor did he touch her. They avoided the topic of their last encounter; both were polite and quiet, waiting, watching each other. The atmosphere was charged with the unspoken agreement of sex to come.

On the way to the car, they heard Latin music drifting from an upstairs club. Without speaking, they climbed the stairs and danced across the crowded floor toward the band. They fell into step, hips locked yet perfectly fluid, whirling, responding to the dips and rolls of the rhythm. They seemed made for each other, for this dance, and then for the next one. She closed her eyes, and the music invaded her, that and his warmth. They stayed late, dancing and dancing, unable to let go of the beat, until they were so tired they could barely stand.

Later, when Stan took her to his bed, he was again the perfect dance partner. Every move in step, every breath an extension of hers. Kelsey felt as though he knew her deepest self, her Iriel self, and that everything he did was designed to bring it out. She stayed with him the rest of the weekend, and Monday night she was there again.

Their guard went down, they started drinking wine, and then Stan asked her casually where she went when they made love.

"I thought you knew," she said. "I thought you went there with me."

He bristled. "All I know is you love it."

"Yes," she said. "I do."

He got up from the table and began pacing the darkened kitchen with its gleaming silvered appliances. "Does it matter that I'm even there?"

"Of course it does."

He put his hands on the table in front of her. "Tell me then."

She had the uncomfortable feeling that she shouldn't, but also must. "You take me to Atlantis."

His eyes glittered with curiosity. "Describe it."

"Beautiful, foreign, like a place on earth, but no earth we know. Mountains as big as the Himalayas, jungle plants, white sand, and fish the color of—"

"And me? I was there?"

She stared at him. "Yes," she said. "I think so."

He seemed pleased. It was what he was after. "And we were together, right? Lovers?"

Kelsey felt herself enter Iriel's skin. *The world is bathed in green glow, the travelers sit in a circle in the misty night, and the crystal spring tinkles nearby, the white star embedded above it. On one side, Jarad waits, patiently enduring her folly. On the other, Gewil holds Muamdi's gemstone, his face reflected in all facets of the spire. She hears her name again and again. Though she craves the crystal like she'd wanted water in the desert, she turns away and calls for Jarad instead.*

Kelsey came back with her hands in Stan's. He was watching her face, wary, hopeful.

"So I was this Jarad," Stan said.

She couldn't tell him the lie he wanted to hear, nor the truth she couldn't face.

He accused her of patronizing him. From there it escalated. She found herself yelling, "Why can't you just stay out of it." And he'd answered. "I'm not good enough to share your special world, is that it?" She'd left, shaken and angry, thinking who, what did she want?

Now Kelsey sat on Marigold's cement stoop, watching the alyssum that lined her walkway, their yellow heads nodding in the late afternoon breeze. The sun had gathered up against the house, and the air was laden with life. She closed her eyes and listened to the birds move from tree to tree, calling out the news. A car door slammed, but Kelsey didn't open her eyes. Only when a shadow fell across her face and the birds hushed did she realize it wasn't Marigold.

Stan's skin was blotched beneath the shade of stubble, and he was breathing hard. For a moment she was fear-charged, believing he could somehow read what was in her heart.

"I need you to come with me, Kelsey."

"Why?"

"He's coming back today. I've got to move into the guest house."

"Who? You mean Miguel? I have an appointment, Stan."

"Please?" He was beginning to tug at her. His eyes, so brown, so human, almost convinced her. Then the doubt rose.

"How do you always know where I'm going to be anyway? Are you following me?"

The muscles of his jaw tightened. "Would *you* ever get around to telling me?"

"Look," she said. "I don't know what you've been doing, but I can't—"

"I said please." There was something not quite right about his eyes now.

"And I said no."

He jerked her arm, started dragging her. Then Marigold's blue Volvo pulled into the driveway and Stan quietly slid his arm around Kelsey's shoulder.

"Can I be of assistance here?" Marigold asked as she reached them.

"This is Stan, Marigold. Stan Dresser. I . . . mentioned him to you." Kelsey took the opportunity to move slightly away. Her whole side throbbed.

"Yes," said Marigold extending her hand.

Stan stared at Marigold's long thin fingers before his instinctual manners took over. He even managed a smile as they shook hands. But the darkness came back into his face when he looked at Kelsey. "Thanks for nothing," was all he said.

Marigold and Kelsey watched the black car slide out of view. Then Marigold touched her shoulder. "What was that all about?"

"I don't know," said Kelsey. "I think he's in some kind of trouble."

"What kind?"

"Drugs?" She remembered the cold sink and Rosemary's close, red face.

"What's he using?"

"Alcohol. Cocaine maybe. Well, certainly cocaine. I don't know how bad it is." Inside, lying on Marigold's familiar futon couch, her head covered with the light Indian bedspread, she told the simplest version of her story, the way it started with the kiss at the party, the strong attraction, the sexual excitement. But there was his jealousy, his lies, his calls to her mother. And finally, her growing chagrin, her sense of betrayal of something, her struggle to understand if what she was doing was right, or terribly wrong.

"OK," Marigold said when she was done. "Women get into destructive relationships all the time. But why in your case? Why keep going back to this man with obvious violent tendencies."

"No." Kelsey shook her head. "He's not violent."

"What do you call what just happened here?"

They sat a moment, and then Kelsey said, "It's the sex. I told you that."

"What else, Kelsey?"

"You mean love?"

"We're not talking about love, are we?"

"Well," the lightweight cloth billowed, then settled on her face, "it reminds me of love."

Marigold's laugh was smoky, as though it too was filtered by cloth.

"In some ways," Kelsey took a slow breath, "I'm like him. It's a side of me. Of Iriel, I think. It has to do with darkness, and temptation."

"What does Iriel have to do with this relationship?"

And now Kelsey had to tell her the rest of it. "I'm getting her story. It's out of order, in bits and pieces, but it's vivid and real. It feels like these are events I've lived through but forgotten. They're part of who I am."

"And you remember them when you're with Stan?"

"Mostly after we make love." Kelsey felt a fresh wave of guilt, the emotion that had dominated the last few days. "I shouldn't have given in to the temptation, should I? It's just that I can't seem to resist."

"You've used that word twice, 'temptation.' " Marigold shifted her thin legs and folded them under herself. "What happened in Atlantis to make you feel so compromised?"

Reluctantly, Kelsey told her about Jarad and Iriel's friendship, their journey to the purple cloud, the swimming, the dolphins, Iriel's appearance in the lab. When Kelsey was done, Marigold sat twirling her glasses. Outside, the afternoon was waning and the wind whipped around the corners of the house. "So it's not exclusive, this Stan connection."

"It's stronger. More immediate, more experiential. I feel . . . as though I'm becoming her."

"And that's what you really want?"

She hadn't thought to doubt it. "I guess it's Atlantis I'm in love with."

Marigold's hands were like butterflies, flitting around each other before they mated. "But what about this darkness you mentioned?"

Kelsey shook her head. "I can't."

"Can't what?"

Now the vision pushed its way in. An ordinary garden, a wooden shed, a hole in the dirt, something long hidden there.

Muamdi cleans the spire so its color emerges. Green like a summer sea, green as moss, green as new grass. I reach. The touch ignites a craving. Then satisfaction. Then deeper craving. Muamdi knocks my hand away; her own lingers. The green light begins to awaken from the depths of the earth, and I understand the size of it. As big as a large cat, and coming to life. Quickly Muamdi snaps off a piece, a small, green, glowing egg. "My truest feeling is that you will need this," she says. Behind us, someone sighs. Like an animal burying its kill, Muamdi throws dirt over her crystal, quenching the light. Then she stands to confront the trespasser. But he is gone. Leaving a permanent shadow, like a bloodstain on the ground.

"Wait a minute," said Marigold. "He was there."

"I thought he was making it up at first. But it's true. He's in the story."

Marigold was silent a moment, almost in prayer, before she looked at Kelsey, her blue gaze drilling for the truth. "You know who he was?"

Kelsey let out the breath she'd been holding. "Gewil."

"And Iriel had some difficulty with this Gewil?"

"She ruined his plans." Kelsey was trembling, reaching toward something beyond her full knowledge. She searched Marigold's open face for clues. She came back feeling disconcerted, realizing Marigold didn't know; she hadn't been there. Then she got a little flash: Iriel leaving scraps for the animals. Some sense of Marigold in that place.

"In what way," Marigold pressed, "did she ruin his plans?"

Kelsey tried to steady her voice. "Gewil and Iriel were betrothed as children. But I . . . she refused him. I think it was public." She pulled the cloth away. "Is that a karmic debt? I've been reading about that. But why was it her fault if she didn't love him?"

Marigold was silent for a moment. "Karma doesn't have to be about fault. I believe we have entanglements, meetings, fates that coincide. Perhaps debt is the wrong word. Did it go further than the rejection?"

"There was Muamdi's crystal. He thought if he brought it to her, she would choose him. And she almost . . ." Kelsey squeezed her eyes shut looking for what came next. When she looked up, Marigold was leaning toward her. "That's just it," said Kelsey. "I don't know."

"Ah, yes," said Marigold, "but you want to."

"I'm afraid if I give him up, I might lose her too. Don't you see?"

"That's dangerous, Kelsey. On more than one level." Marigold slid on her glasses. "There are other ways to find out what Iriel needs to do to be done with it."

"To be done with it," Kelsey echoed.

"It may be slower, but with work—meditation, hypnosis, therapy—we can get there."

Before they wound down the session, Marigold showed Kelsey a few breathing and relaxation exercises to practice on her own. "Whatever you do, don't see Stan again before Tuesday. It's not that long to wait."

When Kelsey got home, it was after sunset, the lingering orange just visible through the trees. "What are you doing out?" she asked Pedro, but he wouldn't come though she held the door open and rattled the bag of cat food.

Surely, she thought, Stan had invaded her space again, but she found no sign of him. Relieved, Kelsey peeled off her clothes and got into bed. She stared at the sagging ceiling, concentrated on warming the cool sheets, then on her breath. It seemed to get bigger like Marigold had said it should—or maybe she hadn't, Kelsey couldn't exactly remember. After a minute or two, something shifted and she felt the chill enter the air.

Soundlessly she slid out of bed and pulled on her white robe.

He was sitting on the banco, shadowed in the crease where the fireplace met it. "Stan?" she called. But the man was younger, his face narrower, his straight, dark hair brushing his shoulders. He wore a brown cape over a knee-length tunic, and his feet were in sandals. It was the way he held himself that spoke to her. Cocky in modern terms, but that didn't nearly describe it: arrogant, solipsistic, the narrow force of his purpose blinding him.

"Gewil," she said, her voice barely above a whisper.

"You call me by my name? Do you come to give me my due, then?"

"You came to me."

He gave a cursory examination to his surroundings. "This is a strange place." Then he focused on her, frowning a little, looking at her naked edges, what the skimpy robe failed to cover. "You are well changed, Iriel."

Now in the other corner of the darkened room she saw a faint light, shimmering like the gaseous tail of a comet. It coalesced just enough so she recognized her brother leaning against an enormous jungle tree. A dilapidated shack stood beside the empty train tracks, and indistinguishable voices, excited and angry, receded into the forest.

Galen was holding his side, fingers woven around a bloody hole. His death wound, she realized with a shock. His face was dirty where he had been lying on the ground, his shirt blackened with dirt and blood, but his expression was of one awakened to a pleasant surprise.

"Galen," she called, and he smiled at her with recognition, then faint amusement at her grown-up self, then delight. She called his name again, but slowly he began fading until only the shimmer remained, then nothing.

Gewil too had seen the apparition. He'd been shrinking from it, into his corner by the hearth. Now, he rose and moved toward her. "Enough of your tricks, witch."

"What do you want from me?" Above all, she dreaded that he touch her.

"Only what is mine, what is ours." His eyes glinted as he pulled a green crystal from his robe. It was the size of his palm at first, then grew until he needed to hold the weight on both his hands. He bent his knees to accommodate the mass, looking up at her, as if it was all so familiar, as if they'd been through it so many times before: this offering, this suggestion of what could be.

The jewel lit up the room with its watery green brilliance. Suddenly she knew the only truth, the most implacable one. If only she had the stone, she could see the past, the future, *change them.* She reached for it, felt its hard surface against her fingers. For a fleeing instant, she held eternity in her hands.

Then the green stone vanished and Gewil captured her wrists.

"See," he said, "how easy it is."

She jerked away, too late. He'd touched her with his cold hands, and she knew he'd taken everything in that instant. Rapidly, he dissipated into vapor, his satisfaction lingering behind.

That night as she went through the motions of her bedtime routine, Kelsey kept coming back to the moment she'd reached for the crystal, believing in its omnipotence. It had felt like the fatal temptation, the tempting of her soul. When she finally fell asleep, her dreams were violent, terrifying images of swirling seawater and faces. Gewil and Stan doing battle against Galen, and her father in there too, shouting above the din. Kelsey struggled against the images, finally breaking free into the waiting torture of sleeplessness. She lay there, barely holding off the terror, until just before dawn, Stan slipped into her bed. His caresses brought a miracle of amnesia.

The Source

Molten tongues twist and curl in the volcano's red mouth. We cling to the earth, the hot ground rumbles, and another bloody display explodes against the night sky. When the smoke clears, we creep closer, crouching just below the rim of the crater.

Why do we linger in this place with its unbearable heat and flying lava? Why do we watch the colored gases with such fascination, even though they choke us and sting our eyes? Because this is the ultimate place, the place we've sought; this is the source of all crystals.

Ever since we entered the cloud, we've been following an abundant trail of crystals that led us here, to the top of the volcano. Beautiful specimens lie on the ground all around us, and new ones form before our eyes. They dazzle us; they bedazzle; they delight; they bewitch.

A whitish mass flies through the air and cools nearby. I gaze fixedly as facets and spires take shape; I'm waiting for the color. A pale orange vapor wraps around the stone and begins to saturate it. I turn away. It is not what I seek.

Green is for healing and minde-link—it's our family color—blue is for spirit, orange for warmth and comfort, the hearth. Red contains the seeds of anger and violence. Purple is rare, the symbol of One-God's power, but white is the rarest and purest of all. It makes me think of a vast star-filled universe, the one that Quiri helped us understand. It makes me think of flying free from the bounds of the earth. Of course, I remember Quiri's white that burned me.

Another burst, and four new crystals cool. All raw, still unfixed; it takes crystle-minde to activate them. That is what the others want from me: to use my talent. I know I can do it; I feel the urge like an itch.

Quiri taught us that a crystal is like a child that absorbs a bit of its parent. An owner's cruelty or sadness can infuse and influence the stone. A crystal will transmute, refract, reflect, but it does not see or think. Yet it has a mind of sorts. It lives; it must feed constantly.

This is another thing: the new-formed crystals cry like blind infants, and we, like so many mothers, turn from one to the next. It is an impossible choice, an unmeetable demand, for even one strong stone can drive a person to madness. This I know, for Muamdi rages in my ear whenever she can break through, crying and begging for the return of her green treasure.

I am boiling with thoughts on the lip of the volcano. I try to sort out my own from those of the others. I am like a seashell held roaring to the ear, amplifying what's around me.

Through Jarad's eyes, I glimpse an arch, a land bridge to the other side. Soon he will give the command to cross it. Can his will, his serious practicality win out over madness?

Everyone else is thinking about crystals. Bracto knows what is here and the power and wealth it could bring him. He's heard of this place from some traveler or trader, or perhaps it is famous in the legends and child-taming tales of the mainland. He and Dtaner have loaded the lecmel with many beautiful crystals, still impotent for all but the lowest work. Since Gewil's betrayal, Dtaner's turned wholly to bad company.

"Bracto knows," I hear him say to Dtaner. "The witch will fix them. She wants to."

"Witch," Dtaner says. He casts a mournful look toward Gewil, then me.

"Witch, she be," Bracto repeats.

I'll never help Bracto, but surely, some seedy sorcerer on the mainland will do his evil deed. Or maybe Dtaner's crystle-minde will awaken soon. He carried Muamdi's green stone all the way from Yabeth, and I heard him speak to it, and it to him. Bracto whispers to him daily; I know they are forming a plan to steal it back.

Gewil is hardest to read, for his mind is complex and darkly foreign to my own. I feel his possessive intent, and his certainty that everything will be as he wants. I have so far resisted him, not easy here in the crystal field. As it was, I allowed him to take the stone away from Dtaner.

Here is how it happened:

Not long after we entered the purple cloud, we came upon a tinkling spring running out of a crystal firmly embedded in the earth. The stone was cloudy white to colorless, with rainbows hovering where the spring ran out. The water itself was sweet tasting and intoxicating.

We made a circle, even She-Beast stayed near, and all of us drank. It was night. We chanted and sang, our thoughts a joyous, spinning ramble, our minds joined like a school of fish.

Toward morning, the dream sorted itself out into a power struggle between Gewil and Dtaner over Muamdi's stone. Bracto and Dtaner sat together making colored pebbles dance into life. Gewil whispered to me to take the stone, beguiling me with words. It was his power that made me get up and lift the green crystal from Dtaner's pouch and set it between us on the ground. That and Muamdi's urging, her need clear and loud-spoken in my head.

Gewil's power was at its strongest that night: his will unbending, his purpose aligned with some universal force. Not One-God, the feminine power of love and creation, Her Will always pressing us toward our truth, this force was a petty handmaiden of some destructive Fate. Fate saw the possible future and pressed hungrily toward its goal. In my weakness and temptation, I lent it my hand. Now I am beholden to change that future, for my dreams have turned violent again: I see ocean, nothing but ocean, huge and troubled, and there is no land.

Something large and invisible is yet undone, of that I am certain.

Chapter 17

They were feeding Kelsey new versions of the organism almost daily, and with Molly out, she was free to take shortcuts and intuitive leaps, to make requests of engineering, and to come and go as she pleased, though she was mainly there, bent over her instruments or computer until her neck ached and her mind fogged. She was working so hard, not to please Crouch, though he'd taken notice, but because she hoped to win back Harrison's friendship, and because she believed Iriel might show up again with another clue.

About 8 P.M., hair still wet from swimming, Kelsey let herself back into the building. She stopped to watch the creatures in the giant display tank. Several new ones had been added: a large angelfish, a pair of black and yellow damselfish, and a banded coral shrimp. They swam lazily in the glow from the tank's light. The angelfish was pale, transparent, and looked almost too fragile to be alive.

In the lab, Kelsey started a set of tests and checked her e-mail. There, among the SPAM, were the familiar letters: HRS@Bioventure.com. Her heart started to race.

Before their quarrel, Harrison had written almost daily, sending jokes, cryptic notes about the work, times to meet for lunch. And though she'd diligently been double-mailing him reports, snail and e-mail, he'd been entirely silent in return. She clicked his message. It read: *I'd like to see more of the CR-799 strain. It may be relevant to the situation here.*

Kelsey reread the message three times, hoping to find some hidden code, some hint of friendliness, then turned away to check her tests. Every one of her specimens was dead, their corpses forming a Picasso-esque face, square eye, nose in profile, mouth sliding off the chin.

Kelsey unlocked her desk drawer and removed her scientific diary. She thumbed back to CR-799; her only note was its rapid rate of propagation. She went ahead a couple of days. *CR-803 is not adapting well. Check CR-799.* She stared at the sentence unable to think about it more deeply, to even comprehend what she'd written. She doodled in the margins of the notebook, her thoughts drifting back to the terrible conversation with Harrison, the love words he'd spoken, subtle as they'd been. Now in light of his withdrawal, she felt she loved him too.

As Kelsey underlined the word "adapting," drew a box, and embellished it with sideways pyramids, the concept penetrated. She'd been doing the natural selection herself, based on her criteria. What if the organisms would choose different criteria? She remembered an article Harrison had given her about population density and evolution. The key idea was that population must be great enough and the propagation cycle frequent enough for an evolutionary change to occur. In the lab, her biggest tanks held only a few gallons.

Kelsey felt something crunch underfoot. A fine trace of white beach sand gleamed on the floor. Alert now, she followed the trail to the lab door. She hurried into the hall and glimpsed a retreating back, heard the swish of fabric. *Iriel*, she thought, but it was only George, the tech assistant from research. The one who was taking her place on the trip.

"I heard a noise," she said when he turned around. "You working late?"

"Um, just going to feed the fish." George was maybe a few years younger than she was, and handsome in a stocky way. She'd noticed a wedding band. Now he spun it on his finger as he faced her. He suddenly grinned. "Hey, how's the swimming going?"

"Fine, I guess." She tugged a lock of hair over her cheek.

"Saw you at the pool a couple Saturdays ago. You were doing some kind of underwater breathing exercise. Getting certified?" he asked. "I just got mine. I'm leaving on Sunday."

"Diving? No, I'm learning how to swim," she said. "It's a little embarrassing."

"Don't worry about it." He smiled, a nice warm smile. "Hey, why'd you scratch anyway?"

She was startled. "I don't know. I guess I was . . . scared."

"Of the ocean?" George asked. "It's just the beach. Everyone loves the beach."

Kelsey slid back into the lab and closed the door. As soon as George was out of earshot, she snuck back into the hall and followed him to reception where she hid in the shadow of a concrete support pillar. Sure enough, he took a narrow cylinder out of his lab coat pocket and using an eyedropper, added something to the fish tank. She recognized the tube. It was the carrier used to transport samples from engineering to the lab.

So he was injecting the protozoa into the fish tank. They were one step ahead of her.

Quickly Kelsey ran back to the lab and closed it down. She was wasting her time, doing the endless repetitive experiments. Crouch already had what he wanted. She was years behind, running her little factory in the lab. Her best progress would come from watching them.

Kelsey arrived early Friday morning. She bent down to greet the angelfish. "My favorite," she told Valerie, the receptionist. By noon, a faint violet tinge had stained the tank, and the angelfish was listing on her side, flapping her lacy fin, her color gone slightly blue. Kelsey tapped on the tank. Why was only the angelfish dying? Or was she just the first to go?

By the afternoon, the angelfish was floating on the surface, and the coral shrimp was not in sight. Kelsey got her first chance at the tank at 4:58 when Valerie left for the day. The angelfish was gone, but she waited until the lobby cleared, then scooped up a sample of tank water in a coffee cup and took it back to the lab.

Every single one of the specimens was dead. She went back to the tank again but could not find one protozoa that had survived. She finally settled for extracting the most varied specimens and pressing them between slides. After 9 P.M. she thought suddenly of the remaining fish; she would see if any of them were acting as a host for live protozoa. But when she got downstairs, the tank was empty and a maintenance crew was scrubbing it out.

"Where you been, Hon?" Stan had his feet propped up, a drink in his hand. He was watching a tiny portable TV he'd brought over from the estate. "You're late."

"I was working."

"What's so all-fired important over there anyway?"

Kelsey stood in the kitchen to listen to her phone message. Though she'd hoped not to hear from Marigold—how could she face her now that she'd canceled two more appointments and was back with Stan?—she'd called back.

"Kelsey, I've felt, in all honesty, rather inconvenienced. But I am also seriously worried about you and your obviously compulsive behavior. So I'm willing to give you another chance. Please think about it and call me."

"Bitch," said Stan, rising from the couch.

Kelsey had been watching the back of his neck stiffen. They'd already argued about Marigold. "I told you I haven't seen her. Besides, she's just trying to help me," Kelsey said.

"Help you break up with me."

"Think so?" Kelsey asked. She thought she saw something else in his face, laziness, a certain lack of will. "I don't," she said, and patted his arm.

Stan pushed past her into the kitchen and poured himself another drink. "She's a bitch," he said again, and went back to the couch.

In the refrigerator, Kelsey found leftover pasta, a cooked chicken breast, and a few not-too-old vegetables, which she sliced and put in a sauté pan. She threw away some runny lettuce and a take-out carton of white rice. It was then she found the letter, buried in the trash.

The envelope was blue, no return address. Her first thought was Harrison, but the handwriting, though tall and slanted like his, wasn't quite the same. And the postmark was San Francisco. The flap was not tightly closed, so she was pretty sure Stan had read it.

She turned her back to the couch, slid the letter out, and carefully replaced the envelope in the garbage.

Dear Kelsey,

I can hardly believe it's you after all this time, but of course you must have grown up. Certainly I remember the incident you asked about. It was pivotal in my life.

"What's for dinner, Hon," Stan's voice was moving toward her.

Kelsey slid the letter under her shirt and spun to face him. "Leftovers."

"Leftover what?"

Kelsey stirred the vegetables, spoon scraping. "Want to make a sauce?"

He kissed the back of her neck. "You're jumpy tonight."

"Watch this for me. I have to pee."

Kelsey didn't dare lock the bathroom door, or even fully close it. They'd grown very free around each other. She wedged the handwritten pages inside a catalog, flushed the toilet, and went back into the kitchen.

It was deep in the night when she finally got her chance. Stan was sleeping, and that was the signal that jolted her out of her own light sleep. She might have put the letter in her purse or jacket pocket and read it later safely, but she couldn't wait. So she sat in the coat closet, door closed, light on.

Lilya had written three pages in a sharp, slanted hand. After the greeting, she went on:

I was working toward my master's under your father's supervision and Myron was going for his dissertation. He and your father had an association, which I, to this day, don't fully understand. They were alternately attracted and repelled by one another, in constant competition, yet always scheming together. In a way, they were like bitter lovers who could not let go of each other.

We were using iridium to promote growth of cancerous tumors in mice with a sporadic, high intensity dosage. In those days we were still on mainframe computers, programming them with punch cards.

On a lark, I tried using a likeness of musical notation (I was always practicing my violin) to drive the exposure. It was a Liszt Mazurka on which we turned a corner into creation of new more virulent type of cancer in healthy mice. This was groundbreaking at the time, and we worked feverishly to duplicate the conditions.

I was lowest in seniority, so I was responsible for the night shift. Dr. Dupuis was usually home in the evenings, but Myron often came into the lab. He loved my musical scheme; he called me a genius and a prodigy. He was only three years older, but acted like a mentor, particularly when your father wasn't around.

Myron wanted faster progress, for his dissertation he told me. Later we discovered he was in contact with Frederick Heinman, a committee member for the Lanmer prize. Heinman planned a confidential visit to the lab. Stretching the rules, but Heinman was ambitious too—he wanted to be the one to discover new work that was ultimately recognized.

This is where things got sticky. Dr. Dupuis was of the old school, but he was seduced by Myron's ways. Surely a prestigious prize would cap his career. Your father was an unusual man, very severe at times, excitable under his reserve. I will say candidly, I was half in love with him.

One night, we were all three there. It was the day before Heinman was to visit, and the results weren't up to par. Myron urged me to increase the dosage, by double, triple, which I did. He asked for tenfold, and they argued over it. Myron won, and I set the dial.

Dr. Dupuis was brooding, watching me from his position near the sink. I remember clearly, for I looked up just as it happened. He was leaning against his cane and his face was half in light, half darkness. Myron said something, and your father leaned forward to hear it. His cane slipped and he teetered. The fear and the vulnerability on his face—I'd never seen it before. He was so open, so childlike; it was as though he first recognized his own mortality. I rushed to him, and somehow left the valve open. I was the one who got the exposure, because I went back and stood there trying not to watch Dr. Dupuis compose himself.

Heinman came and went, whatever happened with him, I'm not sure, but I know they fudged the results and Dr. Dupuis was part of it. You've read most of the rest. I did testify on Dr. Dupuis's behalf, because Myron went crazy. I think it was the bitter culmination of their battle. Both needed to win, and both did in a way, though both were mortally wounded.

It was my roommate Sarah who went to the Dean. She was angry that neither of them came to check if I was well or ill. I believe your mother prevented your father from contacting me. At least that's what I'd like to believe. She never really liked me, that's why I quit the job at your house. It was nice to blame his silence on her, because, you know, it hurt me so much at the time.

She wrote me back after your father's death. She was taking care of his unfinished business, I guess. They'd talked of me often over the years, she told me. Cecil felt guilty about how he'd left it with me. He was sorry. It meant a lot. I was ill then, cancer can incubate a long time in humans.

I went through several courses of chemotherapy, and have been clear of it for five years, thank God.

In answer to your question, I would say yes, Myron Crouch is capable of seeking revenge, even at this late date. It was very difficult for him not to win.

Sincerely,
Lilya Johnson Hendricks

PS. I am no longer working "in the field," as your father used to say. I am a violinist for the San Francisco Symphony Orchestra. Music makes me happier than science ever did.

This last made Kelsey weep. She wept for her brother Galen, her mother, and her father, herself. She clung to the coat hems thinking of her opinionated father, his influence, so strong, but essentially over now.

When she got back to bed, Stan sat up in the dark. "Where have you been?"

"I couldn't sleep, Stan."

"You went out. I heard a door—"

"Shh," she said. "I was sitting in the closet. I was crying."

Somehow this made sense to him. She felt his ropy muscles go soft as he held her, and in relief, she let him. Not all of her, just the part that was afraid. There was a moment, though, after he started to kiss and caress her, when it changed. Maybe his mouth at the base of her hair, or the desire in his eyes, or the way he whispered her name. Something made her open to him. Soon she was moving to his thrill and nothing could have stopped her. The pleasure felt so right.

Ceremony

I search for Muamdi, but she's vanished. Perhaps she is just too small, hidden somewhere below the shoulders, the heads of the crowd that seems not like friends and family, or even people, but so many mouths. Mouths talking, laughing, drinking wine, chewing meaty bones, licking greasy fingers. I focus on two wet orifices closing together for a tongue-entwined kiss. Lips part, smile, and two familiar heads turn my way. To my horror, I see they belong to my parents.

The courtyard smells of charred meat—the smoke that filled it all afternoon still clings to the plaster walls, the bright decorations. Muamdi made fourteen batches of paper for my ceremony of womanhood, one for each year of my life, and dyed them fourteen different colors. She captured the yellow sunrise, the turquoise sea, the many hues of the flowers in her garden. In all of Yabeth, she is the only one with this special recipe for a paper thin enough to fold, yet strong and pliable, able to be transparent or opaque, bright or pale. Father says her fancy filament is good for little save the frivolous. Mama says it is worth less than that—she says the complicated making of it will turn her old before her time. She and Muamdi spent many nights gathering, pulping, pressing, drying, mixing colors. Still, Mama basks in the constant praise those twisted streamers inspire; I catch her smiling as she lights the delicate waxy lanterns, fingers the fluttering flags.

A sudden breeze blows through the courtyard; the lanterns sway and flicker. One catches fire and my father rushes to put out the flame. As though this is the sign he's been waiting for, Gewil kneels at my feet.

His words start low, they are not addressed to me but to the crowd. "My family is happy to announce our acceptance," he says, meaning the gossip about Jarad and me, our supposed lovemaking, has been proven false. My face flames like the sunset reflected in the clouds overhead. "My parents welcome her into the heart of our family. She is . . ." and he goes on to praise my beauty, my purity, my skill in the kitchen, my virtue as a weaver, my strength as a water carrier and wood-gatherer, my swiftness, my courtesy . . . He does not name the thing he prizes most: my crystle-minde, but it is there in his next words. "She may one day become a healer like her grandmother, one of our true treasures."

Lies! All lies!

I stand still as I'm meant to, not yet touching his up-stretched hand, not yet meeting his gaze as I listen to him twist the truth. He does not say that Muamdi has long been shunned, that we in our family are called witch, or cursed, that after the accusation, his parents began to question my character; he does not say that my own mother and father humbled themselves by lowering the agreed-upon price. He does not say he fears that I am wild still, that I climb, and run, and swim, that I am quicker in school than he is, that I have ideas. These things are not seemly, though I'd say he likes them well enough. He thinks he is the one to tame me. He thinks I will carry this wildness into his bed. Soon, he thinks . . . .

And so by the time he finally stops, and the twilight comes and the restless guests are clutching nearly-empty goblets in anticipation of the toast, by the time he's risen—how did he capture my hand?—by the time he stands before me in all his manly splendor, I have my answer ready. His face edges closer, the slice of nose, the dark, close eyes, the low thick brows. He is waiting for what he believes he will hear: that I am honored to be his. I see that in his face, his eagerness, his possessiveness.

Everyone else knows the answer too, the answer I've practiced for days. The yes needed practicing. But not the no. The no just comes.

And so I let the words flood up from my heart. I pull my hand out of his, I engage his eyes, see the sharp panic there as I begin to speak, the creeping glaze of shock. "No," I say in answer to his formal question. "No, I will not have you." And then, when the word, the anguished question escapes his lips, I answer, "Because my soul weeps at the thought of marrying you. Because I would rather die than accept your false love." When he asks who then? I say, "I know no man's love. I may never." And then I push my way through the mumbling guests, past my mother who is leaning in a dead faint against my father, past my slack-jawed almost mother-in-law, through the house and out into the front garden.

"It is always right to speak from your heart," Muamdi whispers.

"I wanted you to say no," says Jarad.

"You are no child of mine," says my mother.

"But Iriel," says my father. "Can't you please reconsider?"

"I will never speak to you again," says Gewil. "You are dead to me."

And so it goes on, the many voices, the anger, the love, the reassurances, the vengeance, as the guests slink away, as the night lowers like a gloved hand, as the inevitable future is set into motion.

Chapter 18

Stan showered and left before dawn, and Kelsey fell back asleep, sleeping through the light, fighting off the coming day. She was dreaming of little covered boxes holding gems, each brighter than the next. The last was a large, white diamond, and as she fingered it, Stan was suddenly there, nodding and smiling. But when she looked again, the box was empty. She began searching, Stan yelling at her to look harder, it was a valuable thing she'd lost, worth half a million dollars. Everything was escalating, her franticness, his voice, until she roared back at him and he turned on his heel and left.

The core of the dream stayed with her as she lay among the sheets. Just for a moment, she pretended Stan was truly gone. It was dizzying, sickening and exhilarating, both. She twisted upright and looked around the room. There was no sign of him; he was tidy, all his clothes were put away, what few he'd brought over. Suddenly her panic deepened. What double life was he leading anyway?

Kelsey thought about calling Marigold, then didn't, then did. She got the message and hung up. But Marigold called her right back. Too late to pretend.

"Kelsey. I'm glad you called. Is there something you wanted to tell me?"

"I guess."

"You've been avoiding me."

"No. Well, yes."

There was a pause. "I don't think this is you, Kelsey."

"What do you mean?"

"I mean I don't think you are the kind of person who breaks appointments, who does not return phone calls, who is, in short, unreliable and rude."

Kelsey felt her face grow hot. "I'm not the kind of person you can insult."

Another pause. "You need to think hard about what you're doing here."

"Don't you think I am?"

"I think you are unconsciously acting. Feeding an addiction."

"That sounds like psychobabble."

"Now you're insulting me."

Again Kelsey came to the same tangled conclusion. She would/could/should give him up. She was not entirely ready. Why not? The answer came in like the breath of a dream. She had more to do, more to learn, more to solve. "I'm not finished, I guess."

"Well," said Marigold, "when you are, why don't you give me a call?"

Kelsey thought about Marigold's opinion a long time, letting her anger rush in and out like waves on a beach. She would not be pushed, she decided, the adrenaline still in her veins. She paced, she sat, she distractedly petted Pedro. She finally left the house.

The day was gorgeous, bright blue sky, the spring wind stopped for good. Everywhere lilacs spewed their old lady scent. Car window open to the fineness, Kelsey smelled change in the air. She drove downtown, walked around, going over and over her mixed-up feelings about Stan. Was she his soulmate as he'd claimed? Were they fated to be together, at least until they worked something out, or was that just an excuse? Kelsey stopped for an iced coffee at a newsstand, and sat thumbing through a magazine that held no interest for her. Suddenly she felt sick, sick of herself, her weakness. She'd go home, wait for him, tell him the truth.

But when she got into her car, she found herself avoiding it again. She headed up to the ski basin, the Karmann Ghia hugging the curves. As she rounded Nun's Corner—where a busload of holy women had once gone off the cliff—she thought how easy it would be to just sail out across the void, flying in her car for a few split seconds.

On the mountain, it was shady and cool. Small plants poked through the soft moist earth: strawberries, the first hint of wild-flowers. Kelsey found the service road and climbed, her tennis shoes growing wet from the soggy ground, and once she stepped through a crusty patch of snow into icy water below. Her feet ached then, yet her determination to reach the top grew stronger. She only wanted to get back to what had started it all, the accident, the first pure Iriel memory.

When Kelsey paused for breath and to look at the view behind her, she noticed a little line of smoke rising from one of the out-buildings. Evening was coming on, and with it the cold. She pressed upward, the last part steep through the trees. She recog-nized a slope she and Harrison had skied in powder. The return-ing memory was gentle, in her body. For a moment, she was back there, feeling the rhythm, the irresistible momentum of the mountain.

She watched the purple sunset spread below her. Then she climbed again, following the spine of the ridge, looking for the place where she and Harrison had plunged down the backside. With only a patchy snow cover, the bowl looked rocky, impossible. Kelsey hurried forward, out of the wind, away from the sight of the aspen groves, the steep, winding gullies.

But now the icy mood was upon her. She began to run down, her frozen feet feeling as though they might break, her breath tight in the thin air. She slid over loose rocks into the shelter of the trees. She caught a tall pine and clung to it, while memory rushed in: Harrison's shout, the avalanche rolling over her.

What struck her this time was the sudden stillness of being under the snow. It seemed a cosmic interruption in her spinning life, a unique opportunity for truth. But what cold truth it was: She'd opened herself to a treacherous person from a dangerous past.

Then Kelsey's sight, her sense of touch dissolved. Of this world, only the smells and the sounds remained: the vanilla pitch of the tree and the forest creaking and groaning around her. Kelsey stopped resisting and let the whirl of emotion claim her. It was baby pain, sweet pure panic, piercing fear, and finally a wide band of grief that rushed forward and engulfed her.

Again Kelsey felt the tree between her hands. She looked up into its canopy and there Iriel's face appeared, not young as she'd always seen it before, but old and creased. Loose hair escaped the gray braids; the face was marked by sorrows. Still the iridescent green eyes beamed out of the tired skin and her exquisite aliveness passed straight through to Kelsey's heart.

Kelsey stood shakily and brushed away the wet pine needles. As she slowly made her way down the mountain, she began to realize that Iriel's life was bigger than one man's and one woman's romantic struggle. Iriel hadn't died young, after all. And in the forest darkness, she thought she heard a quiet plea, from self to self.

Yes. Understand, act, grow. Trust yourself.

The Wave

Waves beating, beating. Pounding against the hull, the retreating shore.

Rain pours down and the sea rises. At this rate, everything will turn to water.

Still not enough to quench the fires.

Another blast. Faraway rock flies through the air and red splits the darkened land. Fire runs like rivers, sizzles into the foaming sea. White cracks in the sky, red cracks in the land. Everything cracked open.

The sea is black, the night is black. Rain pours down. The land diminishes as the Lady Sun is swept across and away. Out. Away. Currents, new currents from under the sea. Pulling currents, faster currents. Too strong. Not right.

Too rough, too choppy, mounting rollers. Big, bigger. Rolling over us. Drowning us. Tipping, flapping, bouncing, diving boat. The Poor Ari, wailing down below, while I cling to the deck and watch everything drown.

Voices. A chorus of voices crying, wailing to heaven. Voices of the dead, the dying. One-God, are you there? Do you hear them? Do you hear me?

A new wave forms out to sea. A wall of water rushes toward us. It towers all the way up to the black sky. I fear it. Why? Can I still fear death, when all my beloveds have perished? With no one left to witness it but me, the great wave roars past. We are under it, we are over it, we ride it toward the shore. Will we be smashed against the cliffs? But the shore is gone now. Vanished beneath the wave. Sunken into its crack. There is no fire, no land, no people.

Only water.

Chapter 19

His car was in the driveway. When she went inside, he was pacing her living room, and his face—puffy and flushed with anger—confirmed her worst fears.

"Where have you been?" he demanded.

"I went for a hike."

"In the middle of the fucking night?"

"It's only eight thirty, Stan. I told you I went up to the mountains and then—"

"Who with?"

"I was alone."

He grabbed her wrist. "You think I'm going to buy some stupid story?"

She pulled away but not before she got a whiff of alcohol. "I climbed to the top of the ski basin. It was cold and snowy. My shoes got wet. See?" Rubbing her wrist, she stared into his enlarged pupils. "Stan, I've been thinking that I can't . . . that we need to—"

He had her biceps. "It's that . . . that Ph.D. fucker, isn't it?"

"Harrison?" A mistake to say his name. She shook her head. "He's not even in town."

"Who then?" Her shoulders were now in his grip, his face looming, the insult sliding out to strike like a snake. "With your appetite, you're probably fucking more than one."

"All I did was go for a drive—"

"Don't ever lie to me!" He hands slid up to her neck. She palmed his chest and screamed.

Stan's face drained of color, and he stood there, clenching and unclenching his fists. Then he began caressing her shoulders through her jacket. "I'm sorry, Kel." His mouth dropped open. "You know I would never hurt you. It's just . . ." He shook his head. "I can't stand it when you're not here. You're never here anymore. And then you say these things . . . ."

She knew then, she'd have to wait until he was sober. For now, she would appease him one more time. "Look, I'm tired, Stan. It's been a hard day. I just want to take a shower and go to bed." She looked down at her feet, then back at his face hovering above hers. "Alone. Just for tonight. Please? Can't you go home for one night?"

"Miguel kicked me out."

How had she missed it? Trembling, she fumbled for her purse and pulled out all the money she had. "Here," she said. "Get a room somewhere. Get cleaned up."

His face worked. He eyed the cash. She knew he wanted it.

"Please Stan. You'll feel better tomorrow."

"Can I see you?"

"Sure," she said. "We'll talk," as his hands closed over the bills.

Kelsey sat at her writing table by the back window, working by the light of the table lamp. She was dressed in her terrycloth robe, and her hair was combed out and drying against her shoulders. Pedro was curled on the rug at her feet.

She'd written three pages in her journal about her evening in the mountains and about remembering the avalanche. She'd gotten a new flash of Harrison's face after he'd dug her out and found her breathing. Still swaddled in snow, she'd opened her eyes for just that one second, long enough to share a look—his relief, hers wonder. What was it? She sat, pen poised over the page.

I was full of something, something I'd glimpsed for only a moment. My understanding was fading so fast, but my heart was full of it. A kind of love, or ecstasy. Nothing mattered except that feeling. I wanted to tell him. But then I was back in my body, shaking so hard, so cold, so scared. He was digging me out, and then I must have gone to sleep.

The telescoping of lives, an instant of stark revelation, a crossing of the veil between this life and that. They'd asked about it at the hospital, but she'd not remembered before now.

Pen on fire, she started writing about Stan and Gewil, and what he/they wanted from her, from Iriel.

It's bigger than romance. Bigger than love and jealousy. He's dangerous, I see that now. His ambitions, his need. It's something big he wants. Something like power.

What about Harrison? She'd left a space, written only his name in the middle of the page. She remembered him pulling the snow away with his hands and throwing it over his shoulder, even after the lights came: ski-patrol wearing headlamps. *I went back to sleep*, she wrote. *I had a dream.*

About Iriel. As Kelsey tried to remember the dream, she stared into the garden at the shrubbery. A wind must have come up because the bushes were thrashing back and forth. A dark shape separated itself and went a few feet along the fence.

Heart racing, Kelsey shoved the diary into the desk drawer and ran into the kitchen. Lights out, front door locked and bolted. Was that enough? She went into the bathroom, and there, like a gift, was the blue key he'd had made, sitting by the sink. Good luck! He must have forgotten it in his drunken state. She slipped the key into her pocket, then tiptoed back into the bedroom and stared out through the glass.

At first, Kelsey saw only darkness. Then black shapes seemed to take form. Was it a man? She ducked deeper into the shadows and tried to think. She could go out and confront him. Or call the police. But what would be her complaint? Her mind whirled until she was sick with the effort. Finally, she shoved her desk in front of the back door and went into the living room to wait.

As time passed, the adrenaline let down, and she grew complacent and weary. Perhaps it had been her imagination after all. She lay down on the sofa. She dozed.

The hiss of the cat woke her. He came streaking into the living room. She heard the doorknob rattle and instantly she was on her feet. The desk legs screeched as they slid across the floor. She heard him breathing, stumbling, patting the bed, and when he switched on the lamp, she shrank against the wall. The desk drawer opened and closed, the trash tipped onto the floor, the drawer again, the pages flipping, his heavy breathing as he read.

Kelsey understood that she had to get out of there. But where was her purse, her car keys? Where had she been standing when she took the money out? She moved toward the kitchen counter, her slippers making a tiny squeak as she went.

"Kelsey?" Stan called out. "You in there?"

Kelsey edged along the counter, feeling her way in the dark. As her eyes adjusted, she could just make out the shape of her purse on the kitchen table. But as she turned, her sleeve caught a glass and knocked it to the floor. It shattered, loud as any explosion. Kelsey had only time to grab her purse and clutch it to her chest before light flooded the room.

He was standing in the archway, her diary in his hand. In two strides he was to her. He tore her purse loose and flung it. The keys spit out, scraping across the brick into the wall.

"Get out of my house!"

"You slept with him! It's right here in black and white!" He was waving the diary.

"No!" she said. "I didn't. I swear."

"Back to sleep! Had a dream. I read it!" He threw the book at the fireplace. It hit the screen and crumpled to the floor.

She felt a moment of confusion as her mind raced back through her reverie. *Back to sleep under the snow.* She took a breath, looked him in the eye. "We're through, Stan. Do you hear me? Through."

He came for her again. His pupils were dilated, and he reeked of cologne. Kelsey stumbled against the countertop as he raised his hand and hit her. She gasped from the blow, and tears sprang to her eyes. "What do you want from me? Just tell me what you want."

"What do *I* want? You're asking what *I* want for a change?"

"Stan . . ." she started, but he had her shoulders now.

"How about a kiss for starters? Yeah, give me a nice kiss."

She shook her head.

"Oh come on, Kel. What's one little kiss? Don't you think you owe me that? After all the servicing I've done for you?" He shook her a little. "You used me. You think I don't know it?"

"It wasn't like that."

"What then? A kiss, a caress, a good *fuck,* and you were off into your own little world."

He kissed her roughly, thrusting his tongue far into her mouth. She gagged and turned and wiped her face on her sleeve. She was shaking badly.

"I want you to go now."

"Don't you think you owe me something?"

"What? What do I owe you? We were two consenting adults!"

"And now you've changed your mind? Is that it?"

"You're not who I thought you were." She was thinking of him in the beginning, his charm, his seductive politeness.

His face colored. "Not that name you called, *Jarad,* but the other one, the bad one."

She hadn't meant Atlantis. But he was right about that too.

"Who was I, Kelsey? Tell me who I was? I deserve that much."

"Gewil," she said. "You were called Gewil."

"Say it like you mean it. Call me it."

"*Gewil.*"

"Say you love me. Say you love Gewil."

She was getting frightened again. She shook her head.

"Say it and I'll leave you alone. I promise. Say 'I love you, Gewil.' "

She opened her mouth hearing the words in her head first, and then she couldn't do it. For a moment, she was Iriel, fighting the forced betrothal.

"Say it!" Stan demanded.

She started crying. "I never consented. I never wanted—"

"Never consented? You were only too willing. So hot, so in love with your so-called visions, your imaginary world. 'You taste like the sea,' you said down in the wine cellar. Remember that? 'I need to feel the sea.' "

She got loose but he grabbed her from behind, knocking her to the floor just short of the keys. The brick struck her in the chin. She saw stars, blackness. Maybe seconds later, she came to with the pain spreading up her face and across her neck. Stan was sitting on her back; he had her arms pinned; he twisted them in their sockets.

"Let me go!" She yelled as he shoved her face into the floor. Somewhere in the room, Pedro was bleating continuously. All she could feel was panic fluttering in her chest, and the old pain in her neck.

He worked at something, his grip on her arms moving from one hand to the other. Once she pulled free, but he grabbed her hair and slammed her into the floor again. Now he threw her robe up over her head and forced her legs apart, lifted her up by the hips. She understood, just as he entered her from behind: He was making her pay. Each thrust pounded her body against the cold floor. She felt the force in her organs. Her blood rose, her anger.

He mumbled names, degrading phrases, *cunt, whore*, but she didn't listen. They were inching toward the keys. She used his rhythm, pushing with her feet, and when she was close enough, reached out, scratching at the brick until she got them. Somehow, she managed to wiggle loose. "Bitch!" he yelled, but he lost his angle and she kneed him, missing the groin, still got him, bone on bone. Screaming, she struggled to her feet. But he pinned her against the wall, and uncurled her fingers one at a time, and threw the keys across the room. Then he held his hand over her mouth until she quieted.

She smelled him again as they slid down, his cloying cologne, the new layer of sweat. He was on top of her, smothering her with the flap of her robe, and started again.

Kelsey remembered the snow, the darkness robbing her sight, cold spreading into her neck, down her spine—imprisonment, death. But it lasted only an instant. Deep in herself, she called upon Iriel. She needed her power, the sheer psychic strength of the crystals to pull her through. She kept her eyes closed and saw a picture. She slid that way, and there it was, the power of the crystal answering her prayer.

Kelsey took the sharp sliver of glass into her hand, sure that Stan would stop her. But he was building toward his climax, and that unleashed her fury. She struck for his eye but instead hit the meat of his cheek and dragged the shard through the skin.

Stan yelped and came to his knees. Lifting his fingers to the blood, he pulled the glassy thorn from his cheek. His face was stricken with disbelief. She stood free.

"You almost blinded me."

She slowly backed away keeping eye contact. Then, casually, she stooped for the keys and ran out into the night.

It welcomed her, cool, alive. The metal of the car door in her hand, the rough fabric of the seat against her bare legs, everything. "Start," she prayed as her engine turned over and over. She watched the front door, still ajar. A shadow moved—Pedro, slinking under the car. She jumped out and grabbed the animal, thrusting him into the seat, his claws tearing her skin, but it felt like nothing. Then Stan was outside. He rattled the passenger door, started around to her side, but Kelsey pumped the gas, cranked the ignition, and finally, mercifully, the engine caught. She lurched into gear and spun past him. His face drained white beneath the jagged bloody cut. Metal glinted in his fist as he raised the knife to strike.

Dtaner's Leap

Hard as it was to say those words to Gewil, to bear his anger and the shock that swept through the boisterous crowd, it is doubly hard now. Neither Muamdi's silence nor Quiri's open protest convinced me to reject the marriage that was already formed in everyone's minds—rather something else, something deep in my throat that I couldn't swallow, something physical, like a stuck bone. Try as I might to soften it with reasons, the bone stayed as solid as though my body had made it. No saliva, no sweet, neither wine nor vinegar could dissolve it. Nothing could fool my body, nothing my heart. I simply had to cough it up.

Now, standing alone on the volcano's rim, I have no such clear signal. Shall I steal Muamdi's stone and return it to her? Shall I let Gewil keep it? Shall I take it for myself, and some future of power? The path of righteousness is as narrow and difficult as the bridge Jarad and I have just crossed over the volcano's mouth.

When Jarad first stepped onto the bridge, he begged me to wait. I would have to take the lead if he perished, that was the unspoken part. But when he disappeared into the smoke, I followed, calling as loudly as I dared. I saw his hand first, extended out behind him, and took it. For just that moment, I didn't care whether we lived or died. When he left me on the far side to wait while he went back to lead the others, I felt as though I would never see him again. Now, I die inside as I wait for him to reappear.

The smoke is multicolored and thick, sunset-red, purple-streaked, bluish-lavender, foggy-pink, a thing of small beauty in this desperate landscape. The heat rises from the caldron, the very air seems to sizzle around me. I do not care, I edge closer to the land bridge—an arched remnant of the former mountaintop—and wait.

Gewil comes first out of the smoke. Behind him, Jarad leads gentle

Gijhaad, Quiri's donkey. She's blindfolded so she can't see the chasm, and each step is as sure-footed as if she were on level ground. I give them both warm tea from my goatskin and lead Gijhaad away from the lip. Her eyes are white with fear when I remove the blindfold, but she seems to know the worst is over.

Jarad coughs, and I rub his back while he works to control it. Then I take out a bit of cloth, dampen it with tea, and tie it to his face like a mask. He squeezes my hand in thanks. The last I see is his palm raised over his shoulder before he steps back onto the bridge.

Gewil starts up again. "I carried it all this way for you, Iriel. I wanted you to have it. You know I love you. I love you, Iriel."

The love words aren't real, they never have been. He knows not how to love.

"All we need is for you to say yes. I have the plan. Everything will be perfect. You owe it to me. After what you did."

He knows this argument creates a little war inside: Was I wrong to reject him? Do I therefore owe him? No, it is only the consequences I regret. The slide back to poverty for my mother—the maid snatched away, the loss of my father's position with Marlane—and worse, the changing opinions of the others. Mama now bears the double shame of an obstinate daughter and a mother consumed by crystal madness. The family taint is back in force, this I know from the pictures I get through Muamdi.

Papa fares better. He is back on the Lady Sun, bringing the catch to Mama for cooking, always fish, little meat. The family eats between that and the kindness of a few neighbors like Jarad's family, who share the produce from their garden and the wine from their vineyard. Still, the luxuries are missing. Soap, salt, paper, candles.

For me, the real temptation is Muamdi's crystal. The stone is my birthright, the family power lurks inside me ready to be born, this I know. I see how even Gewil has learned to use the crystal, or perhaps it uses him. I feel the green power behind his words. "I have what you want," he says.

Jarad bursts out of the smoke, the lecmel on his heels. On the lecmel's back is Bracto wearing the blindfold meant for the beast. Jarad rests only a moment. Then he walks back. Dtaner and She-Beast still have to cross. "Why can't they come by themselves?" I plead. He saves his breath, or maybe it's simply that words would start his cough again. I sense only his will, his solid determination.

"Iriel, quickly now, before Dtaner comes," Gewil begins again. "Say yes to me, say yes to the crystal."

"Say yes," mocks Bracto. "Say yes to me."

Gewil ignores him. "You want it. She wants you to have it. Here, look."

I have resisted this ever since the night at the crystal spring, but now the incessant noise and the shaking ground, my worry, and all the complaining and warring voices loosen my will.

I see Muamdi's shriveled face, her hair gone wild. She jabbers like a jack-bird, by some trick, echoing Gewil's words. "Take it," she says. "Take it. Take it. Take it."

I finger the green spire and the soft base that moves like pooled water. Muamdi, not ill but right again, multiplies inside the crystal. She smiles the way I remember. "Child," she says.

Dtaner's whoop drowns her out. He rushes in upon us and grabs the stone between his massive paw-like hands. Do I let him? I don't know. My resolve is not yet gelled.

Everything will come together at the top of the volcano, *a voice has said inside my head. Is the voice One-God's? I don't know, but I listen for it now. This is the answer that springs into my mind.* You will know what to do, and when you know, you must do it.

Like moving through water, I advance upon Dtaner. He's twice my size, but I have other strengths and so he backs away. Someone calls a warning and Dtaner stops just short of the rim. We are face to face, the crystal between us.

I could touch the stone or maybe try to wrestle it free. Instead, I breathe in the good it once was and what's left of Muamdi. I fold the weak thing into myself, calling upon her bravest part. I must take her pain as well. The first wave is disappointment, next longing, then crystal sickness, rage, madness, defeat, exhaustion, weakness, and at last, the lost child, the rotten core. I feel Muamdi's sorrow and guilt, how she'd like nothing better than to go back and do it over. Then I'm inside that mad child. I accept her pain too: a screaming agony of frustration, animal urges, and the flash of lucid beauty that made her life worthwhile.

When I've done this, the stone flies into my arms, light as nothing. Dtaner shrieks a battle cry, and I'm vaguely aware of Gewil and Jarad rushing forward, but it's the soft advance of She-Beast that brings me the message I need. Her cat-like features, her half-smile, the peacefulness, the loyalty, the compassion. In the flash of the instant, they tell me everything.

That's when I know what I have to do, and in the instant I do it, everything goes right.

When I throw the stone, Dtaner leaps. The luminescent green lights his face as he catches the crystal in his arms, and his body arches so gracefully that for a moment I think he will fly. Then he falls with pure athletic grace into the bubbling fire below. The only sound is the soft hiss of his flesh as the heat claims it.

The first thing I hear is Muamdi's gentle breath, going in and out with mine. I will carry the quiet remains of her existence for a long time. What she will become I do not know. The second thing I hear is the low rumble deep in the mountain.

Behind us, dawn lights a patch of sky beneath the edge of the purple dome. When I turn, I see the silver shine of surf in the distance. "Run," I yell to the others. "Run for your lives!" We do, feeling the earth shake as the crystal sinks deep to its source and makes the mountain start to blow.

Chapter 20

Marigold took one look at Kelsey, dressed in her robe, squirming cat in her hands, and pulled her inside. "You're bleeding. What happened?"

"He raped me." At the sound of her voice, Pedro writhed free and ran down the hall.

"That's OK. He can't get out," Marigold said following Kelsey's gaze.

Watching the spot where her pet had disappeared, Kelsey felt a wash of sorrow. Then Iriel's old face appeared in the dark entrance to the hallway. Now the message came clear. *Everything leaves you in life. Everything! It's all right. It's part of the plan.* Kelsey understood she'd been given a great knowledge, and she turned to Marigold, eyes wide, to tell her. But even now, she could feel the ache in her body where Stan had slammed into her. Her teeth began to chatter.

"You're in shock," Marigold said, gently guiding her into the living room. "Let me get you a blanket. You can't shower, of course."

Candles and a small reading lamp dimly lighted the room, and the embers in the fireplace drew Kelsey in as her mind raced through brilliant details from the last few hours. The mountain trees, stark against the dimming sky, the keys splayed out on the floor—everything seemed beautiful and spare. I've never been alive before this, she thought, then looked up to see Marigold's flat face, the sky chip eyes, the honeyed hair twisting around her wide cheekbones—Marigold seemed the most beautiful of all.

"Good," said Marigold, wrapping the blanket around her shoulders. "Go ahead and cry." She began to examine Kelsey's hands, her arms, her scratched legs where the robe had fallen open.

"Are you still bleeding from somewhere?"

Kelsey shook her head. "It's not mine. I stabbed him."

Marigold lifted her head. "You did? Is he badly hurt?"

Kelsey tried to digest Marigold's expectant expression. Then she remembered Stan, teeth bared as he swiped at the car with her butcher knife. Terror propelled her to her feet. "He's going to come here. He'll kill me. Where are my keys? I have to find my keys!"

Marigold caught her arm. "Listen. Listen to me, please. I'm going to call the police."

"No!" Kelsey shouted.

"But you've been raped. Isn't that right?"

"I've had sex with him so many times."

"Did you consent to it this time? Was it violent? You're quite bruised, you know."

"He kept slamming me against the floor. But it wasn't even me. It was somebody else." Now she could feel the way he'd been absent at the height of it, while he was pounding into her. *You bastard*, he'd said. "His father," she told Marigold. "His father beat him."

"Of course," said Marigold. "Of course you're right." She stood up, walked to the window and back. She slid the chain on the front door, and flicked on the porch light. "I'm going to get my phone."

Kelsey heard Marigold talking, and from the back of the house, Pedro's exploratory meows. *Rape*, Marigold was saying, and *dangerous. A woman, please. We might need protection.* Then her therapist was back. "Tell me what happened as quickly as you can. The police should be here in a minute."

Kelsey could sense Marigold's impatience, as she kept jumping around in her story: her resolve to break up, how it had come to her in the mountains, or maybe on the way down, the vision of old Iriel and something violent about the green crystal she couldn't remember now. She told how she'd been writing in her journal when suddenly she knew Stan was outside.

"He wanted me to call him Gewil." That was when she'd known he was really going to hurt her. She felt the reality heavy in her body, the pain pulsing in each place he'd touched.

Marigold asked about the stabbing. "That's how you finally got away?"

Despite the blanket, despite Marigold's arm around her shoulder, Kelsey was trembling. "It was a sliver of glass. Iriel showed it to me."

Marigold's face clouded. "I've been meaning to say don't mention Iriel to the police, if you don't mind."

"I would have . . ." She held up her hands. A patch of blood covered the right palm and three smallest fingers. "I have to wash it off."

Marigold shook her head. "You can't." She frowned. "How badly did you hurt him?"

"Just his cheek. I cut his cheek."

A car door slammed, and they both jumped up and ran to the window. But it was only a neighbor couple on their porch across the street. Marigold built up the fire, blowing softly until a tiny blaze caught. "I'm going to make some tea," she said. "Try to relax."

Kelsey huddled on the futon, trying to stop the shaking that had set in. Staring into the fire, she felt the other consciousness meld hypnagogically with her own. The red embers, the blue flames—she could feel the heat across the room. And then there wasn't any room.

The crystal feels like a second fire in her hands, a cool green fire. Power feels like this, a throbbing power making her hands warm. The green energy flushes through her body like tingling blood. Then the stone flies up and out of her hands, tumbling spire over bubble, and suddenly the world is filled with sounds: the roar of the volcano, a high angry scream in Gewil's distorted voice, and something big rushing past her shoulder.

Dtaner arches into the air, an impossible dancer's leap. Then the volcano begins to rumble. Deep in its belly, the discontent grows. The gift, not accepted, ready to be spit out again.

Kelsey shook her head. The rhythmic eruptions became knocking, and Marigold was scurrying to the door, saying, "Heads up, Kelsey."

Kelsey ran as far back into the dark hallway as she could go. Pedro darted out of one bedroom door and into another, but she didn't follow. She stared at the textured ceiling, and at the walls lined with Marigold's childlike watercolors. It should be safe here, in the belly of the house, huddled on the carpet, but as she listened to Marigold's voice, argumentative and shrill, she knew it wasn't.

Trying to breathe, the breath catching in her throat, Kelsey tiptoed back up the hall. She'd gotten as far as the kitchen when the teakettle shrieked. At the same moment, a uniformed arm thrust a paper through the crack of the front door. She heard the angry inflections of the police officer. "Battery," was the word he used, and "Warrant," and then Marigold was saying, "I told you we made a call about a rape. We were instructed not to open the door to anyone but Officer Nancy Pacheco. I specifically requested a woman." Then a siren added its voice to the kettle, and the hand and paper disappeared.

Marigold bolted the door and pulled Kelsey into the kitchen. She lifted the whistling kettle from the hot burner and told her quickly that they had a warrant for her arrest. The charge was assault and battery. "You should call a lawyer, Kelsey."

"No!"

Marigold put her hand on Kelsey's shoulder. "Battery's a serious charge. Even though it was self-defense, you'll need a professional to prove—"

"That's letting him win."

"I don't understand."

"I was trying to end it. Now he has a way to drag it out. That's why it was a mistake to call the police."

"Yes," Marigold said, turning slightly away. "But the police *are* involved."

There was knocking again, and Kelsey rushed to the window. She saw two officers now, a large-bodied man and a tiny, neatly-uniformed woman, arguing at the door. The woman's face grew darker, flushed as it was with angry blood. Then Stan's BMW slid to a stop in front of the house. Kelsey shrank behind the curtain and watched, horrified, as he got out and strode up the walkway. She saw his face was bandaged where she'd struck him. Now he was almost to the door, and still the police were ignoring him. Then suddenly the tiny woman spun, set her feet apart, shouted, and drew her gun. Stan stopped just short of the porch stoop and raised his hands; both were swathed in white gauze.

"We want to talk to Officer Pacheco alone," Marigold yelled through the crack in the door. "We want to make our report. We have a rape complaint."

As Marigold slammed and bolted the door again, Stan focused directly on the place where Kelsey stood in the dark window. For a moment, it seemed the glass was gone and he would come hurtling at her. His hands were still in the air, the sleeve of his jacket fell away, revealing eight more inches of bandage on his forearm. Had she cut him there too and blanked it out? But no, she was sure she hadn't, and slowly the implications sank in.

Kelsey let the curtain fall and stood staring at the white cotton fabric, the embroidered eyelets with its pretty scalloped edge. She saw the volcano again, and remembered. They'd run down the flank of the erupting mountain and when they finally stopped near a spring, out of danger, Gewil grabbed her shoulders and whirled her around so she could see his unholy face, greasy with sweat, shining with bitterness and rage. "We could have ruled Atlantis," he yelled, "but you threw it away."

Threw it away, Kelsey thought. *He wants my power. But what power do I have in this lifetime? And then she knew. She could remember. She could change what he couldn't even understand. She could stop this madness.*

Kelsey pushed past Marigold. But Marigold wrapped her slim fingers around Kelsey's hand as she tried to turn the doorknob.

"I have to talk to him."

"Don't give him any more ammunition, Kelsey."

Kelsey's breath whistled out. "I have to tell him it wasn't Iriel's fault Dtaner jumped."

"They'll think you're crazy if you go out there talking about Iriel. And what if he gets violent? What will you do? Attack him again?"

Kelsey had been in Iriel's world, half gone with rage and power. Marigold's words were like a blow to the solar plexus. "You think I hurt him like that? You don't believe me?"

"I saw all the bandages. I thought Iriel, a vision . . . maybe you got carried away." A shadow crossed Marigold's face.

"He did that to himself!" Kelsey shouted. "Just like his father! He's that devious."

"OK, OK," said Marigold, putting her hands out. "I'm on your side. Let's just calm down. Why don't you start by getting dressed? We'll have to go down to the police station anyway. Maybe we can settle this there."

"Settle it?" Kelsey asked, feeling an odd skewing in her brain.

"We might have to make a deal," Marigold said. They were pounding on the door again, and Marigold straightened up. "Go," she said to Kelsey, pointing down the hall. "Look in my dresser. Put on anything you like."

Kelsey stepped into the night. The air felt bracing, and her hands tingled. She'd disobeyed Marigold and washed them in steamy water, watching Stan's blood run down the drain. Now she was clinging to her vision of the volcano. It helped mask the coldness that claimed her the minute she saw Stan standing on the grass, back turned, talking into his phone, one finger plugging his other ear, apparently free and unwatched.

Both police officers were on their radios. They turned when Kelsey emerged onto the porch with Marigold behind her. The man put his hand on his gun and the woman officer approached, her palm out in a stopping gesture. At that moment Stan sensed Kelsey's presence and turned toward her, his mouth agape. Marigold grabbed Kelsey's arm, and in an instant, the woman officer was in front of them, pushing them back, her gun pointed again at Stan.

"She's fucking outside," Stan said into the phone. "And that cunt cop has her gun drawn on me." He listened to a lengthy response. "Your Honor, I apologize. Yes, I appreciate it." He held the phone out to the woman officer. "Judge Jaramillo wants to talk to you."

Officer Nancy Pacheco visibly flinched at the name. "Sir? Yes, Sir. I read the warrant." She listened. "I need to protect her, Sir. He's hostile and dangerous. She's going to press rape charges."

She seemed to get even angrier as the judge made his reply. "Yeah," she said. "But if you ask me, she looks worse than him." Pacheco held out the phone to her male colleague and hissed, "El Rojo wants your ass now, Lee Boy."

The male officer set his feet into a wide stance. "Sir. Officer Leroy Murray," he said into the phone. He listened to the judge. "They wouldn't let me in the house, Sir, but she come out on her own. I could serve her now." He fiddled with the handcuffs on his belt, his sausage fingers tracing the metal loops. "Yeah," he drawled. "She won't make no more trouble for you tonight."

Kelsey had been watching for her opportunity. Now the sinking feeling that time had run out hit her as Murray threw the phone at Stan and instructed her to step down off the porch. "You stand back," he added to Marigold who was still holding Kelsey's arm.

They were all bunched together at the base of the stoop, the night closing in around them, the sounds of breathing loud as the whooshing sea. Kelsey could smell Officer Pacheco's delicate perspiration and Stan's cologne, overpowering and familiar as a nightmare. Murray started reading Miranda in a sonorous voice, and Kelsey lifted her head instinctively.

Just then, the door squeaked open—Marigold must have left it cracked—and Pedro came running out, threading between their legs. It all happened in an instant. Leroy Murray tripped over the cat, lost his balance, and spun away; Pedro howled and hissed at Pacheco who recoiled; Kelsey lunged after her cat, missing him; Stan grabbed her by the hair; Marigold kicked Stan hard in the shin; he roared in pain, then swung at her; Marigold went down clutching her mouth.

And then Kelsey and Stan were face to face.

"You have no rights to me." Kelsey felt the words pour out. "You never did. Nothing that ever happened gave you any right to me."

"You hurt me." He lifted one gauzy hand. "I'll make you pay."

She smelled sulfurous smoke in the air. "You are deluded, Gewil. It's over between us."

He flinched at the other name and the inflection in her voice.

"Our Karma is done. I declare it with the force of my soul and the power of One-God."

She felt him turn into a wall, a wall of denial and will that sent her words ricocheting back against her. Then Murray grabbed her roughly, and she felt cold metal circle her wrists. Pacheco handcuffed Stan, and they were pulled apart and put into separate cars.

Marigold shouted that she'd meet her at the station. Then the sirens came on, whining into the night as they sped away.

One-God

"You have a destiny, Young Master."

"Why do you call me that, Gracious Mother?"

"Because that is what you will become."

I remember a day sitting with Muamdi in her garden cleaning goatsfoot. It was before all this, before the moment I told Gewil "no," before I was sent away for my penance that has lasted now for a year. I have been called in to speak with Gracious Mother for the last time.

"Do you know what your destiny is?" she asks.

Muamdi told me, as we sat plucking and flattening those hoof-shaped leaves, that in big things, fate governs our lives. We are born to it, we must only discover it.

"I do not," I say. I think only that I have avoided the one fate—I am not a wife.

Gracious Mother has wavy white hair that floats to her knees, and a face so lined it looks like sand after a rain. But her youthful beauty still shines through. It is as though a smooth-faced girl sits with the wrinkled one and trades moments with her. One moment you see the beautiful clear face, the taut cheeks, the night-black hair, the next, the web of lines, the drooping jowls. I think the old face may be the more beautiful one. "Have they not spoken of the prophecy, Iriel?"

One evening, Quiri and my grandmother walked on the beach, thinking they were alone. Their talk was free, though I overheard them, hiding behind the dunes. Quiri had just received a communication from Shemmabdis, who had found his way to the mainland. He sent word of a convening of parties, those opposed to the present powers who ruled Phyrius and much of the ruined lands beyond the city. A diverse group, The Society, with whom Quiri associated, advocates of the enslaved mutants, a few Ari who had broken with their kind, some healers, magi-

cians, and mendicants. What united them was the prophecy that someone would come forward to lead them. Someone who had the power to stop the coming disaster.

"Yes, Gracious Mother, I have heard of the Expected One."

"Do you know who it is they await?"

"Master Quiri?" I ask, for that was what I thought as I followed the old lovers in the night. Quiri was preparing for his role. He was begging Muamdi to accompany him.

"And do you believe he is The One?"

I know Quiri's powers. He has disappeared before my eyes. He's shown great physical strength and agility. He reads the old scrolls, possesses long-forgotten knowledge. Still . . .

"You doubt it," she says, and the youthful face flashes a conspiratorial smile.

"Muamdi did not think . . ." I remember her resistance. She said he was foolish and proud. You are not she, no matter how much you wish it. *I note now the feminine usage. Hidden behind the dune, I'd thought it only her way of teasing, asserting herself against his pride.*

When Muamdi and I sat in her garden, the fuzzy goatsfoot greensmearing our hands, I asked her about destiny. "Fate is like the channel of a river, and you are the water," she'd said. "You both cut the channel and are confined by it. You can splash free, you can meander where the banks are soft. But you are still the river." This answer puzzled me, as I was then thinking how to escape the banks my parents and Gewil's had constructed: the forced marriage.

"I have thought of fate while I was here," I say to Gracious Mother. "I have prayed upon it. I know you choose it in a way, and then you are caught by it. But sometimes, sometimes . . ." and here my thoughts form on my tongue and come out fresh, "sometimes you are connected to something big you must do, something you must follow. One-God decrees it."

"Yes," she says, simply. And so ends our interview.

Chapter 21

"Champagne, Miss?"

Kelsey lurched awake. The first thing she knew was everything. The rape, the arrest, the events at the station. She started to rise, felt the seat belt across her lap and the final piece came back. She was in an airplane flying toward Houston for the connection to Belize.

The gray dawn was turning rosy outside her window, and she could see the familiar hump of the Sandias receding below. She'd slept only those few seconds since takeoff, but somehow they made all the difference. It was a new day.

"Would you like champagne, Miss?" the flight attendant asked again. "It's complimentary." Bubbles rose through the blush liquid, the attendant's friendly face hovered above.

"Why not?" Kelsey said and took a glass.

She was in first class, thanks to Crouch. She felt so grateful she'd called him. It had been an act of desperation, but he'd been the only one she could think of with the power to help. Together they'd found that little piece of the puzzle that brought her victory. And after she was free, all she could think of was to flee. Crouch had arranged that too. She'd taken George's ticket. In the meantime, no one would know where she was.

Kelsey drained the champagne and settled back into her seat. After the police station, Crouch had driven her and Marigold to her house to pack and get her passport. Then he'd offered to drive her to the airport. "Don't be silly," he said when she'd at first declined.

The flight attendant balanced her tray against the motion of the plane, and Kelsey reached for another glass of champagne. The first one was doing its work, lifting her head right off her aching body. She felt elated again, a shaky fragile high, new as the day.

Sitting in the police station with Marigold, having endured the scraping of her vagina, the demeaning tests, she'd begun to lose all hope. They brought out her kitchen knife, covered in blood, Stan's blood. She knew they could prove that. They were pounding at her with evidence and questions. At her side was the skinny court-appointed lawyer, telling her she didn't have to answer. Nevertheless, she repeated her theory that Stan had cut himself. She began to feel hysterical as she went on about his father, trying to get them to understand how an emotionally damaged son could have done such a thing.

"How could you prove it?" the lawyer asked her. "It would be nearly impossible to prove." Only Marigold gave her theory any credence.

"I can't stomach him or his kind. They think childhood trauma excuses their brutality. I'm just afraid he'll get away with it. Don't you have someone you can call? With influence?"

That made Kelsey think of Crouch. "I need your help," she said when he answered, bright and awake. "I've been raped, and now they've arrested me for fighting back."

When Crouch arrived at the police station, it was 3:13 according to the old-fashioned wall clock. She'd watched the numbers flip for two hours, thinking, when that clock says 2:00, it will be over. Then she amended it to 2:30, then 3:00, trying not to look again until another ten minutes had elapsed.

"Who is he?" Crouch asked first thing.

"A lawyer," Kelsey said, not wanting to say "my boyfriend" or even "my ex-boyfriend."

"Any influence down here?"

"Knows a judge, I think."

"El Rojo," Marigold added.

"Jaramillo," Crouch muttered. "Dirty as they come. Wait here." Crouch got up and went to the front desk. He spoke at length to the clerk, who summoned Officer Nancy Pacheco. Crouch asked her questions about the warrant. Next, he pumped the skinny lawyer for the status of the case, then fired him as thanks. He substituted Mr. Charles, the company attorney, who appeared within minutes and went to work on Leroy Murray. "We'll get a real defense attorney tomorrow," Crouch told Kelsey and Marigold. "Let's just get you out of here for now."

Mr. Charles, immaculately dressed, was obviously a finer class than they were used to seeing in the police station. When he listened to Kelsey's story, something about his intelligent face, the delicate features, the wire-rimmed glasses made her start to cry.

"What makes you think he cut himself?" Mr. Charles asked.

She was too upset and exhausted to repeat her theory. She just went blank. Mr. Charles waited patiently, polite but acute. Why *did* she think he'd cut himself? She covered her eyes and suddenly saw a picture of Stan pounding on the door, waving the bandaged fists. Then Officer Nancy Pacheco's words came back. *She seems hurt worse than him.* She opened her eyes and said, "I don't think he did cut himself. He's too vain and he can't stand pain. It must be fake."

Leaning back in her seat, feeling the plane bank to the east, Kelsey marveled that the revelation had come to her at all. Iriel's magic had seemed used-up after her speech to Stan on Marigold's front porch. It was as though she had to use ordinary tools to get through the stuck place before she could have the magic back again.

This new version of magic came by way of the unconscious mind, like remembering a word on the tip of her tongue. That flood of relief as the thing came to her, miraculously whole when a moment before it had been hopelessly obscure: He'd dropped the knife and when he bent to pick it up, blood must have dripped onto the blade, giving him the idea.

Mr. Charles arranged for an officer to unbandage Stan's hands on the pretext of photographs for evidence. Kelsey wished she'd been in the room to see it. All of them crowding around as the pile of clean gauze grew on the floor beside him. His mortification as they discovered he had no real wounds other than the small cut on his cheek. She'd only seen his face as they took him into custody: anger, determination, Gewil's solipsistic purpose reflected. She hadn't wanted to press charges at first, but then they found the second complaint, the one from Miguel—damage to and theft of property—and then the old drug charge. Marigold asked, "You don't want him running free, do you? This is your chance to lock him away for awhile."

Outside the airplane, the sky turned morning blue. Occasionally Kelsey glimpsed a patch of sectioned land through soft holes in the clouds. The plane hit an air pocket, and the seat belt sign dinged on. Less than an hour to Houston. Then she would wait for the afternoon flight to Belize City. Only when she boarded the second plane could she relax. Irrationally, she did not feel safe as long as she was on American soil.

Kelsey grew sleepy again. Her thoughts drifted to Marigold and her friend's warm hands as she said goodbye, almost pleading for Kelsey to take good care of herself. The last thing she'd said before Kelsey ran through security was, "I'll put a prayer shield around you."

It was Marigold's way of saying she didn't think Kelsey was ready to be on her own. But that had been the main thing Kelsey was sure of. She *had* to get away, as far away as possible.

Kelsey pressed her face against the window, letting the glass cool her forehead. A headache was starting there. What had it felt like to let go of Stan at last? That moment when she'd walked away, knowing he was glaring at her back, that he was capable of killing her even—did she also feel the instant clearing of her soul, the blessed relief of karmic resolve? No. It was like a stone sinking into deep, dark waters, like a white bird flying into the blackest night. Gone, just gone.

The airplane dropped closer to the earth. Texas was beneath her, a vast state she'd never visited. Crouch had been born in Houston, and his big booming voice still carried a trace of drawl. Despite his help, he scared her too, that and the bargains she'd made. She slid into another image: the car gliding noiselessly down the near-empty highway. The sleek interior, the dash lights, Crouch's hairy hands on the wheel, Marigold in the back seat leaning forward to hear.

Crouch had talked openly about the project. "Staging tanks will be installed by the end of the week. The men are testing different locations around the island, comparing the life-form composition. You'll be working on that part, Kelsey, good thing too. We need help collecting and cataloging. It's just as well George has another week here." Then he told her how they were working with Belizian customs to get the samples he'd carry cleared. They'd of course been granted general permission with the work permit. Now it was just politics.

"Is the location secure?" Marigold asked. "I'm just worried about Kelsey, that's all."

"Secure, classified, one in hundreds of islands. You have my personal guarantee."

"Good," said Marigold.

"You dive certified?" Crouch asked suddenly, glancing sideways at her. "You might want to take a course at one of the resorts before you report to the island."

"Try snorkeling first," Marigold advised, patting her shoulder across the seat.

Crouch named several resorts on popular Ambergris Caye where Kelsey might stay.

"I want someplace quiet. I need time to think," Kelsey said, feeling at the same time it wasn't thinking she needed but something else like knitting her soul back together, or repairing a broken heart.

"Well, sure," Crouch agreed. "Take as long as you need. We're all on red alert here." He fished out his wallet and slipped her a credit card. "And this trip's on me. I owe you that much."

Because of her father. Because he thought he could buy her. The knot of anxiety tightened as the captain's voice came on announcing their final descent toward Houston.

Kelsey hurried toward the international terminal, avoiding what seemed like a plethora of familiar faces rushing toward her. Moments ago, she'd been startled by a man who looked like Stan. He was heavier, coarser; it was only the hint of beard in a strong chin that had fooled her. Yet her heart still pounded as she went over the logistics that could have brought Stan here to this very spot at this very time.

Rationally she knew that only by the most perverse combination of guesswork and luck could he have followed her. Still she worked it out with herself that she could behave in any way that made her feel better. No, better was too big of a concept; she was allowed to do anything that helped her survive for another minute or ten.

She buried herself in the crowd, walking wherever it was thickest. Later, she sat and watched her gate from afar, covered in a sweater and hat. She was checking her phone obsessively. It felt like a bomb about to go off. She'd had one text from Marigold saying she'd found Pedro under Kelsey's car and brought him inside. A second text came in; it was what she'd been dreading.

Kelsey. I'm sorry! I love you!

She jumped up, waving the phone as though she could erase it. He was out of jail! So fast!

I'm coming over. Please let me in. Please, doll. I have something to give you.

They announced that her flight was pre-boarding. She watched the passengers disappear down the jet bridge, first class, group one, group two, group three, group four. She stayed back; she couldn't stand to enter that claustrophobic tunnel with everyone jostling and touching her.

Kelsey where are you? Just tell me. I promise I won't hurt you.

They were announcing her name on the loudspeaker, asking her to check in. When they called her the second time, she ran to the nearest garbage can and threw away the phone.

On board, she walked the length of the plane, checking each face. Still she wasn't satisfied. Back in first class, she rose, ready to bolt. Any other flight seemed better than this one she'd been booked on. The flight attendant made her take her seat and fasten her belt, cooing and tucking sympathetically as if to a frightened child. She'd seen irrational fear before.

But she didn't know. She couldn't.

So Kelsey was left once more to her inner torment. Was Iriel present? Did she still whisper the stories of her life?

No. Sadly no.

PART IV

The Reincarnation of Atlantis

Chapter 22

Dear Marigold,

I found a quiet place on the smaller island, and have been here almost six days now. It's simple, but clean, and because it's almost off-season, there's hardly anybody here.

Kelsey lifted her pen and stared at the sea. It was calm today, not like yesterday when the water had churned up before the rain, and she'd imagined being out there, tossed against the reef. She'd retreated into her cabin like a turtle into its shell, and stared for hours at the thatched palm ceiling, the circling fan.

I've gone in up to my waist the last three days, and yesterday to my chest. The cove in front of the hotel is shallow and like a bath. Further out there is a reef. That's my goal. To swim to the reef and back. I've rented snorkel and fins for when I get up my courage.

That necessary courage flickered today, in opposition to her pain. The pain was like a womb to crawl into. She often sought the dark, uncomfortable place, in her bleakest moments believing the worst: that she deserved the thing Stan had done.

Words don't half describe how I feel. I only know I must act soon, whatever form action would take. I

> *believe I was sent here with a purpose. By here, I mean to this life, and more particularly this place, and this time.*

From where Kelsey sat, she could see a couple playing in the surf, the same couple she'd watched for days. The woman was plump and freckled, with dark frizzy hair, and the man was skinny. He tugged at his wife's wrists, teasing her to go deeper. Every day it was the same. The wife feigned reluctance, and he pretended to drag her out against her will. Now she sank to her shoulders, laying her head back so her black hair fanned across the water. He pulled her then—she floating on her back, he running on the bottom—until he no longer ran but swam with wide frog-kicks. Beyond them lay the reef, a dark line under the crystalline water.

> *I've been thinking about my brother Galen, his short life, and his sacrifice. It makes me think I have to get over what happened. For him. And though I might never hear Iriel's voice again, I hope she's still inside of me, helping me. It gives me courage.*

This last was a straw at which she'd been grasping. Except for a little beat she felt inside, a familiar second pulse that she must have been feeling all her life, Iriel was gone. No stories, no bursts of insight, the memories flat like a movie she'd seen too long ago.

But now she had to face the real purpose of the letter.

> *I'm worried you might be in danger. For the last few days, it's been nagging me, and then this morning I had a dream, just a flash of a knife, and I woke up with you on my mind. It makes sense that he'll blame you. Marigold, I could never forgive myself if anything happened.*

Kelsey was suddenly full of kinetic energy. The letter would take a week to get there, and then it would be too late. For a moment she imagined catching a plane and rushing back. No, she would call Marigold, but the thought terrified her. Why? Because she would be connected to the place where it had happened. Because she would have to think of him. Speak his name.

The sound of laughter made Kelsey look up at the vivid turquoise water and the couple in the sea. The woman was staring, so Kelsey retreated farther under the shade of her porch and took up her pen. But she couldn't sit still; the energy in her body had built to near-explosion.

Snorkeling gear dangling from her hand, Kelsey walked out to the water's edge and let the sea slap her feet. Rooted to the ankle, she prayed for Iriel's help.

The voice she heard was Rosemary's. *The water is your friend. It will lift you up.*

She put on her mask and flippers and went a little ways in. Something yellow darted past her knees. She put her face in just long enough to see a tiny fish pecking at a mound of white coral. Hair streaming, she reset the mask, took the plastic snorkel into her mouth, and pushed off.

Her breath sounded hollow in the tube like someone on a ventilator. Her mind flashed to a hospital room, her father's face among the white sheets, then she was watching a school of yellow fingerlings swim past. She made a careless move, and they turned as a unit. Each time she got close, or even thought of it, the group darted, always together, always in the same instant, as though they'd discussed it telepathically.

The sandy bottom dropped away, and Kelsey felt her confidence soar. A cloud of minnows parted as she dove through—tiny transparent fish, an inch long, hundreds of them. Ahead she caught a movement, a white shape gliding out of the sandy bottom. It rippled into flight and disappeared. At the same time she bumped something.

"Did you see that huge ray, Honey?" It was the frizzy-haired woman.

"Yes," Kelsey said, breathing hard.

"Oh, it's you." The woman treaded water easily. "I guess that means I lost."

"Lost what?" Kelsey's knees pumped, fins threatening to trip her.

"Just a bet. Don't worry, it wasn't money at stake."

Irritated, Kelsey turned toward shore.

"Hey wait! You can't go in! Look. We're almost to the reef," the woman said, pointing a fat arm at the dark patches. "You're scared, aren't you? That's what I said to my husband."

Kelsey sputtered a half-formed comeback, planted her face, and motored out. She passed coral shaped like a huge mound of brains, sea fans, and a white and purple anemone. Fish darted into holes, then poked their heads out to look. A fat-lipped parrotfish showed its beak. She ventured into the coral channel, past the woman and her husband, and dove again and again, accessing a newfound breath-hold and naturalness in the water. The channel led to the edge of the reef, marked with spiky coral jutting above the surface, like piles of dead antlers. Kelsey skirted the antlers and chased another ray rising off the bottom, but it flew away into deeper water. Finally she doubled back, swimming in a kind of visual trance until the water got very shallow and she was aware again of her breath moving through the tube.

Back on shore, Kelsey went for her towel and stretched out on the sand. The couple had gone in, but the minor annoyance of them faded compared with her feeling of delicious accomplishment. She felt the sun on her back, burning away any lingering malaise.

The hotel phones were down, so Kelsey had to go to town to make her call. This involved a shower, shoes, a hot taxi, and a series of hard-to-understand operators before she connected to Marigold's machine. She had nearly completed the message when her therapist picked up.

"Kelsey?" The voice wavered just slightly. "It's just strange you would call today."

"He was there, wasn't he?" When Marigold didn't answer, Kelsey started to panic. "Did he hurt you?"

"It was a little tense, but no, the police came and arrested him again. I filed a restraining order. After the first time."

"The first time?"

"The night after you left. He came here looking for you."

Kelsey felt the kinetic urge again. She wanted to burst out of the room and run down the middle of the street. What then? If he was here . . . . Her gaze skittered over the maps lining the wall of the government office—vast blue punctuated by dots of land and swaths of underwater reef—and around to the uniformed receptionist. She drew a breath of stifling air.

"He's in jail, right?"

"He posted bail. They just called to tell me."

"You've got to get out of there, Marigold. It's not safe."

"I've hired a security guard for tonight. He's got a big turban." Marigold's laugh sounded tinny over the phone lines.

Kelsey thought about this a minute. She shook her head, even though Marigold couldn't see her. "He'll find me," Kelsey said. "He found me in this life. Don't you see? He's clever." *We're connected*, she thought, but didn't say it.

"He's making mistakes. The police are watching him."

Kelsey thought of her letter, which she'd tucked into her purse meaning to mail. She would tear it up. There'd be no postmark to betray her. "You don't know where I am, and I'm not going to tell you. Understand? Nobody knows. I could be anywhere."

"I told him you'd gone to visit your mother. I thought it might distract him for awhile."

"But he knows her! He'll go after her, too!"

"No," said Marigold. "He can't leave the state." But she didn't sound very sure.

Huddled in the back seat of the taxi, head between her knees, Kelsey breathed into her hands. Back at the hotel, she went into her cabin and got under the sheet. She would go into hiding. Move from place to place until he gave up looking for her. She imagined herself a redhead or a blonde, wearing dark glasses and a big hat, sunbathing on the Riviera. But it was no good. She felt the familiar frustration, the anger, and the desperation, the same cycle as all week.

Kelsey lurched out of bed. The sea and the sky had turned pale: peach, aqua, and rose. Watching the colors fade, Kelsey knew her only hope was to leave her fear behind. She'd allow herself a week if she needed that long, then she would go to the island. The decision brought a burst of optimism, and she ran barefoot into the shallow water, imagining the tiny fish she'd seen feeding, their problem basic and uncomplicated, eat or be eaten.

Kelsey felt her limbs shrink away and her neck melt into her shoulders. New, light bones stuck out from her spine. She was whole and small, contained within an oval skin. She darted into a crevice and hovered, fins vibrating as her blunt mouth worked for food. Then the velvet air was around her again, and she felt only mild surprise. As the stars formed in the sky, she felt herself absorb a little more of the other. She stepped deeper into the water, let it kiss her knees.

The resort's dining room, candlelit due to one of the frequent power outages, was a larger version of the cabanas, made of dark local woods, and had a steep thatched ceiling. The fan, at the apex, was still tonight, leaving the air sultry and close. Kelsey thought of the tropics in a nineteenth-century novel—romantic, steamy, and dangerous, fevers lurking. And now the woman she'd met in the water and her grinning bespectacled husband had paused in their meal.

"Hey there! You got away from us. Did you like the reef?"

"Calm down, Honeybunch, you'll scare her away again." The man stood and extended his hand. "I'm Ben. Ben Irving, and this is my wife, Irma."

"Kelsey Dupuis." Too late, she'd already said it.

"Sit down, Kelsey. Won't you join us, please?" Irma asked. "I didn't mean to be rude out in the water. It's just we're the only ones here now, and we were curious."

"She was excited," Ben said. "She gets carried away."

"Have a beer," said Irma, pushing hers toward Kelsey.

"Or a piña colada," said Ben. "Or a rum punch, or a gin and tonic, or some tequila."

It was Ben who convinced her. Just that he reminded her of Harrison in a funny way. He was smaller and darker, and when he smiled it wasn't right, but the curly hair, the glasses, the glibness, something. So she sat.

"What are you doing down here?" Dry, Irma's hair was impossibly big and frizzy. She wore round glasses which magnified her wide, green eyes.

"Just getting away," Kelsey said.

Irma did most of the talking, with Ben chiming in whenever she paused for a breath. They were post-doctoral students, both anthropologists. They had a grant to study Maya culture.

"This has been our lifelong dream. Now we're finally here!" Irma held up her beer to Ben who clicked his bottle against hers.

"Her dream and my dream," Ben said. "Both separately and together."

"We're on vacation for two weeks, then it's into the jungle."

"I read about the Mayans in the airport," Kelsey said, testing her food, always the same, fried bananas, black beans, rice, and fish, the ubiquitous orange hot sauce. "They've been here three thousand years?"

"Actually that's part of our hypothesis," said Irma. "We think it goes back five to seven thousand years. Maybe ten. We have this theory—"

"Hold it, Honeybunch. Let Kelsey have a chance. What do you do, Kelsey?"

"I'll bet you're a tortured poet," said Irma. "That's what I said to Ben—"

"And I said we should just introduce ourselves and ask you."

They did not let her get away with a dodge, so she told them the quick truth: microbiologist. "But tell me your theory about the Mayans. I'm really interested."

Irma and Ben exchanged a look.

"Our theory is that the Maya beliefs are unique in this hemisphere," Ben said. "They're most like the Egyptians, if anything. Belief in the underworld, that's fairly common, but coupled with the scientific foundation to their religious practices—their calendar system, for instance, so complex it had a unit that was twenty-three billion days long—they were way beyond other indigenous cultures. They could predict eclipses with uncanny accuracy."

"I read something about that too," said Kelsey slowly.

"Like the Egyptians, astronomy was for the sake of religion. They wanted to predict big events—the birth of Kings, death of a dynasty, famine, the Spanish coming. They thought it was all written in the stars."

"We don't believe so much in predestination anymore," Kelsey said, thinking of Iriel.

"It's another clue," Irma said. "Who would need to know the future that way?"

"A civilization that had suffered a great catastrophe," Ben supplied.

Irma was talking again. "Conventional theories say the aboriginal people migrated across the Bering Strait, down into Mesoamerica. The Olmecs preceded the Maya who supposedly showed up about 2000 BC. But we think the Maya came here from somewhere else."

"Like the sea," said Kelsey, voicing her newly forming theory.

"Exactly," said Ben.

The three looked at each other. They were alone in the darkened dining room. From the kitchen came the sound of clattering dishes.

"Let's get some beer and sit outside," Ben said.

The breeze was light and the moon was rising over the water. Sitting in lounge chairs under the palms, they drank cold beers that Irma retrieved from amid the last of the ice.

"We believe in the lost continent of Atlantis," Irma said.

"Passionately," said Ben.

Kelsey laughed for the first time in a week. "What an extraordinary coincidence."

"Not really," said Ben. "You know serendipity is just a phenomenon of—"

"Not now, Babe," Irma said, "I want to hear what Kelsey has to say."

"I just can't get over it. Down here in the middle of nowhere, I meet you two, and suddenly . . ." For a frozen moment she thought that Stan had used Atlantis as his entree too. But his claim turned out to be true. Besides, Irma and Ben were innocents, her intuition told her that. She looked from one to the other. "Since I was a little girl, I've had dreams. Of another place. I think it's Atlantis. No, I'm sure of it." She stopped because the curiosity in their eyes made her uncomfortable. "But what about you two? You're scientists. Do you have any hard evidence?"

"I want proof more than anything," Irma said.

"You'll never get it, Honeybunch. It's all washed away. We've agreed that we have to build it up from the Maya side." Ben turned to Kelsey. "We don't think all the Atlantians died in the cataclysm. A few escaped and went east—Egypt probably—but others migrated across the seas to form the basis of the Maya Civilization. They brought some of their legendary advancements such as the calendar and astronomy. Of course, they had to find a way to integrate with the natives. They might not have been numerous enough to be conquerors."

"They came in peace," Irma said. "They weren't a violent people."

"Of course they were violent," Ben said. "They destroyed their homeland."

"Ben and I disagree on this point. I think it was a natural disaster. The Atlantians were inventive, democratic, spiritual seekers. Prideful maybe."

"It's called hubris," Ben said. "Just like now."

"Ben has this crazy theory that the continent will rise again. In America."

"It already has, Irma."

"That never makes any sense, Ben. Our ancestors came from Europe or Africa—"

"You're being too literal, Irma. All the current conditions, the technology race, even the size of the continent is parallel to, in fact, it's a recreation of Atlantis. Our so-called democratic system, the raping of the land and consumption of resources, pollution, disastrous oil spills, wars, imperialism, global warming. I'm telling you, we, right now, are the spiritual descendants of Atlantis, and we need to heed their lessons."

Kelsey felt her own broader purpose open up. "Maybe Atlantians were reincarnated into present day America so we can get it right this time. Not destroy ourselves and the planet."

"That's it," said Ben. "That's what I've been trying to tell you, Irma."

"What have you been trying to tell me?" Irma asked.

"The connection leapfrogged the physical plane. You heard Kelsey. We are the reincarnation of Atlantis."

"I'm OK with reincarnation," Irma said. "I'd like to live again. I like being alive."

"It might be a relief if it was just over," Kelsey said.

"One shot at enlightenment?" Ben asked. "Too much pressure if you ask me."

"OK," said Irma. "I get what you two are talking about. We have a second chance."

"Avoid the cataclysm this time," Kelsey said.

"Apocalypse 2021. Coming to a theater near you," Ben said.

"A spiritual cataclysm," Irma said. "That's what I believe in."

"Environmental," Ben said.

"Both," Kelsey said, and the silence fell around them.

"Can you tell us about your dreams, then?" Irma asked after a moment.

Kelsey looked at the two faces, bright ovals in the moonlight. "I have seen another self. Her name was Iriel, and she lived in Atlantis." Speaking it so plainly brought a surge of energy. Behind that was danger, both known and unknown. She spoke carefully, watching the water as she answered Irma's impassioned questions, and before long, she was seeing a light moving along the coast. It was a boat, zigzagging, threading the reef, closing in on them.

"Do you think she'll witness the destruction?" Irma asked.

"Isn't that kind of like dreaming your own death? If you see it, you really die."

"Stop it, Ben." said Irma.

"It might be true," said Kelsey. "There's a price to it."

Irma turned to Kelsey. "I think your Iriel made it to the Americas and became mother to some of our Maya. Maybe that's why you were drawn here. To find her."

Kelsey felt a chill race up her spine. "Maybe I could."

Kelsey had risen to say goodnight, when suddenly the generators whirred back to life and the courtyard was flooded with light. At the same instant, a second noise separated itself. The boat she'd spotted earlier, the sound of its motor no longer sheltered by the land, had come around the point and was turning into the bay, its headlamp spotlighting the reef. In the boat, a man waved and called to her.

Kelsey ran toward her cabana and the dark jungle beyond. She was prepared to run all night until she heard the voice again. She stopped and turned, watching the tall American say something to the boat captain, and step ashore. She saw the hands go into the pockets. Then she was sure. Harrison had found her.

Chapter 23

They'd covered everything from ear squeeze to Boyle's law to decompression stops. When Harrison started reciting dive tables from memory, Kelsey said, "This is nuts. You're showing off."

Harrison grinned. "Keeps me awake."

They'd traveled all night, first by boat and the last three hours by rented jeep. Since Belmopan the road had grown steadily worse, and now in the light, it dwindled away to nothing.

"Shit," said Harrison, stomping on the brakes.

They drove back down a network of bumpy dirt roads looking for the "highway." The day was already hot, and the air that rushed around them was no cooler than their bodies. Harrison spotted a fruit stand, and pulled over to inspect the meager fare: over-ripe bananas, chunky pieces of coconut with the husk still on, and a few green oranges. They sat in the shade to eat, brushing away the insects. The jungle shimmered. A bright bird hopped from tree to tree, making a sound like a crow. They didn't talk for now.

They'd done enough of that during the night—Harrison telling her about the delays on the project, the lethargy of the men, how things had just now started to break since George had arrived with two duffels full of dive gear. She told him about George's inoculation of the aquarium, and the death of the angelfish. "That's when I realized all my tests were a big waste."

"I'd like to see them anyway," Harrison said.

When he heard she'd sent dozens of reports he hadn't gotten, his eyes glistened. Nor had she received all of his e-mails. "Intercepted," Harrison said. "I thought you were mad at me."

"Me too," she answered.

She and Harrison were off the boat by then, navigating through Belize City. Kelsey closed her eyes to the squalid slums and tried to picture the lab as she'd left it, thinking she'd be back Monday to clean up—which Monday was that?

Regarding her trauma, she'd kept her silence, though her heart hadn't. When Harrison first took her hand, bouncing along in the boat beneath the starry night, she'd had to turn her face and let the tears blow back to sea. Now they sat in the shade a while longer. They didn't look at each other, just rested against the tree, listening to the jungle sounds, his hand supporting hers. She felt she could tell him everything, just through that hand.

"Listen, Kelsey," he said now. "I wanted to give you more time, but it's getting too complicated not to talk about it."

She felt her face flash crimson. When she'd asked him why he'd come looking for her, and more importantly how he'd found her, he'd told her only that he'd hired a P.I. Now he said more.

"You weren't answering my e-mails, your phone was dead, and no one at work knew where you were. They said you'd been out all week. Then George arrived and let it slip you were already in Belize, had been for over a week. I had no idea why you'd changed your mind about coming, or why you hadn't shown up on the island. George, when pressed, said it was a personal matter. Swore that was all he knew. Molly said, as far as she knew, you had gone to the island. She was miffed about the lack of coverage at the lab and her trouble getting day care. So I called your therapist. I had a hunch, I guess."

"Marigold," said Kelsey, letting her breath out. "Why didn't she tell me?"

"She gave me an earful and hung up. She must have thought I was him, or working for him. That told me something had gone terribly wrong. So I asked Dave, my P.I. friend, to check the police records, see if he had . . . well, that's how we stumbled on it. The rest was easy, the company attorney, Crouch's involvement. The credit card trail."

Crouch's credit card. She'd used it instead of her own just to avoid that trail. Stupid! Anyone who knew her boss's name could easily track her down. Kelsey closed her eyes . . . *and smelled again the sickening cologne.* "I wish you weren't involved in this whole ugly mess," she said, and burst into tears.

Harrison's long legs extended in front of him, whitened hair sparkling against his tan.

"I'm sorry," Kelsey said. "I know this hurts you."

He took her hand again. "Much as I was jealous before, Kelsey, it's way beyond that now."

They drove south through the jungle in the heat of the day, drinking bottled water and orange soda pop, talking about his growing concerns as the testing neared. As she shifted again away from her pain, it began to feel like a small kernel inside her, separate from some vastness. She felt a vertiginous sense of looking down on the vastness and the kernel.

Harrison described the private thatched cabanas, Henri, the French chef, hired away from a resort on Grand Cayman at a reportedly huge salary, Crouch's renovation of the old pirate's house. He told her again about the power outages and the construction delays.

"Everyone kind of kicked back once the generator broke down. With no computers and no progress on the tanks, there was nothing for anybody to do, except poor Rodman who kept trying to get things in motion." The scientists thought up crazy things to do in the evenings, like convoluted memory games, and the tallest sand castle contest. "Jersey and Albert got one up to seventeen feet. You should have seen the hole it left. That got them started on the hot tub idea. They rigged it with leftover parts, and it got poured with the other tanks. They even got some tile through the dishwasher's brother."

"Hot tub?" she'd asked. "In this heat?"

"After a dip in the ocean . . . you'd be surprised."

The afternoon was at its peak, and as they descended from the mountainous regions, the air became torpid and oppressive. She was sweating through her light clothes, keeping her belly full of liquid, feeling every muscle in her body surrender to the heat.

"Things started moving again last week," she repeated.

"Parts came in Saturday. Everyone got energized and worked all weekend. The local labor force showed up and we poured Monday, like I said. They should be testing the seawater delivery system today. Though I have my doubts."

"Jersey and Albert think it will work?"

"If the parts had been to their specifications, sure."

They compared Harrison's projections on population with her empirical data, what she could remember of it. They discussed her slides from the fish tank, which she'd fortunately thought to stash in the coat closet along with her notes.

"How did Rodman fix the generator?" she asked suddenly.

"The distributor rotor turned up in the jambalaya rice. Henry Hilton bit into it. He'd been complaining so much—you know he couldn't shave without electricity—so everyone got a big laugh, especially the chef. He could hardly get his breath. They have a thing going about the same name. Henri kept calling him 'mon petit frère.' "

Kelsey laughed. "You think it was a prank then? Henri's maybe?"

"Unlikely. It hurts Henri the most. He lost all the food in the freezer."

"Who else then?"

"Whoever's been sabotaging things in the first place, probably. Though maybe someone else found the generator part and made the joke on the two Henrys."

"Maybe it wasn't sabotage. Someone wanted a vacation. Or it malfunctioned."

He shook his head. "A real coincidence it's all working again now that George is here with the new specimen," Harrison said. "So parallel strains certainly. Crouch didn't want any of us getting ahead of him, like you maybe. He wants control. Absolute control."

"But he was so fired up, having me take those shortcuts, asking to see my extra results." She felt his sharp look. "I didn't see any harm giving it to him. My tests were after-the-fact anyway."

They were passing settlements now, mostly groupings of thatched houses barely visible through the trees, and some ramshackle roadside businesses. The road had improved dramatically, and as the waning day rushed past them, Kelsey noticed her sweat was starting to cool almost as fast as it sprang from her skin.

"Perhaps it was a two-way street." Harrison said. "Engineering was taking your self-selected specimens and riffing from there."

"No," she said. "He never took samples."

"So you're saying you trust him."

She colored, thinking how she'd turned to him that night, and he'd been so willing to help her. "But who can we trust? Have you leveled with Rodman?"

He shook his head. "Though I'd imagine he's thinking the same thing we are. Rodman gets his satisfaction from a job well done, so the delays frustrated him terribly. He must be looking around for reasons. He must be seeing that people aren't being straight with him."

"And you believe Franklin's a saboteur? He seems like a fuck-up."

"Drinking too much, sleeping in, loud obnoxious behavior? It reads like an act to me."

She was spinning, weighing his theories against the impossibility that anyone, even Myron Crouch, would take such risks . . . what Harrison had said about George and the diving.

"Maybe George isn't too smart," she said, "but I guess he'll do what he's told."

"That's why we need to watch him every minute," Harrison said. Which got them back around to the dive manual in Harrison's head.

They got down to the sea at sunset and checked into a rustic hotel near the water. They'd already decided to wait until morning to hire a boat out to the island. After dinner they walked down to the end of pier, and sat, feet dangling over the water.

"I've been wondering if I should go back." Harrison said.

"No."

"Your notes, your slides—" He was still sitting erect after all the driving.

"Shh." The night was dark, the stars snuffed out by thick clouds; she could feel the moist air breaking against her clean skin. She didn't want anything to change at this moment, not even the tight little kernel of pain she could still feel buried inside. It seemed to fuel the rest.

"It's a beautiful night," he said after a time. "The air is so soft."

Suddenly the kernel expanded. "Harrison, why did you come after me? Once you knew?"

He took off his glasses, folded them into his pocket. His eyes were colorless in the night. "I thought you might need me."

"Plus you knew I couldn't still want—"

"Him? Shit, Kelsey." He turned slightly away, staring past her at the black water.

"You must hate me."

"No."

"Because I was with . . . because I chose him." *Over you*, she thought.

"I didn't understand. I don't."

She clutched her knees to her chest. "I was stupid," she said, "weak. It's part of the answer."

"What are you trying to do, Kelsey? You made a mistake. It's over. Let it go."

She was thinking of the persistent attention and flattery, Stan's obsession with her. That was only the bait. "It's like you know something about them deep in your gut, and then you realize you're just like them." Still not enough. "I had secrets. Even from myself."

"Iriel?"

"More than that. You know I wanted to kill him that night. I tried."

"You cut him with some glass?"

"I struck for the eye."

"Blinding him maybe, but not—"

"You don't understand. I saw it going to the brain." She was trembling. "I didn't know that about myself. That I was capable of killing. Now I do."

"What made you stop?"

"I missed, that's all. So you see, I *do* owe him something."

"That's pretty twisted, Kelsey."

"Listen, Harrison. The very strange thing is that he was truly connected to her, right from the beginning. I thought he was making it up, but he wasn't. I know who he was, and what he wanted." She thought of Gewil's face, thick with disappointment.

"Who was he?" asked Harrison, showing a bit of that same disappointment.

Now the night's resistance thickened too, but still she went on. "They were betrothed. She . . . I . . . refused him." After a moment she said, "I think he followed Iriel across the ages for some kind of reckoning, and it's no coincidence he found me. I sometimes wonder if I was meant to do this, to, you know, draw out his venom. What happened is my penance, in a way. Iriel's penance. Does that make any sense?" Behind them most of the town's lights had gone out. There were only a few teen-aged boys, voices drifting on the wind from the basketball court, and the sound of the ball bouncing off concrete.

"She laid something out for you, for your fresh perspective perhaps."

She wanted to think about that. "There's more coming, don't you see? The whole environmental disaster. Do I have to relive it too, just to know what happened? Because I'm sure I'm meant to. I'm sure that's the important part."

"That's actually pretty scary," Harrison said, "in light of what's going on."

As they were walking to the hotel Harrison said there was something he needed to ask. The night's velvety air, with its hint of heat, wrapped her. They'd stopped by the hotel's tiny pool, a cement plunge surrounded by plants in plastic tubs. "You're planning on seeing him?"

She shook her head. "No. I'm terrified."

"But you're not done." There was something new in his face.

"I tried to confront him, tell him it was over." She was starting to shake again. "But how could I convince a madman? If he's not done, how can I be? Even if I shot him dead, he'd find me, somehow, in another life, and it would be worse. Because there's been violence now."

They stood in the squalid little courtyard while the night lengthened into its darkest hour.

Chapter 24

On the same pier, daylight revealed a business they'd missed in the dark—a little shack advertising seaplane rides, jungle trips, snorkeling, and scuba. Kelsey sat dangling her legs over the water. She felt strangely calm after Harrison's revelation at breakfast.

"And what should I be doing while you're back at BioVenture?"

"Keep your eyes open. Do your job."

"Follow George?"

He shook his head. "You can't dive."

She pointed to the little building. From this side they could see a faded PADI sign.

"It'd take three days minimum to get you certified. You'd still be a novice."

"You could teach me in one, I bet. You just gave me the crash course."

"Theory only."

"You could though," she said. "Then you leave tomorrow, and I'll go on to the island."

"I'd be responsible if you got hurt."

"I could stay here and take a class," she said. "Or you could come to the island with me and follow George yourself."

He glanced back at the building. The wooden flap had gone up, and a bikini-clad woman was setting up shop. "Would you promise to get a manual and study it like crazy? And practice your skills in shallow water. Practice until you can do them in your sleep. And let me be the judge of whether you're ready or not."

"Anything," she said.

He slicked his palms against his shorts. "You're sure eager for someone who couldn't swim a month ago."

She stared back. "I know I'm ready."

Harrison rented the gear and tanks, and they started going over the equipment. Then they swam a little ways out into a quiet part of the bay, a roped-off area that must have been set up for the very purpose they had in mind. With all the gear on her back, the weights pulling her hips down, the inflation around her chest buoying her up, Kelsey rolled along like a barrel. They bobbed on the surface for a few final instructions, then began to breathe the tank air, deflated the BCD's–buoyancy control devices—and dropped under.

At first she felt mild panic, but Harrison got her to sit on the sandy bottom and watch the surface, fifteen feet above them. After a moment she relaxed, and the underwater world began to enchant her. It felt like she was inside a glassy kind of air, and there were two worlds, and she was in the real one. The other, up there, was over-bright, and things happened too fast. She, Kelsey, was going to live forever in comfort at the bottom of the sea, watching the slow dance of the grasses and the occasional finny creature flying by.

She practiced going up and down with her bubbles, clearing her ears, flooding and clearing her mask, throwing away her regulator and recovering it. Later, Harrison started teaching her buddy breathing. For some reason, it made her laugh. When he gave her the out-of-air hand signal, she got mixed up and threw away her regulator when he threw his, and the momentum made her float into him. His eyes widened behind his mask, and as their faces came together, he gave her a funny little underwater kiss, sideways, masks bumping, then he had her in an equipment-complicated embrace, and she thought she was supposed to give him her air, so she let it all out at once into his mouth. They came to the surface sputtering, then she over-inflated her BCD, and it made a guttural, spitting sound, and they both lay back rocking in the water, laughing up at the sky.

By the time they'd used up the first tank, she couldn't stop grinning. "This is so much fun. This is the best thing in the world."

"Wait until we go out to the reef."

They hired a boat for the afternoon. The captain, Max, was a thin black man who talked incessantly about his brother who drove a cab in Manhattan. It was a beautiful, breezy day, and the water was clear and only a little choppy. Despite the morning's practice, Kelsey's heart was racing by the time they were anchored over the reef.

She made it through the back-roll entry, and when Harrison signaled OK-to-go-down, she let the air out of the BCD and felt herself sinking. She swallowed a few times to clear her ears, then looked up; the boat was small above her, and the sun came through the water.

If only Iriel could see this, she thought, then, quite clearly, she saw the girl free swimming, tunic flapping in the current, bubbles streaming behind her as she vanished around a bend in the reef. *I must be doing the right thing!* Kelsey thought as she followed Harrison over a complicated coral garden. A school of yellow and blue grunts passed by, flying like birds.

One fish after another caught her eye, the colors rich in the sunlight. Then they were at the edge of the wall, and Harrison was pointing downward into the blue, and she felt her ears popping again. Above them, the boat idled, stuck on the sun-dappled surface. Below, the waters were shifting murky blueness. They sailed along in the current, searching the open waters for big sea animals. Harrison liked to drift out there, hanging above the void, but not Kelsey. She was drawn to the blue depths, feeling that glorious letting go as she descended. She wanted to sink away into beautiful oblivion, be delivered into its dark relief. It was the seduction of the infinite, of death.

The dive had lasted forty-two minutes, and she came up with plenty of air. Harrison praised her natural ease in the water, and she thought, Yes, I have Iriel's water spirit. They took their surface interval floating on the boat in the sunshine, the afternoon hot and sleepy.

On the second dive, Harrison showed her an eel, and she spotted a lobster hanging in a cave. It was a nice dive, a pleasure, but already almost routine. After a shower, they went to town and bought a whole set-up of dive gear, from wetsuit to BCD to fins to wrist computer. The total came to over two thousand dollars and they charged it to Myron Crouch.

⁂

They had a late lunch at a café facing the sea. The breeze felt delightful on her sunburned face and she was famished. She dug into her lobster salad with a vengeance.

"Kelsey," Harrison said, "I have to leave right after lunch."

"What! Why?"

"I can't fly after diving so deep. Not for twenty-four hours. So I thought I'd drive to Belize city tonight and catch my plane tomorrow."

"Can't you just wait another day? I don't understand the rush."

"You read Molly's e-mail. And you said it yourself. The environmental disaster. It's major. Plus . . ."

She knew he meant Stan. He wanted to check up on Stan, make sure he hadn't made any connections as to her whereabouts. He'd call her mother too, though from the brief phone call they'd had, Kelsey knew her mother was fine, still in her bubble of infatuation with Stan, unaware of where Kelsey was, or what had happened because Kelsey didn't tell her anything. Stan had called her of course, which made Kelsey's blood boil. But she didn't let on.

"I don't understand how my old notes from February can be so important," Kelsey said. "Don't you think we have the newest strain here?"

"Maybe. But I think there's more she's not saying."

"Like the money thing, you mean." Molly had accidently typed a $ sign in her e-mail instead of an "S." At least that's what Kelsey thought. Harrison had argued that it couldn't possibly be a mistake, that it was a subtle message about something going on, something she'd found out. "I don't know," said Kelsey. "Molly is pretty straight-forward."

"Which is why I need to talk to her in person."

⁂

It was cool and dark in the room, and Kelsey flopped onto the bed and closed her eyes. She'd helped him load his gear into the jeep, he'd promised to check up on her house and pick up a few things, she'd listened to his admonitions about being careful, and told him the same. Then she reluctantly let him go.

Kelsey had been counting on the evening; they'd talk, it would be gentler, the difficult things behind them. Maybe they'd kiss again. But he'd seemed so distracted as they said goodbye. She'd pressed the letter to Marigold into his hand—she'd not torn it up after all, had added a note that Harrison was helping her, that Marigold should tell him everything—then the tears had sprung up when he kissed her cheek. They'd already gone over their plan, the revolving e-mail addresses they'd set up, the dive details. Last, the unspoken part: Thank you. Be careful yourself. Don't mess with him.

The air conditioner gurgled, and Kelsey realized it had been annoying her for some time. She left the room and walked at random through the seaside town. Smells of fish cooking and smoky fires scented the air. Tall black men, whittling, or lounging on their porches, grinned at her and spoke unintelligible greetings.

Beyond the village she came upon a stretch of beach and an odd resort: about twenty plastered huts, painted like Indian tepees, their deserted porches littered with bathing suits, drying shirts, and dive gear. Around the point Reggae music blared from a bar—everyone was there, laughing and dancing. Kelsey threaded her way through the crowd, absorbing the physical contact, the jollity, bought a beer and walked away down the beach until she could no longer hear anything but the echo of the bass and the occasional shout of laughter.

She found the remnant of a hammock in a grove of palms, and sat in it to watch the sunset. The beer tasted sweet, and the water was turning pink. She'd lost her melancholy on the walk, and now she let herself savor the moment. A strong thought came flashing in: *She was here where she belonged.* Kelsey heard a splash and looked at the flaming sea. Then she was on her feet, bottle still in hand, wading through the offshore grasses.

The dolphin jumped again. It was gray and fat with a strong, short tail. It seemed to be moving into shore, and she was going out as rapidly as she could. The sandy shelf dropped away, and in one delicious moment, she felt her cotton clothes float away from her body. Then she rolled onto her back, kicked to stay afloat, and took a sip of beer.

Proceeding this way, Kelsey soon found a second sand bank where she could stand. With her ear still in the water, she could hear the dolphin clicking and squealing as it moved from one side of her to the other. Once, it came up quite close, and she saw its eye and an x-shaped scar across the crown of its head. It smiled and clicked a greeting, then nodded and disappeared under the water. She watched as it surfaced again and again, rapidly leaving her behind. Perhaps the glinting bottle had attracted its curiosity, or the joyfulness of the human who'd come into the sea.

Back in her room, Kelsey turned off the offensive air conditioner, threw open the window, and climbed up on the little writing desk to get the breeze. Except for the stub of candle she'd lit, the room was in shadows, and she felt a trance poised to come, for this place felt deeply familiar. She took a breath. What Irma and Ben had said reverberated: Some had survived. Some had crossed the ocean. Had Iriel? Kelsey could imagine she had come to these shores.

A painted vase, shaped like a woman, stood on a low bureau across from her. As Kelsey stared at it, she saw the woman more and more clearly until a real woman sat opposite her. Past middle age, though not yet old, she had streaks of white in her black hair. Her olive skin was still flawless. Muamdi!

Grandmother! You are so young. How can this be?

But look at you, child. What of this baby you carry? Your time is near? You are well?

The child is the only reason I live.

Are they not kind to you here?

They are strange and savage, though I am learning to speak their tongue. If I use my stone—

Muamdi's fingers stop just short of the glowing crystal. The crystal slips back into its pouch. The light dims and the image fades.

Kelsey found herself leaning into the corner, head against the wall. Her belly shrank to normal, but the ghostly outline of Iriel's pregnancy was still with her as she lumbered down from the desk. Outside a bird squawked. It could have been in this world or Iriel's.

I am here, Kelsey thought. I am ready to know.

Before sleeping, she tried to imagine how it was: huts in the jungle, cooking fires, Iriel and her baby among the small dark Maya people. But all she could see was the painted tepee resort with its crop of lively gringos. The last image that came was a small x-marked dolphin jumping in a rosy bay. It had come across the entire sea, to guide its human friend.

Mainland

We begin to see the mainland after only two days at sea. The channel between it and our island turned out to be quite narrow, so we are quickly in sight of this mythical place, Phyrius, after all our longing to see it. But this morning our view is still obscured—a fog encases the mountain that seems to rise straight from the sea.

Jarad and I stand on the deck and watch as the sun burns away the fog a patch at a time. First we see the jagged peak, then the caved-in mountain face, and last the tight bay rimmed by dirty white rocks. As the morning heightens into noon, we enter the bay, and the shore comes into better view. We begin to understand that the rocks are not rocks but crumbling buildings, temples, dwellings, large, once white, now grayed with ash. Only one is gleaming, washed clean.

"Look," Jarad says. "It must be where they meet."

The white place, Quiri had told us. You must find the members of a group called The Society. They will expect you. They will help you.

The day grows hot and still, and the captain drops anchor, waiting for something, some permission to proceed, I gather. The mountain's shadow retreats so we are bobbing on the sparkling sea under a fierce sun. Then, out of the sparkles come apparitions, strange shiny objects rising from the water like slow flying fish. They are big as small boats, and made of metal, the substance Quiri brought to our classroom once, a substance that shines in sunlight, is heavy and dead as rock. So how can they fly?

The metal birds rush up and out to attack us. They swoop close to the deck making a buzzing sound like a horde of bees. Horrified, we shrink away. The captain, a friendly sort, just laughs. "Aircars," he tells us. "They fly for pleasure."

"They feel pleasure?" Jarad asks.

"No," says Captain Notale. "Those inside receive the pleasure."

"Who rides upon such wingless birds?" Jarad asks watching them go.

"They ride inside," the captain explains. "It is the Ari."

Yes, the Ari. Quiri told us of them too, a race who came from the stars and now live on the earth. Slender, very tall, so white you can almost see through them.

"Beware the Ari," says Captain Notale.

"Why?" asks Jarad. "Are they wizards?"

Captain Notale laughs. "No, not wizards."

Gewil is with us on the deck, as he has been much of this journey, listening closely.

"Do the Ari own the air-creatures?" he asks.

"Oh no." The captain laughs again. "No one owns them."

"They are alive then?" I ask.

"Not alive." Another one swoops over us. I duck and watch its underside. I see clear windows with pale faces pressed against them.

"They are giving us permission to enter," Jarad says.

"Not them," says the captain. "Those who control them. Those who watch remotely."

"The owners?" asks Gewil.

"No," says Captain Notale again. "No one owns the aircars. They are controlled by one faction or another. It depends upon the day. Upon who is in power. But always, the Ari ride."

"I wonder," says Gewil. "If such air-creatures could be mine to command."

Chapter 25

The wind was calm, the sky gray, the ocean fog-bound. Slowly the clouds blushed and lifted to reveal an azure sea. Already sweating, Kelsey stepped onto the boat with her bags. She hadn't understood why Max, the captain from the day before, had refused to take her to the island. He'd sent a man named Cal instead.

They passed several small atolls, some inhabited, some not. Then, in an open stretch, out of sight of the shore, they came upon a small dugout occupied by a man so old his skin was as gray as his frizzled hair. Once their wake settled and the water was disturbed only by the occasional dip of the paddle, the toothless old man spoke animatedly with Cal in his native Garifuna. Kelsey got the impression she was at least partially the topic of conversation.

She leaned back and closed her eyes, listening to the light slap of the water against the hull and the garbled words. The image of the morning sun burned through her eyelids. For an instant, the red ring became the fiery rim of the volcano, and she jolted upward. But she saw nothing except water and the mounds of islands on the horizon. She almost dozed again, and then the sudden rocking of the boat and the old man's excited shouts roused her. Cal stood in the stern—the two boats had drifted apart—and the water between them was bouncing.

"There," said Cal, gold flashing in his mouth.

Behind the canoe a pair of dolphins breached, one gray, one all white. After a silent minute, they came up again between the two boats. The albino flipped its tail, and the outboard rocked. Chattering, the creatures sank back into the water. Kelsey was leaning, her hand in the water, and almost instantly, the dolphins came up. She saw the gray's black eye and the cross on his forehead, felt the electric shock of his skin against her hand, heard his clicking voice. She almost understood; he was saying friend, friend, friend, hi, hi, hi.

The old Garifuna was quiet until the dolphins breached a hundred yards away. Then he too burst into rapid chatter.

"The small one, all white, special good luck," Cal translated. "Old Man say he never sees them like this, so close, letting you touch. You, a stranger."

Of course, Kelsey had recognized the gray dolphin with his cross; it could be no coincidence. But how had he followed her, and why? The boat took off again, the dolphins leaping in their wake. She suddenly remembered her bizarre morning dream: dolphins sitting around a bonfire telling stories of humans and their follies. Then something about spaceships flying out of the water. That had been more real.

"Burial Island," Cal said when a larger green island popped into view. "Where you go, Miss. I give you special tour."

"Did you say Burial? I thought it was a pirate hang out."

Cal shook his head. "See over there, look like mountain? Stone temple." He pointed to a small tree-covered promontory with a sheer drop-off toward the sea. "Many bones hidden."

"Mayans brought their dead here?"

"Not Maya. Others."

But Cal would not say what others. He drove the boat along the deserted west side of the island, pointing out a long white beach, the pristine reefs. As they rounded the north point, she saw a two-story limestone house with a crumbling widow's walk. Scaffolding was erected on three sides and a supply of lumber was piled in the clearing. The long pier, newly built judging by the unstained wood, extended out to the reef. Cal looked proud. "Pirates," he said.

This must be the place Crouch was having reconstructed, but no one was working except one shirtless, pony-tailed gringo, a red bandana knotted over his head.

"Archeologist," Cal said, putting the emphasis on the middle syllables.

"What's he doing?"

Cal shrugged. "Digging."

The last side of the island was rocky and deserted for a mile or two until they turned into a sand-rimmed bay facing the open Caribbean. In the shady, palm-choked interior, the thatched roofs of the settlement were visible. Several boats were anchored in the bay; on shore, workers moved in the sun. Centered on the beach, the three tanks formed the eyes and nose of a mute, unsmiling face.

"Big holes for growing fish," Cal commented. "Fish grow fine in ocean." He raised his palms to the sky as if to say, Crazy Americans.

The sand was deep and soft, and the beach rose steeply. The locals paused in their work—laying lengths of pipe between the sea and the tanks—just long enough to watch Kelsey struggle by with her bags. Cal had refused to come ashore, though she'd tipped him generously. To her left, a funky cement building with a long wooden porch faced the open ocean. She could hear voices and laughter from around the bend to her right, but she kept going toward the three white men huddled near the tanks, their bronzed backs facing her.

"Hello?" she called out.

The men, two fat and one skinny, wore only shorts, baseball caps, and flip-flops. They turned; their expressions were of boys caught at something. She recognized Rodman, the skinny one, and Henry Hilton. The third had startling red hair, peeling skin, and a large, hairy belly.

"Kelsey?" Rodman came forward. His glasses were taped at the bridge of the nose, and when he wiped his sweaty forehead, he left a streak of sand. "We kind of quit expecting you." As an afterthought, he dusted his palms on his shorts and reached out to shake. "I guess you heard about the delays?"

"Things look like they're coming along now." She gestured toward the three holes, which were lined with something black and shiny.

"The natives aren't trained for this kind of work. Neither was I, for that matter." He was regarding her with the same open curiosity as the other two, rapt gazes generally planted on her face but sometimes sliding off toward her legs. She suddenly understood: These men hadn't seen a woman for weeks.

"We probably don't have work for you today," Rodman was saying, "but tomorrow or the next day, we'll get the tanks filled. I guess you can get yourself set up in the meantime. Computers are in the back of the dining hall. Land lines work intermittently, internet, rarely. You read the memo about phones. Well, maybe not. I have the only permitted satellite phone. Security reasons. Cells don't work, anyway."

"I was told I'd be cataloging," Kelsey said, nodding. "Anything else you need me to do?"

"Know how to set up a pump?" Henry Hilton asked.

"The field lab is there," Rodman said, pointing to a larger tent beside the tanks.

"Wickstrom's territory," said Henry Hilton. He had his arms crossed over his stomach and his feet planted wide.

"I didn't realize he was here."

"We didn't either," said the red-haired man, "until he crawled out to eat one time."

"He's working hard," said Rodman, "unlike some others around here."

"Hey." The red-haired man raised his palms. "You got two of the world's finest chemists out here in the hot sun helping you jury rig a pump."

Rodman picked up her bags suddenly. "I'll show you your tent."

She followed him along a winding path through the palms past a number of cabanas—tents on raised platforms with an outer structure of poles and thatched roof—each with a porch and hammock. Harrison had described them, but the tents were bigger than she'd pictured.

"How did you find us then?" Rodman asked, looking over his shoulder.

"Crouch gave me pretty good directions," she improvised. "Cal, who brought me, luckily knew the island. He called it Burial Island. I hadn't heard anything about that before."

"That's another problem," Rodman said. "The workmen found some bones near Rafael's place. It seems the government is very sensitive to archeological matters." He'd stopped in a clearing near an isolated cabana-tent, and went up the wooden steps to the door, a zippered canvas flap with a second zippered mesh door inside. "You'll want to keep it closed to keep the bugs and sand out, though that's impossible really. They sweep every day."

Inside, the light was dim and the air musty. A double mattress on a box frame occupied most of the space, and a wooden crate served as a nightstand. Rodman unzipped the window flaps. "I'll get someone to set it up for you. Like I said, we didn't know you were coming."

"Oh." He paused at the door. "We'll have to figure out the bath arrangements. Well, make yourself at home. Dinner's at seven, but most everyone shows up by six for cocktails." He rubbed a long-nailed index finger over the tape on his glasses. "You didn't cross paths with Stillman by any chance?"

"No," she said. "He's not here?" They had agreed she'd feign ignorance.

"Left last Friday. Thought maybe you'd been in contact or something." It was a question.

"No," she said again, looking at the floor.

"OK then." Rodman turned and left, flip-flops flapping down the path.

Kelsey had only just unpacked when a man appeared carrying bedding and towels. She found the two-sided bathhouse, one door labeled with a bare-breasted hula-skirted woman, but it was clear the men had been using it, for their wet towels and razors were everywhere.

In the dining hall, a nice array of fruit sat on the long serving table, and some drinks were nearby in a cooler. The chef, a compact Frenchman with typical dark features, came out of the kitchen.

"Ah. Bonjour, Henri? Je suis Kelsey Dupuis."

"Enchanté, Mademoiselle."

Thus ensued a long conversation and instant friendship. Henri insisted on making her a Salade Niçoise, "à la minute," then sat with her while she ate. He was from the countryside south of Paris; his parents were vintners, and though he loved wine, the work hadn't suited him. He'd taken his training and moved to New York where he apprenticed at several restaurants, famous, he said, but unknown to Kelsey. Henri said he'd open a nice wine for her if she came back at six. Thanking him, she hurried off toward her cabin.

The bed looked inviting with its yellow flowered sheets and pink cotton blanket. She'd just flopped down when she heard a light knock. The same man was back, this time with a young helper carrying a mirror, a clothesline, and a hammock.

Kelsey found a path that disappeared into the low vegetation behind the cabins. Perhaps it led to the pristine beach on the other side of the island. She'd lie in the soft, warm sand and stare at the sea, then take off her clothes and go for a lazy swim. She hadn't gone far when she came upon a clearing with hastily constructed shacks made of leftovers from the camp: sea-encrusted tires, a torn tent, and even a round of piping sliced open to make a shallow washtub. Faded hammocks were draped between the trees, small shapes swung in them, probably children. When a Maya woman came out, baby on her hip, Kelsey turned away.

A faint side trail took her west to the top of a small rise. From this vantage point, she could see the two camps, the black pits, and the aquamarine bay beyond, but not the west side of the island, so she continued north, picking up the trail that disappeared and reappeared in the low vegetation. Out of the trees, it got dryer and sandier and hot. She began to regret her lack of foresight: no hat, no water.

After a time she came upon an old rank cistern. Stunted banana trees and a few scrawny avocados surrounded the clearing which contained the remains of a dead garden. She picked up a fallen fruit; it oozed over her hand, and tiny bugs swarmed out. A huge iguana moved suddenly—it had been invisible a moment earlier—and Kelsey bolted.

She ran now, over spongy ground, wiping the slime on her shorts. The island was only four miles long, Harrison had told her, and on a good trail she could cover that in thirty minutes. Running became her purpose—rhythmic breathing, the surge of blood through her tissues. Still, her brain was overheating, and the sweat beginning to turn sluggish and salt-saturated. Again the image of the volcano superimposed itself on the landscape, then she was gliding in an aircar above a wasteland of lava: burning heat, the rock of the explosions, the massive earth on fire below her. Then the land gave way to water, nothing but water, and Iriel on the vast surface, clinging to the crippled boat. Barely alive, she only wanted to throw herself in and drown. Yet she was unable to do it. Unable to die because of the life she felt quicken within her.

I have no one to love but you, my child, and you are as yet unborn. I fear it will be soon, for today your weight dropped, and now my womb tenses and shudders like a hand making a fist.

The pain! Surely this is not right! I wish Muamdi were here. But I have only these strangers who have taken me in.

They have given me this house with its rope bed and enough food: fish and fruits and flat, tasteless pancakes with which they scoop everything into our mouths. They care nothing for comfort and pleasures, only religion; they worship stone carvings, vast heads and other idols.

One-God, eater of idols, did I bring You here with me or did You die with everyone else?

Oh! Do you feel this pain too, my child?

There is a beauty to this sea, green and shallow, and the land so lush, with its trailing plants and hard unyielding fruits. Each day it rains, the same rain that washed away my thirst and kept me alive. Us alive. I must be grateful for the rains. That and the dolphin who nursed me at her breast and brought me bits of fish to eat. Or did I dream it?

Though I wish it every day, I tell you we can't go back. My father's poor boat was torn to bits on this shore. Besides, everyone is dead, washed away. There is nothing left. Nothing. Do you hear me? I am so hot. I cannot breathe. I will hold my stone. Perhaps it will help.

When I use my crystal to help me speak their language, they bring me their own green stones, small and hard and without light. Besides their fineness and beauty, these gems have no power. They also hoard gold-colored metal shaped into heavy jewelry, all of which they say belongs to Man-God. They want to take me to Man-God who lives in the jungle with his many slaves. They would have me be his concubine. They think it a great honor. Do they not know I've betrayed the world for less?

I am like a caught fish in this net bed. I must go forth into the light. Ah brightness. Ah pain. I am dying!

The water feels so cool. If the people come out, I will flash my crystal, and they'll back away. But the one called Chichi is brave, and kneels behind me. Now the day grows dark as night. The others hide. They think I've caused this.

I fear this false night too, only because it is a strong omen. Will you be born a king, or man-God? The earth is round, Quiri taught us; the heavenly bodies cast shadows upon each other. One night we watched the moon being eaten, me standing between your father on one side and my betrothed on the other. Now it is the sun that dies. Chichi trembles and says her words. I sink below the water.

Day breaks a second time, and Chichi is at my feet, floating my knees on her shoulders. Another woman holds my head, and I feel you squeeze out. We rock in gentle waters. You, my firstborn, my baby son. I will name you Rotan for my father, your grandfather. I will not name you for your father, as I could not bear to say his name every day.

Oh, Jarad, I miss you so. Will you never see us again? Not even glimpse your son?

Never is so terrible a word.

Kelsey sat in the cooling Caribbean, feeling her body temperature come down. Behind her, the pirate's house cast its shadow. The sun, still bright, contained the volcano, that fiery icon of destruction, just as Kelsey now contained Iriel. She felt branded by the image; she felt like the one who'd been born.

Chapter 26

The man with the red bandana was wading toward her. "You get stung or something? I heard you come crashing through the brush."

When she asked for water, he took her to the back of the house where he had a hammock and a makeshift kitchen set up. It was a tangle of shrubbery and trees, bougainvillea, banana, orange, untended now but probably once lush and lovely. He handed her his canteen. "Drink it all. I have more."

She drained it, feeling her tongue soak up the water.

"Hey, man, how about an orange soda?"

"That would be heavenly."

He reached into a metal cooler. "Name's Keith."

"Kelsey."

"You know, you should watch this sun. You're bright red."

The soda was not ice cold, but it eased the drama that had gripped her body. She no longer felt the contractions in her uterus, or the burning fever, or the weight of a newborn baby in her arms. Just the lingering sweetness.

"You're the archeologist." She nodded in the general direction of the scientific camp. "I just got in today."

He sat opposite her, swinging in the hammock. He was about thirty-five, nice looking, brown hair in a ponytail, his bronzed skin and bandana making him look like a pirate himself. He told her he'd been working on the mainland, and had gotten a call when they hit bone.

"Did you find anything?"

"A complete skeleton, well preserved, maybe two hundred twenty years old. Want to see?"

He took her to a hole near the foundation where the skeleton was laid out on a tarp.

"How'd he die?" she asked.

"She, by the size and bone structure." Keith held up a rusted ax blade. "This was here," he fitted it against the skull, crushed, she saw now, "completely imbedded. Feel. It's still sharp."

She backed away, so he carefully replaced the metal implement next to the bones.

"I thought he made his mistress walk the plank," Kelsey said.

"Raphael? Probably buried a whole harem of them. But I'm out of here tomorrow. I'm not that interested in the pirate era."

"What about the ceremonial site at the other end of the island?"

"How'd you hear about that?"

"My boat captain. But he wouldn't say who was buried there. Not Mayan he said."

"They're so superstitious." Keith cleaned his hands under a plastic water jug. "Hey, how about I give you a boat ride back to that camp? I've wanted to check it out anyway. Big secret doings, I hear."

While he gathered his stuff, she poked around the house. It had once been elegant, judging by the wood paneling, the brass work, and the chandelier sitting in the middle of the dining room floor. She climbed a grand winding staircase, railing missing in places, to a second story. Perhaps here the women had been imprisoned, for the space was broken up into cubicles. Someone was in the process of tearing down the partitions, stripping away wiring and yellowing layers of wallpaper. Below the wallpaper, dark mahogany gleamed.

Keith's voice startled her. "People used to give sightseeing tours from the mainland, historical significance and all, until the dive operation bought it."

They climbed to the third-story widow's walk—they could see all the way back to the mainland. To the east the sea shimmered in the late afternoon sun, unbroken by any land.

He moved naturally into her space. "The natives say that burial site is haunted."

"Seems like this place might be haunted too."

"Yeah, but they're more scared of their own kind. It seems someone had extra-ordinary powers, so they were buried out here to keep them from pulling tricks once they were dead."

"They believe that's possible?"

"I know," he said. "But something interesting happened on a dig a few years back."

He moved in again, touched her arm and she shivered under her sunburn. There was something about him other than his sweaty smell that she didn't quite like. His energy was too invasive.

"This was, oh, maybe late '80s, and the site had never been excavated. One of my professors was on it. They were out here a month, camped by the ruins, and the whole time they were harassed. People would come out in boats at all hours of the day and night and start shouting. Half-warning, half-threat. The Maya leader talked to them, and they usually went away, but the camp got tense. And then they kept losing things—bones that had been dug up the day before, pots and pans, articles of clothing, no real pattern to it."

"Someone was stealing?"

"Never found out. But there were dreams. Everyone had them. My professor's was of an old medicine man chanting around a fire repeating the same few Mayan words. The closest anyone could translate it was something like 'Follow the star to the west.' "

"Did they find anything?"

"Not much. It was just a burial site; no one ever lived there. They ended up putting everything back where they'd found it. The Maya leader had a dream about it. Funny, he wasn't superstitious beforehand. Now here's the weird part. You know those bones they'd lost earlier? Guess where they turned up? Back in the graves along with the pots and pans."

The scientists were gathered on the dining hall porch when Keith pulled the boat into the bay. They waved and cheered, with even a few catcalls and whistles for Kelsey as she disembarked. Keith anchored in the shallows alongside a heavy hose that was now attached to the last segment of pipe. The hose, buoyed to keep it on the surface, looked like a black sea snake undulating in the tide. As they were wading ashore, Henri came running up.

"I will delay the dinner for you, Kelsey. We are not yet seated."

"I need a quick bath," she said in French. "Mes cheveux sont sable."

"Yes," he answered, "you will be even more beautiful with clean hair."

Though the men's things were gone from the women's side of the bathhouse, and it had been cleaned, she hung her bra on the door as a sign she was there. As the water ran through her hair, Kelsey closed her eyes. She didn't replay the afternoon's scenes, just the feelings: acute grief, poignant joy. Tonight her own life seemed a distilled reflection of Iriel's, the hardened emerald within the green crystal.

Half in the other world, Kelsey stepped out of the shower and dried herself, wrapping the damp towel around her hair. An exposed bulb hanging from the ceiling cast a crude circle of light. She passed through it, to the gleaming row of sinks. There, in reflection, she saw the image, not unfamiliar, of a man watching her. Enjoying it. She screamed and George recoiled, then spun away, leaving her gasping at the blank place in the mirror.

Night had fallen by the time Kelsey entered the dining hall. The scientists, seated at two round tables, looked up at once. A few gave her polite nods or hellos; most kept their greetings silent. They were engaged in other business, listening to Keith talk about the dig.

Kelsey made her way to the first table and sat in the empty chair next to him. Rodman was across from her, and the man called Red. The blond man to her right was introduced as Albert; to his right was smaller, dark Jersey, and then she knew Franklin, of course. They'd all dressed in better shorts and clean shirts, all but Franklin who was sloppy in cut-offs and an old shirt pulling against his belly. The extras, Henry Hilton and a sullen Wickstrom, bent over a diet coke, sat at the second table. George was not there.

Henri rushed over with a chilled Chablis from his parents' own vineyard and a small plate of lobster pâté and mini-toasts. After some wine, she began to loosen up—it was nothing, she could put it right out of her mind, nothing had happened. Under Henri's protection and constant fussing, she began to feel safe again, even when George returned and sat at the far table, even when she caught him looking.

They ate family style, a delightful fish stew, French green beans, sliced tomatoes, and miraculous fresh baguettes, served with ice-cold slabs of butter. Henri and his helpers brought the food out in covered china dishes and set them on the tables. When they were done serving, Henri squeezed in next to Kelsey. Red retrieved a handful of beers, and Kelsey and Henri shared the rest of the Chablis.

"Almost out of Mexican," Franklin said as he opened a Corona for himself.

"That's because you drank them all," Red said. He too had grabbed one of the Coronas.

"I guess I could become a wine snob like Kelsey and the Frog," said Franklin.

Next to her Henri stiffened. Rodman, still nursing his first beer, eyed the men.

"You don't have the palate," Henri said, "to be a connoisseur of wines."

"Yeah," said Albert. "You're a real pig, Franklin."

Franklin had been attacking his stew, dipping big, buttery hunks of bread into it. He looked around the table at the faces. He seemed almost hurt, for his pale eyes watered up. "What do you know about my so-called palate?"

"Well," said Henri after a moment. "You like my food. I vote that in your favor."

Everyone laughed except Rodman.

"What's new back home?" Albert asked Kelsey. His pale blond hair and wire rim glasses made him look fragile. She thought he was a microbiologist too. She'd like to tell him how all the fish had died in the tank, but not yet.

"It was getting nice. The lilacs were out."

"Flowers," Franklin said. "What about the playoffs?"

"Maybe she likes flowers," said Albert.

"Yeah, Franklin. She's a girl," Red said. "But you probably don't know any."

There was a pause, everyone waiting to see if this was going to pass.

"Wrong time of year to come to the tropics," said Jersey. "Right, Kelsey?"

She thought of him as working in the depths of the building, electronics, maybe equipment. He and Albert made an interesting pair, one dark, the other fair, both physically small but likely mental giants. Friends too. Maybe more.

"Rainy season," Albert supplied.

"Yeah," said Red. "Rainy season brings out the bugs." He nodded toward Franklin.

"June is the official start," said Jersey. "Just a week away."

"Last year I was in the jungle," said Keith. "It rained fourteen inches in a month. We were knee deep in mud, and the mosquitoes were a bitch."

"There's a storm coming this weekend," said Jersey.

"What day is it anyway?" Henry Hilton asked from the other table.

"Wednesday," said Rodman. "Is it a big one?"

"Just some rain. Choppy seas. Supposed to last two days."

"Crouch is coming Friday," Rodman said. "Maybe he'll be delayed."

"You wish," said Franklin.

The dessert, a pudding made from a brick-colored fruit called sapote, was long gone. Red had brought another round of beers, and Henri had opened a second bottle of wine. He put a glass in front of Franklin and poured him a small portion. Franklin made a show of tasting, his little finger up in the air. "Mighty clean little brew," he proclaimed.

"Hey, let me try that." Henry Hilton had pulled up an extra chair.

"Of course, En-ry," said Henri. He went back toward the kitchen.

"You've been in the country a week, Kelsey?" Henry Hilton asked her. "What have you been doing?"

"I learned how to dive," Kelsey said.

"You're a diver?" Rodman asked. "Great. That will free me up."

"What is it you're doing out here anyway?" Keith asked after a pause.

"Cataloging fish," Rodman said.

"All of you?" Keith asked, looking around

"Hell," said Franklin. "He probably knows anyway. We're testing a product to clean up environmental spills."

"What kind of product?" Keith asked.

"Organic," said Jersey.

"What are you talking about?" Henri had returned with a wineglass for Henry Hilton. He poured and Henry took a sip, then gave a thumbs up. Franklin held his glass out for more.

"They're telling me what they're doing out here," Keith said.

"Well," said Henri, "it is simple. They are planning to see if their paramecium will eat up all the bad things without killing the good things."

"Paramecium!" shouted Henry Hilton. "Where'd you learn such a big word?"

"In my kitchen," said Henri. He was rewarded with a roar of laughter.

"I heard some rumors," Keith said after the laughter abated, "that you were going to release an engineered organism in Belizean waters."

"No," said Rodman, "that's why we have the tanks."

"I'm surprised you have permission. Government permits are hard to get, especially for foreigners."

Everyone was quiet at the table.

"Money will oil all kind of wheels, non?" said Henri.

"Sure," said Keith, "I know people, but who gets paid off on this one?"

"This discussion has already been too free," Rodman said, and the talk turned to the hot tub which Jersey and Albert planned to finish the next day, if someone named Martin showed up with the parts. They had already rigged a rainwater collection system, so Jersey was hoping the storm would fill it. There was speculation about Crouch's reaction, who he'd fire, maybe Jersey and Albert, maybe just Rodman. Maybe everyone.

"Hey, Kelsey," said Henry Hilton, "want to see it?"

They left the dining room in a bunch. The night was breezy, almost cool. There were no lights across the middle of the beach with its three gleaming holes, but the workmen had lit lanterns in the pathways, and a couple of the tents glowed so the place looked like a tropical fairyland.

"Kelsey, don't you see what's going on here?" Keith had pulled her into the trees. "Those tanks right in the middle of the beach—you get a high tide, a storm surge, and the thing washes into the ocean. Or someone dips his hand into the little pond, that paramecium gets all over his skin, then he goes swimming, or even just takes a shower. Where do you think that water goes? Down the drain?" He was close, breathing on her, had hold of her arm.

"You know people in government," she said slowly as she pulled away. "Why don't you register a complaint?"

"Kelsey!" A chorus of voices took up the chant. "Kelsey! Kelsey! Are you out there necking with Keith?"

As they walked toward the noise, she was praying she'd done the right thing. They came up on the tub high on a point overlooking the water. It was just another dark hole in the sand.

She-Beast

On the second day after our arrival, we come upon the camp where they've taken She-Beast. Quiri laid a spell when he left us in the mountains, a spell of knowing and foreknowing, a spell that contains his memories of the mainland, a spell to guide us as we elude our followers and seek those who await us. Our path to this sanctuary is wild and erratic. Running, hiding, ducking through abandoned structures, asking a question here or there, unsure of whom to trust. But when we notice an enormous grape hedge gone wild, and a partly hidden archway leading through it, we know we have found the place where the mutants live.

The talking stops immediately as we enter—we had not known She-Beast and her kind could talk—but she greets us in a high-pitched cat voice which seems to make a question of every word. Love? Happy? Come? She leads us to a simple shelter and gives us fig-sized grapes and a little goat cheese and some rough bread. Then she takes us to meet the others.

They are varied in composition and health. The most desperate do not seem able to do the simplest things for themselves. These are tended by the others, hand-fed, daubed with medicines, wrapped in leaves or sea-bandages as they lie on nests made of forest moss and straw. The worst have parts that do not match. A human leg of one size is paired with a cat leg of another, a bird head perches on a man's body, some have broken wings, no arms, fingerless hands. One is so diminutive I hardly see him at first, though he squawks at me repeatedly to bring him a little fish. He is part fish himself, and seems consumed with fever despite the pool he lies in. Even the more normal ones limp or wince, their faces contorted by scar or beak. A few are massive, with teeth curving to their chins. One has ears as long as my arm.

I take out my herbs, and after a while my small green crystal, and tend to them until night falls. We stay long enough to hear their stories, the work they did in the mines, the losses of beloved friends—they have no family, for they are infertile and do not reproduce themselves—the deprivations of the camps, the ostracism and violence they suffer on the outside.

Someone has made these, I think as we move away into the cover of night. Someone who wanted a slave to do his bidding.

In my heart, I know this is very wrong.

Chapter 27

It was already hot, and a fly was buzzing her face. She heard the motor again—it was not the fly that had awoken her—and rolled onto her back, staring at the sunlight coming through the tent, bright red where the canvas was thin, like glowing rubies, like fire.

She trudged by Keith doing yoga in the sand—he'd stayed overnight in the camp, too drunk to drive the boat, he'd said—and on to the bathhouse where someone in an adjacent stall was relieving his bowels. As she threaded past the tanks, Rodman's voice, loud with irritation, rose above the noise of the pump. In the dining hall, she gratefully took her coffee to the porch where the wooden shutters were open and the breeze blew off the water.

The sea was a brilliant turquoise; she watched it heave and flow, and drank the strong coffee. One by one, the others left until only George sat across from her, reading a book. He looked guileless this morning, and he kept his head down, absorbed, it seemed.

Keith came in, wet from the shower, showing no sign of a hangover. He was all business this morning, wrote down her e-mail, and told her he was leaving for the city that afternoon. He knew just who to talk to. George was watching them, his expression half curiosity, half devotion. She got her food and took it out of sight of the porch. So entranced was she by the quiche and the fruit, that she didn't notice George until he was standing by her table with his book under his arm.

"Sorry I've been staring, but you look so much like my wife I can't help it." Up close, with his big brown eyes, his bristly hair trimmed short around his square but boyish face, he was as appealing and innocent as a puppy dog. He asked if he could refill her coffee.

"Henri's gone shopping," he said when he returned with two more pieces of quiche, "so we'd better eat up the leftovers." When Kelsey waved the food away, he consolidated the helpings on his plate, set his book face down on the table, and sat.

"What are you reading?"

"Just some sci-fi." He flipped it so she could see its title, *The Asteroid Robbers*.

"Any good?"

"Kinda sucks, I guess." His smile revealed large white teeth. "You know, it's uncanny, you and Cindy. Same hair, size—well she's gained a little. But the way you move when you talk. I was watching you with that man. My wife looks just like that when she's mad."

"You must miss her."

"She and Josh are having a hard time."

"Your son?"

"He's ten months old. A real handful." Soon he was telling her about Cindy's troubles going all the way back to the birth. Josh was big, and the labor had lasted twenty-three hours, culminating in a C-section. Cindy, exhausted, had gone into a depression that even now she could not seem to shake. "She's not strong," George said, "emotionally, I mean. She's just that sort of person."

"The baby's healthy?"

"Perfect." George went through the quiche one bite after another. "We talked about her getting a job, but Josh is so young. She hardly goes anywhere. And now with me gone . . ."

"Do you call her, e-mail or anything?"

"She doesn't know how to work the computer. But she writes me letters when Josh is asleep, sometimes in the middle of the night. Really long ones. I wish the phone worked." He waved his cell phone at her, some kind of game on its face.

Just then, Rodman entered the room and crossed the distance to their table.

"Good," he said. "I wanted to talk to you both." Kelsey had the inclination to stand at attention or salute, but instead offered him a chair. He perched on the back and glanced at his watch. "I need you both suited up and out in the water by eleven."

"What time is it now?" George asked.

"Ten thirty-five."

"OK," said George, looking over at Kelsey. "We'll be there."

"We need the tanks filled, fish in them and cataloged by the time Crouch gets here. That means a lot of work for you two." Rodman frowned and stood up. "No goofing off."

"He's sure been touchy lately," George said. "He makes everyone uptight." He had a question on his face. "So you're diving with me? I thought you just learned to swim."

"I guess I liked it and kept going. I'm a novice, sure."

"You have gear?"

"New," she said.

"Me too. Crouch bought it for me."

"Me too," she said watching the smile cross his face.

Kelsey walked down to the beach toward George, wearing her new wetsuit and carrying her gear. Jersey had opened a dilapidated shack that must have been the old dive shop. He was running a noisy compressor, filling the tanks with air.

Her nervousness focused on one worry: that Rodman would ask for her non-existent dive certification card. She occupied herself with the equipment, and in short order he was standing over them, giving his briefing. The objective today was simply to fill the three tanks with seawater. All they had to do was guide the hose underwater and make sure nothing got stuck or jammed as the pressure came on.

"Get the water as clean as you can. No fish if you can help it. Get set up on your end, then give me a signal."

"Like what?" George asked.

"Think of something."

George circled his arm above his head like he was throwing a lasso.

"Fine," Rodman said. "And try to conserve your air. I want you to go until you reach three hundred PSI. You're going no deeper than twenty, twenty-five feet, so I'm not too worried about a decompression problem. You both have computers?"

Kelsey's was on her wrist, but she had no idea how it worked. Harrison had said only that it was water activated and that any monkey could read it.

Rodman looked from one to the other. "I know you're both novices, but it should be a very easy dive. Look out for each other, and if you get into trouble, come in. Any questions?"

"Are we going to fill the tanks one by one?" George asked.

"There's a network of valves between them, as you should know, so we'll be going for all three at once." Rodman turned to Kelsey. He'd been glancing sideways at her equipment, and now he was giving it his full attention. "By the way, you'd have to have your face on the back of your head for this to work." He pointed at the regulator connection. "Turn it around. It's backwards."

Kelsey felt the cool water seeping into her wetsuit. She and George were on snorkels following the hose out into the bay. To their left a large mound of reef erupted. She could see the fish pecking at it. Some of these fish will be captured, she was thinking. Some might die.

George grabbed the end of the hose which was buoyed at the surface. "Let's swim it over that way," he shouted as he treaded water. "It's deeper, and the water's cleaner." Meanwhile, his rhythmic pedaling was stirring up the bottom, making their current location unacceptable. She took a length of hose and started swimming sideways, but it wouldn't move—it was anchored at the buoys.

"OK. Let's go down and move the anchors," George shouted. "I forgot about that."

By the time they got the hose into a suitable location, Rodman was down by the water again, his hands in the air in an exaggerated "what gives" gesture. George gave his signal, and Rodman tromped back up the beach. The motor cut on, then off again, on, then off. They waited, but nothing more happened. They could see the backs of the men, working over the pump.

"I think maybe it's broken," George said. "We'd better go talk to him."

"You go. I'll wait out here."

After Kelsey got bored looking up at beach with the milling scientists, the choppy ocean in front of her, and the pale, cloudless sky, she put her face in and watched the few fish that swam by. Finally she put the regulator into her mouth. Breathing underwater, she began to inch along the bottom of the hose. In one spot, a chain of cleaner shrimp was marching up and down, busily waving their antennae. Kelsey thrust her flippers into the air and hung upside down from the hose, counting her breaths before she saw a small purple and turquoise fish on the bottom. Swallowing to clear her ears, she made her way toward the coral.

The sea grasses swayed in the current. Green light filtered through the water. Again she hung upside down and watched things from this perspective. Suddenly, clear as daylight, she heard a voice in her head.

Hey Hi!

Disconcerted she tucked her legs, spun, and righted herself. A large creature was coming toward her out of the gloom, but she didn't panic, for she got an instantaneous second message. The word *Friend* jumped into her mind, and she knew him.

The dolphin, the one with the cross on its forehead, hovered five feet in front of her. It seemed to be blinking, waiting for her to do something. She thought it wanted to see her spin again, so she did a back somersault. The dolphin spoke in rapid clicks. It was praising her.

Then there was a moment when her mind went absolutely clear and brilliant, and she understood that God was speaking to her. This magnificent animal was the conduit. She got the words again that weren't words.

No creature harm.

You? Harm you? For that was unthinkable. She loved him.

All. None.

She understood the absoluteness of the request, and she knew it meant *now, this, here.* The dolphin twisted away and shot off so fast she could barely follow its progress. She surfaced in time to see the gray and the albino breach together, a hundred yards out.

On shore she heard the scientists yelling. Some of them were wading into the water and pointing to her. She thought they meant the dolphin, had she seen the dolphin? She tried to shout back, yes, wasn't it incredible, then she noticed Rodman doing the cowboy movement, and George lumbering toward the water. She had only a moment to grab the hose in her hands as the pump came on. She felt it grow heavy. She sank toward the bottom and held on, feeling like the traitor she was.

When Kelsey entered the dining hall, a group of the men were gathered behind the buffet, abuzz with the success of the day. Franklin was handing out beers.

"Hey Kelsey, what's your pleasure. Corona, Negra Modelo. Or are you holding out for the fancy stuff."

She shook her head. "Are the computers working? I'd like to check my e-mail."

"Ah, come on. Franklin spent all day getting this."

Someone handed her a Superior, cold, the bottle sweating. She made her way back to the computers. She was disappointed there was no message from Harrison, only one from Keith. *I lodged a formal complaint against your operation with the Belize Department of the Interior.* She forwarded the message to Harrison's new e-mail account, then rejoined the group.

Rodman pulled her aside. "Jersey says you came in with nine hundred PSI of air in your tank."

"Is that unusual?"

"After five hours in the water?" Jersey asked.

"It was her second tank," Rodman said.

"No. I only refilled George's."

George, at the sound of his name, joined them. "Yeah. I used that up too, just trying to keep up with her."

"There must be a mistake," said Rodman. "Five hours, even only half of it under water, on two-thirds of a tank? That's physically impossible."

"What's impossible?" Red asked.

"Kelsey didn't use any air," said Albert.

George smiled at her. "What gives, Kelsey? Did you grow gills under there?"

She'd sat a long time on the bottom with the heavy hose in her arms, occasionally glancing at her air gauge and responding to George's inquiries with the hand signals Harrison had taught her. She was making bubbles, but the gauge wasn't going down. The third time she gave him the same flash of twelve fingers, he checked it himself.

Was she even breathing? She was relaxed, perhaps even meditative. She'd gone in and out a few times, she knew that. She kept looking toward the deeper water, hoping to see the dolphin's bulky shape, feeling connected to him still. Some of the time, she'd been far out to sea.

"I spent time at the surface," she said now. "George was down some of the time."

They were at the center of the group, Franklin, Hilton, and even Wickstrom, hanging at the fringes.

"Maybe her gauge isn't working properly," Rodman said. "A whole tank in, say, two hours, shallow depths with little swimming, would still be remarkable, but not unbelievable."

"My equipment's brand new," Kelsey said.

"I'll test it just in case," Jersey said.

"Why don't you bring your computer in too," Rodman said. "I'd like to check the log. There might be a safety issue. Do you have any symptoms?"

"I feel fine. I think I was relaxed," she added. "Maybe I just wasn't breathing that hard."

They'd pulled the two tables together. Henri brought out a conch ceviche which they ate with homemade tortilla chips, then four large platters, red snapper, and fried jumbo shrimp. He'd made French fries too, which he plopped down in front of Franklin, who almost broke his face smiling. He immediately stuffed several into his mouth, making exaggerated noises of pleasure. Last came the vegetables—baby carrots in butter and a small ratatouille which Henri placed in front of Kelsey. He opened a beer for himself and took his usual place beside her to eat.

"Ca va?" she asked him. "Ca c'est bien passée aujourd'hui?"

"I was shopping. For that, the food is fresh tonight."

"Les carottes sont délicieuses," she continued.

"Maybe tomorrow I will swim with you. It will be my day off."

"Who cooks then?"

"Alberto. I am training him."

The men were having some kind of joke as they passed the food, each piling generous helpings on their plates.

"Goûtes la ratatouille. I think the others will not appreciate it properly."

"Only our getter of beer."

They laughed at this. The chef's small face wrinkled around the eyes.

"You two telling secrets?" Red asked. He was sitting on the other side of Henri tonight.

"I just tell Kelsey about Franklin, a gentleman today."

She realized they must have gone to the mainland together.

"Was not," Franklin said.

"Helping with the shopping, bargaining the price, carrying the boxes. He makes a good selection of fresh fish."

Franklin, to show his pleasure at this praise, produced a loud burp.

"Do you do yoga or anything?" Henry Hilton asked when the subject of her air came up again. "Yogis can hold their breath for hours."

"I meditate a little. And I run. With the altitude difference . . ."

Wickstrom had been quietly eating throughout the dinner, nursing his cola. Now he pushed his plate back. Alberto's assistant, Juan, stepped forward and snatched it up.

"I've read about a phenomenon where the need for oxygen in the human body is greatly reduced in the face of certain stimuli," Wickstrom said. "A person can temporarily take on a state similar to what the yogis achieve after years of practice. It's completely spontaneous, in reaction to, say, a great fright, perhaps some kind of religious experience. In fact, now that I think of it, it's analogous to our organisms radically changing their chemistry in response to different compounds. Evolution in an instant."

"You're saying Kelsey is evolving into a fish?" Franklin asked. The group laughed.

"Like adrenalin," said Jersey.

"The opposite," said Wickstrom.

"An out-of-body experience," said George.

"A low description," said Wickstrom, "since the body has actually taken over. The directive is self-preservation."

"That is an interesting theorem," Henri said.

"Theory," said Henry.

"The-ree."

Did she need to answer? "I didn't say anything before, but I saw a dolphin."

"We saw it too," Jersey said. "A pair. One was an albino."

"No, under the water. Close in."

"What did you do?" Rodman asked.

She smiled, remembering. "A somersault."

"Somersault?" Franklin asked.

"She did a somersault," Henry Hilton said, his face cracking into a grin.

"This is what?" Henri asked.

Kelsey mimed the action.

"I would like you to teach me this summer salt," Henri said.

"How close?" Rodman asked.

"As close as you are to me."

"That's a strange thing to do," said Red. "I mean basically you turned your back on a large animal that might have taken your movement as an act of aggression."

"I didn't feel any fear," said Kelsey. "In fact, I felt the opposite. I was . . . at its whim, and maybe I was proving that I trusted its benevolence. I can't really say why, just that I thought it wanted me to do it. Then it praised me with a series of clicks."

"But how did you know it wanted you to do the somersault? Its whim, as you called it." Rodman was leaning on the back legs of his chair.

She looked straight at him. "I felt it speak telepathically."

"Consistent with the syndrome," said Wickstrom. "The subject has a high belief—"

"Hogwash." Rodman rocked forward, the front legs of his chair banging on the floor.

"I know it's unbelievable to you," Kelsey said. "But there's more to life than a scientific explanation for everything. Sometimes . . ." She stopped.

"Sometimes what?" Rodman was intently watching her.

She opened her mouth, closed it again.

Finally Rodman spoke in a voice that was startlingly gentle. "I'm not saying your experience is invalid, rather Wickstrom's interpretation of it. Some things have a scientific explanation, and others don't. I've learned that much."

"Science will eventually explain everything," Wickstrom said. "Religion, the paranormal. We just can't measure it yet."

"No," said Rodman. "Some things should never be explained. How else can we enjoy the beauty of the universe in human terms? In God's terms?"

"These discussions always come down to God," Wickstrom said.

"Get me a beer, will you?" Rodman said to Franklin. "I feel good tonight. I have a story."

Franklin motioned to Juan who was clearing the table. "Dos cervezas, por favor."

A few of the other men raised their hands, and before long the fresh bottles were opened and passed around. Wickstrom retreated again into his quiet.

Chapter 28

After Henri brought out a plate of brownies, proclaiming that "Henri" Hilton had baked them, after Henry's jowls had grown visibly heavier under the praise, after Henri had taken orders for "sleepy tea," and it had been served, Rodman took off his glasses, and placed his folded hands on the table in front of him.

"What I'm going to tell you doesn't leave this room. Not that it's a big secret, just personal. I want to tell you one very strange experience of mine. My wife is constantly having these experiences. She would verify that what happened to Kelsey is true and possible if we remember to look at it without the distortion of the lenses of our rigid reality."

"You mean science," Kelsey said.

"And skepticism." He looked at Wickstrom. "Not that you aren't entitled to it, Wick."

"This is weird," said Red.

"Too weird for me," said Franklin, but he didn't move.

"My wife, Gloria, comes from an unorthodox family. I like to call them witches and hippies." Rodman's face softened further. "I think of them as inhabiting a different world than you or I do. When she's in her true self, things happen. What else can I say?"

Kelsey felt a warmth start on the right side of her body.

"We met when I was taking care of my sick mother back in Baltimore and Gloria was a nurse in the hospital. Mom had a particularly virulent form of lung and throat cancer, and could no longer smoke. She had always been difficult, but now she was impossible. She'd be screaming with nerves and then be heavily sedated for days. I had to make a lot of decisions. My father was long gone, my younger sister was tied down with her babies, and my older sister hadn't spoken to my mother for fifteen years.

"Gloria was living in a communal household then. I'd go over for dinner, and we'd sit up late drinking jug wine, and smoking. I'd perversely taken it up at that point. We were both the same age, in our twenties, but I felt she could rescue me. And she did. But not in the way I imagined. Nothing ever happens the way you imagine."

"Wait," said Henri. "Go more slow."

"He's just getting started," Red said.

"It makes me want a cigarette, just talking about that time," said Rodman.

"Want one?" Franklin asked. "I can get you anything you want."

"Pot?" asked George.

"The thing is," said Rodman, "once Gloria gets on an idea, she keeps repeating it. I've learned that it's better to go along with her from the beginning. Her idea that summer was that I needed to listen to Mother's pain. She kept on about it. My mother was really an impossible woman, you see. When we were little, she'd criticize us kids, always goading us to do better, and then when we had something to be proud of, she'd find a way to cut us down. I was particularly vulnerable because my game was over-achieving. I kept believing that if I just did something really spectacular, she'd love me. Of course it was never enough."

"That's sad," said Jersey. "Really."

"Sounds like you need therapy," said Franklin.

Rodman shot him a look. "Oh, I got it, believe me."

"So what happens next?" asked Henri. "With this terrible mother."

"My sister and I had an argument about bringing Mom home to die. She said, 'Don't do it, Johnny, she'll suck you dry.' And she was right. Just I had the hubris back then to think I could handle her. You see, Gloria agreed to come live with me and help.

"You wouldn't believe how awful that was, trying to feed her, hydrate her, keep her clean. Mom was hardly human, more like some kind of deranged monkey. I wanted to knock her out with drugs, but Gloria wouldn't let me.

"The thing about the pain came to a head when the summer was at its most beautiful. Life was abundant, flowers, fruits, and tomatoes hanging over the fence from the neighbor's yard. A tiny kitten adopted us. The light trying to get in, Gloria said. It was really strange, because we were blackness inside: curtains drawn, speaking in whispers between her tantrums. Gloria kept spacing out the doses of pain medicine. I was begging her for those shots almost as much as my mother, and once she stuck me, just to let me see how it was, how I drifted away and couldn't think, how depressed I got afterwards. It was when I came out of it that we had our revelation.

"Mom and I were sitting together. She had completely lost her voice. I was exhausted too. For a moment, looking at her lined face, I thought I knew how it must have been, raising us kids alone when she was raging inside. I was able to take her hand, usually I was too angry for tenderness. I was going to say something, to try to forgive her maybe, when I swear this blackness came right out of her like a visible cloud. It was so ugly and big, swarming over the entire room like bees. We both watched it absorb into the curtains and the wallpaper and the carpet and the bedding. It was monstrous, all fear. I felt that fear in a way I've never felt fear, not even in Nam. Mama just kept those steely eyes on that cloud of fear and so did I, and after a very long while it lightened up, just a little. It felt as though we were doing something together, by holding hands, by not letting it out of our sight. We were a force, that one time in our lives, and slowly the thing went away, like a bad pain that just fades. It was exhausting work, but maybe the best thing I ever did in my life. And it left me feeling like I could float off the earth. I felt that way for days, and if I need to, I can still access that lightness.

"She returned to herself the next morning, no less vehement, and died a few days later, never acknowledging what had happened. Who knows, maybe it didn't happen to her in the same way it happened to me." Rodman was silent for a while, then he said, "You know, I think I will have that cigarette."

The group divided into the card players and the smokers—Franklin, Henri, and Wickstrom with his pipe, and tonight, Rodman. Kelsey followed them out to the porch, and George came too, making noises about the joint, which Franklin produced right out of his pocket.

"Is your wife still a nurse?" Kelsey asked after they'd all lit up.

"A healer, not so much Western style anymore. She calls it energy work."

"You mean a psychic healer?"

"Helping people die was her specialty, though now it's more those who aren't yet ready to go. She reads body auras and tells people what they need to do, often bizarre things." He took a drag on his cigarette. "She sent one woman with an inoperable brain tumor down to a remote Mexican village where the people didn't speak English, or even much Spanish. She was there for months. When she came back the tumor was almost gone."

"What cured her?" Kelsey asked.

"This woman was a Hollywood executive, an incessant talker. The tumor was on the language part of her brain. According to Gloria, she just needed to quit talking for awhile."

"Awesome," George said. He tried to pass Kelsey the joint for the second time.

"How does she do it?" Kelsey asked. "Has she described it to you?"

"She stands back, and something else steps in. She just follows along, mimics the moves she sees. She described it once as following a very gentle dance partner."

"I wonder what my aura looks like," George said.

Kelsey narrowed her eyes. "I see . . . a smoky haze."

Rodman laughed. "You can develop raw abilities, you know. Maybe you'd like to meet my wife."

"I'd like that." Again she felt the warmth at her side.

He stubbed out the cigarette. "That was no good. I can see why I quit."

"I feel good," George said.

"How about eight in the morning?" Wickstrom asked.

"Shit," said Franklin. "That's fucking early."

"Nine," said Rodman. "We're starting collection—"

"Let's not talk about it," Franklin said. "It's too depressing." He stretched his legs out. "You know, this is the good life. Getting paid big bucks for doing basically nothing. Henri cooks up a storm every night. Good drugs too." He offered the joint to Rodman.

"No thanks."

"Want another cig?"

"No."

"No now or no forever."

"I'll let you know."

Henri got up. "I go to bed." He gave Kelsey a little kiss on the cheek.

Franklin stood too. "I'm getting another beer."

"Bring me one," George said.

"Do I look like the fucking waitress?"

After they'd both gone inside, Wickstrom fooled with his pipe, cleaning, tamping, and finally lighting it. Sweet smoke drifted over Kelsey. It was a beautiful night, a little breezy. Half the stars were out, the rest of the sky was smudged with clouds. A lone gull cried, piercing the quiet, and inside, Franklin's voice rose above the slap of the cards.

"So," said Wickstrom, "are we going to sit here all night contemplating our navels?"

"Just a while longer," Kelsey said. "I haven't finished my tea."

"Go on, Wick," Rodman said. "Spill it."

"In front of the infant?"

"No need for insults. How old are you Kelsey?" Rodman asked.

"Thirty-two."

"I have children older than that," Wickstrom said. "Grandchildren."

"Petey's no more than seven." Rodman snorted. "How old are you, Wick?"

"Sixty-four in November. If I live that long."

"Still got you beat," said Rodman. "So what's on your mind tonight?"

Wickstrom made a show of lighting the pipe again. "I've been working with George's sample," he said. "Still not what we're looking for."

Not what we're looking for. Kelsey felt a chill now, same side.

"Shit, I wish I hadn't lost 876."

"What happened to 876?" asked Kelsey.

"Freezer accident," said Rodman, glancing sideways at her. "Is it still the lifespan problem? What're you feeding it?"

"Herbicide components mainly."

"I thought it was nitrogenous fertilizers," Kelsey said. "Petroleum bi-products."

Wickstrom shot a glance at Rodman.

"New client," Rodman said. "We've been developing a second strain for the last month."

"I figured that out actually, about the second strain," Kelsey said.

"Clever infant," said Wickstrom."

"If I didn't need you diving and cataloging, I'd have you working with Wick."

"I don't need any help." He blew out a fragrant stream.

"I'm worried about safety," Rodman said. "We need time for that."

"I've been working on safe for months," said Wickstrom. "I've spliced safe characteristics into the cells. I've made generations of safe. I've lived and breathed safe."

Partly because of Wickstrom's bragging, and partly because she trusted Rodman after his story about his wife who she could still feel sitting beside her, telling her to go ahead, she let loose. "What about the fish tank then?"

"What about it?" Rodman asked, the habitual annoyance back in his voice.

"George injected something in there, and all the fish died. I watched him do it. It had that same violet color," she added. "I'd seen once before. In the beginning."

"We have no violet coloration in any of the organisms I've worked on," Wickstrom said.

"Sometimes I see things in the lab you might miss at the top."

"You're saying there's a third version of the organism?" Rodman asked. "One that we haven't even—"

"Who's doing the work?" Wickstrom broke in. "Supposing for one moment she's telling the truth."

"California, Wick, who else?"

"This is our project, Johnny. How dare they end run me?"

"Maybe they thought you'd object," Kelsey said, "if your priority is safety."

Wickstrom knocked his pipe against his chair leg. "I'm going to talk to George, that little punk. I'm going to wring his neck."

"He's wasted, Wick. Besides it's coming from the top, you know that." Rodman rubbed his brow. "I appreciate you telling us this, Kelsey. Anything else unusual?"

She took a breath. "Crouch doesn't care about safety or science. He takes shortcuts. That's his MO. I've seen—" She stopped herself.

"We're seeing it," Rodman said slowly. "You're saying we're seeing it now."

Wickstrom had his gaze fixed on her face. "I want to know where she's getting her information. Who she's in cahoots with."

"I do my job," she said. "I observe."

"From your elevated position as laboratory technician."

"Wick," said Rodman, "try to be civil."

Wickstrom stared at her. "Isn't it time for your beauty rest, Sweetheart? Isn't that how little girls stay so pretty?"

She stood, angry now, and Rodman stood with her and shook her hand. Wickstrom went back to his pipe and didn't look up.

Kelsey woke, moments, it seemed, after she'd finally fallen asleep, with the sensation that she'd said or done something she must immediately rectify. She could smell the incoming rain and feel the heaviness in the air. Then a crack of lightning brightened the gloom, and rain was drumming against the canvas. She thought of all the chances she was taking—Keith, the forwarded e-mail to Harrison, and now what she'd said to the two senior scientists.

The storm tortured her, the rain pounding, driving the bad thoughts deeper into her aching head. Then gradually the squall passed, and the wind became only a rustle in the dripping trees. She pulled on her shorts and ran barefoot over the damp path, so smooth that she made it to the dining room without stepping on a pebble. As soon as she cracked the door, she saw the light. But now he'd seen her too.

Wickstrom's wiry hair was loose tonight, thinning and gray, flying around his face. His bare feet sprawled out from the hems of his pajamas. He peered at her over his glasses and raised his bushy eyebrows.

"The storm woke me," she said.

She sat in front of a computer and began typing a message to Harrison. She kept glancing at Wickstrom; she had the sensation he was seeing every word she typed. It was crazy paranoia, she told herself, but then when he gave her a little self-satisfied smile, she impulsively deleted the message and went to the phone instead.

Because Wickstrom was listening, she left her full name and a business sounding message about not much; she wanted to talk long enough for Harrison to wake and pick up. Then they'd arrange another time, or somehow she'd make him understand using code or innuendo.

"Stillman not there?" Wickstrom asked.

"What makes you think I was calling him?" She was set to deny it.

"Jersey activated the log for me last night. It tells me who is calling whom. For example, George called his wife at 11:03 and talked forty-seven minutes."

"Are the computers bugged too then?"

"If you want them to be, my little Mata Hari."

"What gives you the right to spy on people? What gives you the right to question my integrity?"

"How can I be sure of you? How can you be sure of me? Well, the cat is out of the bag, Ms. Kelsey Dupuis, daughter of Cecil Dupuis, and you can't stuff it back in now."

She stared at him, his wild hair, the half-smirk she was coming to hate. "How dare you talk to me like that! You're a pompous shit—you know that?—and nobody likes you." This last felt childish, but also, like the cat, couldn't very well be stuffed back in.

"I'd be hurt," he said, "but it's not the first time someone told me that." He went back to his computer and she stood watching him, waiting for an apology, an acknowledgment. But he didn't look up again.

Chapter 29

Kelsey felt no better in the daylight, bouncing along in the boat with no breakfast in her stomach. She was groggy from the deep sleep she'd finally fallen into at dawn, and breathless and embarrassed. They'd all been waiting when Rodman deposited her and her gear at the boat. Only Henri's presence cheered her.

George got sick over the side as they hit some chop, but now he'd settled in beside her, chomping on his gum, his square jaw moving against the sweetness. They were cruising out to a bounteous reef where they'd find many beautiful fish, their captain had assured them.

George began to talk, first in a mutter, then more loudly. Cindy was having trouble with the checkbook, she'd gotten two notices for bounced checks, and now she was frightened of even going out to get the mail. "How can that be?" George kept asking. "I make plenty of money."

He smelled slightly sour and beery, and though he kept adding fresh gum to his mouth, it didn't erase the aura of the night, with its mistakes. Kelsey finally took some gum at his insistence—he had four packs of it—and somehow, chomping along with him, got caught up in his story.

"I told her to call the bank, or she's going to worry all weekend," George said.

"Can't she balance a checkbook?" Kelsey asked. "That's basic."

"It's on the computer," George said. "She doesn't know how to use one. I told you."

Well, she's a ninny, Kelsey thought. "You should teach her when you get home."

"She must use the credit cards until the cash is there at the first of the month," the chef yelled into the wind.

"How can she spend so much money when she hardly leaves the house?"

"Internet?"

"But she doesn't know how to use the computer," Kelsey and George said in unison.

"Never underestimate a woman," Henri said, "for spending the money."

"Oh come on," Kelsey said. "That's chauvinistic."

George tried not to smile. "The doctor said it's postpartum depression. She used to work. She did the shopping. She took exercise classes. She kept herself up. She's still pretty, but now she's gotten a little—"

"Fat?" Henri asked.

The boat swung suddenly and stopped. As their wake died, they could see the reef below.

"Well, anyway," George said, "it helps to talk about it."

Kelsey was surprised to learn that Henri was going to make the dive with them. He told them his brother taught diving, but he didn't like to dive in France because the water was cold.

"When did you make your last dive?" Wendell, the captain, asked.

"Three months I go one time," Henri said. "Before then, two, three time a year maybe."

"I'll watch over you then," said Wendell in his crisp British accent.

Kelsey and George began making plans about signals and specimens. Wendell's wife, Shirley, would keep the boat running and follow their bubbles, should they need to surface to deposit their catch. They had two underwater cages set up beneath the boat, and there was a covered tank to transport the smaller samples.

Kelsey had the most training in marine biology, and she had briefly consulted the fish book that Rodman had stuffed into her hands before they shoved off. That made her the expert in charge of selection. George would carry the slurp gun, a device that allowed them to suck fish into a clear plastic compartment, and with a reversal of the gun's action, deposit them into collapsible plastic containers they each carried attached to their belts. Their mission was to gather a diverse sample and get them back alive. Rodman was going to do some additional collection offshore, a quicker process but expected to yield more ordinary specimens.

"The boat follows, so we don't need to turn round. We'll go straight out until we have three hundred PSI left, then we'll take a ten-minute safety stop on the way to the surface. We'll get a shark in the shallows on the way back if we're lucky," Wendell said by way of a dive briefing.

Kelsey felt the now familiar pleasure as the sea enveloped her. She sank dreamily through the water watching the others. Henri was skinny in his wetsuit and had a look of surprise on his face. George, struggling to clear his ears, pulled his regulator out of his mouth and spit out the wad of gum. It floated serenely toward a parrotfish, which gave a nibble and rejected it.

They drifted to the reef at about fifty feet. It was pristine and healthy and loaded with fish. Kelsey spotted a juvenile squirrelfish feeding near George's right shoulder and signaled him to take it, but he spooked it, then went for the more common snapper. Too big for the gun, the fish darted back to the safety of its school.

George began to take shots at random, ignoring Kelsey. By luck he pulled in a pair of grunts then lost them in the transfer to her container. She signaled that she'd like to try, but his jaw muscles set and he pulled the gun closer to his chest.

The reef became shallower, and they watched a small ray flush out of the sandy bottom straight into Wendell's net. He must have set up the capture, because it was so smooth and easy. He gave the thumbs up and rose to the boat, which was nearly overhead, and put the ray into one of the cages while Shirley took his collection bag to empty.

George was creeping toward a rocky place at the edge of the reef, and as he disappeared over the wall, Henri caught Kelsey's eye. He was circling his finger, miming a somersault, so she smiled, tucked her legs, and did one, then signaled him back. Henri pulled his legs up and pushed his arms, but couldn't spin. He looked like a little pod thrashing backward in the water.

They were laughing now, streams of bubbles rushing up from their mouths.

Kelsey demonstrated and Henri tried again with the same result. She helped him tuck into a tight ball, then she reached out and spun him. He caught the water with his arms and went over again. Then they were doing slow motion back rolls, side-by-side.

Upside down, she spotted Wendell re-entering the water. He sank leisurely in their direction, his descent elegant and practiced. The net floated above his head like fluttering hat ribbons. Inspired by the graceful line of his long body, Kelsey arched out of her final spin. The movement took her over the wall. George's bubbles, rising from the depths, caught her eye, and the slurp gun resting where he'd left it on a shelf of coral.

Suddenly, she heard the dolphin's warning repeating in her mind. A swift kick propelled her to the gun. She gave a second flick of her fins and was over the wall in time to see George tuck a small vial back into his BCD. There in front of him, a small violet cloud hung suspended in the water.

George's face registered her presence, and he gave what passed for a shrug of innocence. She pointed the gun at him and he put his hands up. But, of course, the gun was useless as a weapon, and both she and George realized it at the same time. He turned lazily toward her and she toward the sample.

The purple cloud of one-celled life was still a tight blob, but the edges were dissipating. She stuck the nozzle into the color, pulled the trigger, and slurped it all up.

Kelsey swam fast, making what she hoped was a wide circle and simultaneous slow ascent to the boat. Her first impulse, to bolt to the surface, had been thwarted by the beeping of her dive computer and Wendell's frantic arm motions. George was behind her, not gaining but steadily following. If he caught her, he was certainly capable of wrestling the gun away. Behind him was Wendell. She'd seen him on the one backward glance she'd risked.

They were over open water now, sprinting into the blue. She had the gun tucked against her suit to minimize its drag, so she had only her legs to propel her and those heavy fins. She was wide of the boat, but if she turned too sharply, George could cut across and catch her, or if he was smart, he'd go back to the boat and wait for her to come up. But he hadn't thought of that.

Her thigh muscles burned and her breath wheezed through the apparatus. Then suddenly, she felt herself metamorphose into a more powerful swimmer. One kick of her tail and she made the turn, feeling the flood of relief as the boat came in sight. Shirley had followed their bubbles.

But her tail caught on something; it became once more a right flipper and a left and then an ankle, and he'd caught that too. She bent at the hips, thrashing, ready for a fight. He let go and just before she bolted again, she recognized Wendell in the foaming water. He was pointing at his air gauge, then at hers, making a calming motion with his other hand. Thirty yards behind them, George was making a slow emergency ascent. He was out of air.

〰〰〰

Kelsey handed the gun up to Henri. Wendell had heard her panicky story in the water, and for now he'd agreed to take her side.

"It's not true," George had said once but then had gone silent and brooding, hanging onto the anchor line until Wendell let him on board.

Wendell insisted on releasing the ray and collapsing the underwater cages before they left the reef. During this time Kelsey had only Henri and Shirley to help protect her cargo. But George didn't seem aggressive anymore. He was sitting with his elbows on his knees, his head in his hands, dripping onto the deck.

They took off, still in silence. Shirley piloted the boat, and Wendell came to sit by Kelsey. "What is it?" he asked, pointing to the gun cradled in her arms.

"A bio-engineered organism capable of killing many fish. And the reef too."

"Why did you release it in the water?" Wendell asked George.

"I was doing my job. Following orders."

"Who told you to do this?" Henri asked. "The boss, Rodman?"

"No," said George. "Mr. Crouch. The one who pays your salary."

"But didn't you know that all the fish died in the tank?" Kelsey asked. "I saw you put the organism in there."

"They've solved that problem." George unwrapped a piece of gum and put it in his mouth.

"Who?" she asked. "Who's working on it?"

"They don't tell me everything." George shrugged, his powerful shoulders bulging out of his open wet suit.

Kelsey had a sudden intuition. "Are you getting paid extra for this?"

He raised his eyes to her. They were red from the salt water, and he had a mask imprint still on his face. "Cindy wanted to buy a house, OK? This was a way to do it. It's only a demonstration anyway. What could that hurt?"

She lectured him most of the way back to shore. She told him the organism could easily spread and multiply, that it could kill every fish in the ocean. She said he should tell them everything he knew to help make up for what he'd done. George's head hung lower; he chomped on his gum.

Back on shore, Kelsey raced toward the holding tanks, the slurp gun in her arms. Behind her, George had somehow gotten free, and was climbing off the boat. She shouted and Jersey came out of the dive shack.

"Where's Rodman?"

Jersey reached for the gun. "Want me to empty that into Tank One?"

"No!" She clutched it tighter to her chest.

George was powering up the beach, yelling for her to wait. Jersey glanced at him, then back at her. "Hey, how'd you do on air today? Want me to analyze—"

"Not now! I need to talk to Rodman!"

"He's in the water, doing collection."

"Wickstrom," she said, feeling she had no other option. "And don't let George near me."

She burst through the door of the lab. Wickstrom, surrounded by a messy array of printouts and equipment, looked up from the microscope. Only his broken concentration and his astonishment seemed to slow the rude remark that was almost visibly forming. Not waiting for him to speak, Kelsey pushed the gun into his arms; its contents had bloomed bright fuchsia.

"That's mine." George crashed in, shaking Jersey off his back. Wickstrom gently deposited the slurp gun on his workbench before coming around to face George. He arranged his gangly limbs into an impenetrable barrier.

"He released it at the reef," Kelsey said. "I think I got all of it."

"Good girl," Wickstrom said. Then, frizzled eyebrows twitching, he focused on George. "You say this is yours? Because if it's what I think it is, you're in serious trouble."

George glanced at Kelsey as though she could help him with this trick question. "I was only doing my job. I was . . ." George's bristly hair poked up like a beaver's pelt. "Just give it back. I'll . . . I'll destroy it. I wasn't supposed to . . ."

"What? Let us see it?" Wickstrom's eyes were piercing.

"What if I lose my job?" George asked. "Shit. Cindy's going to kill me."

"It's more than just your job on the line," Wickstrom said. "You understand that?"

"Yeah," Kelsey said, "it's the whole . . ." She stopped because Wickstrom's smirk was dancing on his lips. "We need some security, don't we?"

Jersey slid around George. "Albert and I will take him over to the hot tub. If he tries anything, we'll push him over the cliff."

"Well, maybe if you both sat on him," Wickstrom said.

"Who's sitting on whom?" Rodman's head had appeared at the doorway to the small space. His gaze lingered on George, then took in the others. "What's going on here?"

Kelsey stepped away from the table so he got a clear view of the slurp gun with its bright contents. "George released this," she said, "on the reef at fifty feet."

"You're shitting me," Rodman said. Then, half under his breath, "This is all I need."

"Well, he did," said Wickstrom, "so deal with it, Johnny."

Rodman pushed his breath through sunburnt lips. "How much did you get, Kelsey?"

"All that was visible."

"Who touched it? Who was in the water?"

"Me, George, Henri." She pointed to Wickstrom, not wanting to say his name. "He handled the gun just now. And Wendell, the captain."

"We need to get everyone cleaned up in case that's an issue. Wick, how fast can you do an analysis?"

"I can have the main characteristics within two hours."

"I want to know what happens when it has contact with the air, with human skin. How about the boat?" Rodman asked.

Jersey stuck his head out the door. "It's leaving now."

"Well, get them back here."

The surface of the pools reflected the clouds skating overhead. The few fish swam in circles inspecting their new, stark environment. George and Kelsey, standing in bathing suits, were waiting for Rodman. The breeze hit her skin. Next to her George had goose bumps.

"What's going to happen?" he asked.

She ignored his question. "So Crouch told you to release it? What was he planning? And how did you ever expect to find it again?"

"I had an inflatable marking device."

"Jeez, George. I wish you'd said something."

"I didn't mean any harm, Kelsey."

She looked at him shivering. "I just don't understand why he wanted it way out there."

George looked uneasy, but just then Rodman came out of the lab. "Call me when everyone is assembled." He went off to talk with Jersey who was carrying the dive gear into the lab. Behind it, the groundskeepers were trooping off toward the forest camp.

"Siesta time," George said.

"What I'd really like is some food."

Suddenly a boat rounded the bend and roared off toward the pirate's end of the island. It was riding low in the water, from cargo or a lot of people.

"Are they working out there again?" she asked.

Now the others were coming toward them from all directions like insects converging on a sweet. As they got to the tanks, they asked the same question, "What's up?" They addressed Kelsey, as though she was the instigator of this. As though it was somehow her fault their day had been interrupted. As though she was somehow in charge.

"OK," said Rodman. "Here's the deal. We have an unknown generation of the organism on the island, and Kelsey has told me she thinks it's related to a version that killed some fish back in the decorative entry tank. Wickstrom is doing analysis on it right now. I'm going to make some calls and I want everyone to reconvene again at," he looked at his watch, "let's say 5:00 P.M. in the dining hall. In the meantime, you're all confined to camp. Stay in groups or pairs, out in the open. I want you in sight of each other at all times."

"Are we under suspicion of something?" Franklin asked.

"Yes," said Rodman.

"That sucks," Franklin said.

"Yeah, well, you suck too," said Red. "You suck eggs, Franklin."

"What's so bad about a new version of the organism?" Franklin asked. "That should be good, right?"

"George released it on the reef," Jersey said.

Red and Franklin chose to look at each other and smile. It was an exchange of surprise and shock; the smile faded into anger in Red's case.

"It's out there?" He pointed to the turquoise and white behind them.

"Kelsey gets it all up in the suck gun," Henri said.

"This is bizarre," said Franklin.

"I don't want you gossiping like a bunch of old women," Rodman said. "I'd forbid it if I thought it would do any good. On second thought, I'm going to assign groups. And the water's off limits."

"It's going to be wickedly hot," Albert said.

"How about the hot tub?" Jersey asked. "We got it filled in last night's storm. None of us got near the specimen."

Rodman sighed. "Oh hell, I don't care. Just the ones who are clean, though."

"What is it that you think you have in there?" Albert pointed to the lab.

"When I know, I'll share it with everyone at the same time. At the meeting."

"Are you going to talk about me?" George asked. "Am I going to get to defend myself? I want to make a phone call."

"I'm making the calls," said Rodman. "Then we'll determine the rules at the meeting. I'm not taking any chances of this thing getting out of hand."

"I have rights," said George. "I'm an American citizen."

"This isn't America," Rodman said, displaying his temper for the first time. "As far as I'm concerned, you're under house arrest." He looked around at the glum faces. "Until we know what we have, I'm keeping a tight control on this situation. That means all of you."

Wickstrom came suddenly out of the lab. He was holding the vial and George's wetsuit. "This thing is all over the place," he said. "You're going to have to clean up really carefully, and disinfectant may be the worst thing. If we've come anywhere near our goal, it's going to thrive on chemicals. Choose something mild if you can find it. Contain the wash water."

"I took my bath already," Henri said. "But I didn't touch a thing under the water."

"I handed you the gun right at the beginning," Kelsey said.

"Let me check you in the lab," Wickstrom said. "You'll be my first guinea pig."

"Where is my friend Henri Hilton?" Henri asked suddenly.

"Oh shit," said Rodman, "he's missing again, isn't he? I counted you as one of the men." When he asked if anyone knew where Hilton had gone, no one did.

Chapter 30

They bathed with natural mint soap, and collected the runoff in the rain barrel. Afterward, wearing a clean beach towel and nothing else, Kelsey went into the lab.

Wickstrom gave her the raised eyebrow then returned to his microscope. He circled his long arm for her to come look. Under the powerful magnification, live protozoa, the color of lilacs, wiggled among the dead.

"It's the result of a process similar to diatomic fluorescence. Look at this." He dropped a bluish substance onto the slide. The organisms began frantic movements; some of them burst apart, forming new animals, fringe of cilia wiggling. Once they were stable and whole, only the nuclei pulsed, as though to some cosmic rhythm, forcing the color across the cell.

"What was that you put in?"

"A paste of common cleaning powder."

She raised her head. "So it's working."

His gray-blue eyes twinkled back at her. "Now watch this."

As he put another drop onto the slide, Kelsey saw the animals puffing against the confinement of their outer selves. Those unable to break open their skins paled and died. Through the lens of the microscope, she saw the magnified eyedropper tip shaking as it leaked out another dose of poison. After the seventh drop, the remaining animals had gotten fatter; their color was a vivid, lovely amethyst.

"The population is stable," she summarized. "Fewer are dying. Births are rarer."

"What do you conclude?"

"It's evolving," she said. "You're causing it, but it—" She stopped. How to explain her feeling that the organism was conscious?

"I can't believe this is the first time I've gotten a look at the real animal," Wickstrom said as he rubbed the back of his neck.

"Where do you have the rest of it?"

He gestured toward a row of labeled jars scattered about the lab, their contents ranging from royal purple to pinkish-white. "I can keep making new generations, but it's all empirical at this point."

"How are you going to protect it?"

He waved toward a cot in the corner.

"You're going to sleep here? That's your entire plan?"

"Who's going to steal my jars? And what for—to sell it to the North Koreans?"

"At least hide your best samples. I can imagine someone coming in here and smashing everything." She saw the shattered lab, glass everywhere, the color draining through the floor.

"No real scientist would do that," he said. "It would be like desecrating the Mona Lisa."

"I don't understand."

"Can't you appreciate the breathtaking beauty of what you just saw? Aren't you moved by the sight of life reinventing itself? I think it's the most beautiful thing I've ever seen in my life." Gone was the cynic, the ironic misfit. His eyes were shining, his body leaned toward hers, awaiting her reaction.

"I think . . . your dedication is beautiful."

He responded with a look of curiosity. "OK," he said, "let's see if you're clean."

He took samples using Q-tips and cotton swabs from the first aid kit, clipped some of her hair, and scraped her skin. She was instantly reminded of what had happened at the police station in the dedicated back room, with the rape specialist.

"You're feeling ill maybe?" he asked. "Because we can't have that."

"I didn't get much sleep, and I haven't eaten all day."

"Don't worry. It's coming back negative." He was looking at her over his glasses which were perched on his nose; she could smell the pipe smoke clinging in his hair.

"Did you ever want to be a doctor?" she asked after he went back to his swabbing. It grounded her to talk, to remember where she really was.

"I started med school a year behind my brother. But he was so perfect at everything, I couldn't go on with it. Had to do my own thing, be my own man, you know."

"That's so sad." She felt her eyes brimming over.

Wickstrom got up and went back to the microscope. "Yeah, well, my brother got AIDS from one of his patients. That's a lot sadder."

She could see his head was turned so he could pretend the tears weren't tracking down her cheeks. "I'm sorry," she said, "it's just that you remind me of my father."

"Is that good or bad?"

She took a few more breaths. With him farther away, the pipe smell was diluted.

"Look," he said. "This won't take much longer, then you can go play."

"You don't want me to stay and help?"

"You'd just be in the way." But he said it kindly.

He took a second swab from under her chin. She could remember the gun's nozzle pressed there when she was swimming. "This seems to be the only area that was affected besides your wetsuit. I'll want another sample in half an hour. You have a hair dryer?"

"Why would I?"

"Go see if anyone has one, will you, Doll Face? And bring me a sample of the wash water."

She smiled back at him. "Which do you want me to do first?"

"Get dressed. You're indecent."

She had the urge to flash him. And then she did.

The hairdryer, neatly printed label identifying the owner as Henry Hilton, worked very well: Kelsey's throat was pronounced clean with the stipulation that she come back later for a final check. George's hands had actually gone under a flame. The hair on the back of them was singed off, and he'd clipped his nails to the quick. That was where the concentration had been; he also had no remaining sign of infestation.

Once she'd found him again, Kelsey wasn't letting George out of her sight, so they traipsed from her tent to his, then into the kitchen where they lunched on mini ham and cheese sandwiches before joining Jersey and Albert and Red at the hot tub. After an initial discussion, George was allowed in, and Kelsey went to lie in the hammock that had been strung up nearby.

Kelsey swung in the shade and listened to the men splashing and talking. It was delicious, with her stomach full and the afternoon warmth blanketing her body. She let it all drop away, the adrenaline of the day, everything she should be worried about, any emotion except for a nascent happiness. Just for a second. She started awake because the sun had dropped below the palm fronds and was now shining into her eyes.

The voices had changed—quieter, edgy—and she sat up, making no new sound, keeping the gentle swing of the hammock, pushing off with her toes.

"Is he going to fire me?" George asked. "Because if he fires me, I'm toast at home."

"He can't. Not without H.R.," said Albert.

"Plus you've got the big man on your side," said Red.

George groaned.

"So," said Red, "how much was that bonus? You got paid extra to put it in the water?"

"To bring it here," George said. "But no one was supposed to know about it yet. The demonstration was supposed to be a surprise."

"Like a birthday surprise?" Red asked.

"How much?" Albert asked. "I'm just curious."

George lowered his voice. "–thousand."

Albert whistled. "Why didn't he ask me?"

"Would you have done it?" George asked.

Kelsey pushed out of the hammock and went to the blue edge of the tub. They'd snaked a river of broken turquoise tiles through the black and around the tub's rim. "What were you demonstrating anyway? And for who? Is Crouch planning some kind of spill?"

"What if he's right?" George asked. "What if he can prove it?"

"He's got a point," said Jersey, "if this thing's all it's cracked up to be."

"You can't go introducing new bioforms into a delicate ecosystem."

"That's the whole point," said Albert. "We already are, all over the planet. This was supposed to be the solution."

She looked at the flushed faces. "We've barely gotten started with this phase and now he throws a whole new generation at us. This so-called demonstration is dangerous and ill-conceived. I'd say the whole project is."

"So what's your game, Kelsey?" Red asked. "You seem to have everything figured out."

"I hope I'm not the only one," George said. "I bet I'm not the only one."

Jersey and Albert exchanged a look.

"Hey, what time is it anyway?" Red asked.

Kelsey looked at her watch. "Four fifteen."

George sank deeper into the water. "I wish he'd let me call Cindy."

The men didn't talk anymore, except Jersey and Albert who fussed with the bubble-making equipment, but it seemed to Kelsey that they were speaking in code, assessing their position in the group, their loyalties.

Kelsey climbed out on the rocky point. The low cliff marked the southern tip of the bay and she had a good view of the south end of the island and out to the unbroken horizon where the sea shimmered in the heat. The water was flat except for an occasional wave that broke against the side of the cliff and the eddies along the little riptide where the current and the calmer bay water met. A field's length away, the water circled back in a giant arc.

It was still sunny and warm, but the sky was not cloudless. Suddenly this tenuous moment resonated. Kelsey could almost feel the turning point, like the wheel in the water, bringing fate back upon itself.

I must ask them to give up their inventions, their flying cars, their crystal weapons. I must speak for the mutants that wander this ruined city living in misery and filth, or live in harsh camps. Gentle, loyal, and shy creatures. She-Beast, with her bird feet and furry cat face and altogether human hands saved my life on two occasions. Tonight I will speak for her and her kind. But will they listen?

It was Quiri's charm that got us in here, to this hall, and the histoire that foretold a coming—strangers from an isolated island, with little to recommend them except the purity of their thoughts and a talent for crystle-minde. It was said they'd be traveling with gentle beasts, pursued by evil, bearing crystals, bathed by fire, carried by kindness over water, tested and proven lucky. That is our story so far.

Strangers meant to save a land from disaster. We are expected; we are destined.

But will they listen?

As Kelsey felt her alter-ego recede, she absorbed a massive guilt, a global guilt. Could what happened to Atlantis happen again today? Widespread destruction, entire continents, or perhaps entire oceans? Would it be a slow death or a sudden one? Again, Kelsey heard the sighing sound of a million souls dying at once.

Then she was back in the hall, the words tripped off her tongue haltingly. The language was foreign, even to Iriel, but the words came, just as she needed them. Her plea met a block, an opposition. Something more powerful than she'd ever imagined. Gewil and his army had arrived to oppose her, to absorb her. They had found the white crystal. The massive white crystal that started all the wars and set off the destruction. Lyticia's power source.

Brothers, Sisters, it is imperative that you hear me and join together to stop this evil. We are at the brink of disaster. It is impossible, I tell you, to control such force. Not even the ancient queen and her dwarf could hold it in their minds. We must stop . . .

"Hey Kelsey," George called. "What are you saying over there?"

She turned, embarrassed, and walked back to them. "Was I talking?"

"Practically shouting," said Red. "It sounded like Chinese."

"We've been calling you. We wanted to know what time it is," Jersey said.

She looked down at her pink wrist. "Twenty 'til." She looked up to see the four men bathed in light from the sinking sun, their skin glowing, their heads crowned with bright halos. They looked like angels. They only lacked wings.

"I'm getting out," said the first angel.

"Not yet," said the second.

"You going to stop me?"

"Yeah," said number three, his halo dimming just slightly. "It's our job."

"This should be fun to watch," said the angel with the red hair and the peeling shoulders. His halo slipped down over his right ear.

"Well, watch this," said the first angel, the big, strong boy angel. He sank below the water. He spit fountains at the two skinny ones. He sank again, shot wide of the red angel.

"Hey," said Jersey, wiping his eye. "I don't want your bad breath all over me."

"I'm cooked, anyway." Albert pulled himself up on the pool's edge.

"I'm going to call Cindy," George said. "And no one's going to stop me." He looked up at her. "Hey, Kelsey. Get me a towel, will you?"

She shook her head, but his smile, his square head, his bristly haircut were still appealing in the fairy light of her receding vision. She stood, holding his damp towel by a corner, waiting for him to get out. Instead, he slipped under the water. Only when he rose, the mischief clear on his face, did she get her warning. The mouthful of water began to arc skyward. She saw the pink inside of his mouth, his white teeth, the fountain coming at her. She too was moving slowly, sliding backward along the tiles. The water hit the turquoise rim and pooled there.

She dropped his towel into the puddle.

PART V

A Second Chance

You Change

I whisper my pain. Do you hear it? Do you see the darkest moment when I could not change another's mind? All the magic I could muster didn't work; my greatest trick, the time loop, failed, and failed again.

I can still hear their cries, a million souls dying at once. You've heard them too—their final moments of agony preserved forever in my memory. All because I could not fulfill my destiny. What failure was it? Lost nerve, weak will, or just some simple action that I overlooked?

If I could try once more, I'd ask One-God's intervention. Could I then restore the vanished world? Ah, prayer. It has become my perfect pastime. I do it mostly between lives.

Between lives, when peace is simple. Not being, not doing. Not undoing.

So where am I now? Certainly not wedded to the Light. Rather in some limbo of reincarnation, clinging to you, telling you my bits of truth. I am not free of life's misery, yet I do not fully live either. I am only a fragment, a disembodied memory. I cannot act; I only remember. Can I progress? It is not the usual way. It is most unusual.

Whether I called you, or you me, I know not. But you are the one who makes the choices, feels the world licking your face, tastes the dream. I can sometimes feel the life you have. Then you feel my life too. It is a strange gift we share.

Can you free me from this torment? Can you free yourself?

Try.

Chapter 31

Kelsey spent the last few minutes separate from the others. She'd chosen not to go into the claustrophobic atmosphere of her tent; instead she squatted behind it, hidden from the camp. A blue and yellow bird began to scold. The sound was vital, raucous and rhythmic, completely unabashed; it seemed bent on driving her away with the sheer assault of its voice. Then after a moment the bird burst into song, its serenade as sweet as its complaint had been strident.

Inside the hall, tables had been moved aside and chairs set up in rows. Rodman was already there, looking through his papers. Though it was past the hour, the hall was empty except for George, the bristly top of his head visible behind the row of computers.

"I let him have his call. I hope it calms him down." Rodman bent over his notes again. Dismissed, Kelsey wandered toward Henri who had come out of the kitchen.

"You're not getting your day off?"

"I am not making the dinner." He looked at her closely. "You are OK?"

Kelsey shook her head. "Un peu nerveux."

"I'm going to listen. I asked Monsieur Rodman." Henri lapsed into French. "Parce que, I told him I know everything already. I was here from the beginning. From before the beginning. After I finished Valentines in Cayman Islands, I came here. Avant le début."

Kelsey switched back to English. "So what was it like?"

"We have to make the kitchen. To clean everything. The people from before, they do not like your boss, Mr. Crouch. They leave a big mess."

Out of the corner of her eye, she saw Albert and Jersey come in. "You met him?"

"We speak on the phone many times, then he arrives to start the repair of the house. He did not see it before. Even if it was a ruin, he say it was nice, how you say, bonus. A very good price, he say that many times. He talks much of the many fine woods in the house."

"How long was he here?"

"Only one night. I cook a meal, we eat together, we have cigars and look at the ocean."

"Did he say anything about the project? Anything that might be important?"

Henri's face was pinched. "I will try to think for you."

At the back, George knocked over his chair. Sweaty and red-faced, he strode over.

"You're not going to believe this, Kelsey."

"You talked to your wife?" she prompted him.

"Shit, yeah, I talked to her. You'll never guess what she did."

Kelsey wondered what new twist his difficult wife had put on things.

George's straight teeth showed. "After our talk last night, I must have gotten her fired up, because she got up at eight this morning, packed up the baby, put on her good clothes, and went down to the bank. She wouldn't settle for the teller. She got all the way to the Vice President."

"That's good," said Kelsey. "Isn't it?"

"And you know what?"

"She tells them her mind?" Henri said.

"The thing is, my last paycheck never cleared."

"What do you mean?" Kelsey asked. "It bounced?"

"Not bounced, was never put in. It was supposed to be a direct deposit, you know, but it never went into the bank account."

"I don't understand," said Kelsey. "Payday was a while ago."

"I got no bonus," said George. "It was the fucking bonus check."

"You mean the extra for—"

"—and you know this is maybe good because it means I'm not liable or anything, for what happened because I didn't get—"

"But I don't believe it," Kelsey said.

"Maybe he runs out of money," Henri said. "Maybe he already spends too much on the pirate house. This is what he tells me, Kelsey, that he have so very much money to do whatever he want on the island, but you know sometimes people say this when it is not true, it is only—"

George cuffed Henri's shoulder. "So listen to this. She marched right down to BioVenture and read them the riot act, and you know what? They acted like they'd never heard of this check."

"Who did she talk to?"

"Those eggheads in accounting. Crouch's secretary. She was down there all day."

"With the baby?"

"Hey, Kelsey, George, let's get started," Rodman called.

"We can talk more later," Kelsey said, but George grabbed her arm.

"You know what I think? I think maybe Henri's right. I bet I'm not the only one who got stiffed. It's payday on Monday, and I bet all hell's going to break loose."

"OK," Rodman said. He and Wickstrom sat at the front, facing the rest. "We have everyone except Hilton. I guess we'll have to start without him."

Franklin reached down for the beer he had under his chair.

"No," Rodman said. "No alcohol."

"That sucks."

Rodman ignored it. "OK," he said. "You all know why we're here. I think it best to start with the new facts. Dr. Wickstrom?"

Wickstrom's hair escaped his gray ponytail. His glasses hung on a chain around his neck. "I would classify the new organism as different from the last strain I tested, CR 878, or first island generation, in three main ways. Let's call the new one G-1000, for George, who claims ownership." George, beside Kelsey, gripped his chair seat.

"First," Wickstrom went on. "G-1000 is in a different subfamily, Amerticitis, rather than Paramecialita. This has some important ramifications, the main being that the former classification tends to be more parasitic than the latter. Second, it is more adapted to warm temperatures. The third change, and this is important, is that it is adapting rapidly in response to any number of different chemicals. It seems able to grow, reproduce, and change some of its basic characteristics in response to the food source, to show a kind of sustenance preference, if you will. Given enough time, it will shift its preference to a second chemical. I had not been able to achieve that with any of the 800 series." Wickstrom coughed into his hand. "The other question, whether we have a problem with G-1000 and its toxicity to life, is a broad subject which, in my view, will require quite a bit of prudent research."

Kelsey unconsciously ran her hand over her throat.

"Estimated timetable?" Rodman asked.

"Years," said Wickstrom. "Decades. How many creatures are there in the sea?"

"That's ridiculous," Franklin said.

"We need answers now," said Red.

"You money guys are all the same," Wickstrom said.

"I don't like this fuck-up any more than anybody else," said Red. "And yeah, sure. I'm concerned about job security."

"Look," said Franklin. "We achieved our primary goal. That should count for a lot."

"Which goal was that?" Wickstrom asked, his eyebrows thrusting outward like horns.

"You were the one who got all misty eyed over 876. And you couldn't even keep it alive."

Wickstrom's mouth drew into a sour look that must have been characteristic over much of his life. "Who do you think is responsible for the power outages? I have my own suspicions."

Franklin's face grew red. "What are you saying?"

"OK," said Rodman, "I don't think this is going anywhere. What do you know so far about the toxicity of G-1000? Any hypotheses, Wick?"

"I obviously haven't been able to test any ocean life yet."

"What about the fish tank?" Red asked.

"We're looking at different subspecies," Rodman said. "Right, Wick?"

Wickstrom had his glasses back on and was studying his notes. "We can make no such assumption."

"How do you propose we proceed then?" Rodman asked. "How about the cleanup?"

"Our best option is to go back to the tanks and begin to run the tests we were sent out here to run in the first place." Wickstrom nodded toward George and Kelsey. "Without better equipment, and real medical tests, we can't be sure. I have skin and hair samples, covered with dead organisms, but don't know if any penetrated the skin, and if so, would they cause a problem? Regarding internal organs, we have no way of knowing. We're waiting for any symptoms to appear. We hope not."

"What if it's virulent?" asked Jersey. "How can we find that out? Quickly, I mean."

"Short of dissecting a human subject . . ." Wickstrom peered over his glasses at Franklin.

"What about the open water," Jersey asked, "where it was released today?"

"My best guess is that it will have nothing to feed on in the relative desert of the Caribbean. This is my hope anyway."

"Explain yourself," Rodman said.

"Warmer water is less oxygen saturated than cold," Albert said, "so it supports very little life other than in the specifically adapted environments like the reef. There's very little plankton, for example, compared to the Pacific. You have big lifeless expanses of water. In poetic terms, it's like a desert."

"The water is the sand?" George asked.

"I have a theory," said Wickstrom, "that the specimen seems to propagate best in high concentrations. That means tight spaces. Containers. Not the open ocean. Maybe they have some way of communicating at close range," he added.

There was a light laugh from one of the scientists, but Kelsey was thinking some form of mass consciousness, like a school of fish.

They argued about the practicality of going back to the dive site. George, strangely enough, seemed the most determined, despite Wickstrom's theory. "And if they did survive, you'd risk re-exposing yourselves."

"I want to go," said George. "I'm the one responsible."

"You're just the lackey," said Red.

"It won't do any good anyway," said Albert. "The probability of finding them again, with the currents and everything, is basically nil. They're part of the sea by now."

"I think we should get on with the tests," Franklin said. "Get ready for the boss."

"You want to stage a parade or something?" Red asked.

"Yeah," said Jersey. "What's the boss going to say about this?"

"I talked with him today," Rodman said. "A few times actually."

"Hey," said George, "I have something to say too."

"You'll get your turn," said Rodman.

"Why don't we take a break?" Wickstrom said. "Cool off a little."

Franklin had his beer again, and Rodman didn't say anything, so Red got one, then George, then Jersey. The group mood relaxed a notch. George told everyone about the missing bonus check, and Kelsey watched the reactions. Franklin cussed and slapped George on the back. She thought he might be covering, probably was. Rodman also seemed shaken by George's revelation. His face colored slightly above his beard. That was more interesting.

"So he was paying you extra?" Wickstrom had obviously been out of the loop on this bit of information. "To do what exactly?"

"I was supposed to bring the new samples here. I was keeping it secret so he could arrange the demonstration." He looked at Kelsey. "I wish now I hadn't done it."

"He offered me money today," Rodman volunteered.

Wickstrom's face grew long. "Why, Johnny?"

"Keep things quiet?" Red asked. "Not let it leak that we had an incident?"

"We talked about a lot of things. We should sit down. I have notes."

"No," said Kelsey. It was the first time she'd spoken. "I think this part should be informal."

"Off the record," said Jersey. "That's cool."

So Rodman told them about the calls, the first unpleasant, giving no details. "He still wants to do his demonstration. He might bring another organism from California. I told him there would be resistance from this community if he tried to inject it into open water again. He assured me he had no such intention. He implied George had acted without authority." Rodman paused. "That's where he wanted my . . . uh, support."

Kelsey felt the blood rush to her head as she decided what she wanted to say. "I'd like to know where everyone stands. Who was getting money, besides George?"

"Why would anyone admit they were taking money?" Franklin asked.

"Because we're going to find out anyway. Because this whole thing has gotten so far off track we can't go back to the way it was before."

"She's right," said Jersey.

Rodman looked around the group. He asked them one by one if they'd either received or been offered money by Crouch. They all denied it.

"Don't lie, Franklin," said Red. "We know that's how you got that hot car."

"You son of a bitch."

Franklin grabbed at him, and Red threw a block, a flash of white flesh—the underside of his arm—and Franklin's beer went flying. Now the smell was everywhere, the bottle spinning on the floor. Then, in an eye's blink, Wickstrom had a palm on each chest and the two were standing breathless and apart, nursing spots.

"He insulted me," Franklin said.

"You tore my shirt."

"Want to go sit in the sandbox awhile?" Wickstrom asked. "Plenty of it out there."

Franklin was panting still. "My sister died. That's how I got the fucking car. I wasn't smart enough to hit up the boss."

Red's face was crimson still, but the color slowly drained away. "That true?"

"Sure," said Franklin. "I swear on your mother's grave."

"I'm sorry then. My mistake. I apologize."

They shook, still wary, still hating each other—maybe not as much though.

"So if you didn't get any money," Red asked, "who did?"

Rodman cleared his throat. "I took money. Right at the beginning. I thought I was earning it for heading this project. There were no conditions. It was simply an extra check."

"Look," said Kelsey, "that doesn't really matter now. This project's basically over."

"What, we all just quit and go home?" Franklin asked.

"Not quit, we have a lot to do still, like Dr. Wickstrom said. We just know we can't meet the original commercial goal as it was lined out. Can we agree on that?"

"I don't get your reasoning at all," said Franklin.

"Don't you see? Crouch's action will go before the board of directors, and it will be questioned. What he did, what he had George do, is not in any way ethical. The EPA will make a stink about this. This project will be shut down. Maybe even the company."

"Not if we don't squeal," said Franklin.

She thought now of her own complicity, the shortcuts in the lab. Harmless perhaps? And then she thought of her father. And Lilya. "He's dangerous," she said, deciding so again. "What he's done, what we've helped him do, is dangerous."

Franklin waved his arms, and his smile came back. "My point is this was just a little internal incident, a slip up, a mistake. The important thing is the organism does what it was supposed to do. We've achieved our primary goal. Don't you see what our co-operation might be worth to him?"

"You're suggesting group extortion?" Wickstrom asked.

"Stock options. If this goes big, it could be worth some bucks."

"So what you're saying is," said Jersey, looking at Albert, "that we test it, it's safe, it has a commercial value, it gets patented, widespread use, fortunes are made. A lot of ifs."

Franklin had a new beer. "Just think of the applications. This could make us all rich."

Henri broke in. "That's what he said to me, Kelsey. I did not want to tell you before."

"What are you talking about, Henri?"

"That he was going to make so much money. He wanted me to—how you say?—put money in for seed."

"Invest?" she asked.

"I have some money from the vineyard sale. I give him that. For the company. Plus my salary, three months. That is for stock too."

"You didn't," Kelsey said.

"I did." The chef's face had gone white. "Maybe you are wrong about this, Kelsey."

It was after six now. Alberto put his head out the kitchen door, but Henri waved him back. Outside, they could see the flicker of the lanterns being lit.

"You did the projections, Albert," Jersey said. "What do you think?"

The chairs were in a circle. "We were looking at populations," Albert said carefully, "which is where I get my ideas about the dispersion patterns of the organism. I basically agree with Dr. Wickstrom that they will not thrive in low-oxygenated water—maybe in the surf—but probably not deep water. Also, we did analysis of population explosions in projected ideal conditions."

"You and Stillman," said Rodman. "How did that come out?"

"It was very rapid propagation," said Albert, "in the case of a contained environment. The ocean, of course, is a practical infinity."

Unless, thought Kelsey, *the ocean became the container*.

"Weren't you supposed to be projecting the absorption rate of different chemicals," Rodman asked, "adaptation of the specimen, that sort of thing?"

"Stillman had already done it, I think."

"I'd better talk to him," said Rodman.

"He seemed mostly concerned with population control. He seemed to be asking a lot of what ifs: what if there's a spill, what if the population is too large, what if there's a storm and it spreads." Albert looked up and his eyes seemed smaller. "It's almost like he was prescient."

"Maybe he's the one taking extra money," Franklin said.

"That's not fair," said Kelsey. "He's not here to defend himself."

"He your boyfriend?" Franklin asked.

Rodman put up his palm. "I have a couple more quick things, and then we'll eat. Crouch is in California for the weekend, having meetings, dinners, what not. He plans to play golf with the chairman of the board, and someone else." Rodman looked down at his notes. "Esquibal, someone named Esquibal, I think."

"Don't know him," said Wickstrom.

"He was glad we had fish in the tanks, wanted to see something Monday when he gets here. So I had Dr. Wickstrom make the first injection just before the meeting."

"I remember now," said Wickstrom. "It's not Esquibal, it's SK Bell. They're the new client. My guess is those guys are coming. That's why he wants to put on a good show."

There were voices outside, laughter, then someone shushing. The door to the dining hall darkened with several figures.

"Hey," said one of them. "What's going on everyone? I thought you'd be eating dinner."

"Where the hell have you been?" Red asked.

"Down at the Pirate's house, Mate." Henry Hilton gave a group salute. He moved toward them, tripping over something. He turned to the group in the doorway and laughed.

"Who's that with you?" Rodman asked. "This is a closed meeting."

"I didn't know about any meeting," said Hilton.

"You've been gone all day," said Rodman.

"Hey, I brought dinner guests. Friends of Kelsey's."

Kelsey recognized Keith, but the other two were behind him, their shapes masked. The image of the passing boat flashed into her mind. The dark figures, a bit of red. Kelsey moved toward the couple. They were grinning as they came into the room. The big frizz of hair, the mismatched sizes: friends indeed. Each took a hand.

"We have so much to tell you, Kelsey," said Irma.

"You're not going to believe what we're doing here," Ben said.

"What?" Kelsey asked. "Certainly not the pirate dig." And then she knew. "You're going back into the burial mounds, aren't you? You're going after Atlantis."

Chapter 32

Kelsey had been afraid to ask Rodman for permission to call Harrison—even if he granted it, he'd know of their alliance. Then she did ask, and he denied her request. It turned out he already knew from the log that they'd had communications. He gave her a lecture on fraternization and sent her away. "Everything is out in the open from now on," he'd said.

She was staring into Tank One—only a hint of the telltale color remained—when Wickstrom and George came out of the lab. Wickstrom, wearing gloves, was holding an empty test tube with a tong. He bent to take a sample.

"Is the organism still alive in there?" she asked.

"Last sample was down 32 percent. That was over an hour ago."

"Why, do you think?"

"Not enough concentration. Plus I can't introduce any chemicals without Hilton's explicit approval. And he's disappeared again."

"How about an interim-sized container?"

He smiled. "Come back into the lab with me, Sweetheart. I want to check you again."

"But hurry, Kelsey," George said. "We have a lot to do still."

The lab was messy, the live specimens declaring themselves by their shimmering colors. Wickstrom whistled a tune as he examined her throat and upper chest with a magnifying glass.

"How's George today?" she asked.

"Complained of a sore throat."

She was startled. "It's related?"

"Probably not. I checked out his mouth pretty thoroughly and didn't find anything. He said he smoked pot last night, so that's probably it."

She squinted, trying to remember. "Did he hold the vial in his teeth to open it maybe?"

"Now that's a theory. But no, he said he hadn't. Was a little scared, though, by the throat thing. Doesn't like to admit it. He's just a mixed-up kid, you know."

"I guess I better talk to him." She slid down from her stool. "Want me to help today?"

"Maybe tomorrow, Doll."

All morning, as Kelsey and George cataloged the tanks, boats crossed the bay. Irma and Ben helping Keith move out of the pirate's house, workmen getting it ready. Mid-afternoon, as arranged, Keith stopped by to take her to see the dig.

"They've got five carpenters and a bunch of guys cleaning up and painting and stuff," he told her. "Besides there's all those boxes to unpack. Irma checked it out. Expensive stuff. Silk sheets, crystal, the works."

They hugged the shoreline, following rough terrain, impassible by foot. They passed a gorgeous cove, a real beauty cut into the rock with trailing vines and a narrow white beach. Not far beyond it, Keith tied the boat to a small tree and they climbed the cliff, hands and feet, to get to the path through the jungle. "We found this trail on our second trip today," Keith said. "It's much more reasonable access than the point. A little overgrown, but I've cleared it up some."

They walked half a mile through low-growing vegetation and twisted palms, complaining about the heat and humidity. When they neared the camp, Irma ran out to greet them. She pulled Kelsey into the camp, a shady grove where two big tents were pitched. One was the kitchen, the smaller was for sleeping. They had an outdoor fire pit, three hammocks, and a minimally constructed lean-to for the tools. The dig, not far away, was on a rocky outcropping overlooking the sea.

Standing in front of the temple, Kelsey felt an immediate sensation: a fragility in the air like at high elevation. The jungle had encroached on more than one side, its tentacles spreading under and around the rocks. One vine had entirely surrounded a stone and lifted it aside. Something ran out of the hole—a bright green iguana—and scurried away.

Kelsey was drawn to the most intact face of the structure. A shaft of light penetrated the trees and illuminated a carved inscription. She could make out the symbols of a man and a woman and a cat-like beast, and a radiating star. The glyph covered two large stones, and the third seemed to interrupt the story, for it cut a symbol in half with its blank face.

"You found it quickly," Keith said. "I only knew about it from the papers. See how it's almost disappearing as the sun moves?" Last night he'd told them that he couldn't get the idea of the site out of his mind, so he'd contacted his old professor who'd posted his work on the web. "Amazing, isn't it, how this dig just came together like instantly? I was supposed to pack up, but for some reason I didn't. I just took off and left my tools. Then these two were at the airport, like they were waiting for me. I think we're going to have better luck this time."

"Sure," said Irma. "Kelsey's here."

Kelsey ignored this. "What does this say?"

Ben approached the writing. "Here lies dearly departed . . .."

Irma punched him. "No, Honeybunch, read it like you did this morning."

Ben put his thick glasses back on. "East to West, then something like star and boat, travel by sea. This here," he pointed to a box with a slash across it, "means death, no—early death, and this circle means many. The first of it is cut off." He looked up. "You read it right to left."

Kelsey felt a chill. *East to West*, haven't I heard that before? She moved her finger over the glyph, starting from the middle of the blank stone. "It says a great storm came to a far land and caused many to die an early death, then those buried here traveled to the west by boat, or star boat. A man and a woman." *Or it could be a woman and her unborn son.* She paused, her hand hovering over the picture of the beast. It seemed the strangest of the pictures. "What about this?"

"A jaguar. A symbol of power," said Ben. "This was someone with power and status, a tamer of beasts. A ruler. Man-God. Woman-God. You tell me."

She touched her fingertip to the glyph and got a little jolt.

The great cat sits placidly beside the pyramid door waiting for my Man-Son, Rotan. When Rotan brought the cat back from the hunting trip, snarling on a rope, I tamed it with my jewel. But the beast is not my friend, despite my magic. It loves only Rotan, licking his face with its sandy tongue, gnawing his hair, and purring so loudly I can't sleep. It's black as the night it watches, and its eyes are pale green, like my stone. The beast frightens everyone. Someday it will grow a taste for human flesh.

"Are you getting a connection, Kelsey?" Irma asked.

"I think so," said Ben grinning.

"I saw the jaguar. It was kept as a pet, but it wasn't tame. It was terrible and terrifying."

"It would have been legendary," Ben said.

"That is so cool," said Irma, taking her arm. "Here we are in the jungle, and you're getting pictures in your head. I can't believe it's happening, can you, Honeybunch?"

"Well, sure. We knew that Kelsey—"

"From the moment I set eyes on this place I knew it was the one. In fact, from the moment we met Keith and knew we were coming here, that you were already here, I was just so excited. Tell me everything, Kelsey. Do you think it's your people? Was it maybe even you, from the past? Have we found your grave?"

Putting it that way gave Kelsey another jolt. Irma had her by the shoulders now. "We're going to find something. I just know it. We're going to find proof that you lived before."

"Honeybunch," said Ben, "we've talked about this. Irma, remember?"

"No, Ben, you're wrong this time. I have a real hunch."

Keith had been watching with an uncertain expression. "Hocus pocus aside, we'll never know anything if we don't get started."

They began to number the loose stones and move them aside. Keith was planning to apply for a grant to restore the pyramid, but first, he wanted to see the bones and any artifacts that might be buried there. They had moved maybe five stones and were just beginning to scratch at the cool earth when Ben hit bone. It was better even than that—the shine of gold was quickly apparent.

The artifact was revealed as a finger joint encircled with a golden ring; strangely, it was unattached to any hand. But the ring seemed authentic enough: a flattened circlet with an empty setting, the tiny bone speaking of a time when people were smaller. Keith identified it as the middle joint of an index finger. They went back to digging.

Surrendering to the meditation of the work, Kelsey let go of the eerie sensation that had clung since Irma's comment. A few bones were not going to prove anything. Instead, it seemed a mirror was there in the dirt, reflecting her doubled life.

"Wow," Ben called, "look at this." He was squatting with a flashlight at the hole the iguana had been in. He pulled out a slice of stone.

"Hey, I looked in there this morning," Keith said.

"Yeah, well this was lying right on the surface." Ben shone the light across the front of the hole. "It practically bit me."

Keith, obviously irritated, snatched the tablet, and the others gathered around. It was the size and shape of a poetry volume, made of hard, shale-like stone and covered with writing.

"What is it?" Irma asked. "Can you read it, Ben?"

"Looks like a map," said Kelsey, brushing some of Irma's frizz out of her face.

"A star map. See this?" Ben pointed to lines that linked several points and a little drawing at the base, something like a compass.

"Yeah," said Keith, "An ancient star chart—for navigation. Wow."

Kelsey felt a chill run up her spine. This *did* feel familiar.

Irma jumped up and down. "It's proof. Real proof."

Ben was watching his wife. "Could be Maya, Honeybunch."

"I've not seen anything quite like it, though," said Keith.

"It's them," said Irma. "Don't you think so, Kelsey?"

But she felt only a cold touch when she held the tablet in her hands, the distant past, dead ones, no message.

"I don't get it," said Keith, shining the flashlight into the hole. "This was the first place I looked yesterday. And this morning, twice at least. I kept checking, like a compulsion, you know." He turned to Ben. "Are you playing a trick on me?"

Ben frowned. "Why would I do that?"

Keith was rolling the flashlight between his hands. "It's not right. Something's happening. Something creepy."

"I think we're getting help," said Irma, opening her palms to the sky.

Keith started pawing the opened earth. He came up with another small bone, which he held aloft, the third joint of the finger. He started spinning, the bone pointed obscenely toward the heavens. "You think you're fooling me? Come out and show yourself. I'm not scared."

The rest of the afternoon produced more bones, and in the hole, a potshard, a feather, and just before dusk, a turquoise stone. They began calling it "the mailbox." Despite the joke, everyone was keyed up and nervy, and they only broke for supper due to the failing light. Ben was cooking his famous vegetable stew, and Kelsey was invited. Now she and Irma sat dangling their feet over the sea, watching the sunset.

"There's a weird energy here," said Irma. "Like poltergeists."

"I agree," said Kelsey. "It feels haunted."

"Keith is pretty jumpy. Do you think anything bad is going to happen?"

"No," said Kelsey. But the rocks below looked suddenly treacherous.

"How about back there?" Irma pointed over her shoulder meaning the scientists' camp. "I've been watching you. You're worried."

"Maybe I should have gone back tonight."

"You're not really one of them, though." Irma rubbed the rosy flesh on the inside of her knees. "Something's off with you. Is it a man? I think it's a man. It has to be a man."

Had the poltergeists gotten hold of Irma's tongue tonight? "No. Well, that's over."

"That man who came to get you?" Irma asked. "You acted terrified that night."

"Harrison? He's a friend." Kelsey looked out to sea. "It was someone else. A relationship that went bad. There was violence."

"Wow," said Irma, her eyes gone big.

Suddenly a motorboat could be heard rounding the point and Kelsey stood. She'd been caught up in the larger trouble, the pattern of repetition she was seeing everywhere, but now, the personal felt near at hand, ready to spring back into the forefront. She felt a rush of relief as she recognized the man driving the boat. Henry Hilton. His wake settled, circling back to the cliffs.

"Henry!" Irma shouted over the sound of the motor.

He tied the skiff and started climbing. Irma was yelling instructions about the handholds. The cliff was difficult; Henry was winded and red-faced by the time he got to the top.

"Hey, Kelsey. They sent me out to find you," he said between breaths.

"She's staying for dinner," said Irma. "You can too, if you want."

Much to Kelsey's surprise, Henry pulled a satellite phone out of his pocket and called Rodman. On the way back to the campsite, Kelsey asked how he'd gotten the phone. It seemed a flagrant violation.

"I offered to do delivery co-ordination for Rodman. Business only." He seemed about to say something more but grinned instead and told her the latest news: George and Wendell had come up with zilch on the reef.

That night, they danced wildly to music on Keith's boom box. Everyone drank too much, and laughed and sweated. Henry Hilton grew breathless and red in the face and had to lie down. Then Irma and Ben started arguing.

Long after the others had quieted, Kelsey could hear them talking in their tent, then making love. Henry was snoring. Still, she waited. She'd found Hilton's phone—his shirt was hanging from a twig and the phone was in the pocket—and now she tiptoed past the pyramid, out to the point. She could feel the cool stone, the promise of more contact with the dead. For a moment she felt tempted to touch it, blindly, in darkness, commune with those within. Instead she stayed in the open and dialed Harrison's number.

"Kelsey! I can barely hear you."

"I can't talk very loud," she whispered. "What have you found out?"

He told her he'd just gotten home from California, and that he'd had a long, frank talk with Rodman just moments ago. They'd come to an understanding. Rodman was playing it straight until after the visit, then he'd co-operate with any investigation the board entertained.

"What about Molly?"

Harrison laughed. "She's good, Kelsey. Been going through all your notes, systematically documenting the multiple strains. That will help in the end."

"That purple coloration," said Kelsey. "I had that early on. Then they took it to California. That's what Wick thinks."

"Wickstrom?" A note of surprise in his voice. "Listen, Kelsey. Money's the thing now. This new client is demanding a faster timetable and tangible results. That's why Crouch told George to go ahead with the demo."

She told him about the discussion of wild profits by some of the men.

"Not likely," he said. "Basically Crouch is way over budget, and it looks like he might have cooked the books—that's what this accountant told me—and unless he gets an infusion of cash, they're going to shut the project down entirely. And somehow the Belizean government got stirred up and is giving him a lot of trouble. By the way," he said. "I'm flying out early tomorrow. Should be there mid-afternoon."

"That's great news. I'll have them clean up your tent."

Harrison paused. "Thing is, Crouch fired me. I've got to be underground. I'm prepared to camp out."

"Fired? But I need you."

"Maybe it's better this way. I can get more done if he doesn't know I'm there."

"I think we should protest."

"He's getting desperate, Kelsey. Be careful. Don't tip your hand. Don't piss him off."

"What can he do? Fire me too?" she said. "Sounds like it's over anyway. Maybe we should go to the board, lay it all out for them."

"No," he said. "I need you on the inside. It's the end game now. There's a lot at stake."

She remembered the dolphin message, *No creature harm.* "Like my father," she said. "Only it's a lot bigger, and it's our job to stop him this time."

"Right," he said.

"You could stay at the dig," she said after a pause.

"What dig?"

So she told him about the temple and Iriel's strange connection to it, the magical flying bones, Keith's panic, everybody's heightened energy. She must have been too enthusiastic because she didn't notice at first that he'd gone quiet.

"What happened, Harrison?" she asked, knowing as clearly as if a gong had gone off that it was Stan. "You saw him. Something happened. Tell me."

"I can't talk anymore right now, Kelsey." He was suddenly whispering too. "Everything is going to work out. Just one more night then I'll be there." The knot in her stomach clenched, as she told him to please, please be careful.

"Don't worry," he said. "I'll see you tomorrow."

Kelsey made a nest on the floor in the kitchen tent, between Keith's cot and Henry Hilton. The ground felt hard, the Mexican blankets scratchy under her legs, and just as she began to doze, Henry started snoring again. She woke with a start. She could hear the trees rattling in the wind and thunder approaching.

Why was she so frightened now? Harrison had said everything was fine, hadn't he? It was the proximity of the grave, she told herself. She could feel Iriel—no longer vibrant and defiant but weakened, half dead already—reaching out with skeletal fingers. Death, patiently waiting, enticing, with its promise of eternal decay.

Something is following me. I begin to run, though I know that is wrong. I am old, too old. My breath comes hard, my knees ache; blood rises in my head, and everything turns dark and unfamiliar. Lost again! Now I hear a rustling at my heel. I spin and lose my balance, but my stone jumps into my hand. Its beam ricochets off a rock; I smell singed fur, and the beast slinks away between the trees.

Suddenly Kelsey could smell Stan's skin, salty and pungent from lovemaking. It was so real she thought he was in the tent. But it was just her senses playing tricks.

Now the rain drummed down. Here in the close tent with the two sleeping men, she twisted deeper into the scratchy blanket and felt the hard ground under her bones. She wrapped her blanket over her head to block out the snoring, but it was to no avail. She had to live the night, the endless hours of tortured thinking, waiting for the dawn.

Chapter 33

The next morning while Kelsey and Wickstrom and Henry were working on the chemical sequence, Rodman came by and confiscated Henry's phone.

"I have deliveries coming in," Henry said.

"This is a scientific operation. Try concentrating on that." Rodman flipped through the phone's log. "You call Stillman last night?" he asked.

"I swear, I didn't."

Rodman gave Kelsey a look. "You want to tell me what's going on here?"

She shook her head.

"OK," said Rodman, "but I've got my eye on you two."

They had cultures going in Tanks One and Two, no fish. They had all been moved to Tank Three. Wickstrom had told them his concerns: the organism was changing in unpredictable ways, and it was not particularly geared toward the list of compounds Crouch had provided. "It's highly volatile," he said.

Still they made progress throughout the day, Kelsey providing the link between George at the tanks and the field lab. Wickstrom was at last listening to her ideas. They were using some of the same chemical combinations she'd discovered in the lab at BioVenture. Hilton, by clever substitution, was getting closer to the noxious by-products that the new company, SK Bell, wanted to dump into the Gulf of Mexico somewhere east of Houston. Or was already dumping.

The clouds built, and conversation threaded through the work.

Kelsey learned that Wickstrom had a daughter in Denver, a single mother who was running for a legislative seat, and that his nine year-old grandson was already studying high school science. Hilton told them of his interest in science fiction, and his nascent attempts at writing. Then he confessed he'd made a little money handling orders and deliveries for the camp.

"Of what?" Kelsey asked.

"Parts, supplies, frozen foods," Hilton said. "Whatever we need."

"So that's what you've been up to," Wickstrom said. "You sly dog."

Later George came in to tell them a crab had fallen into Tank One and died. Dissection proved a parasitic invasion had shut down its nervous system. The poor creature's flesh had turned a lovely cooked blue.

About three o'clock, Rodman gathered those he could find to announce that Crouch had called from Belize City. He had flown in a day early on a private jet, and they were refueling at the airport at this moment. They would be flying to another island which had an airstrip, and from there taking a seaplane. All this was expected to consume three to four more hours. They were hoping to beat the dark.

"First thing in the morning," said Rodman to Wickstrom, "have something ready to go."

"You want me to stay up all night?"

Rodman looked at him. "If necessary."

"All right Johnny, we'll put on a great big effort the rest of the afternoon. We'll be out here working when he arrives. I just can't seem to keep it going in these frigging tanks."

"Well, think of something. Don't let me down." Thunder sounded in the distance, and Rodman looked up. "What's going on with this weather? Anybody know?"

"If you'd let us have a phone line, I'd check it out," said Albert.

Albert and Franklin were paired up to use the computer. The two looked at each other while Rodman went over his checklist of everyone's afternoon assignments.

"How about Henri. We need dinner. More formal, I think. Everyone dress up."

"He's sulking," said Albert. "He says he won't cook."

"Well, he picked a hell of a time. Somebody go talk to him, please."

Kelsey found the chef lying on his bed, reading. When she told him that Crouch and his guests were arriving that evening, Henri barely moved. He said he wasn't cooking.

"Because of the money?" Kelsey asked.

"He will have to give it back before I cook one pea for him."

"He's bringing guests."

"They can eat sand."

Kelsey staunched her laughter for she saw the chef was serious in his distress. "It will all work out, Henri," she said. "The company will be responsible for its debts."

"I gave the money direct to him."

"What, in cash?"

"I write a check with his name on it. I get no receipt. I am a stupid, stupid man." He fell back on his bed and took up his book.

Rodman had taken Franklin out to the pirate's house, and they'd been gone two hours now. Red was in the lab helping Wickstrom compile characteristics and chart a progression of evolution. These were the questions Wickstrom most wished to solve: how did one evolution lead to the next? what mysterious mechanism triggered the rapid simultaneous changes in the individuals? Henry and Kelsey were working outside when the rain came driving in, a deluge, sheets of rain.

As they were struggling with the wooden tank covers, Jersey and Albert ran over, shielding their faces with their arms. "We need something to cover the tub."

"Kelsey, you go," said Wickstrom, "Take the tarp. I need Jersey."

As they ran through the rain, sandals slipping on the muddy trail, lightning flashed all around. Kelsey began picking up rocks to use as weights. Holding them and the flapping tarp, she bent to the tub's edge. Something wasn't right. The water, rain bouncing on its shimmering surface, was tinged a rich violet pink.

"Did you get it covered?" Wickstrom's ponytail was dripping down his back.

"The tarp is torn. It'll leak. Does that matter?" she asked

"Not much, I guess. Well, we'd like to contain it, that's all."

"I'm really, really worried."

"OK," he said. "Who got into the tub besides the dynamic duo?"

"I don't know. Did anyone get in last night?"

"I never go near the thing." Wickstrom's eyebrows twitched. "So it must have been George then. It must have been in his throat all the time. Did he spit in the tub or something?"

"He was making fountains."

"Stupid," said Wickstrom. "The fucking environment is perfect. The heat for one thing. Why didn't we think of that? And chemicals? They use any chemicals?"

She held up the plastic container of Tulip Tub.

He was staring at her with his pale, intelligent eyes. "I'll have Hilton analyze it. Where'd he go anyway? Where's Albert?"

"Where's Jersey?"

"Still tracking the storm. The U.S. weather bureau is calling it a low-level disturbance, but he saw something on one of his sites that got him interested. Some renegade weather station out in the eastern Caribbean predicting it might develop."

"Into what?"

"Nothing, Doll Face, just a little rain. We sit tight, ride it out. No problem."

She spoke carefully. "What about people traveling?"

"You worried about the boss?"

She shook her head.

"OK. Don't tell me your little secrets." But his manner was friendly. "You going to check on George now? Bring him here, would you, Luv?"

As she went outside, the storm was lifting. She saw light at the horizon, a patch of blue. She found George sleeping on his bed wearing only his under-shorts, a sheaf of papers clutched in his hand. His forehead was blazing hot.

He kept asking about a fire truck, if she'd seen a fire truck, if she'd gotten down the license plate. He was frowning with effort and vexation as she told him, no, she'd missed it.

"Damn it, why can't you do anything right?" He fell back on the bed, his head rolling from side to side. She feared he was going to go into some kind of a fit, but he focused again. "I'm glad about the baby, Cindy, really I am. Maybe it'll be a girl this time."

"We've got to get his fever down," Wickstrom said when she told him.

"That's what I was thinking. I was thinking ice. Anything else?"

"Aspirin, if you can find it. We're ill-equipped here. Besides . . ." He let the sentence trail off. She knew what he meant. They weren't dealing with an ordinary flu bug. "We should probably get him off the island."

"Maybe we can get him stable for traveling," she said, "then take him to the nearest hospital as soon as the seaplane arrives."

"That's Belize City." Wickstrom's face was wrinkled with worry. "Of course, the states would be best. I don't know how much time we've got."

Together they bathed George and changed his sheets, then settled him in the bed again. He was cold now, and they covered him with his blanket and left him sleeping. When they got outside it was late and the sky was bright and clear again, and a light breeze was blowing. Kelsey said she needed to go out to the dig to see if Ben and Irma had any of the jungle medicines they'd studied.

As she was looking for the camp's boat, finding only the rowboat, beginning to curse her luck, Keith arrived in his skiff. He had a big grin on his face, a kind of now-I-know-what-you're-up-to grin, so even before he told her, she knew that Harrison had arrived.

Harrison and Kelsey sat together on the outcropping near the anthropologists' camp. He seemed to be studying the weather to the east—perfectly clear except for a low bank of clouds at the horizon.

Kelsey was studying him, trying not to show it. It was the indeterminate interval before she was to return with Ben, Irma, and Keith to the scientists' camp. Henri had become expansive at the end, the more people to eat his feast, the better. Dinner was presumably on hold until the seaplane arrived.

Harrison had refused to talk about the "little problem" he'd taken care of," beyond the basic facts. When he'd gone to her house to collect her things, Stan had been there, living there—the horror of that still made her queasy—but Harrison had gotten him out, and it was over. He kept saying that: "It's over, Kelsey. You can forget about him."

"But how?" she'd asked. "What happened?"

"Let's just say I had him removed," Harrison said. "He's got bigger problems than you right now."

So she thought Stan was in some kind of legal trouble, maybe drug trouble. She thought he was immobilized by whatever Harrison had done. She both wanted to know more and didn't.

"I guess we should go back soon," Kelsey said now. "I just wish you'd come, that's all."

"Irma will be more help than me."

Irma, it turned out, had been a nurse in the Peace Corps. At this moment she was studying her books and selecting tinctures, herbs, and jungle remedies from her supplies.

"What I meant is," said Kelsey "there's really not much advantage to hiding. Not with George sick."

Harrison shook his head. "Crouch is like a cornered dog. Let him have his night of glory, let him hang himself, if he's going to." Suddenly he put his finger to his lips and turned back to stare at the sea.

She saw nothing new, heard nothing, just the light chop slapping at the cliff. Perhaps that was what interested him, the subtle change in the weather, the freshening breeze. The white cloud, bright in the lowering sun, was slightly closer now; it looked like a tumble of surf. Kelsey imagined it that way, a massive wave crashing, rolling in to engulf them. She let herself go into that moment of terror, and then it passed. If there was more to face, she would. There was no question of that. That's when she felt Harrison looking at her. He put his arm around her shoulders and she leaned into him; then his lips were at the corner of her mouth. It lasted only a second before they were interrupted by the sound of the distant engine. They stayed, cheeks touching, as the seaplane descended toward the ocean, its headlamps lighting the water and the irregularities beneath.

Minutes later, Kelsey and Harrison and Keith were standing by the pyramid. Keith was lamenting the rain; they'd had a good morning, most of the rest of the skeleton had turned up, but now their holes were muddy. She tuned him out. She wanted to show Harrison the inscription. Though she couldn't see it in the near darkness, she went right to it, hands outstretched like antenna. She traced the outlines of the cat, the moon. Harrison ran his hands over the stones until he got to the blank one. He knocked, the chamber echoed.

Suddenly Kelsey knew there would be a weak corner. "Here," she said. "Help me."

Harrison took out his knife and pried the stone loose.

Bones of the cat came out, tail first. She could almost hear its snarl and feel the menacing coil in its legs. She knew the cat had outlived Iriel and so been buried with her son, Rotan. The important thing, the treasure that still hung around the beast's neck, Rotan had, of course, inherited from his mother.

The ribbon and pouch had long since decayed, but the stone had not changed in ten thousand years. It was pure green energy. It was Iriel's crystal.

Chapter 34

"What makes the light? It's so pretty." Keith came toward her, reaching for the stone which was indeed casting a pale green circle of light across her palm. "It'll be the foremost piece in our collection. In a museum, of course, it's museum quality, just stunning, an incredible find, and you'll get the credit, naturally."

Kelsey dropped the stone into the pocket of her shorts.

"Hey! That belongs to the dig!" Keith reached for the pocket; Kelsey sidestepped.

Whirling away from Keith, Kelsey kept her hand protectively around the little crystal. Although it was smaller than an egg, bigger than a marble, it was surprisingly heavy. And warm. Buzzing with warmth, almost talking.

"Kelsey." Irma came forward. "Let me touch it. Please." She was smiling, beguiling, completely un-trustworthy. Kelsey knew this from the stone.

Irma and Keith started circling. Suddenly Irma lunged. Ben grabbed her, and Harrison took Keith; a kind of shock went through the group.

"Honeybunch! I've never seen you act like this. You were almost physically violent."

Irma looked abashed, but she seemed to be formulating another argument as well.

"I don't feel anything now," Ben went on. "The phenomenon seems worse when it's visible. Perhaps you should keep it in your pocket, Kelsey."

"She can't keep it in her pocket," said Keith. "It belongs to the world."

"You mean you," said Ben.

Kelsey finally spoke. "Remember last night? You were dying to know what was driving the magic, the unrest? Well, this is it. It belonged to my . . . my ancestor. It's my birthright. And now it's been returned."

"That's baloney. You can't steal artifacts."

"You think this dig is baloney? The inconsistencies, the strange occurrences, the ease?"

"She's right, of course," said Irma.

"She's just saying," said Ben, "that all this wouldn't have happened without her magic. Who knows what more might come to light if we stick it out? I'd say you better get a grip on yourself if you want to finish this dig. I'd say if you don't straighten out, some arm bone is likely to conk you on the head in the middle of your solar shower."

Keith was left behind with Harrison, and Irma, Kelsey, and Ben headed back to the scientific camp in Keith's boat. They used the searchlight to illuminate the water, and each time Irma alerted Ben to the presence of reef, he brought the craft to a full stop and came forward to inspect the channel. They finally settled on the best method of navigation: Irma driving from the stern while Ben called out instructions to her. In this way they finally found deep water. Then Ben took over and Irma sat in the bow, her hair billowing behind her.

The moon had escaped the clouds at the horizon. Not quite full—it hung heavy and low in the sky, misshapen still—the unusual yellow color made the face appear bilious and sallow.

Whenever Kelsey touched the crystal—to reassure herself of its safety—she felt her perception enhanced in some way. The water upon which they rode seemed to be expanding—a seething power, waking now from its bed beneath the surface. The salty wind, the purpling clouds, foretold rain. The rain future, she did not like. The other future, the evening ahead, seemed paradoxically scripted but unwritten. And George? She got no answer. Her probing seemed to offend or tire the little stone.

George had been sleeping when she left, and his body had cooled almost back to normal. She and Wickstrom had had a hopeful conversation. George had likely introduced the organism to his mouth with the stick of gum. Perhaps that was why he got sick and the others hadn't. But as they approached the lights of the camp, she felt worry concentrate in the pit of her stomach.

The seaplane, with its peeling paint job and scummy surface, was anchored in the bay, perched on its pontoons like an ugly water bug. As Irma and Ben carefully maneuvered around it, she could have reached out and touched it. But with her hand on the crystal, she felt a violent vibration, as though the plane had crashed once, or would, and she shrank away. As they disembarked, George staggered toward them through the thickest part of the sand.

"What are you doing up?" Kelsey put the back of her hand to his forehead.

"Oh, Kelsey, I thought for a moment you were my wife. You see I dreamed about her. She's pregnant again, did I tell you? I must have slept too long because I can't seem to wake up."

"You don't remember having a fever?"

Irma had him by the arm and was leading him toward the dining hall. "I want to take a look at your color," she said, "in the light.

Extra lanterns had been placed on the path leading up to the dining room, giving it a festive air, and they could hear voices coming from inside. Only after she followed the others through the open door did Kelsey think of her torn shorts and windblown hair, her sandy bare feet.

Myron Crouch, wearing a red Hawaiian shirt and holding a champagne glass, was facing her, talking with Rodman and two other men. One, tall, his suit jacket removed and tie loosened, was listening raptly. To his left, a stocky Asian man in immaculate golf clothes shifted his stance and looked away. Crouch, though staring straight ahead, seemed not to see: His gaze slid past her and out the door. She half-turned, but no one was there—only the empty evening.

All the scientists were dressed in their island finery; even

Franklin had on a button-down shirt and loafers instead of his toe-less tennis shoes. Rodman followed the gaze of the short man that was now fastened on her—the money guy, Kelsey figured—and hurried over.

"Kelsey. Put on a dress, for God's sake. I thought you were sick," he said to George. "Well, thank God you're up. What are these two doing here?"

"Irma's a nurse," said Kelsey. "Besides, Henri invited them."

"You're feeling better?" Rodman asked George. "Well, maybe everything's going to be all right, after all. Crouch liked the hot tub, by the way, Tank A we're calling it."

Kelsey stared at him in amazement. "You made that out to be a good thing?"

"Don't be a naysayer tonight, Kelsey. Please."

"Who are those two guys?"

Rodman told her they were Mr. Stevens from SK Bell and Liu, CFO of BioVenture, Cal Branch, and that Wick was preparing some demonstrations. No fish. Rodman actually looked a little chagrined. "OK, with George better, things are looking up aren't they?"

"But after the demonstration, then what?"

Rodman shook his head. "That hasn't developed."

The crystal was throbbing in her pocket.

"I was never very sick," George piped up. "I just had a little headache and took a nap."

Rodman's face darkened. "You had us worried."

Kelsey showered and dressed quickly, fashioned a pouch for the crystal and secured it around her waist under her sarong. When she re-entered the hall, cocktail glasses had supplanted a number of the flutes, and the noise level had risen. They had their buzz, so who cared if dinner was delayed? Several people noted her entrance—Irma, who was talking with Henry Hilton and George, Crouch, with an ironic nod, and Wickstrom, who looked trapped with the bosses and their important guests. Franklin broke away, picking up another champagne flute from Alberto's tray.

"You're looking well, Kelsey." He clinked his glass against hers.

"Thank you," she said, sipping the wine. It tasted very fine.

"Where have you been today?"

"Here. The dig."

"Find anything of interest?"

"What did Irma tell you?"

"She said you had a piece of jewelry that might have dated back to ancient Atlantis. She said it had irresistible magic powers."

"Can't believe everything you hear."

"But you're into weird shit, aren't you? That talking dolphin?"

Kelsey smiled and rubbed her champagne glass against the roll of her sarong. "So what did the boss have to say?" She was making her way to the group clustered around the appetizers. She took one, a bacon-wrapped lobster bit on a toothpick. "Everyone put on a good show?"

Franklin tittered and raised his glass. "To Kelsey, who's managed to hang onto her cynicism in the face of our success." The others turned toward her, everyone looking rosy.

"She's not the only one," said Red. "What's taking Henri, anyway?"

"Hey," said Jersey. "Speak of the devil."

Henri had come out of the kitchen wearing full chef regalia, a tall white hat and long apron.

"We've been betting against him," said Albert. "He was in a mood."

Henri tapped a champagne glass with his spoon. He didn't look in a bad mood; he looked jovial. "The dinner is served."

To her relief, Kelsey found herself at the second table, away from the boss. She'd greeted him with a somber handshake; that part was over. Now she was sitting next to Mr. Liu. Her table included Jersey, Red, Wickstrom, Irma, and Ben.

"I understand we're having lobster," Jersey said to Mr. Liu.

Liu nodded.

"Mmm," said Irma, "I love lobster."

"You love butter," said Ben.

"Have you met everyone?" Kelsey asked Liu. He was wearing

gold jewelry: a fancy watch, a chain at his neck, and several rings, including a jade pinky ring. The stone was bright and clear as her crystal. "You're at the L.A. branch of BioVenture?"

"Yes," he said.

As she asked questions about his career, he warmed a little and told her about his last position with a Tokyo toy manufacturer.

"I also do some consulting for a consortium of third wave dot-coms."

"That must be interesting," Jersey said. "Still have a high failure rate?"

"Of course," said Liu, smiling. "All but one."

"Which one is that?" Ben asked.

Liu mentioned a company that sold software allowing ISPs to collect and analyze data, and when Ben pressed him, went on, "The edge is the analysis, which, instead of throwing out the outlier data, spins a commanding profile to predict possible future consumer trends."

"What's that mean?" said Irma.

Liu looked bored.

Ben spoke up. "Let's say you order collared shirts for $19 each and an Adirondack Chair and some pottery knick knacks, and book tickets to Orlando or maybe Washington, D.C., and your wife buys beige and white towels and Oprah bestsellers, your kid downloads some games, little sis gets monogrammed, green-friendly water bottles for everyone. You meet certain demographic statistics, you have a profile, right?"

"Typical middle-class American soccer mom family," said Red.

"Well then, let's say someone in your household visits a porn site late one night, or makes a bid on an item like an old plastic coffee cup that Marilyn Monroe once owned, or takes a tour in a psychic chat room, or orders a free sample of vitamin X cream, and it just happens once, this piece of information is rejected from the system because it doesn't fit the pattern. It's called outlier or renegade data."

"Right," said Liu. He was looking at Ben with interest.

"So what your software does, and this is hot, I think, is to make some projections based on just this oddball or renegade data, not only for you but for others, and it creates a marketing profile that opens you up to SPAM which is meant to tickle your fancy and get you to indulge that oddball whim. The theory is that a person is more likely to spend a lot of money on something his wife might disapprove of. He might do it before she finds out, might spend more because he's sneaking it—maybe he thinks, hey, it's his money after all—and he wins a big argument in his head with her. If you can target his hidden desires, you can score with him."

"You don't even have to be online," said Red. "Their cookies collect data, like from your checking account program or your credit card."

"Really?" asked Irma.

"Sure, Honeybunch," said Ben, "cookies are everywhere."

Liu looked at Ben. "You have half of it, but there's more."

Just then Alberto appeared with the first course, a creamy soup. He looked very nervous and almost spilled Mr. Liu's before he scuttled away. He returned with a bottle of Chablis and some crackers.

"Lobster," said Irma, tasting her soup. "I was hoping that would be the main course."

"So," said Ben, "you're thinking that these bits of outlier data might match up with other outlier data, until it's not outlier anymore but mainstream. This is what your software looks for."

"Renegades start trends," said Mr. Liu. "The successful businessman watches trends, the hugely successful anticipates."

"Renegade behavior is an important predictor of future behavior in biology," said Wickstrom. He raised his eyebrows at Kelsey.

"How do you know which renegades to follow?" she asked.

"Simultaneously occurring correlatable repetition," said Ben. "See, if our middle-class wife orders that free sample of Vitamin X, then Joe, a weightlifter in Cincinnati, buys Vitamin X, and Sarah in California goes to a web site selling French Vitamin X Cream for cellulite reduction, and then Mrs. Smith in a Dallas nursing home gets the equivalent from Avon, and this all happens in one week, then you've got something going."

"That means the product already exists," said Irma. "How avant-garde can that be?"

"Every product already exists," said Liu.

"No," said Kelsey, "people invent things."

"Of course they do." Liu turned toward her. "But if you have to wait for someone to invent something, it's too late."

"An inventor could make money," said Irma, "if they could figure out what to invent."

"There's statistically very little money in product development."

"Right," said Red. "The poor creative slob who thought it up gets shafted."

"That's not fair," said Irma, licking her spoon.

"The money comes in the later stages typically," said Liu. "It's a waste to get in too early. Actually, in my view, it's all about marketing."

"That's a real commentary," said Red.

Lobster soup was followed by lobster salad. The chef appeared momentarily to watch his helpers serve. He was drinking wine, smiling over the scene. Then he disappeared inside the swinging doors.

"How do you feel about our situation here?" Jersey asked. "The so-called product we've developed."

Liu expression soured. "No comment."

"Are you here to make an assessment?" Kelsey asked at the risk of further annoying him.

"As long as the client is involved, we've green-lighted it. That's all I can say right now."

"We have reason to believe the project is over budget."

"That's an issue," said Liu, "that we're looking at."

"We're all toast," said Red.

The table was silent while Alberto served them lobster tails with drawn butter and another bottle of the same wine. He left a second plate of crackers.

"What do you think the chef is trying to tell us?" Red asked, pointing to his food.

Liu raised his eyebrows. "I can't imagine his motives for this unpleasant meal."

"You'd be surprised," said Jersey.

"Well, I'm eating mine." Irma had tucked her napkin into the neck of her shirt.

"Maybe we can get back to the other discussion." Wickstrom leaned back in his chair. "I found it interesting. Let's see, we were talking about simultaneity of ideas, product development and demand. Perhaps you have another question, Madame? And no doubt you have another answer." He nodded at Ben.

Kelsey, like the others, turned to Irma. It seemed the dinner's success was in her hands.

Irma wiped her fingers on her bib. "Let's see," she said to Ben. "You were saying it's a chicken and egg thing, between the product and the demand?"

"Virtually simultaneous," said Ben. "That's the cool part."

"I don't get this simultaneous thing." Irma took a tentative poke at her food.

"You see," said Ben, "the product is going to be developed by different people in different locations at the same time, that's just how it works. It's the theory of collective unconscious; ideas, stories, themes, inventions arise simultaneously in many places. And likewise, the demand arises simultaneously as well, only the consumer is going to be lagging behind the inventor because he is less creative in general, and he's slow to recognize his desires until they are pointed out to him, in fact flashed in front of his face multiple times. That's the theory behind modern marketing because we have become so desensitized. It's why this approach is necessary."

Liu's eyes were glittering like the stone in his ring. "You should come to work for me."

"I'm an anthropologist," said Ben.

"So this collective unconscious," said Irma, "is basically telepathy of some kind?"

"You could think of it that way," Ben said.

"Telepathy," said Wickstrom. "Of course."

Kelsey stared at him again, but he was bent over his crackers, rearranging the fragments on his plate.

The lights in the dining hall were suddenly extinguished. At the next table Rodman pushed back his chair and stood up. But before he had time to make a move, the kitchen doors swung open and Alberto and Juan came out carrying dual flaming deserts. Blue-gold fire danced around the edges of the plates. Alberto carefully set his dish down in front of Kelsey.

While Alberto served, Kelsey watched the dying flames. She could smell cognac, and, in fact, Henri was making an appearance with snifters. He spent a long time with Crouch, who seemed to have accepted the joke. They ended up sharing a belly laugh before Henri moved on to Kelsey. "Did you enjoy your meal?" he asked as he placed a brandy before her.

"Where did you get your inspiration tonight, Henri?" she asked in French.

"Monsieur Rodman's request."

"The sweet?"

"Lobster ice cream," pronounced Ben.

Henri sat at their table and, perhaps because of that, they ate the dessert, which was tolerable, would have been good even except for their satiety with its flavoring ingredient.

"What will you do with the leftovers?" Irma asked.

"I have just now chopped and frozen the bits," said Henri. "You will have them again some day."

"I ate mine," said Irma.

"You were the one?"

"Was this a protest of some kind?" Liu asked.

"Non," said Henri. "I am perfectly happy with my investment here. I am celebrating it tonight with this first class dinner."

Liu's eyes darkened. He had gotten the information bite.

After dessert, Crouch and Henri and the other smokers went out to the porch for Cuban cigars. Kelsey was surprised to see Wickstrom join their group. She'd have to wait to talk to him.

The night was warm as a bath, and the moon had a gigantic ring around it. Ben and Irma had decided to stay over in Harrison's tent. As Kelsey was saying good night, they were startled by voices in the jungle behind them. A large shape came out of the darkness—several people carrying something, a boat.

"Hey," Irma called out. "Where are you going?"

But the natives ignored them. They were a family: parents, a grandmother, four children, plus a baby. Kelsey recognized the man and the oldest boy, the ones who'd set up her tent. These two helped the women and children into the boat, then pushed it into thigh deep water and jumped in. The craft had no motor, merely oars which the man took up.

"Where are you going, Sir?" Ben asked. The group had followed the natives down to the water.

"Shore," the man said.

"Why at night?"

He pointed to the sky. "Storm coming."

"Will it be bad?"

The man shrugged. He pushed off and began to row.

They watched the moon disappear behind clouds, and speculated about the storm. By then the skiff had arrived to take Crouch and his party back to the pirate's house. Kelsey had the bad feeling again as the pilot disembarked. He was a large black man with a wide grin, and he seemed perfectly friendly. "Did you all have a nice supper?" he asked.

"Lobster," Irma said.

Ben laughed.

"You don't like it?" The man looked confused. "Most like it."

Now Ben and Irma seemed rooted to the spot, rehashing Henri's joke and the dinner conversation. Kelsey too felt stuck in the soft sand, in the hot night. Then the men spilled out of the building, and suddenly Crouch was next to her, his hand cradling her elbow.

"You were in a heap of trouble last time I saw you. Over it by now, I trust?"

"I'm well, thank you."

"You know, your father would have understood the significance of our discovery here."

"Yes, but there was danger, even then."

"That's life in the grown-up world, Missy."

The men piled into the boat and sped away. Kelsey watched them go.

⁂

"Have you been wondering how the organism made the jump from saline to fresh?" Wickstrom asked. "Or why it has become suddenly parasitic, then perhaps benign?" He showed Kelsey samples from George's throat, one from five P.M., another from seven-thirty. The organisms on the second slide had shrunk, their color putrid, like a bruise.

"I wish I had better equipment. I didn't know what we were getting into." He smiled at her. "Have you been thinking of that dinner discussion?"

"No," she said, "but I could see the gears turning in your mind."

"These changes happen instantaneously, like those fads that come out of nowhere. They somehow decide, oh, let's be parasitic now, or no, we think we're going to turn into elephants."

"You think they're communicating this intention?"

"Yes," said Wickstrom, "and I'd say telepathy is as good an answer as any. Of course, you'd have to be one of them to talk to them."

"Or have a great translator." Kelsey laughed. "I think I'm getting punchy."

"Go to bed," said Wickstrom.

"What about you?"

"I'm not a big sleeper."

"What are you working on tonight?"

"Crouch brought another generation with him. 'Course, it pales beside mine." He gestured toward the rows of violet waters. "But he must be planning something."

"Stevens, the client, did you get a range on him?"

"I was stupid enough to show off for him. The boss brings that out in people. But you're yawning. Go get some sleep."

"In a minute."

She sat and talked to him while he worked. She was unwinding, settling her mind with the absolute clarity of science; the explanation, a rigid truth, was there, somewhere. Wick began talking about his life, his disappointments. He told her he was sorry he'd let his marriage go. "She was a good woman. I just didn't stick it out. I was an ass. Well, that was the thing with my Dad, he left, and I duplicated it. Poor sucker."

"Why?"

"Nobody loved him. He was a shit all his life. How could he expect it?"

"He's dead?"

"Bad heart." He rapped his chest, like it was for good luck, like it was wood.

"And your ex-wife. Where is she now?"

"Remarried, living in Dallas. She has her own life."

"So you're alone."

He hesitated. "I did meet someone a few months ago. She may have moved on by now."

Somehow she doubted it. "What's she like?"

"Odd, a misfit." He laughed. "Like me."

"You're nice."

The light was bright in the small, close room, and Kelsey found herself blinking to keep her eyes open. "What are you going to show the boss in the morning?"

"Tank A. Hilton has his list. They'll see it clean up a spill."

"And these in here?"

"My renegades," he said smiling, "are in here somewhere."

Chapter 35

Kelsey recognizes the little cove. Her recognition goes beyond the sense of something pretty glimpsed, remembered, even yearned for—it's as though she's found home. Harrison, too, is like she first saw him, bearded, the eyes behind the spectacles rich with humor. She leads him to a shady spot where they sit and bury their feet in the warm sand. The water in front of them is dappled, aquamarine, sparkling in the sun.

"I'm glad you're back, Kelsey," he says.

She understands him to mean she is herself again. She feels a shaky relief, a settling of her emotions, as though a recent disturbance has safely passed.

Together they unravel the nuances of her transformation, their thoughts forming simultaneously or in complementary succession. She recounts the events, he provides the analysis; he remembers details, she adds the subtle twists. She is soothed, peaceful; the words die out.

Harrison begins to make love to her, and what was calm is now disturbed. She wants to swallow him, but she cannot quite. She feels his breathing inside her own chest. The sky opens and they are bathed in gentle rain.

Kelsey woke to the sounds of the closing storm: thunder and something flapping in the wind. She was at first disoriented; the afternoon with Harrison, fresh in her mind, seemed real, no dream. The trouble was she could not fit the rest of her memories around it.

The flapping sound persisted; the tent door had come loose in the wind. She stepped outside and a streak of lightning illuminated the bay—whitecaps with their silvery ruffles, the bobbing seaplane tethered to the water—and the approaching curtain of rain.

It was pitch black as Kelsey made her way along the pathway toward the bathrooms. Clouds covered the moon, and the lanterns had all burned down. She thought it must be late because no one was stirring, not even Wickstrom. Then she heard moaning.

George's forehead was hot and dry. He struggled against the twisted sheet, pronouncing incomprehensible syllables, before fainting back into deep sleep.

Kelsey ran through the rain and woke Irma, who rose instantly, pulling on shorts and turning her back while she fastened her bra under her shirt. She asked but two questions: Was he sweating and were there sufficient washcloths and clean water in his tent.

Ben and Kelsey went for the water, ice, bowls and cups in which to mix the tinctures, clean towels, bedding, extra candles. There was no one in the dining hall, not even Alberto who usually slept in the storeroom off the kitchen. The lights did not work; the electricity was out.

Irma applied ice to the back of George's neck and knees. She forced him to drink cup after cup of water laced with remedies. His eyes were open wide now, the whites red again, his face puffy and flushed. He remained quiet except to answer Irma's questions—his responses still incoherent, though prompt, earnest attempts—and he took the water as if it was his job. Finally he began to sweat. They kept wiping him down, all three of them at once, squeezing out their cloths and reusing them. They refilled their bowls from the tent's runoff, dumping the old water into the sand. Kelsey worried that it might be contaminated—could the organism come through the pores alive?—but there was nothing she could think to do.

George shivered, his big muscles convulsing. They changed the sheets, then put him back to bed and this time he slept less deeply, waking almost immediately to urinate into a bowl. Irma held the liquid up to the lantern's light. It was tinged a dark kelly green.

That was scary enough to send Kelsey off to wake the others. She entered the darkened lab, calling for Wickstrom but he didn't answer. She found a candle stub and lit it. The bed was empty, slept in, the sheets flung wide. A diary lay open on the bed; it was filled with chemical equations. A container of violet sample sat uncovered on the table—that didn't seem right—and a second beaker was on its side, contents dripping off the edge of the table.

Now Kelsey ran into the pouring rain, searched the bathroom and the kitchen and the dining hall. Finally, she woke Rodman, who made her wait while he dressed and put on his slicker.

"Did you look in his tent?"

"He hasn't slept there for a week."

"Go check anyway. I'm going to look in on George."

"Irma's there. He's stable. I think he's going to get better."

"You're not making sense, Kelsey. A minute ago you said we needed to evacuate him."

"I'm worried about Wick. I think he might be sick."

Rodman was staring at her, his face in the shadow of his rain hood. "Might be?"

"I don't know. Just a hunch. A strong one."

"Right," he said. "OK."

They went together through the camp, searching the public spaces, then the tents, waking the occupants in the process. Kelsey knew she was exuding panic, but she couldn't help it. She'd begun to shiver; she was drenched. Somewhere along the way, she got handed a poncho.

"He's got to be outside," said Red when they'd gathered in the dining hall. "We've looked everywhere inside."

"How about the village?" Rodman asked. "Anyone go over there?"

"Deserted," said Hilton. "They've all left."

"We saw the boat leaving after dinner," Kelsey said. "They're afraid of the storm."

"Kitchen staff too," said Hilton.

Rodman was grim. "Let's say they have a point. That means we'd better find Wick before things get worse. We don't want him wandering around in this rain."

Kelsey traipsed through the jungle in the oversize poncho hoping Wickstrom had had the sense to go inland rather than toward the sea, the slippery cliffs. Near the native village, she saw several big sneaker prints filled with rainwater. This gave her a spurt of hope until she remembered Hilton had been here moments ago.

The wind was gusting and the rain driving sideways, so she took shelter in one of the huts. The palm roof shook and a piece flew off, revealing the night sky. The moon shone through a thin place in the clouds before the darkness descended again, and the rain. It was all familiar, the storm, the meager shelter, her sense of urgency, her fear.

I am huddled in a dark corner of the stone temple, scared, an old woman, alone. It's a fierce storm, perhaps it will be one of the bad ones that last for days, roughing up the seas, tearing apart the houses, and scouring the sand from the beaches. Where are the others? I've crept in here on hands and knees after my fragile roof blew away. But I'm no longer agile. My skin is scraped; my palms sting; I bleed.

A low growl in the darkness. Rotan's evil beast smells blood and has followed me. Can the crystal ward it off one more time? I can send no killing ray, I quenched that long ago. Instead I put up a weak shield of pale green light. The greenness illuminates, but that won't matter to the cat: It works by other senses. Now I can smell its meaty breath. The stone gives a faint murmur, it has been doing that of late: speaking of its own volition. Telling me what to do.

Remember.

Yes, I remember the night the storm of all storms was set off. This stone temple smells like the catacombs. We'd escaped that night, not from the storm—it hadn't started yet—but from the angry crowd. I'd plucked Jarad from the stage where we'd just been condemned to die, and transported us both through solid walls and air and time, escaping by magic, disappeared, dissolved, reconstituted in the cool tunnels beneath the city.

Claws click on the stone floor; a paw finds its way under a corner of my shield; I've lost my concentration and let this happen. A crack of lightning, the green eyes blink, and the paw withdraws. The cat thinks the trick is mine. He associates me with such tricks. For the moment, he is afraid.

I creep sideways, easing toward the entrance, using one hand to hold the crystal at my belly where I can focus its power. Each movement compromises my knees, my lame hip. The cat moves with me, wary for the moment, but it will not last.

That night we ran easily through the corridors, following this same green light that extended in front of us like a beacon. We tested symbol engravings to see if they would open doors, we ducked into chambers to catch our breath, to hide. I had a sense of the evil ahead, Jarad less so. He was always pure of heart and direct of purpose. He knew what we had to stop. I feared we might not be able.

The white light was blinding when we got close. No pure radiance, no love source, only the blare of ego, greed, confusion. Gewil's gang lay unconscious around him on the floor. He too was stunned, prone, but his nose for me made him lift his head. Jarad, somehow immune, was already at the base of the crystalline shaft. It crackled as it rotated, turning its flat eye-face to meet him. He reached to touch; I yelled a warning. Then Gewil was by my side, whispering those words of love and temptation. Join me. Together we will possess, we will control . . . ultimate power . . . the world at our feet . . . love.

The cat catches my leg, a long, ugly tear before I can close the shield around its paw, giving it a minor shock, a little burn. The cat sits on its haunches and licks my blood off its claw. It has a taste for me now.

My time is short. My mind clears like the sea in a dead calm. I must look down and see the white bottom. I must think of those things, things I do not like to think of, things I can never make right.

Kelsey huddled in the corner of the poor shelter, feeling the rain against her face. What had happened to Iriel in the chamber of the monolith? But the vision was gone, extinguished by the noise of the storm, the urgent present. The missing man.

Kelsey ran over rocky ground, calling, slipping in the mud. She was heading for the open water, when Rodman caught her at the door of the dining hall. They'd found him in the tub, he told her, naked, singing like a drunk.

"Then he's sick."

"Others too."

While she'd been wasting her time in the woods, Rodman had been busy. He'd stacked the tables against the walls and moved all the beds into the mess hall. In case the winds got worse, he said. They'd put up the storm shutters and gotten the generator working, and now there was light, harsh to her eyes, and the air-conditioner running for the first time since she'd been on the island. In the sick beds were Jersey and Albert and Red and Henri and Wickstrom peeking out from under his sheet. George came bouncing in from outside.

"Well," said Rodman, "that's a relief. We're all here."

"Now what?" she asked.

"Anyone want a cigar?" Franklin asked.

"Outside," said Rodman.

Kelsey helped Irma—her hair coming loose, her face rosy with heat—as she assessed her charges. Jersey was sweating profusely, Albert sleeping but hot, and Henri complained about his throat. Red had vomited and Ben was cleaning up the mess. Wickstrom kept sitting up in the bed and flinging himself backward like a kid on a trampoline.

Kelsey took a chair beside his bed, took his hand. He started singing.

"That's nice," she said though he was way off key.

Someone asked what time it was. A voice called back. "Ten after three."

"Someone dim the lights, please," Irma said. "Some of us should try to get a little sleep."

The storm was growing noisy, and Franklin came in reporting winds gusting to fifty miles an hour. Irma sat down by Kelsey. "If we're lucky we'll see the same quick cycle of fevers we saw in George. If we can get them all to break. I don't know, Kelsey." Irma wiped the back of her hand across her forehead. "I wish we had proper masks and gloves. Antiseptics."

"That might not stop it."

"Anyway, how does this thing travel?"

"In liquids."

"We're handling bodily fluids, sweat, urine, vomit."

"Maybe not that way. So far it's isolated to those who soaked in the tub."

"And him." Wickstrom made little noises as Irma bathed him: the quick intake of breath, cooing, like he'd put something delicious, but too hot into his mouth.

"He was working with the samples."

"I talked with him earlier," Irma said. "I got the impression he's careful."

Kelsey thought of the spill in the lab and frowned. "Well, maybe he made a mistake."

"Don't talk about me like I'm not here."

His lucidity was back. A good sign. "How did you get sick then?"

"I guess I just deserve it."

"You do not."

"How do you know?"

She could think of no honest answer, so she said nothing.

George was feverish again but sleeping. Franklin and Henry Hilton were also asleep. Even Rodman dozed off in his chair, and Ben had almost convinced Irma to lie down for a few minutes when Henri woke up moaning about his throat.

"He says it's on fire," Kelsey said. "What can we do?"

"Have him chew this root." Irma dug out something that looked like a desiccated carrot.

Now Jersey was awake too, and Red. Franklin began sweating profusely, so Ben moved another bed into the middle of the room, announcing that the supply of clean sheets was almost depleted. So the second round had started. Wick was a different story. Though his fever did not seem as high as the others', it had not broken; he remained hot and dry and quiet. He seemed to be dreaming with his eyes open.

"I fear it's in his brain. I don't know. Nothing seems to be working," Irma said.

They left Wickstrom and started making up Franklin's bed. "This is getting bad, Kelsey," Irma said when they were out of earshot. "I think we're all likely to come down with it before the day's over."

"How do you feel, Honeybunch?" Ben asked.

"OK. How about you two?"

"Just tired," said Kelsey. "Maybe I'm immune." She was thinking of the sample she'd put her finger through the first time she'd seen it. "Perhaps we'll be lucky. George seems to be getting better with each cycle."

"We need resources," said Ben. "Doctors, equipment, drugs."

"We won't be able to evacuate or get supplies for a day or two, not by the sound of it. By then it might be too late." Irma brushed impatiently at her hair.

"They'll find a bunch of decaying corpses," said Franklin, "all bloated and stinky."

"Stop it," said Irma. She turned her back and addressed Kelsey from close range. Her eyes were snapping. "There is something else I thought of. The crystal . . ."

Kelsey patted her waist, felt a momentary panic. She'd left it in her tent.

Irma pressed her arm. "Do you think you could do it? It may be our only hope."

"Being overdramatic, Irma," Ben said.

Irma ignored him. "Well?" she asked Kelsey.

"I don't know. Yes, I'll try. I'll go get it."

"No need." Red-faced, Irma reached into the pocket of her shorts and produced the crystal on the palm of her hand. "I can't do anything with it. I already tried."

Kelsey closed her fingers around the stone and for a moment she and Irma were in a tug of war. *It was starting all over again, the desire, the stone soaking up the attention, making a play for the new admirer. Look at it glow.*

"Irma," said Ben, taking his wife by the shoulders. "You've got to give it to her."

Irma opened her fingers. It seemed to cost her an effort. "Will you let me watch?"

"Sure," said Kelsey. She was staring down at the stone, which seemed to be laughing like a gleeful imp. This was a new side of it; it hadn't been like this with Iriel. "Help me then," said Kelsey suddenly understanding that she needed backup. "You too," she said to Ben.

They gathered chairs around Jersey's bed. Kelsey wanted to start with him because he seemed childlike, sleeping on his back, sweating lightly as if in a warm bath. They took up their positions—Ben and Irma on either side of the bed, Kelsey at his head—and she closed her eyes and concentrated on her breath. Nothing happened. Her inner screen was blank.

Kelsey tried touching Jersey with the crystal, but couldn't find the right place, so she placed the cool stone against her own solar plexus. Was she being pretentious to think she could do this? No, she realized. It wouldn't be she. Nor Iriel either. A greater force would come to their aid if it were willing to help.

Are You willing? Please heal these sick men.

White light washed over Jersey. She could see it pouring from the crystal and felt again the particular vibration of the stone, an innate thing, stubborn yet malleable, a two-year-old child.

"Hey, what are you doing?" Franklin called out.

"Shut up," Irma said. "Can't you see we're concentrating?"

"Is this some kind of New Age crap?"

Ben turned around. "If you don't shut up, you'll be last to know if it works."

All this time, Kelsey was suspended, like she was about to roll downhill. She could feel the impending rush. The stone had grown heavy—it had been light as a balloon before—and she let it sink against her legs.

"OK," said Irma, "want to try again?"

This time the whiteness formed a rectilinear block, the energy strongest at Jersey's head, held square on the sides, and dissipating at his feet. Jersey's eyelids twitched like he was dreaming. This was all happening in Kelsey's mind, and she didn't know if anyone else was experiencing the same thing. She opened her eyes.

"Feel or see anything?" she asked Irma.

It took Irma a moment to come out of her trance. "Yes," she said.

"I'm tingling," Ben said.

"So am I," said Irma, "and I saw a white light."

"Me too," said Kelsey, "so we're on the same page."

"My feet are cold," said Jersey, waking suddenly.

"I think we need someone sitting there," said Ben.

"That's right," said Kelsey. "Of course you're right."

Rodman jerked awake when Kelsey touched his shoulder. She described what they hoped to do. By now there was a little gray light coming in the cracks at the windows, but not enough to make the night seem over.

"You've done this before?" Kelsey asked.

"I know something about séance," Rodman said.

With Rodman at Jersey's feet, the healing took on a sense of professionalism. He lent the same solidity and practicality he brought to his leadership, but without the edge. He suggested candles and physical contact with the patient, a light touch of fingers all around. Now the white light reflected back from him making a tight circle of energy. Kelsey found she could open her eyes and see the same thing as when they were shut: the concentrating faces, the white light around and under the patient and then Jersey was lifted from the bed, his color blanched as though the molecules of his body were dancing.

The light tinged violet and Kelsey knew they'd reached the level of the organism. She concentrated on clearing the color away, and it did lift, leaving the pure, shimmering white. She thought she heard squealing—the protest of tiny voices—and then they were slumped together over the patient and Jersey sat up saying, "Hey," and looking from one to the other.

By now it was noticeably lighter. Kelsey felt a sense of urgency, and pressed the others to skip the rehash. She placed the crystal on Henri's throat, and everyone took their places.

I find myself in a white room, surrounded by tall pale beings. Star Ari, they call themselves, born of the star gods, children of heaven, highest among creation. On the streets of Phyrius, I saw many of them clamoring to get on the crystal-powered airships, hoping to make their escape from our impending doom. Some were not full-blooded; they made their faces white with powders, falsified their height with stilts and lifted shoes. These were turned away.

But here is the largest concentration of high-caste Ari I've ever seen. They parade back and forth in their finery; shiny metallic decorations cover their long, white bodies. Though bloodless and white like the stars from whence they proclaim to come, these are not the healers, the holy ones, bleached by the use of their stones. Where the purest of their race are full of One-God, these Ari are unholy and pretentious.

Gewil sits beside me, watching the show. We are in a hard-edged room with an enormous spire ceiling. Its mirrored walls reflect the ghostly migration of the Ari, the crystalline furniture, and the blazing cold fire. The room shrinks. I feel feverish and wrongly energized. I realize with horror that we are trapped inside the white abomination. Lyticia's crystal.

Why are the Ari ignoring us? Gewil tries to get their attention, but they will not turn their long necks. He steps into their path. They pass right through him, shades, ghosts, memories. The edges of the room press inward like a coffin. The Ari pass elegantly back and forth in the narrowing hall. I think they are looking for the doorway to death.

Kelsey came out of her trance. Something had gone wrong. Henri was staring wide-eyed with fear, choking under the weight of the little stone. She snatched it off his Adam's apple, and he caught his breath with relief. The others frowned at her.

"I felt evil," said Rodman.

"Merde," said Henri, clutching his throat.

"I'm sorry," she said. "I can't control it."

"You'd better try," said Rodman.

"Think of God," said Ben.

Kelsey wanted to crawl into a corner and hide. Only Irma seemed to be gazing at her impassively, the others looked cross and blaming. She and Irma rose together, exchanged places, and sat back down.

The room is back. The Ari shades glide around in their long robes, headdresses riding high. They are not really here, she thinks; remember that.

Maybe we aren't either.

Outside the room she hears a noise. She goes toward it.

It was the crash of a wave somewhere out to sea. Kelsey pictured a deserted island, palm trees blown inside out like umbrellas. The wave repeated itself, overrunning the land. Then she was back in her body, feeling her breath rise into her chest, feeling Henri's with hers, and the others exhaling in time. She opened her eyes; they were all slumped forward in the aftermath of healing, and she understood they'd not stirred, they'd not judged her, they'd not been in the white room, and she and Irma had not exchanged positions. She'd been through it all alone; it was her separate vision, Iriel's vision, and the faraway wave was just a dream.

"It's too much," Irma said. "You're tired."

"No," said Kelsey.

"The work energizes the channel," Rodman said.

"I am better," Henri said. "I think you must continue. I will help you."

The healing was getting mixed up with Iriel's traumatic night in the awful chamber, and she mustn't let it happen again because the place was a stuck place, a trap of the mind. "Hold the stone," she said to Irma. "I need your distance."

Green calls white, and white cancels violet. She'd simplified her thinking. She sat with Irma, partners at Albert's head. Henri and Jersey had joined the group. Franklin's protests had been ignored.

Irma was too aggressive. The white energy simply flew out of the stone. Kelsey was sure it would soon be depleted. Then she felt a secondary source feeding the white wave through the channel Irma provided. Behind that, of course, was the primary source, and so she settled in.

Albert seemed to have an agenda at odds with their purpose. He resisted; his limbs grew incredibly heavy. Kelsey felt again the sense of someone behind her. She twisted around to see.

A compact, gray-haired woman wearing a faded, flowery dress sat, spine upright, in a chair. She was small, like Albert, and as plain as a boy. This was her son, lying on the bed with the circle of people, and she was making a decision. Did she want him to live or die? He was waiting for her answer, ready to obey, and she was deciding to keep him with her forever.

Alby, she kept saying. *You're first in my heart. I think you want to be first with me.*

Kelsey saw a cropped photograph of the two, mother and son, bent over a book, heads almost touching. Behind them was a curtained window, a kitchen window.

Alby, my Alby, you were always first with me.

The photo slid back into the leather wallet. The wallet slid back into the jeans pocket.

Will you come to your Mama?

No. The answer was of earth plane origination, not ethereal.

Who is speaking?

He's a vital person, said Jersey. *He has a life.*

You dare come between me and my son?

I dare.

Let him choose then.

Albert sat up, still in Kelsey's dream.

Mama, I don't want to come now.

The woman rose in a fury. She became huge; an angry man took her place. He burst out of the flowered dress. He wore hip boots and carried a hunting rifle, two limp ducks hung from his belt. A small boy cowered before him, crying, but did not look away. The man raised the gun, pointed it at the boy, and pulled the trigger. Still the boy did not flinch. He took his medicine like a man. There was a cascade of flowers, a rain of petals, of dust, and it was done. Albert remained.

Red was the easiest of all. He simply sloughed off a mantle of violet and sat up, grinning at the group around him. George relived his wedding, renewing his vows to his bride before the witnesses in the room, and Franklin renounced his addictions. The promise was this: he would agree to die, but knowingly, in the future if he ever resumed his habits. By this time Kelsey was dressed in gauzy green, and the glowing stone had lit the inside of the hall a bright kiwi color. She was Iriel, and Irma was her double. The two held hands, the cooing crystal lodged between them, and sat like twin queens at Wick's head. He'd been awake, a presence in all the other healings, pushing away their attempts to work on him. Now they told him it was time to accept their gift.

I'm finished, he told the twins. *Save your breath.*

Why? Asked Kelsey/Iriel.

Because my heart is already leaking.

We've saved the best for last. Let us try.

Too late, I'm already dead. See for yourselves.

Kelsey looked around the bed at the bent faces. Wickstrom was indeed still and breathless. Everyone was somber, but Galen was smiling. He lifted Wick in his arms and flew away. The morning was complete.

The Wizard's Bargain

If you judge me by my accomplishments, I am failure. My work is incomplete—does that mean it is as if I never lived? Now that I'm part of the fabric of many, the All-Are-One, I see that a single soul's journey is but a breath, a breath inhaled and held for the next eternity.

But, Oh, the one time I was grand.

Listen. You are grand yourself. You must not think otherwise, for your time is now. The future rests with you as it once did with me.

Listen now. Here is the part:

I am trapped with Gewil inside the giant, white crystal, Lyticia's abomination. She renounced it too late, for the Will was long since cast. In the prime of her power, she'd set the Will, infused the monolith with all her desire and ambition and determination to rule. Did she regret it? Perhaps yes, perhaps no, for history played a strange trick on her. But that is another story.

What is Lyticia's Will? Perhaps it was her way of protecting herself, or of getting revenge. Perhaps it is the bastard child of her former intentions. All I know is the giant crystal is moving now, grinding into position, ready to fire on some target, to unleash the unholy forces stored inside.

In the time it takes the Will to manifest, we are powerless, Gewil and I. Or more truthfully balanced, at odds, canceling each other out. We have different ends in mind—his is to rule, as Lyticia ruled, mine is to save as she saved, in the end. The two halves of her nature live on in us. We didn't know until too late that the Will was the fatal middle ground. If either had let the other win, the Will would have been thwarted. But the struggle consumed us. And so the Will had its way. But I digress to the result. The story comes first.

The Ari with their splendid clothes pass proudly back and forth. As I watch, bits of the crystal's truth come to me. Once Lyticia lived inside this pretty chamber, hiding from the destruction she'd unleashed. The Ari were her court, and so they still promenade, vacant reflections, endlessly trapped.

Gewil and I sit knee to knee on identical golden stools, immobilized by the battle of wills. Our profound disagreement manifests in pictures we cast upon the crystal walls, first me, then him. And as our pictures war, the chamber tilts, the weapon aligns on its target.

In the aftermath of the last destruction, the lowliest, the mutants, the injured, the poor, the sick, and the reverent believers of the Society suffer. These are the images I throw against the sides of our prison: poor creatures wandering the streets in search of food or uncontaminated water, homes in ruin, learned men at manual labor.

Look closer and you will see a child's dirty face, stained with tears. She clutches the ragged hem of a bearded man as they move along the street, winding in and out of the booths; he is lame—see his mangled foot, his wince as someone bumps him? When they approach the back of a booth, the proprietress frowns and passes a crusty bit of bread. The man divides it and the two wolf it down. The man again taps the old woman's shoulder, but she turns her back this time. The girl cries because the scrap of food only ignited her murderous hunger.

Gewil shows me the palaces of the rich—the Ari, the Minister of Justice—and the soldier camps, clean, and well lit. I see a covered reservoir where water is kept, and food grown under crystal lights. He shows me the glistening arsenal, and the soldiers of the Crystal Force who guard the crops. This last makes me angry, for I did not realize there was such bounty in the midst of suffering, nor had I understood the corruption that keeps it in the hands of the few.

Gewil reveals his plan. He sees the crystals, the ancient and raw joined together into a powerful new force which he and his coalition will use to "protect" our lands. I think vanquish, conquer, squelch dissent. On crystle-sci he is eloquent. He believes he can change the shape of the earth, destroy volcanoes, stop earthquakes, even turn the climate to our advantage. Doesn't he know the plan of which he speaks, and the hubris with which he speaks it, are not new? Doesn't he understand the earth storms are One-God's warning to us?

Some have said Fate is cast, and it is too late to heal the world. I see the way Fate cuts like a river. The channel is deep but can still be changed. Can we not turn away from greed toward generosity of spirit, human love, and peace?

Gewil says, as though reading my thoughts, Fate has brought us to this moment.

We cannot work together, I say, except in peace.

Don't you see, Iriel? You control the Crystle-Minde and I control the soldiers. Together we can stop the earth storms and punish the trouble-makers. We must start with the islands, and one by one, absorb them into our plan. Then we rule . . . .

Not rule, lead.

Yes, lead, rule, it is the same. He swallows his temper, for he senses an opening. Listen, he says, my wizards are waiting. Trained crystle-mindes. The finest . . .

His wizards? How has he come to such power in so short a time? But now I think maybe together we can do the thing I came here to do: destroy the Giant White Crystal, Lyticia's Abomination, before it destroys us.

Hurry, I say, together we can disarm . . .

I see by his sly smile that he has no intention of disarming. Rather, he means to make the abomination the pinnacle of his arsenal.

I run at the transparent slab. Jarad is on the other side fighting to make his way in. I match my palms to his. With a giant leap, I am outside the crystal's walls and Gewil's men are inside, sleepily positioning themselves around their commander as they eye their new surroundings.

We embrace. Still holding me, Jarad points to the crystal. The shining monolith is steeply angled at the heavens. A trapdoor has opened in the apex of the room, revealing the night sky, the distant stars. The firing mechanism engages but suddenly grinds to a halt.

Three wizards file into the room, one white haired and ancient, like Quiri, the other two short and dull, unremarkable except for the glistening of their pendant stones and their jewel eyes. They are wary, but they do not move to seize us, nor do they block the exit.

The wizards speak their bargain without words. If I give up my struggle with Gewil, if I help swing the balance of power in his favor, they will help me subjugate the Will. The inevitable terror will not be visited upon our islands.

My heart beats faster. Is this my destiny then, this wizards' bargain?

They say they cannot hold on much longer. I must trance myself; I must allow the stone to absorb me; I must stay permanently linked. This is what it will take to change the course of Fate.

I pray to One-God. Her answer comes in a squeeze from Jarad's hand. He knows this is a tainted bargain. Maybe the people won't die today, but surely our children and our grandchildren will, for under Gewil's program Nature's insult will not be remedied. We speak only of a delay.

The worst is that Gewil has his way.

Gewil and I are locked inside the stone again, alone in our vital battle, no wizards, or soldiers, no Jarad to help me think. The crystal grinds; The Will resets itself.

What would you do now? Gewil asks.

Convince you to destroy this abomination before it's too late.

Why destroy the greatest power there is?

No one can control . . .

We must join together. That's the only way. It pleases the gods.

Which god? Do you no longer follow One-God?

And so we sit here, going over the same old ground while the Will manifests.

What Will is stronger than my life purpose, you ask? Gewil's, Lyticia's? Perhaps they were only Fate's pawns, as I was. But that Fate has run its course. The river turns.

You can still turn back to the light.

Chapter 36

The morning sun streaked over the cloudbank at the eastern horizon. A few patches of rainbow shone where the rain still fell, but otherwise it was clearing. The sea no longer crashed against the cliff but bounced as though with glee, and the wind had gone still and breathless.

The washed-out smell and the sun on her eyelids wounded her. The screen door banged. Kelsey looked away when George spoke her name, and when he made a comment about the weather, she cut him off. After a time he thanked her for saving his life. He said he felt so bad for what he had done, for what he'd caused. He was sorry about Dr. Wickstrom.

"And?" she asked, glaring at him.

He lowered his gaze. "It should have been me, I guess. But, Kelsey . . ."

"What?"

"I feel like God . . . if there is a God . . ."

"What does God want with you, is that it? Why were you spared and not him?"

"Don't be mad."

She softened. "I can't stand it, that's all."

"Everyone's saying you performed a miracle. Everyone's in awe."

She shook her head. "It wasn't me."

"OK," George said. "I know what you mean."

She remembered his fevered cheeks, how he'd closed his eyes when she brought out the crystal. The glaring green light had blinded her too. It had been so strong and eager, the force behind, so pure.

"I prayed last night," George said.

"I feel like I'm still praying."

"It was so weird Kelsey, like I was high and sick at the same time. But the last time I got the fever, I knew I wasn't going to see Josh and Cindy again, so, you see, what you gave me, what He gave me, is a second chance. Not many people get one, and I know I don't deserve it." Here he choked up, and she felt her heart go with him finally. "I've been focused on the wrong stuff, and Cindy—that's the worst thing—I haven't treated her right. Sure, she's messed up, but I am too. I'm going to try a lot harder when I get back. No, better than try. I'm going to *be* better."

Alone again, Kelsey watched the sea. The calm had set in so the water was swelling and shrinking, not breaking against the rocks. She should get up, check her tent, maybe go get Wickstrom's diary, she had an itch to do that. But how could she touch his stuff so soon? Then Rodman came out and told her they were going to have a little ceremony.

She nodded. "I was thinking of going over to the lab to clean up."

"Have you looked over there?"

She followed him around the corner and saw the devastation. All but three of the tents had blown away, and the lab was open to the air. Even from here, she could see that many of the samples had spilled onto the sand.

"I'll help you after we finish. We won't have much time." He was guiding her inside. "We're still out of communication, so we don't really know if the storm's over or not. This might be something like an eye, but it looks like a good chance." Rodman glanced toward the darkness still brooding at the horizon and the lines across his forehead deepened. "We're going to try and evacuate the island."

"Evacuate?"

"Your choice, stay or go. I want to get the body to shore, that's the main thing, and I think some of the others will leave too."

"Do we have room in the boats?"

"Not unless someone wants to row." He smiled. "But seriously, if you want to go, you have a place."

She thought of Harrison on the other end of the island and shook her head.

"Well," he said, "I'm not taking this as a final decision."

Wickstrom's body was covered by a white sheet. Kelsey kept thinking he was going to sit up and say something, counteract any false sweetness. Rodman spoke about knowing him for thirty years, about his struggle with alcohol, his dedication to science. He said he didn't know a better man. George repeated that Wick was truly a better man, that he should have been the one who lived, and then he choked up again. Even Franklin spoke.

"He and I didn't really get along, but that was probably me. I can be a real dickhead, I know that . . . . God, I'm sorry I ever went to work for this shitty company."

Kelsey said, "I wish I'd been his friend longer. He was a deep man, good, he hid his goodness." And then she couldn't go on.

Irma took her hand. "He died bravely. He waited for all the others."

"I should never have taken the generator part," said Henry Hilton in a low voice.

"What?" Kelsey asked. "You took the part?"

They were interrupted by the sound of the front door slamming.

"Let me through." Myron Crouch, ruddy and windblown, thrust them aside and pulled the sheet back. "What happened here? Who else is sick?"

"We were just having a moment of prayer," Kelsey said, "and we'd like to finish."

"By all means."

Crouch had left Wickstrom's face uncovered, and it was Franklin who pulled the cloth back over the bloodless skin. The group silently regarded the inert bundle.

"May God rest his soul," said Rodman. There were scattered amens and George crossed himself. Crouch laid his hand on Wickstrom's chest and turned to question Rodman.

"We had a miraculous turnabout after I talked to you, Sir, a remarkable turnabout. Thank God everybody is OK, but . . ." Rodman's mouth closed into a flat line.

Suddenly Crouch lifted his hands. "He contagious?" His head

jerked back. "How about an antidote? Is there an antidote? Remember, I own this research."

"Do you own this?" Franklin poked Wickstrom through the cloth.

Crouch turned on him. "Why wasn't I informed of the seriousness—"

"Hey," said Red, nodding at Rodman, "you gave him some runaround last night."

As they closed ranks, Crouch turned from one to the other, trying to maintain eye contact. "I demand to know how this man got sick. What was he researching? Anyone? George?"

"Sure," said George, "I'll talk." He started telling Crouch what they knew about the bonuses, the missing funds. "You lied to me, you used me, and look what happened. You're responsible for his death as sure as if you used a gun."

"I don't like your attitude, any of you," Crouch said. "There'll be an investigation. You can bet on that." He made a move toward the door.

"Hold it," said Rodman.

"He's hiding something," Kelsey said.

Crouch fought, but George and Franklin quickly pinned his arms behind his back and Jersey slid his hands into Crouch's pockets. He pulled out a slim notebook.

"It's Wickstrom's diary," said Albert as he handed the book to Kelsey.

"I have every right to that," said Crouch.

"The company has a right to it. Your interests are diverging," said Rodman.

"I bet it wasn't going to find its way into the hands of interested parties," said Red.

"Into the shredder, more like it," Franklin said.

"Destroying evidence," Kelsey said to herself. *Like he's done before.*

But Crouch heard her. "Little Bitch, you set me up with this group."

Just then, the seaplane's pilot entered the room. "We ready?" he said, looking from his struggling passenger to the men holding him.

"He's flying out?" asked Rodman.

"He told me ten minutes. It been twenty now."

"Get Liu in here," Crouch bellowed.

The pilot looked skeptical. "What he do?"

Rodman pointed to the body. "Can you take us to shore?"

"I full," said the pilot, backing away from Wickstrom. "Can't fly safe with more weight."

"Well, someone needs to stay behind. This is an emergency."

"I got plenty emergency today."

"What's the holdup?" Liu, looking immaculate but cross, covered the distance between the door and the group with short, swift strides. "Myron, let's go."

"Seems these characters mean to hold me against my will."

"He killed a man," said George.

"That's an outrageous lie. In fact, these men, due to their negligence—"

"Sir," said Rodman, addressing Liu, "I'll make a deal with you."

Though Crouch protested, Liu moved with Rodman toward the back of the room. After a second Kelsey went after them, and George followed. It shocked her to see her boss rendered powerless, and all his hatred focused on her. For a moment she was a small child in her father's study. She'd read it then too: the will for revenge, the measure being taken of her father's character, the plan brewing, maybe already in motion.

Kelsey turned back to the group. Liu was no taller than she, and his face was within a breath's distance. George towered behind like a bodyguard.

"A man has died as a result of Mr. Crouch's policies," Rodman was saying. "Others were endangered, and only by . . . a set of fortuitous circumstances has a large-scale disaster been averted. I think when you delve into the situation, you'll find hard evidence of wrongdoing."

Liu began twirling the emerald ring. "You have this evidence?"

Rodman pulled out Wickstrom's book.

"This is?"

"A scientific journal. Dr. Wickstrom's."

"He was logging the differences between the two strains of the engineered organism, the one official, and the other ... not," said

Kelsey. "There were shortcuts. I was ordered to take shortcuts. And then there was the matter of the money."

Liu frowned. "You alleging mishandling of funds?"

"Bribery and payoffs," said George. "I'm willing to testify."

"What do you want me to do?"

"Take me back to the states. With the body," Rodman said. "Let me press charges."

"In return?"

"We won't name you," said Rodman, "if you co-operate. We won't name you in our complaint."

"Can't fly six. No way," said the pilot.

"Let me keep Crouch behind," said Franklin.

"Too much liability." Rodman faced Liu. "What about you?"

The small man looked surprised. "I need to get back."

"We'll get you back. I promise."

"Why not Stevens?"

"He's the client," Red said.

"What am I going to do here?" Liu looked around at the others.

"Take a day off," Red suggested. "Play some cards."

"Can't take five and all that extra stuff," the pilot said. "We too heavy coming out."

"What stuff?" Kelsey asked.

"All that I pack up for this guy."

Everything from the lab, equipment, vials of samples, had been packed into two large crates. Even the stained sand had been scooped away. Kelsey was amazed once again at Crouch's bravado. His escape was planned, only a quick set of instructions to Rodman while his pilot did his dirty work, then he'd have been off. How could he imagine he'd get away with it?

"Take this stuff over to the dining hall," said Rodman, and the group split up. Kelsey wandered up to the point by way of the hot tub. As she got closer she was thinking maybe the organism had died out.

To her horror she found the sea had broached the tub during the night. Pinkish water pooled on the surrounding rocks, and down below, the froth was tinged as though with blood. Already fish bodies floated on the surface, white bellies up.

Kelsey pulled Rodman off the plane. He was sitting in the back next to Stevens, and she could make out Wickstrom's body curled into the cargo space behind the seat. They stood on the cliff overlooking the tidal pool. Rodman fidgeted as he watched the circular flow of water. "This is a pretty strong eddy," he said. "Maybe it won't spread."

"There's no guarantee of that."

"Maybe the temperature will be too cold to sustain it for long."

"Don't you remember Wick talking about a single sufficient favorable condition? The oxygen in the water may be the favorable condition now." She thought of his stiffening body.

"I don't know, Kelsey. I agree it could be serious. But I have to leave you with this. I have to take Wick off the island. That's my top priority. We'll send someone back in with better equipment. The government will have to get involved. In the meantime you have Jersey and Albert, Red. Good God, we need Wick. He was the best."

"Animals are dying," said Kelsey.

"Well, maybe you can use the nets, get the carcasses on land, use the slurp guns for the organism, I don't know."

"That's just a Band-Aid solution. Plus we can't get into the water ourselves."

"You're right," he said. "Don't do that then. It was a bad idea. I wish I had an answer." He stared at her. "Well, I still think getting help out here is the best thing I can do."

"Go then," she said.

"What will you do?"

"I'm going out to the dig."

He lifted his glasses and rubbed the back of his hand across his eyes. "To the spiritual source?"

"My crystal?" She fingered the stone and shook her head. She felt a headache starting as she watched the foam circulate below her. "No. Harrison is there. He'll help me."

"Stillman? Great. Wonderful. I thought he might . . . well, after your call. Make him in charge of science. You take my role. The men will listen to you. Can you handle it, Kelsey?"

Suddenly her stomach tightened, and she wanted to hurry. Suddenly everything wanted to be fast again.

Kelsey and Irma and Ben watched the plane take off into the wind, rocking in a gust until it settled down, silver silhouetted against the black bank of clouds. Then they piloted the boat toward the east end of the island.

"Which access?" Ben asked.

"The jungle," she said, then changed her mind. "No, the cliff."

"Which is it?" Irma asked.

"The jungle," she said again, going back to her first instinct.

Irma and Kelsey disembarked below Keith's ladder, and Ben took the boat around to the cliff side at Kelsey's insistence. Why was unclear. Kelsey simply had a sense that the boat should be there but that she should be here, approaching the camp in this way, the old way Iriel must have come. She was following her gut.

Her gut was churning. She needed to find Harrison. She felt as though she couldn't get to him fast enough. Something else was nagging at her, something she'd heard or seen in the last hours, something about Crouch or the plane, Rodman, the phone call. She began to feel as though someone was watching her from behind the trees. She half expected the jaguar to leap out and sink its teeth into her neck. That was it, she told herself, Iriel must have run barefoot along this same trail, eluding pursuers.

The forest was eerily quiet, and she and Irma didn't talk as they stepped over roots and pushed aside the wet vegetation that seemed to have grown up overnight. Kelsey stifled a scream when the underbrush rustled as some animal fled. She heard her own breathing loud in her ears and the sound of her tennis shoes hitting the spongy ground.

Kelsey outdistanced Irma and entered the silent camp first. She ran into Irma and Ben's tent, then the kitchen tent, both still intact. As her eyes adjusted to the gloom, she saw something move—behind the cots, what she'd most feared, what she'd somehow known would be there—Keith and Harrison slumped together on the floor.

Kelsey knelt beside them, trembling and crying so hard she could barely see. Keith was unconscious, his face battered, bleeding from the mouth. Harrison was worse. His shirt was blood soaked; he'd been shot or stabbed. The wound must have gone into the lungs, for his breath came in gurgling rushes. He was doubled over, pressing the weight of his body into his own fist, which was balled into the hole to staunch the bleeding.

When she touched his brow, his eyes opened. The brightness stunned her, and the knowing.

Suddenly Irma was helping her, then Ben was outside calling their names.

"Tell him to be quiet," Kelsey said. But it was too late. A figure darkened the doorway.

"I knew you'd come." Stan had a small black pistol pointed at them. "You can watch me finish him off." Then Ben called again, and Stan vanished like an apparition.

Kelsey and Irma separated Harrison and Keith then Irma pulled bedding off the nearby cot and propped Harrison upright while Kelsey held his hand, praying. All the while Kelsey watched the door where Stan had stood moments before. One of the things she was praying for was Ben. *Please let him be safe, let him do something, let him save us, let him save himself.*

Irma was tearing the sheet into long strips, when they heard the gunshot. Irma rose up as though hit herself and lurched out the door.

"Careful," Kelsey said. "Irma."

But her concern for the others blacked out as she bent over Harrison. He'd fainted again and his fist had dropped away from the hole under his right ribs. It was oozing at an alarming rate. *Too much blood.* She felt the wetness soak her shirt as she pressed her body against his. Her heart beat an extra beat into the wound. The crystal was throbbing between them.

She heard the words *I love you*, though neither had spoken, and they sounded as familiar as breathing. *What a mistake I made*, she said back. *I didn't recognize you.*

No matter, we're together now.

Harrison's breathing suddenly relaxed, and for a moment she feared the worst, but it came back without the gurgle. What's happened? she wondered, confused by the sound of voices internal and external—Iriel and Jarad at their final moment of separation, Gewil coming between—a cacophony of yearning, and vows for the future. *I'll find you.* She heard herself saying, wait, wait please, and the crystal sighed. Outside people were shouting.

"You'd better go," Harrison said. "I'm all right now."

"No," she said, "I need to stay with you. I don't know if I . . ."

"Yes," he said, "you did. I dreamed all this, Kelsey. He can't find us together."

"But what should I do? What can I do?"

"I don't know," he said, but the light in his eyes gave her courage.

Stan had Irma and Ben trapped against the pyramid, and they seemed to be arguing. Irma's hands were in the air; she held something in one, her glasses, flashing light. Ben was talking fervently while Stan listened, pistol drooping a little.

Irma gave a little start at Kelsey's approach, but somehow Stan missed it. Irma was taking loud stiff intakes of breath through the nose, and sweat stains were growing under her arms. The stones of the pyramid blurred through the prism of her fractured lenses.

"No, no," Ben was saying, "it wasn't like that."

"What did she tell you?"

"Oh, she's reconsidered, right Honeybunch?" Ben pulled Irma's hand down to her side, and the glasses dropped into the dirt. "She said you were . . . that you might get a little . . ."

"Fragile," Irma supplied. Her nose was running. "Intense."

"No," said Stan. "We're wasting time."

"She said you were the best lover." Irma pressed closer to Ben.

"Sex?" Stan said. "It was spiritual. We're soul-mates. She knew that."

Kelsey had crept close enough to make a play for the gun, but just as she reached, Stan spun and pressed it to her temple.

"Kel? Did you say all those things? Are they lying to me?"

"Please," she said. "Don't hurt anyone else."

He saw the blood, Harrison's blood, staining her shirt. He pushed her toward the others.

"Don't make a mistake," Ben said. "You'd regret it. Trust me. If you give up the gun—"

"Shut up."

"Can't we go somewhere quiet? Just us? To talk?" After her first instinct to run, to go with Harrison, Kelsey had planned this. A distraction, to buy a little time. Even if it meant putting herself at risk. She couldn't let him hurt anyone else. Not on her account.

"Don't be stupid. I'm not letting them go."

The uneasy triad sat against the pyramid near the place they'd found the artifacts. Ben was holding Irma's hand. Pale freckles had appeared across her blanched cheekbones and the bridge of her nose. Without her glasses, her eyes looked smaller and dense, like river stones.

Stan stood over them at first, but his gun hand was trembling, whether from fatigue or emotion, and he soon squatted in the dirt beside Kelsey, cradling the gun in his lap. She thought he'd been sober only a short while. She recognized the unrelieved tension in his face and the darting restlessness in his eyes, which he couldn't keep off her.

Kelsey tried to speak around the egg in her throat. So many avenues seemed treacherous. "You're a big part of my life," she said. "I've realized that."

He moved his head and his brown gaze drifted, milky with yearning.

"I've learned . . . I don't know. I just don't think we're done yet."

"Right," he said. "Right on."

"Just that I'm willing to work it out somehow."

Watching his lean sallow face, his body, thin around the muscle, the long legs in the creased, still-clean jeans, she thought he was not the same man she'd known: neither the man who'd seduced her, nor the one she'd buas in a warm bathilt up in her mind until he had a terrible, paralyzing power over her. He was someone in between, a hurt someone, a struggling addict maybe, violent and volatile. But when she thought about what he'd done, her hatred rose like bile in her throat.

Then there was a sound, a twig snapping, the rush of flight, some disturbance in the dense part of the forest, and Stan moved. Kelsey's heart was loud in her ears as he pushed her into the tent. But only Keith was there, unconscious on the floor near the bloody bedclothes.

"What did you do with him?"

"Nothing, I swear."

"Don't lie." He lashed her in the head with the gun, so she staggered and lost her balance. Her skull was throbbing when the stars cleared.

"He can't get far." Stan pressed the barrel into Kelsey's ribs. "Go!"

There were no signs of Harrison's passing, no drops of blood, torn clothing, shuffling footprints. Kelsey willed Stan to keep going on the cold trail; time was her friend, time for Harrison to get away, time for Ben and Irma to escape. But it was Stan's enemy, and he knew it. Cursing under his breath, he pushed her back toward camp. He stopped only once where the vegetation seemed trampled, a faint animal trail leading into impossibly thick underbrush.

She'd had but a moment to pray, *Harrison, hide*, for she knew he'd gone that way, when they heard a sound—rock rolling on rock, gathering speed as it fell—then sudden silence as it was absorbed by the sea. They came out north of the ruins. Keith's skiff bobbed in the water below them, and above it, three figures inching down the rocks.

She yelled a warning just as the gun popped. Ben and Irma looked up, then bent their heads and kept moving in the same painfully slow manner. They were in the most treacherous part of the climb and Keith, woozy, dangled between them. Irma hung from the rope with one hand, supported most of Keith's weight with her other. She was practically doing the splits as she stretched for the next foothold. Then Ben had Keith by the thighs. A second shot ricocheted, and Irma spidered down the rope toward her husband. Stan cursed as he spun spent cartridges onto the ground and pulled bullets from the pocket of his jeans.

He was close to the cliff. If she pushed him, he'd fall. She took a step.

The crystal has fired once. We three are caught inside: me, Gewil, Jarad. The abomination aligns itself, trembles, readies to fire again. This we have lived three times; the time loop ends always the same way. The volcanoes ignite, the earth cracks, the storm unleashes, the terrifying wall of water rushes to shore. Then the aircar appears, just in time.

I have no weapon save my small, green stone. I feel it gathering strength for its next task: our escape. I reach for Gewil with my bare hands. Murder is my intent. The material manifestation of my anger—a sharp dagger—forms out of nothing. I raise the knife to strike. Yet cannot. Yet must. Jarad stays my hand, and I weep with relief.

I can't do it, Kelsey realized. *Violence isn't the answer. Rebirth has no limits except change.* She watched Stan fumble the bullets into the chamber. If they don't hurry, I still might do it, she thought, praying again. *God, God, God.* I'd do it to save their lives.

Irma had the anchor. For an instant her heaviness left her, she was airborne, then the boat rocked violently, and Ben was leaning over the side to compensate. Keith managed to start the engine, but it was Ben who took the wheel. Steering blindly, he roared away, his wake cutting a perfect swath through the middle of the narrow channel. As the boat grew small, Irma raised her hand to Kelsey. Then Stan dragged her into the woods, keeping the gun in her side.

The Fifth Man

"Who was that other guy anyway?" Red asked. "He didn't even come ashore."

"Maybe he worked for the pilot."

"Nah," said Franklin, "He was a gringo."

"I saw him this morning early," said Jersey, "wandering around the camp."

"He was picking stuff up," said Albert. "I think he had one of Kelsey's bras."

"That guy?" said Liu, "Myron picked him up in Belize City. Some flunky Myron knew."

"What the fuck?" asked Franklin.

"You think we ought to go find him?" Jersey asked.

"Kelsey said she'd be back in an hour," Henry said. "It's almost that now."

"We better wait a little longer," Albert said.

"I raise you three," said George, fanning his cards.

"Fold," said Red.

"You yahoos have any money?" Liu asked. "Or is this just for fun?"

"I will bet my salary," said Henri, "on these cards that I have in my hand."

"Does that mean they're good or bad?" asked Red.

"Probably bad," said George.

Chapter 37

Crouch had been happy, Stan bragged, to meet him at the airport in Belize City and take him to the island—once Stan had told him all about her plan to avenge her father. Stan had made a case as good as any he'd presented in court. He'd found the letter from Lilya, his research assistant had uncovered the story, and from there it was easy to invent the details of conversations the two of them had never had. Then early this morning, Crouch had told Stan to "go ahead and take care of business." Kelsey chose to see and think, rather than listen to this. Covering the open ground on the rocky spine of the island, she was formulating a plan. Stan was telling her now how he'd been watching Marigold, and one day, Harrison had appeared and handed her a letter through the door, and he'd begun following him. Stan told her he'd gotten so smart, so unbeatable. He'd raised some money, a few drug deals. Here he spit. "All I had to do was pay off a few people, and then your boss was so willing to help."

The clouds had been building; the sun was long gone, and the wind swirled around them. They'd just descended into a gully, an old coral canyon by the look of it, when the rain hit. They ran, covering their faces, and then Stan spotted a small cave above their heads.

"Just until it lets up."

Claws scrambled against rock as she entered, and she smelled the animal, then Stan came in behind her, breathing hard. Minutes passed; the rain fell harder.

"It's not going stop anytime soon."

"Why do you always contradict me like that?"

"We're not safe here. It might flood." She watched his lips part.

"What are you trying to do, Kelsey?"

What was she trying to do? But he suddenly began talking.

"You think you're so smart, but you don't know shit. You don't know what it's like to be dirt poor, to have the meanest son of bitch for a father, to have to lie just to survive."

"You told me some of it."

"Some," he echoed.

Rain blew on her face, smelling of the sea; it was as though the whole sea was falling from the sky. Stan was staring again, and for a brief moment she met his eye—just long enough to catch his mood—then she turned back to the curtain of water.

He'd gone mad again, without the mellowing effect of the drugs and drink. It was like he was turned inside out, his demons dancing across his face.

"Tell me about him," she said, thinking it might relieve him. "Tell me what he did."

"Killed Ma." Flat words.

"Your mother?" Dumb to repeat, dangerous.

"I watched him." Was he seeing it again, out in the rain? If she tried, she'd see it too, a bloody hole in a woman's chest.

"They were drinking, he's all comfy in his plaid shirt he always wears, and Ma takes offense at something and goes and gets the hunting rifle. Nobody threatened Pa, was what he said." Stan voice slowed, the drawl crept in. "She was in that hospital four days, and all this time he's coaching me on what to say and working things out. 'A nigger come and done it,' that's what I told them at the trial. But I messed up. Said his shirt was red one time, blue the next. D.A. made me say plaid, so then everybody knew. He was brilliant, that D.A."

"So your father was . . . ?"

"Convicted? Nah. Jury let him go." He stared at her again, his jaw slack. "He went nuts without her. Came at me like I was her sometimes."

"You were dealt a bad hand," she said softly.

"Is that what you think, Miss European nanny, famous daddy, and all the rest?"

Something Marigold said came back to her. *Childhood trauma does not excuse brutality.*

"Can't you see what's happening, Stan? This gun, this violence. You're turning into him."

He shoved her into the wall of rain, and before she could run, jumped down on top of her.

By the time they entered the camp, she was too scared to yell out. Stan had roughed her up in the trees, though she'd done nothing more to provoke him; she'd just gone too far; he was too broken to fix; she'd understood it all through his fists. Her only defense was to stare back after each blow, letting him see her pain, hoping he'd feel ashamed. And he had finally, watching her with his breath laboring, mouth red and open.

They came upon the tanks with their few circling specimens moving listlessly beneath the rain-pocked surface. He was raving. He'd find Harrison, hold her witness to the killing. She shut him out and listened inside. She heard fish crying for help and turned toward the sea.

The ocean was whipped up and foaming now, and gray as the sky. Spray flew off the whitecaps, waves spewed against coral, and the tide, steadily rolling in, was eating up the shore. She could see blue fish bellies choking the surf, and she tried to go, but he was winning, dragging her toward the dining hall and his plan.

The men, sitting around the big table playing cards, looked up when they entered. She took in their smiling faces like medicine: Red, Jersey and Albert, Franklin drinking a beer, and Henry Hilton looking surprised. No Harrison. *Thank you.*

"Hey," said Red, half-standing. "Kelsey."

Jersey stood too. "Liu went in the big motorboat, but we waited for you."

"I hope he makes it," said Albert. "I told him he was nuts."

"What happened to your face?" Franklin asked, coming forward. "Hey! It's the guy. The fifth man."

"Don't anybody move." Stan showed the gun. He saw Franklin's beer and made a move toward it, then seemed to change his mind. "Get me one. You."

"Poison anyway," Franklin said, not moving.

Stan took the bottle. He cleaned the lip, tilted it back and drained it, wiped his mouth. He seemed momentarily stunned. Then he spoke. "Tell me where that Ph.D. bastard is."

"Lots of Ph.Ds. around here," Jersey drawled.

"I don't have time for this shit." Stan was moving in again, waving the gun in their faces, when a noise came from the back. He pressed the metal to her jaw, used her as a shield, but there was no other sound except the storm.

Kelsey brushed the gun away and moved closer to the men. She was heedless now to all but her anger. "Is everyone well?" she asked. "No relapses?"

"What are you talking about?" Stan asked. "No talking unless I say so."

"We had an epidemic here," said Franklin. "You ought to be scared. You saw the fish."

"Bullshit," said Stan. He squinted at the dirty T-shirt, the fat belly. "Show me the guy in charge. I want to talk to the bastard."

"That man died," Kelsey said carefully. "They took him away on the plane."

"Stupid suits." But Stan was nervous now.

"It affects humans," Jersey said. "Worse than Anthrax. Quicker than Aids."

"We're all inoculated," Albert said, "except you."

"You get hot, start sweating," said Red. "Pretty soon you're out of your mind."

"Wickstrom's eyeballs exploded," Franklin said.

It was close in the room, no A/C, no fans. Stan, sweating now, demanded the vaccine, and the men played along. They said they'd go get it from the lab, but Stan wouldn't let anyone out alone. They'd all go, he said. Just then, the noise at the back repeated itself. Henri and George, both wearing rain slickers, came in from the porch and pressed the door shut behind them.

"It's getting rough out there," said George. "Hey, Kelsey!" His face lit up.

"Watch out!" she shouted.

George ducked and upended a table as the wood behind him splintered. Stan loosened his hold on her to aim again, and she struggled free just as Franklin hit him from behind. Henry Hilton and Red jumped on top. The gun fired once into the floor.

"Who the hell are you?" Franklin asked for the second time.

Stan, after the initial outburst of profanity, remained silent. He was seated at the table, Franklin and Red behind him, the others close. George was trying to stare him down, but except for an occasional accusing glance at Kelsey, Stan kept his eyes averted.

"You know him?" Red asked Kelsey.

She shook her head. She meant no, she wasn't able to talk about it just yet.

"She's upset," George said. "Leave her alone."

"How'd he get here?" Henry Hilton asked.

"He's Crouch's goon," said Red. "They left him behind."

"Crouch is pissed at Kelsey," asked Albert, "so he sends this guy to rough her up?"

There ensued a discussion of what to do with him. The possibilities included feeding him the sick fish, or stripping him naked and hanging him from a tree. They finally decided to tie him up and wait out the storm, with the implication that he'd be their amusement in the long night ahead. Albert and Jersey put on slickers and went out to find rope.

Now that it was over, Kelsey kept clutching the crystal through her shirt, seeing swirling visions of Gewil and Jarad and herself as young Iriel. George rubbed her neck, but Stan glowered whenever he touched her, so she gently pushed him away. Outside, the wind grew louder and the waves battered the rocks. The afternoon was waning, another night coming on.

"Sucre," Henri said, when he brought her tea and cookies, "revitaliser."

"Merci." Then she added, continuing in French, "I am grateful to all of you. He is a bad man. A crazy man."

"He hurts you?"

"He . . ." she couldn't think of the French word for rape. "He wants to own me."

"He is your lover?"

"He is from my past. My long ago past."

"From . . ." He said a word she didn't understand. "World, he is from the lost world."

How did he know? Then she remembered she'd seen Atlantis when Henri was being treated. A voice came. Muamdi's. *He's one of us.* She feared for a moment Stan had heard it as well. He seemed to be developing a perverted sixth sense. *Just as Gewil had.*

"Henri," she said. "This is important. My friend, the man I love, is here on the island. This man shot him. Il est gravement blessé. Il a perdu beaucoup de sang. I helped him with the crystal, but you must find him, you must—"

"The dive shack's gone." Jersey and Albert had come bursting through the door. "We were right there when the water took it."

"We've got to get to higher ground," Albert said. "It's rising fast."

At that moment, a wave struck the back porch and tore the door off its hinges. Water swirled across the floor. Everyone was up, including Stan.

"Quick," said Jersey. "The next one might be bigger."

"We need supplies," Henry Hilton said. "Matches, Flashlights, water, food."

"No time," said Albert. "Just get outside."

But Kelsey was rooted, staring at the gray churning water. Lightning flashed, and the clap of thunder closed the sky. The world seemed to be ending and she was held witness, hearing, repeated, the sound of all that death. It was like a sudden intake of breath without exhale.

I've got to stop it!

Someone threw her a slicker. She was putting it on, moving toward escape, when Stan shoved into her. Franklin still had his collar, but Stan got her, daring Franklin to pull the trigger.

Only seconds had passed since the wave.

"Help me," Franklin yelled, "someone," just as another slicker came his way. Franklin put out a hand to deflect rather than catch it, but Stan snatched the black raingear out of the air and disappeared under it, like a magician, taking Kelsey with him.

"Shoot him!" George yelled.

"He's got her!"

She was fighting her way out from under the stinky rubber. Her feet slipped and then the gun was against her skull—she didn't know how Stan had gotten it—and he dragged her onto what was left of the porch. The sea gathered itself up and came at their heads.

Kelsey surfaced far from shore, cut face burning from the salt. She caught glimpses of the wreck of the dining hall—the whole back wall was gone—and figures moving up the beach. She struggled against the riptide, getting nowhere, tiring herself. Minutes later something large floated past—the rowboat—and she managed to grab the gunwale and cling.

Then the crystal around her neck began to buzz as cold fingers wrapped her wrists and a face materialized above her in the boat. He was smiling, enjoying a final moment of victory, of possession. He was both Stan and Gewil; they'd merged.

Incarnation of Fishes

Daughter. Hello!

Father, I've missed you so much. Where are you?

Here, in the water with you.

How is it I hear your voice but don't see you? Do you yet live?

It was like a miracle. One instant we were dying, filled with agony and fear, the next our eyes opened to a new life. So much better here, so much simpler than before.

You mean after the destruction, Father?

What other before and after is there?

But where are you?

Ishja and Gaethy are over there, and the boys. Marlane, the teacher, Shemmabdis. Almost the whole village of Yabeth is with us. Don't you remember how we used to go out on the Lady Sun . . .

But Father . . .

. . . and catch the likes of us? Ha ha!

You are the fish?

Yes, we are the fishes now.

Chapter 38

Stan loomed over her in the black raingear. The next moment she seesawed above him, gripping the sides of the boat. The gun was gone, so what was to keep her from jumping him? She would, she decided, as soon as she caught her breath. Meanwhile, he was rowing hard, driving them out to sea.

She thought of it again—how she'd rush him when he was off-balance—and tasted the fear like bitter iron in her mouth. His gaze was fixed on the receding shore, but the moment she edged toward the middle of boat, he raised the oar.

"I just want to talk," she shouted over the wind.

"No more talk."

"We're going to die out here. It's too rough."

"We can get around the island. It'll be better."

A big sea lifted the boat. They both threw their weight and then they were safely down the back of it. She picked up the rusty bucket that was under the seat and began to bail.

Stan bent again into the teeth of the storm, his neck straining, the heat of the work showing on his skin. *Beauty, his gift in this life.* The thought slid away, like the land was sliding away. She turned to the island and saw only water. Gray, angry water in all directions, and night was coming on.

Endless night, endless sea. The world is swallowing, and I am in its gullet. No hope, the sea is grown too big.

Kelsey bailed now, helping Stan balance the bucking boat against the troughs and valleys of the waves. They were a team again, their bodies working together, up and down, spinning with the boat, around and around. Even the water seemed to respond, like some crazy, tilting dance floor. She marveled again at their symmetry, their perfect fit. Perhaps it was meant to be: Stan and Kelsey, Iriel and Gewil.

If I had it to do over again, would I say yes instead of no?

But I did say yes, and look where it got me.

It was your karma to say yes this time.

Then she understood that "yes" was on the path to this moment, this opportunity, and that she still had a chance. She could stop this dance, however beautiful, however fated. It was what she'd been born to do.

I am ready to die, if that's what it takes. She didn't say it, barely thought it, only stopped helping. *Stan's plan.* Then she knew he had no plan, only blindness and drive.

"Bail," he shouted.

"No!"

It felt better to sit there in the boat, her fear edging at her throat like a knife. She began to shiver, but that too passed. She felt nothing. Then it burst wide open.

I cannot think of it. I will not think of it. Dead. All dead. Dear Jarad. How can I believe I will never see you again?

A wave came over the bow and pushed Stan toward her.

Gewil shouted, You did not give me my due!

Voices, too many voices. She rushed toward life again, feeling her stinging face and the rope of fear twisting inside her. She prayed, mouthing words she'd never been taught. Childhood words praising One-God. *Oh Perfect Presence. We ask Thy Grace, Thy Intervention.* Stan bailed now. He'd left the oars flying behind him, still tethered in their locks. The boat was swinging wildly, and another wave pitched them nearly on end. The bucket flew into the water, Stan leaned, and suddenly Kelsey was alone in the boat.

Alone, so many nights blurred into one, the sea heaving, me with my grief and the precious Ari. I've saved her instead of you, my love. That was Gewil's fault, you see. He took my thoughts away, just long enough for me to falter.

She took up the oars, righted the boat. A hand—the short, dark fingers instead of the long fine ones—grasped the side. Gewil's face appeared by her knees.

Take me! Choose me!

Had he been shouting those words all her life and she'd just now heard them?

The moment I time-jumped from the doomed aircar to the Lady Sun with Gewil's plea ringing in my ears, the Ari was on my left, you, Jarad, on my right. I flinched at his words, forgot my concentration, my careful spell. This is why I took the fragile one, not you. I thought we had a chance, but we'd already said our goodbyes. As if you knew.

Can you ever forgive me? I only looked his way.

Could she have looked away? She couldn't now. She raised the oar to strike, and then she put it down and hauled him back in the boat.

"Give me the oars," Stan said when he'd caught his breath.

"No. We're going in."

"You're not strong enough."

But he did not force her. She worked her way around until she was pointing back to where she thought the shore must be. Stan watched from the bottom of the boat. There was something new in his face.

"I thought you hated me. I thought you wanted me dead."

She had no breath to waste on him. She meant to get back and turn him in. She'd go through it with him, help him until he understood.

She didn't understand herself; each moment was unfolding fresh. Her actions took no premeditation from the past, only its knowledge, embedded in her cells. That and the voices, repeating their words and memories until she no longer could do anything but act.

I can't blame him for all my woes. I only let him sway me from my task. He had his own. It was contrary to mine. It's time to forgive.

There was a little lull in the storm. The water, though big, had more roll to it, less pitch, and a red sky opened to the west. Kelsey placed her hand over the stone, still riding between her breasts.

Time! For you.

Stan rose from the bottom of the boat. "You never said it."

"Said what?"

"That you loved me."

No, of course not. Even when they'd been deep in their affair, she'd willingly taken his words, his love, never thinking to return it. She still had her hand on the crystal, and it was guiding her. "I could tell them you escaped. That you drowned. You could put all this behind you. Start over."

"Start what?"

"Anything."

"I'm nothing without you." He watched her with his broken eyes. "Kelsey, I wish you'd say it. Just once."

She let the boat pirouette on the oar so for a moment she was facing the shore. Was that a bit of land? Yes, the high part of the island, bobbing into view.

"You have to let me go, Stan." Anger clouded his face, so she hurried to say what was rising up from her heart for him. Not pity, not anger, but something pure and true. "We're so deeply connected that it's beyond love, greater than love."

She could see a white place. It contained them both. They'd been there for eons at the foot of One-God, preparing for this life, this meeting. They were supposed to help each other.

"I love you, and I thank you," she said, "and you have to let me go now."

"I can't—" He stopped mid-sentence. He was terrified, stripped down to nothing.

She thought at first it was what she'd said, then she saw his gaze was fixed behind her head at too high a point. She had no time to react. The wall of water flipped the boat like flotsam.

〰〰〰

Tangled in raingear, reaching for the air. Another wave tumbled her, dragging her down to the death she no longer wanted. She clawed at bubbles, her lungs bursting.

I didn't die in water! This is someone else's death!

She swallowed water, not air, the salt burning her lips, her lungs violently expelling. Tangled in time, lost in blackness, going into the tunnel. She saw love's light, and she was flying toward the stars. It was so beautiful, so free. And she *knew. Everything.* But then she glanced back at the earth, the dense water, her limp body sinking into the depths, and that was enough. She re-inhabited her body in an instant, and then the press of flesh arched her toward painful birth. Lungs screaming, she lay limp and gasping against the creature's back.

Each breath was wretched and painful; they were coming with terrible regularity. Something kept bumping underneath her, helping her float, or did she only imagine it? She thought she saw the arch of white, and her ears were full of poetry. For a time she was gone, dreaming of the pretty cove with its fine white sand and soft sunshine.

She managed to get free of her clothes until she was wearing only a T-shirt and the crystal, a white beacon around her neck. She was exhausted, floating again, taking tiny strokes against a current which seemed to be bearing her somewhere far away. She'd lost everything in that moment of inattention, Stan, the boat, her way.

Swim now. For your trial is almost done.

It was dark and Kelsey was so cold. She kept hitting fish bodies, and somehow they kept her awake. The water had grown calmer, but she was lost, swimming when she had the strength, drifting when she didn't. Sometimes she would sink, wanting nothing more than gentle surrender, then something would nudge her again, and she'd be back in the struggle.

There were stars and a bit of a moon. Where was Stan? She grieved for him, like Iriel had grieved for the poor Ari. The wrong one, but can't one feel love nonetheless?

Fish Poem

Small fishes we once were, small fishes, dumb and blind
who grew and got a sandy taste, and filled new lungs and minds
We liked the sky upon our skins, we liked to bite the air
We liked to dive beneath the sea, to dolphin's watery lair

And then one year it came to pass, we spoke one common mind
Our single voice sliced through the seas, that parted just behind
We came to know the face of God, the twisted shape of time
But when we learned of legged man, our thoughts turned more
sublime

Oh legged ones, why must you weep?
You conquer air and foul the sea, take rock and plant and every tree
What makes you think this world is yours to do with as you like?
Do you not know the sea spits out what she cannot swallow?

Time swims like an eel with its tail in its mouth
never ending, never beginning
If you see with the eyes of your soul, you can swallow the eel's tail

Look! Love is everywhere
Float in the light of our love and become the God

Chapter 39

Kelsey saw the star fade and the clouds part like cotton candy. She'd been dreaming. Muamdi and Quiri were dolphins, one fat and pure white, the other marked with the cross of God. Wiser than humans, they danced upon the waters in one incarnation after another speaking in telepathic verse.

She was close to the beach now, and the dead fish were thick. She felt the sand come up and strike her knee. She was too weak to stand so she crawled through the lacy surf talking to the smallest of the swimmers.

You must help each other, she told them through the crystal. *Help your fellow creatures, do not kill them. You are part of the sea now.* Repeating. *Do not kill. You must not kill.*

She could hear their tiny micro-voices as they gathered their purple selves toward a new purpose. They found their way into gills and bloodstreams and ate up their old versions, their destructive selves. They were gleefully chattering, this new voice growing so loud it melded with the roar of the surf, until Kelsey heard nothing but water. It was midday before she saw feet in the sand and knew where she was.

"Jarad," she said.

"Kelsey, you're alive."

"And so are you, my love.

I Go

I go now into the quiet recesses where All is One and One is All. I am no longer I but you, and he, and she, and everyone who lives and ever lived. Together we are pure Love. Nothing more, nothing less.

For a while I was an angel, with wings brushing the earth, eyes open to the world. Yes, that is how I can explain it. And you were my living replica.

I had not understood before you lived it again, before you took your own way through, that your choice was not wrong. Your mistake was no mistake. Your foiled attempts, your sacrifices, not in vain. Each was necessary.

As were mine.

Before you lived it, I had not known that we were halfway up the spiral of enlightenment, and that each attempt is perfect and blessed.

I had not known that where there is murder, there is forgiveness, where there is hatred, there is love, where there is failure, there is success. In death, there is birth. And rebirth.

For now, you live. Your humanity is so precious and troublesome, so vibrant and personal and mystical. Your eyes are a little more open, and the future is my gift to you.

So go now, knowing that I am part of One-God, and We are always at hand. Notice me when the invisible becomes suddenly visible, notice me in the silent stillness within, notice me in the sudden and unexpected answer to your prayers. Notice me in love.

I bless you and I thank you. Now go in peace.

Epilogue

"Do you think they'll ever find the body?" Kelsey and Harrison were sitting on what was left of the beach, looking out at the sea, turquoise and sparkling again, though when the wind was offshore, the smell was strong.

"I don't see how, with all that mess out there. The sharks are having a field day."

She watched the government boat launch again. "Do you think any of the charges will stick to Crouch?"

"Fraud maybe. The Belizean government is pretty riled up. They're still holding him in Belize City according to Rodman."

"Mr. Charles will get him out."

"Not likely. The company is working on severing him. Rodman told me he's loosed an independent team of lawyers on BioVenture, first and foremost. He's got an ironclad contract, that's what Rodman said, but it's still going to cost him if he thinks he can hang on."

"I bet he's got a bunch of money squirrelled away."

"Likely. But they have a way of freezing the cash once they've sniffed it out."

In a dark patch of water about a hundred yards out to sea, a dolphin jumped once, twice. Kelsey smiled and changed the subject. "Irma told me in her e-mail that she and Ben are coming back to close up the dig. She said Iriel wants them to."

He turned as much as his bandaged chest would allow. "Iriel's talking to Irma now?"

Kelsey laughed and shook her head, though it still ached to do so, even these many days later. The doctor said she had a mild concussion, maybe from hitting her head on the boat, maybe from the beating. A wonder she'd had the stamina to swim all night. A miracle.

"And she told me Keith's coming back Friday. Then Franklin to head up the BioVenture cleanup team. That's an interesting choice, don't you think?"

"He's really fastidious in his work," Harrison said. "I had a chance to see some of it."

"I guess this means we won't be alone anymore."

He kissed her shoulder. "We have plenty of time for that."

In the last few days, quiet and clear inside and out, they'd decided a few things. New work for both of them. Kelsey was going to medical school but with the intention of becoming a healer as well as a doctor—why waste that scientific talent?—and Harrison would start his own environmental foundation, something he'd been thinking about for a long time. And something else. Daring at first, but now it seemed perfectly natural. They'd be married in the spring.

"I still expect him to reappear, maybe blue and bloated, one last attempt at shocking me. He couldn't have survived out there, could he? I did, though. That's just the point."

"You had help."

"But he's good at surviving. How did he get away from that sting you set up, for example?"

"He paid off the cops. They were in on it all along. Stupid of me not to think of it."

"It's like he's Houdini or something. He could have made it."

"You sound like you almost wish it."

"No," she said. "I mean I hope he didn't suffer." She listened to the water lapping at the shore. *Hush, hush.* "It's just that I feel this blank place inside where he and Iriel always were, this place of struggle. I think I've been anticipating him since I was a child. It's like having an infected tooth removed."

"Or a bullet. I don't miss it much, though."

She laughed in delight. "You're so funny, Harrison."

"I can say anything and you'll laugh."

"I just feel so happy here. The two Henrys will make it nice, don't you think? With all that black market money."

"Maybe we can come back. Could you stand that?"
"Our honeymoon."
"That would be nice."
"You think so?"
They laughed, because it already was nice.

Muamdi's Lullaby

Child, Are you awake?
Is that you, Soul Grandmother?
I've come to visit, if you'd like.
I'd like it very much. But how—
The rules allow these moments.
I meant now that Iriel's gone.
You have her gifts.
Can I call for you then? Will you come anytime?
I am sometimes busy.
Being a fish?
You know we breathe air.
Of course. I'm a biologist. Well, not anymore. So strange this change, so much I'm leaving behind, so much I'm learning. But I do love magic. And healing.
One-God's compensation.
Will you sing me more poems?
Poems, yes. But I rather prefer stories.
Yes, the story of me. Of Iriel, I mean. I want to know everything about her life.
Yes, she was my truest treasure. Shall I begin, then?

Laura Davis Hays

Laura Davis Hays is a California native, the only child of a theoretical physicist and a librarian. As a girl, the family's weekly trips to Huntington Beach tapped into a deep chord of ancient memory and fear for her. Riding into the waves on her father's hip, she sensed other, connected worlds. Later, Hays's father nurtured her love of mathematics and books, teaching her algebra, and reading adventure stories at the dinner table every night. His early death spurred her intense desire to understand the realms beyond this one and the possibility of life after death.

Hays's fiction employs flights of fancy and complex structure, weaving an elaborate tapestry in which her characters come to life. Her prize-winning body of work includes a forthcoming fantasy series, the *Atlantis Material,* and a collection of linked stories set in Denmark, her ancestral homeland, in the early twentieth century.

She has a grown son and two granddaughters, and is active as an accounting consultant, a performing pianist, a composer, and a skier. She and her husband live in Santa Fe, New Mexico, with their two cats, Rufus and Dexter.

Made in the USA
San Bernardino, CA
04 March 2016